THE WORLD CHRONICLES BOOK THREE

CHRIST'S REIGN AND THE LAST HARVEST

JOHN JOHNSON

Paperback ISBN 978-1-960007-12-4
eBook 978-1-960007-13-1

Orison Publishers, Inc.
PO Box 188
Grantham, PA 17027
717-731-1405
www.OrisonPublishers.com
Publish your book now, marsha@orisonpublishers.com

Printed in the United States of America

Other books by John Johnson
The Byzantine Chronicles series
- The Blade – ISBN 978-1945169-29-8
- The Brothers of the Blade – ISBN 978-1945169-40-3
- Sons of Light – ISBN 978-1945169-45-8

The World Chronicles series
- In the Shadow of Babylon – ISBN 978-1-945169-55-7
- Babylon Revealed – ISBN 978-1-945169-72-4

The Silver Cord ISBN – 978-1-945169-87-8

For to us a child is born, to us a son is given;
and the government shall be upon his shoulder,
and his name shall be called Wonderful Counselor,
Mighty God, Everlasting Father, Prince of Peace.
Of the increase of his government and of peace there will be no end,
on the throne of David and over his kingdom,
to establish it and to uphold it with justice and
with righteousness from this time forth and forevermore.
The zeal of the Lord of hosts will do this.

—Isaiah 9:6–7

Blessed and holy is the one who has a part in the first resurrection; over these the second death has no power, but they will be priests of God and of Christ and will reign with Him for a thousand years.

When the thousand years are completed, Satan will be released from his prison, and will come out to deceive the nations which are in the four corners of the earth, Gog and Magog, to gather them together for the war; the number of them is like the sand of the seashore.

And they came up on the broad plain of the earth and surrounded the camp of the saints and the beloved city. And fire came down from heaven and devoured them.

And the devil who deceived them was thrown into the lake of fire and brimstone, where the beast and the false prophet are also; and they will be tormented day and night forever and ever.

And I saw a great white throne and Him who sat upon it, from whose presence earth and heaven fled away, and no place was found for them.

And I saw the dead, great and small, standing before the throne, and the books were opened; and another book was opened, which is the book of life; and the dead were judged from the things which were written in the books, according to their deeds.

—Revelation 20: 6–12

PREFACE

This book is the final work of the Chronicles of the World trilogy, consisting of *In the Shadow of Babylon*, *Babylon Revealed*, and *Christ's Reign and the Last Harvest*. Favorite characters return from the first two books, and new characters are added in this, the third, book. The relentless and driving prophesy of the end times finds fulfillment in Christ's reign upon Earth, the last harvest, and Satan's eternal torment in the lake of fire.

The trilogy is not an attempt to convert Christians to a particular interpretation of the future. I used a millennial interpretation soundly rooted in the scripture and my own suppositions and extrapolations as to how practically such knowledge could manifest itself to the participants. I took the "what if it is literally true" approach and made the process a meditation on the possibilities of the Word. It is my belief that end times interpretations are totally within the realm of the individual and that person's relationship with the Lord. What you believe the prophetic future will be like has no bearing upon your position in Christ. You are heaven bound and sealed by the Spirit, regardless of whether your end times interpretation is correct or incorrect.

I believe this book will increase believers' zeal in loving God with all their hearts, souls, minds, and strength and loving their neighbors as they love themselves.

Rest in Him. Enjoy your imagination, owned by God and miraculously bound to His Word, and explore the future.

CHAPTER 1

Tim Johnson gazed upon John Johnson, and John contentedly studied the face of older brother, Tim. They smiled almost to laughing, as neither had held a gaze for so long, studying eyes, nose, mouth. They could see the shared and unshared features of their genetic code, their ancestry through to their grandparents. The more they gazed, the greater the delight. This was the Lord's new world, the old burned and gone. Brothers could look upon each other, seeing no past hurts, no sibling unfairness, no jealousy—only the joy of relationship and all the good times when they had backed each other, defended one another, talked honestly, communicated tough words for their God, who was all truth—and here was the payoff.

They sat on chairs that had been designed to mold to the body's contours. They sat upon an eminence of stone, white limestone, a hilltop among hilltops. The limestone sparkled in the sunlight and seemed to reach forever. They sat within the land of Abraham, Isaac, and Jacob, the land of the Davidic covenant. Israel! The air held a pristine clarity; the sky the bluest of blues, the beauty of delicate wispy clouds gave perspective to the immensity of space; the blue air seemed to wrap around them as if the presence of God. The air smelled of grapes—coming from the empty or nearly empty glasses, throw-away plastic cups, on countless tables. Thousands of people stood, sat, meandered, collected in small groups. This was the last day of the marriage feast, the seventy-fifth day since the Conqueror Christ had taken back His kingdom. The bride—resurrected members of the Church, complete; joined with the mortal redeemed of the Tribulation, had met the groom—Christ. The gathered families, friends, individuals, all spiritual brothers and sisters in Christ, heard the music from near and distant bands, ancient music of praise performed by their Jewish hosts. Spontaneously, many people danced, some in vigor and ecstatic praise, others softly embracing, moving slowly with their God and with each other. The talk from countless mouths, laughter, was the sweetest hum within the ears, like the delicate wine within the blood or the warm sun upon the skin and the ancient stones.

"I think we can gaze so long because there is no guile in our hearts. There are no hidden hurts and weaknesses we need to hide. The Lord our God has washed us clean," opined Tim.

"The way it was supposed to be from the beginning," said John as his sight flowed to the radiance of the newly rebuilt temple.

"A new beginning," added Tim.

"Of a thousand years." John sighed. His mind wondered, then his eyes grasped the scene of Jerusalem spread before them. Who would have thought—defeated, empty of spirit, running from a battlefield murder charge in a foreign country—his life would know the ultimate victory of God within him and upon the world? The vanity of humanity's willful reign cast away by the overwhelming love in the Creator's heart. John Johnson, resurrected, here now, a witness! John's eyes scanned the beauty of the scene. His eyes locked onto the radiance of his dearest friend and resurrected partner, Diana, who was engaged in conversation with Tim's wife, Mary. The two were barely moving on their walk—so engrossed in conversation were they.

Mary enjoyed Diana's company—Diana's unbounded joy was contagious. Diana thirsted for an older woman's perceptions and understanding, and Mary was happy to fill that need. They had first met seven and a half years ago. At Christ's return two months ago, they had only exchanged pleasantries and praise. The first meeting had been before the Tribulation, in Tim's professorial home; back when Tim was someone in the "world," and the Johnsons were ignorant oafs to the truth and their Lord. Mary would not allow her mind to dwell on the past—the hurt was too great, but Christ's forgiveness was overwhelming in power. She felt movement in her womb—the child was seventy-six days old. A girl, they would name Hope, a boy, Timothy. The child had been conceived the day before the Lord returned. Mary knew the happiness of her pregnancy radiated upon her; but Diana was in her resurrection body—she glowed. All those resurrected glowed with the radiance of the Lord. John matched his partner's glow.

"You have a little girl coming." Diana's pleasure soaked into her tone. She could have no children, and outside of her resurrection body had not wanted any till she had met John and his Jesus. Now, she was content again without her own child.

"How do you know we have a girl already? The test is weeks away," said Mary in a tone of astonishment.

"In this new body, I see and feel things ultrasounds cannot detect. I apologize if I frightened you; I thought surely a resurrected friend would have offered her insight."

"No, no, this is welcomed information. Don't be embarrassed. This new life is strange to all of us." Mary hugged Diana in reassurance, and a sadness came to her. Diana was unable to have children in the resurrected body. She thought of speaking on this matter, a condolence, or an observation on the endless possibilities of nonmotherhood. But she would stick her foot in her mouth. She would just be silent. Instinctually, she began slowly walking back to Tim.

Diana began to speak, and happiness was upon her face. Mary was such a kind soul. "I am content with not having my own children. The resurrected have no desire for birthing and raising children. I can't explain it, except to say the truth is that kids were never ours—humanity's—from the beginning. They belonged to God, and mothers and fathers were caretakers—a very important job when values needed to be taught; where dangers lurked, physical and psychological, for the young ones. Your child will never know want, and the Spirit of God will teach her. The dependency stage will be greatly shortened. You will be needed, of course, to steer her along and to provide that deep friendship and instruction. But think of it—no more months of potty training, feeding; no more perverts, no more murderers, no false and harmful information coming from anyone's mouth, no crazed animals, no accidents waiting to happen. Everyone—the entire population of the world—is tuned into the life of children and watching over them with the desire to protect and help."

Mary smiled broadly—the resurrected could read thoughts—and laughed in contentment, knowing her Hope would be safe and loved. "Thanks for those words…that knowledge. This old lady will need all of that."

"And think how good the Lord has been to you that both your children knew Him and did not fall under the spell of the deceiver." Diana paused. Mary thought of her Mat and her Katie—the best kids a mother could have had. Diana resumed speaking. "How does the Lord salve that wound of loss in a mother's heart?"

Mary saw Diana's troubled brow. "But He does, my dearest. Let us love Him more for His kindness." Mary remembered when the Lord had allowed little Emily, the grafted orphan daughter to her family, to die during the Tribulation. The desolation had made her angry, insane with grief—even knowing Emily was secure in Christ for eternity. Emily had been resurrected and remained a joy in their lives—would remain a joy forever.

"Amen and again amen." Diana smiled as she spoke, experiencing the healing Mary had undergone with Emily's loss. The women were back at the table of their partners.

John's hand reached out to Diana even as he continued his talk with his brother. Diana reached out and grasped his hand. Mary realized John may have felt his partner's distress or unease, even when seeming oblivious to her presence. Or was he just glad to have her presence by his side? Mortal Tim had discerned nothing. John leaned over to now-sitting Diana and kissed her tenderly. Mary was touched by the tenderness and remembered John as a teenager, who seemed as cold as ice. She always suspected it had been a ruse to hide a tender and breaking heart. But in those days before the Tribulation, everyone seemed as cold as ice, unless they wanted something from you. Mary realized sitting was not what her mind needed, and she spoke. "Let's walk up to the observation building. The roof has tables and food service." Mary stood; Diana followed her lead. Tim said, "I will stay here and order food, if possible. Don't be long." John added, "I'll stay with my brother."

Mary smiled at Tim. "Okay," she said and took Diana by the arm. "Tell me about these resurrected bodies. Eventually, I'll have one." Their walk began. Diana spoke. "Yes, at some point in the millennium, within these thousand years, you will leave us for a short time. It is thought an eight-hundred- or nine-hundred-year life is possible for those who lived through the Tribulation." Diana clasped Mary's hand. They seemed like sisters, the sister Diana had never had. No, Mary was like Miss Ames, the teacher, prior to the Tribulation, who had once been a nurse and had cared about her students like an old-time mother.

Diana glanced at the crowds gathered around long banquet tables or grouped in quiet clusters in alcoves or on sunny piazzas. The day was glorious. Their Jewish hosts, waiters, kitchen staff—so kind and attentive. Israelis had embraced their Messiah, in these last days, with zeal and gratitude in amazing numbers. The citizens of Israel had asked to serve; they wished to show the hospitality of the land, the nation of Yahweh's Israel. Scientists, mathematicians, biologists, surgeons, doctors, field hands, and janitors, all humbled by their salvation, infused with God's love, wished to serve. Even if only to cleanse dishes, scrub pots, and ensure restroom sanitation.

The wedding throng was immense. Christ forbade the counting of the guests through a formal census. The gathered could have their opinions—this was expected and natural. The "many are called, and few are chosen" adherents believed seven million to twenty million were saved from the entire planet from Christ's birth to the Tribulation's end. Many in attendance were just happy to be present, and knowing their own unworthiness, they imagined many more were saved and attending this feast. All believed that from Moses and the law through the prophets, fewer were saved. From first man, Adam, to Moses, even fewer were now present.

All the redeemed were now gathered, scattered over the warm land already bearing grapes. Stitches of young tree seedlings had been planted; fields were being cultivated. The gatherings were organized by nationality and time periods. New robes given by the hosts to everyone present were worn, and these were marked with the year of the wearer's birth and the name of his or her nation. The land mass of Israel was one vast, outdoor party, holding the only human life upon Earth.

Mary stopped with Diana, and she, too, studied the beauty of the hilled and rolling land and sky, felt the warmth, and smelled the sweet-scented air. They saw tens of thousands of people covering the earth. What a glorious time to be alive. She wished to taste the day, the land, roll it up tightly, place it into her mouth, and absorb God's mercy, His kindness. She was saved by her God for this day and days into eternity. She, Mary, the slut, the pill addict, and derelict mother of a family of sweethearts—of a loving son and daughter and a faithful husband. "Oh, Lord, I love you." She spoke under her breath, but Diana heard. She smiled and took Mary into her arms, seeing Mary's horrors and personally knowing the degradation of sexual impurity. Tears came to their eyes. Mary spoke in a whisper. "How good He's been to us. How did we deserve such a Father?" They embraced snugly and they cried tears of joy. In time, Diana spoke. "Come on, now. Let's do what we set out to do."

John's eyes followed the women and saw them stop and embrace. "Look at our partners. I'd like to hear those words." John's head nodded forward, pointing as Tim's eyes followed. Tim spoke. "We went through much, John… during the Tribulation. I almost lost Mary to Satan's wiles…and myself. Mat was separated from us for almost a year there, at the end."

"All the more reason to love our Lord more," said John solemnly.

"Yes, of course, and we do. We will love Him forever." Tim became reflective. "Twenty million souls at most, for all of God's efforts, His sacrifice of His son. Doesn't He deserve more than this? Why weren't we—mankind—any better than this?"

John answered, "God knows that answer. He knew the number before He began, and He thought it worth it. Besides, your number is a conservative guess. Triple the number may truly be before us. All is going according to plan. Enjoy His plan."

Tim weighed his younger brother's words. Younger by ten years—they were more like uncle and nephew. Yet, John had not been beguiled by the world and came first to Christ. It was John and Gramps who had confronted him with the truth. The truth was Christ, and the Truth had led his family through the Tribulation. "Yes, yes. I will enjoy." He moved back to his thoughts. He sensed the effort God had had to expend to turn a prideful lump of animal flesh named Tim into a being who could even grasp the plan of God. It was a wonder anyone was saved. Live in the present. Tim spoke. "Where are you staying this evening? Our hosts say it will be seventy degrees tonight, no wind, no rain. Same as all the other days. I am told our chairs stretch out into satisfactory beds. Blankets, pillows, even a mattress will be provided. Mat and Katie and little Emily are to rejoin us from their wanderings, and Gramps and Great-grandfather Jeremiah. There is a fire pit already stacked with wood. Stay with us and, of course, Diana too."

"Yes, these chairs are unique—first I've seen since being here. We've been sleeping upon warm sand topped with the foamiest of mattresses," said John, and he added, "Our hosts won't mind?" For the past seventy-five days, the Johnson clan had slept in the designated location for the Johnson lineage of central Pennsylvania. The days had been spent wandering, or on sightseeing tours of the Holy City and environs, as well as participating in formal events, such as the reopening of the Jewish temple, the individual awards ceremonies, the national awards, and the wedding celebrations involving the true and eternal Church.

Tim spoke. "They do not mind now that the formal itinerary has been completed. I asked." Without waiting for an answer (he wished to give John time to decide), a new topic was presented. "Tell me about Diana and your resurrected body." Tim knew in time, at the end of the thousand years, he would have such a body—all humanity would.

"My resurrected body?" John laughed in delight. "I am never for a loss for energy. I can remain awake for whatever length of time I choose. I can eat whatever I like and as much as I like. I can feel excess calories being stored upon my body; I visualize tight packets of micro-sized energy, with all essential vitamins and nutrients, no water. When the energy packets reach their preplanned limit, I stop eating. Period. No desire for more, no feeling of excess. My joints, my muscles move and work without complaint; I am supple. My mind is sharp, quick, and many streams of thought are running like a river through me, and one stream can be brought to focus with an amplified clarity and depth, or two or three or four streams simultaneously. Colors and shadows jump into my eyes, it seems, with the same clarity as my thoughts. I wish I could paint a thousand pictures a day. I can fly! I can pass through material objects! I can read thoughts, to a point!"

His amazement stopped his speech. He regained his composure and continued, "I am privy to a well of knowledge that is the mind of the Holy Spirit, Himself." John stopped abruptly, afraid of boring his brother, or wandering into boasting.

"Go on! Give an example!" Tim's excitement had him leaning off his chair.

"I saw some common, everyday house sparrows dusting themselves beside the roadside, just down the road from here. I wondered about their survival through the seven years, and I wondered at the sparrows back in Harrisburg. The Harrisburg house sparrows came from Europe in the 1800s. Prior to that, only native sparrows were in North America. Many times, as a youth, while driving the big ag machines, I wondered if the sparrows I saw were the descendants of sparrows that Gramps or Great-grandfather Jeremiah might have seen. If we could trace the genetic code, the generations, what did these sparrows see in their lifetimes? I remembered the line in the scripture when Christ told us God even sees the sparrow fall.

"In an instant, the wanderings, the generations of a single sparrow I had seen back in my youth, flashed through my mind as a huge map—even nesting locations, food eaten, newborns raised. The scenes slowed when humans, early settlers, the whole panoply of mankind intersected. I even saw the ship the sparrow's ancestors had come across the ocean on, and the tracking would have continued through Europe and deep into time had I not cut off the flow.

"Yes, God the Creator was keeping track in infinite detail—is keeping track even now. Nothing escapes Him. All is important to Him, and it is all alive continuously and constantly. He wishes to share it all with us. That's why He made us—to share. And the phrase, 'For nothing is hidden, except to be revealed; nor has anything been secret but that it would come to light'—Mark 4:22—took on new meaning."

Tim saw the tears streaming from John's eyes—tears borne of utter amazement. Tim spoke. "The scientists of our day always said the human mind's potential capacity was barely being used. Now we know why. It was built for eternity, and knowledge is always growing."

"Yes, yes, exactly," John answered. "He had it all planned, has it all planned. Do you know I can pass through solid objects? Do you know I can move through air and space? I said that already. Do you know I am impervious to germs, viruses, falls, blows?"

A waiter stood beside the two men at a respectful distance from their impassioned conversation. The waiter's robe tag gave Israel for nationality; an apron hid his date of birth. He was a man in his thirties with a dark beard and naturally curly hair. He came with a platter of thin bread, hummus, and thin slices of lamb. "A small repast, gentlemen?" His eyes are kindly, thought John, and he had been interested in their conversation. John's mind sighed in relief. For his entire life on Earth, a stranger listening in had been a cause of wariness, even dread. Every person wanted something, an advantage, and every mind seemed depraved. Now everyone could be trusted, everyone meant well, everyone had all they needed from their God. God had made them clean, in their right minds—minds washed of sin.

"Did you hear our passion? We were talking of your God and ours," said John. Then he added, "Us—together—our God. The only God there is, our I AM. Such great and good news." The waiter smiled and tears came to his eyes. Tim added, "Thank you for this food. May we take it all? I've just realized I haven't eaten in hours."

"Certainly, take it all."

The brothers noticed an emotional welling within the waiter that he wished to calm. The waiter took two bottles of water from his apron flap. "Water to wash it down."

"Most certainly, good host." John reflected on how easy it was to express the inner heart of thankfulness and kindness in this new reality, this new world.

The waiter spoke. "Yes, I heard your words and was appreciative of your sentiments. Have you gentlemen given thought to where you will live and what work you will do?"

Tim answered, "Some. We both plan to return home to the eastern United States, Pennsylvania. We are brothers, John and Timothy Johnson." He pointed as he gave the names. "I have two grown, unmarried children, another on the way, and hope for spouses for them and grandchildren."

"Yes, a good location. The rivers are flowing, the rainfall now dependable. Needed are agriculturally leaning citizens to grow crops and raise livestock and geologists to explore new deposits of ores and minerals uncovered in recent geologic turbulence. You could establish homesteads along the Susquehanna River, or the Juniata, or the many creeks that flow into them, and live and grow in peace." The waiter's eyes softened in tenderness at the scenes upon his imagination. "Your children will find good spouses, and your descendants will be many." The waiter seemed to be prophesying. By his eyes, they knew he had gone into a world hidden from them. His mind left the future and returned to the present, as he said, "See these chairs? I designed them. I once was a carpenter, making chairs, benches, tables. Watch how they unfold." He took a nearby empty chair and, in swift moves, converted it into a bed. "Made of scrap metal scavenged from the great battlefields of this region."

Tim and John chuckled at the ease of assembling and the sturdiness of the bed. John spoke. "Come visit us…in the future. What is your name?"

"Joshua."

"Yes, Joshua; come and visit us. You seem to know our area," said Tim.

Joshua quickly rejoined, "I had workers there; the leader was a Joshua also." Joshua looked across the broad piazza. "Mary and Diana are returning, and the rest of your party; they, too, will be hungry. I will return with more food." Joshua smiled as he left.

"How did he know their names?" asked John.

"How did he know so much about our home?" asked Tim. Did the waiter know his Joshua? The Joshua who had spread the salvation message during the Tribulation, who had taught his family, who had shared meals with his family, and who had been burned alive as a heretic? He had been from Israel, one of the 144,000 Jewish evangelists who had preached Christ's salvation to the dying world. Tim's mind calmed from the traumatic memories. He had completely forgotten to look up his Joshua. Through the course of eternity, they would meet again; of this he was certain. Neither of the brothers' minds worried or were dismayed at the waiter's knowledge. Perhaps he had previously served Mary and Diana.

"Your waiter friend is bringing food," said Tim as Mary and Diana approached.

"Who?" asked Mary.

"Your waiter—he knew your names and where we are from," Tim said determinedly.

Mary and Diana sat by their men. Mary spoke. "We don't have a clue as to what you are talking about."

John calmly deflected from the impasse. "No matter. He's coming back. Really nice guy, Joshua, honest and clever. He designed these chairs." Having seen Tim perplexed, he had decided to add support to Tim's reality.

A retinue returned—staff with blankets, pillows, mattresses for nine. A waiter set down a tray of food and said, "More is on the way."

"Where's Joshua?" inquired Tim of the man who seemed in charge.

"I do not know. I was given a message via text to deliver these things to you and take care of your party tonight. The request had the usual management signature," the man said pleasantly.

"Hey, we're here!" A raucous but decidedly feminine voice resounded across the stone of the piazza—Katie. Mary smiled, her precious Katie, once a quiet little girl of great kindness and depth of understanding, had found her joyous voice in the new world. Emily, Mat, Gramps, and GG (Great-grandfather) Jeremiah straggled behind, not from fatigue, but from conversation and the panoply of history grabbing their eyes. "Is that food for us?" asked Mat, as he came to the gathering.

"Yes, help yourself," said Tim to his son.

John questioned the new arrivals. "Do you know a waiter named Joshua, around thirty, black beard—not long. Curly, black hair. Any of you know him?" Heads shook in the negative.

Katie suddenly became animated, stiffened her posture to full height. She threw her hands into the air, pumping them up and down. "Dad! Mom! Uncle Tim! Aunt Diana! Don't you know our Savior, Our King when He stands right in front you? Just like the road to Emmaus. The whole world is under His authority. He's been meeting His people, appearing and disappearing, not wanting to collect a crowd. All gathered know this…except for the Johnsons!" Katie began pacing, in an attempt to lessen her emotion, as Mat and Emily laughed in joy and amazement.

John looked quietly at Tim, searching his eyes for the import of the moment. Jesus, Messiah, God's Son—who had suffered excruciating physical pain and humiliation on the cross, tormented by the worst in humanity, so that John and Tim Johnson would be acceptable to God and so could be sitting here at this moment—had just served them.

"Let's see if we can take the chair He designed with us," said Tim. The chair would have great sentimental value, if not monetary worth. He thought of the Son of God, who had died for him, speaking to him, moments ago, as a friend. The king of Earth and Heaven, of all that is or ever will be. How many times had he called to his Jesus in times of need, in times of greatest stress and danger. The desire for the chair ceased. A greater gift was his: his Lord lived within his being. "Those last words of mine were never spoken," Tim sheepishly commanded his brother.

"What words?" asked John.

"About…" Tim's voice faded away as he laughed. "You got me."

CHAPTER 2

John and Diana settled into the seats of the massive jetliner—top deck before the wing, with window views. The passengers were all bound for Harrisburg International. What level of infrastructure and amenities existed at the airport and within the area were unknown to the passengers. Nor did they feel the need to know; they were going to a new and beautiful life. Hardships would be overcome, and assuredly God's help and provision would be ever present. John did know that for the last seventy-six days, scout teams and infrastructure teams, both resurrected and angelic, had been working. He knew not everything had been destroyed on that final day of the reign of Satan; the jetliner was proof. God had planned, of this John was certain. The liner was full, one thousand settlers returning to central Pennsylvania, a thousand more to follow within weeks.

He had spent two years living with Gramps in the Harrisburg area and working in the ag fields of central Pennsylvania before enlisting in the army. He had illegally returned as a murderer from the Polish Conflict with Diana in tow for a two-day stay before taking up Gramps's trail of the missing satanic unholy book. He remembered that flight so many years ago. He vividly re-experienced his fright, fear, and desperation of that time. Diana had been his rock and his delight as she discovered their Lord and God. He took her hand; felt the long, smooth fingers, the narrow wrists. She leaned into him, her head on his shoulder, and they began the silent exchange of talk between their spirits and souls that only the resurrected knew.

Although the resurrected neither married nor were given in marriage, nor had any matrimonial obligations as far as the law was concerned, the formerly married or engaged would not be forced apart and could remain together through eternity if that was their wish. They understood that work assignments would be offered them that might involve parting for lengthy amounts of time, but they did not need to accept. Their reproductive days were past, but the deep, internal bonding and the sublime assimilation that was seemingly magical—or perhaps miraculous—was not gone. One could mentally disappear into another and find rest and love. Sensations of spirituality existed in place of sensations of the physical body, like those in the past world, where physical seed needed to be transferred.

Diana reviewed with John their history, the search, when they were new to each other, for the unholy book that would split the old World Church and instigate the Rapture. How glorious it had been to have the Holy Spirit upon her and within her. How glorious had been the release from sin and having a purpose greater than oneself. In the jetliner, unknown to any of the passengers, they communed with the Spirit and each other. Bathed in the clear water of holiness and the welling of the springs of life, they gave praise and thanks for the thousand years on Earth that God had granted.

Tim and Mary sat beside John and Diana. They saw the peace on the couple appear as a divine radiance and remained silent in respect. Mary held Tim's hand as he pressed a button with the other that automatically pivoted their seat to face the window—a window running continuously the length of the hull. Katie and Mat had yet to board, and little Emily was always with Katie. Gramps and GG Jeremiah had already entered and were sitting with the earlier Johnsons from the 1700s, 1800s, and early 1900s. One was a Civil War veteran, who had died from wounds in a hospital before the war ended. Gramps and GG Jeremiah had slowly parted from their wives during their stay in paradise. Their wives had chosen to live with their families in Minnesota and Virginia.

Tim wondered what Gramps and GG Jeremiah thought of this end to the world, the coming millennium. They had played a major part in the unraveling of the World Church fabric that presaged the Tribulation. GG Jeremiah had discovered the satanic bible and had hidden it before his untimely death. For generations, the evil book had remained hidden. At God's ordained time, Gramps had found the satanic bible clue left by GG Jeremiah and sent fugitive John to retrieve the book. This revealing of the unholy bible had led to the split of the World Church—a key historical event in prophesy. He wondered if this schism had prompted people to question their salvation and walk with the Lord. He needed to talk to them again, to relive that tumultuous time in his life when he had backed John, Diana, Gramps—and, unknowingly, Christ—and not the church.

Miraculous how everyone on board spoke English, no matter what their native tongues had been. Yet, there was the tower of Babel, that supposed story from the Old Testament in which God purposely confused mankind to thwart the evil plans of their hearts. Now the world was of the same heart, mind, purpose: serving and praising God—not Satan, the world, and the flesh.

Tim noticed a family who all shared jet-black hair and a mildly brown trace in skin color. The father had a patch on a well-tailored deerskin jacket that said: Native American, Susquehannock tribe. Another patch on the left breast gave his name as Andy Springs with the dates 1680–1765. Andy's wife had exceptionally long, braided hair. The two sons—boys becoming young men—had the same black, shining hair, cut close, like their father's. The sons, like the father, wore modern, rugged clothing styles. The wife wore a full-sleeved shirt and a simple, modestly tailored dress from waist to ankles in the cut of her past time on Earth. Her clothes were of rugged quality, the dress plain, the shirt checked in earth-tone colors. Tim looked forward to a conversation with them.

Tom Burnell and Tish, with their kids, were aboard. Who would have thought that a chance, violent encounter on a commuter train would have led to an enduring friendship with Tom and his family? Tim loved watching the expressive faces of Tom's adopted daughters.

History was on display aboard the jet: a scattering of Native Americans, whites from Europe, blacks from Africa, Jews from every continent, Hispanics, Asians. Most had chosen modern fabrics and clothing styles, some kept hats or vests or pant styles and shoes from their time on Earth, a few traditionalists wore only the clothes of their time. From every race and tribe, every nation, they had been chosen, all had suffered for their God; all had clung to the name of Jesus, and all now had their reward. Everyone upon the jet knew forgiveness, mercy. They lived with love, joy, peace. They had patience, kindness, a deep goodness. They were the faithful people, and their gentleness and self-control were beyond reproach.

Tim began to weep. Why had God been so kind to him as to place him in this band of the faithful, upon this plane, upon this adventure of a thousand years—a thousand years in the span of his eternal life. He reached over and felt Mary's tummy for his little Hope. Mary had conveyed Diana's knowledge of the child's sex just last night.

"What moves you, Tim? Our little girl?" she asked.

"I am thankful for her, but it is these people on our plane. I feel unworthy to be among them."

Mary spoke softly. "God decided who would be upon this plane. No one was worthy. Not one of us. All of us had been blind and stupid as to the Lord. All of us…all these people…lived contrary to His ways. You and I, thinking that being in the World Church made us better, made God our personal genie, and the church, our stepping stone to an ego-driven life of material comfort and praise. Everyone on this plane was blinded by the world, the flesh, and Satan. Why did we make it, while others failed? Because we got a piece of the truth—only when all was stripped away—and the Lord in His mercy built upon those little pieces of truth till we had so much truth we were compelled to go forward."

She looked at her husband. Should she go on? Yes, he needed to hear. "You are worthy, my clever man, because you were not afraid to face yourself, your sin, and hypocrisy, and you endured. Endured to the end. All these people have the same basic story with only circumstances and personalities different. Look at Winkie, your trusted friend. He was a priest of the World Church, wanting to help people, yes, but unable to see Father God even as God intruded upon him daily—I'd say hourly. God doesn't make mistakes. He has chosen. He gave a fair and equal opportunity for all His creation to know Him. He rewarded those who sought Him with more truths. Many preferred themselves, the world's lies, over Him. They could never see the truth, because deep down they didn't want to."

Tim kissed his wife, lingered before her lips and eyes, and whispered, "Thank you."

She squeezed his hand. "Thank you for appreciating me."

Katie, Emily, and Mat entered the aisle. Tim and Mary's happiness heightened. Katie saw the pleasure that her entourage produced in her parents and relatives. Katie grabbed her dad's face and cheeks, a hand upon each; pinched gently, then wiped away the tears her dad had shed when his kids had entered the plane. She moved on, knowing Dad might cry more if she remained. Tim reached for Emily, next in line, held his hands against her head, tickled her ears with his little fingers till she mussed his hair. That was their ritual, and she smiled. Katie, looking back at the interaction, laughed in joy and said, "Daddy and Mommy love their kids. And we love you back. The joyous days are here."

Katie's posture livened, her back stiffened, giving her full height, as she called out over the seated people, "Give praise to our God! Let our joy be endless and deep, people of the Lord!" Katie raised her hands in praise and sang hallelujahs in her rich voice. The listening ones smiled and raised their hands. Hallelujah and amen choruses erupted. Mat's deep amens resounded. Emily's ethereal voice repeated a chorus of praise; enthralled with His holiness, her range increased in power and depth. Katie felt so free, and she remembered the times when her actions would have caused a person to be beaten and arrested and likely sodomized by masses of angry, humanlike creatures. All those were in Hades waiting for their judgment at the end of the thousand years. They couldn't stand to hear the name of the Lord or imagine praises to His name. She lived to praise His name!

Tim and Mary were both aware their little girl had grown, not only in height but in stature. Tears of joy and amazement came to them. The scrawny-legged girl, who never complained and always stayed balanced and poised within the Spirit of God had bloomed like a field of the brightest-colored wild flowers. The praise of the Lord welled from every pore. Little Emily was still a silent girl in demeanor, as if she studied all of life's moments and movements. But her voice in praise—so pure, sweet—was the voice of the temple of God, the sound of incense, cleanness, purity, and holiness. The little girl who'd been whipped to scabs and scars had been healed, made whole. The Lord dwelt within her, and she saw through His eyes. And Mat! Tim remembered how he had ached for Mat, feared that his son would have no children, never be a daddy, never work or find purpose upon Earth, as the millennium was unknown to Tim at that time. Mat had been his rock during the Tribulation, with his physical strength and his savvy mind that read situations correctly. Tim had spent countless hours worrying for nothing. God had been in control of it all.

Victory had come at its appointed time, which was known before humanity even stepped foot upon the earth. Known before the serpent, Satan, had even opened his mouth of unending deceit. God knew there could be no completion to His creation and proof of omnipotence without the victorious earthly kingdom of God upon the world. A thousand-year reign to show Satan—the adversary—and mankind—the saved and coming unsaved; He had planned it all from the beginning. The so-called learned men of religion thought the game could end without time expiring; without the scoreboard showing the countless points of the victor; without the winning team and teammates and fans upon the field; without dancing, and shouts, food, and drink. When you win, you celebrate; you take the trophy home. This was unacceptable to the clever theologians, who had sliced up the Holy Word into fragments, and imbued their foolish thoughts in the remains. God's hard-won people, redeemed by the blood of the Holy One, would celebrate. No gloating, no boasting, no snide remarks for the fallen, just sadness for the failure of the unredeemed. Satan received the disgust, the righteous indignation, the hatred. None could find sympathy, though he was just a created being, for the pain and torture he had inflicted upon mankind.

Truly, to the frontline Christians—to those who had declared the Holy Words to Satan's kingdom, by voice, by written words, by song, by debate and argument, by actions, and godly lives; to those grunts in the trenches who had borne grievous wounds of body and soul, who had been harassed, belittled, tortured, and slain—it had not been a game, but a war. It had been a brutal, deceitful, ever-changing, relentless war, for the adversary never rested. He only slunk off the field of battle before returning in greater fury to hurl himself at humanity and the Lord's redeemed. Torture, mockery, death was what Satan demanded. The unknowing bowed to his demands and kissed his ring and lived a lie, while the people of truth soldiered on through dark and bloody storms, through winter's snow and ice and hunger, knowing their Redeemer lived. God's people had been mangled and broken, their physical bodies burned and mutilated; and the pain within their hearts sometimes seemed overwhelming. Yet they had endured. The tears that came with knowing it was finished would never leave them. Thankfulness had no expiration date.

Mat spoke. "There's Dan and Barb in the back." He waved and began weaving and twisting down the long aisle, with Katie and Emily following. His eyes were focused on the brother and sister. He had seen Barb just days ago. He would marry her.

That is what the Spirit told him. She had a peaceful spirit rooted in unwavering faithfulness. She had beauty and poise and liked children—liked the way they thought. She had patience and gentleness while in their presence. The times of worship during the Tribulation, with Katie, Dan, and Barb, at Carl's Camp, had been the happiest of his life until the millennium. Dan had been his brother in arms; they had trained together for over a year. They were in the same personnel carrier the day of battle. Somewhere, soon after the carrier's door opened, they had lost contact. Dan's dad had needed special attention. Dan's dad had had his pelvis removed by a high-explosive round. He had died, and not belonging to the Lord, he had gone to Hades and was waiting for the judgment sentence to the lake of fire. Dan had been shot in the eye by an enemy sniper as he lingered over his father, and Dan, too, had died. But he had been resurrected completely intact, as all resurrected were.

Not many knew yet that the resurrected could, when they wished, show their old, wounded, and broken bodies in their natural states. Dan had shown Mat his—the missing eye, the skull blown apart in the back. Mat had not asked nor wished to see (he had seen Dan's corpse on the battlefield), but it seemed to mean something to Dan—perhaps that he was accepted in all states of his being. Dan, being resurrected, could not marry, and neither Mat nor Dan knew whether Dan would feel a sense of loss. He had urged Dan to talk to other resurrected about this matter.

As they neared Barb, she held up a hand-sized device, and said, "Recordings of our old worship songs from the Camp." They had sung their fears and troubles away with praises to their Savior. Mat sat beside Barb, moved close to Barb; she did not move back from his closeness. She even closed the small gap he had left. He looked into her eyes to gauge her intent. She winked—something she had never done before, even with kids. He laughed. She unflinchingly held her gaze.

He spoke. "Do you know what you are doing?"

Her gaze was looking into his soul.

"Yes, I know what I am doing. Do you?" she said, as she noticed he was not letting go of her gaze. All sound aboard the aircraft stopped. They were the only two onboard.

"Will you marry me, Barb?" She had been chosen by God; she was all he ever wanted, all he ever needed.

"You know I will." There was no better man than Mat for her. They were of the same being.

Their hands reached out, touched, clasped. They kissed.

"Whoa. This is too much for me," said Katie, waving her hand as if to dispel the heat of passion. The noise on board returned.

"Me too," said Dan.

Emily, a twinkle in her eyes, laughed. Then, calmly, matter-of-factly, she said, "Okay, let's start the music and sing."

They did sing, and the people around them listened in appreciation. Tom Burnell, his wife, Tish, and the kids, near to Mat and Katie, listened intently. Tom found great beauty in Katie's voice, a succinctness in the words, a clarity in the notes. Even her improvisations were carried perfectly. He was overwhelmed by it all—from their place among the redeemed, to the marriage supper in the land of Israel. He constantly said to Tish, "Pinch me." Then Tish knew how overwhelmed he was. He asked himself repeatedly, "How did I get here?" A loving wife, three beautiful kids, and eternity before all of them. He needed to say something, do something; needed to lay something at the feet of Jesus to show his appreciation.

All he had was his life, and that had been an awful thing. A hateful man, a drug addict, intimidator, killer. The only good within that story was what Jesus had done. Jesus had done it, the miracle, through the darkest days the world had ever known—the big trouble, the Tribulation. His girls, his Tish had to know. They had to know the past, because the future would be so bright, they might never remember the darkness. They needed to know the darkness. He would tell them his story. They had to know the darkness, or the light and gaiety would lose its sharpness, lose its poignancy. They would forget their pains, the darkness, and then what? What could they teach their children and their children's children?

Barb passed the words to all the surrounding phones. Then all sang, and the singing spread as the hearts of God's people welled with emotions of thankfulness. All one thousand voices sang, including pilot and copilot, crew; prayers came; hopes and prophesies were given utterance and sang themselves. Tom Burnell sat and quietly wept as his girls—Tanya, Anya, and Flo—mesmerized by the singing of Katie, Barb, and Emily, joined their voices. Tom saw the joy in their eyes, the radiant happiness, and knew that he had to protect that happiness and light in their eyes. A new world was waiting, a new beginning. Life would be lived the way it should have been from the beginning—before Satan entered. He turned to Tish, saying, "Pinch me," and they laughed together through their tears.

CHAPTER 3

The jetliner descended through the light puffs of white clouds; the air quality was pristine—the great fires that had burned the world seemed to have burned the sky clean. The passengers could see greenness spreading upon the earth. On high ridges, mountaintops, anywhere the topsoil had been stripped away, the green faded, and the light-brown–colored sedimentary rocks, the white-gray limestone, the granitic boulders were seen. By depressions, rills, brooks, streams, creeks, and small and large rivers, the greenness had darker shades and thickness; shrubs and small saplings rose above the uniformity of grasses and grains. Bamboo hybrids were thickening and spreading up veinlike gullies and ravines that sparkled with trickling, rushing waters. Small saplings of every variety were emerging. They saw the great Susquehanna riverbed covered with the thinnest sheet of water. Islands and even many sandbars were covered in dense shades of green. The angelic hosts had been busy the day after the great conflagration, seeding the earth, reintroducing insect life, restocking oceans and rivers and streams with fish, crustaceans, mollusks, clams. Grain seeds had been scattered—corn, wheat, millet, rye, every variety the earth had known. All dropped from the air. The ice caps that melted during the Tribulation had not raised the ocean levels but had been absorbed into the air and fell as rain.

Unseen by the passengers, the American and Canadian prairie land, the plains, the high plains before the Rockies were the recipients of the increase in rainfall. Lakes formed, rivers flowed, green prairie grasses sprouted and would soon be grazed and farmed again. The eastern regions received elevated rain levels that would cover the Appalachians and piedmont and coastal plains in forests again. This was God's gift to Canada and the United States during the judgment of the nations, held immediately after the Tribulation's end. A judgment of punishment and reward to which few modern biblical scholars had given thought or credence. The nations had been judged; not for the good works of men and women who were elected officials, as mostly all were corrupt; not for national policy, as atheistic globalism had been the policy; not for hardworking, inventive bureaucrats, as all had been selfish, lazy, and indifferent; not for altruistic ideals, as all were venal; not for enlightened religious standards, as all had worshipped humanity; not for Olympic Game wins, as all were cheaters and steroid abusers; not for notable entertainers and actors, as all were devoid of values and morals and preached humanism; but for the number of individual men, women, families who held to common, immutable decency and the God-given rights of the Lord's creation. His people, His workers, who had kept their love alive and had loved their neighbors as themselves. The citizens, the people who had given to the hungry, helpless, downtrodden during the Tribulation; the people who had kindness, mercy, empathy, and the boldness to follow what they knew was morally right. To their nations more was given.

As the jet banked, John, Tim, and Mat, sitting together, saw the airfield—naked bands of concrete running lengthwise along the broad river. No outbuildings, no control tower, no hangars were seen, only a few waterproof coverings over crates, boxes. "Looks like a combat zone," said Mat as he remembered his tour of duty in India and the Middle East. John wondered if the concrete runways were those he had landed upon in his flight from Europe, before the Tribulation, with Diana doggedly one step behind. It was her fainting-spell distraction that had probably carried him past the security measures.

Tim commented, "Primitive but sufficient—no potholes, no debris on the concrete." He remembered his past as a field geologist, when rough runways in underdeveloped areas were the norm. Those days seemed like another lifetime. He had flown to and from Harrisburg as a kid, visiting Gramps. His college days and life thereafter had been based in New York State.

Mat commented, "No structures anywhere on the land. All were burned. Where did this luxuriant regrowth come from?"

"How many angels are there?" John responded.

The Native American family had occupied the seats behind the Johnsons. The large man, the patriarch, had been listening to the discussion, and he added in a friendly tone, "Hundreds of thousands of angels seeded North America, and some of the resurrected helped. It only took two weeks."

"How do you know the number?" Mat asked, an incredulous shyness in his voice.

The patriarch smiled approvingly, his eyes gleaming with excitement and pride in the task accomplished. "It came out as an offhand comment by a man who had authority, at one of my briefings." He reached for a handshake. "My name is Andy…a corruption of *Andaste*, the Huron word for the Susquehannock tribe and used by the French. Last name, Springs. Was born by several springs, relatively near this location."

The three Johnsons wondered at Andy's briefings—apparently, Andy knew things. Andy's boys were off their seats, with cupped hands blocking the glare from the window. Mat had heard them being called Puck and Tuck—characters from a Shakespeare play, according to Diana. The jet was circling, moving east along the mountain ridge.

The son named Puck turned from the window in excitement and addressed his father. "There's where Snake Town was, Dad! In the crease in the mountains."

Mat located the mountain gap below; he knew these boys had lived upon this land before he did, at another time in history. Mat studied Puck's eyes—vibrant with life. His brother, Tuck, had the same gleam. What an adventure for these boys. "I know that place as well. There once was a training camp run by one of America's last patriots near that gap. His name was and is Carl Stasic. The Camp existed during the Tribulation." He saw twisted metal on the summit of the ridgeline, the remains of the wind turbines.

Tim spoke. "Used to be called Indiantown Gap at one time in the nineteen hundreds. It was an army training ground."

"How appropriate," said Andy. "It was filled with westward-wandering, fleeing Lenni-Lenape and was a Native American town, with a sprinkling of European traders and craftsmen, in my time."

The boys listened to the comments from the men of the other family and their dad. The jet turned west for the descent into the landing.

Tim said, "That's amazing, Andy. Your boys know their topography."

"They've seen maps in paradise and since our return to Earth. They are attentive, observant young men, qualities which have great value."

John, who had been listening quietly to the conversation, watched the boys straighten in delight and pride at their dad's praise, and his heart was warmed. It was apparent the boys had a deep love for their father.

Tim gazed at Andy, who seemed to be connected to a higher level of decision making, and asked, "Do you know the game plan?"

"Yes, the air crew will unload supplies, shelters. We will remain by the airstrip tonight, and tomorrow air platforms will show us homestead sites. But really, you may choose any piece of land. Flat, fertile land, for farming or hilltops and ridges for views. You may have waterfront property or even land near the cities and towns for commercial purposes as well as living. There will be plenty of land left for future settlers and commercial farming operations. The rich lowlands, plateaus will be for agriculture or grazing ground or even left untouched for forests until the future need arises for more ag land. The first people to come back were chosen because they wanted land—that's why so many are from the early days. Land was the dominant desire of their time. I stress that you will get to *choose* your land. We are ranked as to order of choice, based on what we accomplished for the Lord's kingdom."

After a pause, Andy said, "I know all this because I am in charge of this settlement process. I had much experience with my people and other tribes during my eighty-five years on Earth." He thought for a moment. "Food production and exploitation of natural resources is a priority. The urban people will be coming in a few weeks." With that said, Andy moved quickly, with a forest-hunter suppleness, to the front of the aircraft and stood before the pilots' cabin doors. Held up his hands, placed his phone on speaker, which then keyed into the plane's sound system, and addressed the air-bus passengers.

Andy formally announced his leadership position. Tim listened to Andy's words. He was a natural leader. A tall man with an impressive physique, much like a South Sea islander's, with large bones and bulging muscles. His boys were wiry but not yet done with their growth.

While studying Andy, Tim realized, with an intellectual jolt, that the inhabitants of paradise did not resemble the ages they had reported. Andy died at eighty-five, yet he appeared as a vigorous forty-year-old. His boys appeared to remain at the age at which they had entered paradise. He had not recognized the phenomena in John and Diana, as they had only been parted from him for seven and a half years. Upon reflection, Gramps was no longer appearing as an eighty-year-old but instead as a man in his fifties. Tim concluded that normal growth and aging of the young would resume on the new Earth. A thought that the new normal human life-span had been elongated—that people would live ten years for every one year of old Earth time—entered his mind as fact. This had been deduced from an Old Testament prophesy. Earth's inhabitants might even reach the age of Methuselah, who lived 969 years. Tim's mind faded into musings, but from the words of Andy he picked out that: only canopies were needed for sleeping, and a few blankets; the winds were light, and the rains, if any in this season, were gentle; and no mammals had been restocked yet, though some had survived the burning and existed in the wild state. The musings turned to dreams of the land he might own, the house he would build, the lives they would all live in this new, pristine world.

***

The cooks and kitchen help were breaking down the food-service line. Andy stood, asking for attentive minds. He requested a cheer for the good food and the orderliness of the meal presentation. The culinary workers received a standing ovation. Everyone was full and content as the sun was setting, and yellows and oranges tinged the sky. The gathering had been laid out in six circular encampments, clustered near the airfield. The circle consisted of three concentric rings of eight smaller circles, each of four families or four groupings of singles. Each of the eight circles had a leader. Andy doubled as a circle leader and the leader of the entire group of settlers. Each family or group was supplied with a sturdy inflexible but lightweight canopy. Cots had been provided. The canopies, cots, blankets were now the responsibility of the families and would follow them to the new home sites. The families broke apart and returned to their campsites.

Every family grouping had a fire pit with manmade logs rated to burn for four hours. Andy's grouping included the Johnsons, Emily; Dan Smith and his sister, Barb; and the Burnell family. Andy gave his boys permission to start the communal fire at dusk. The families collected. Tim noticed nine-year-old Tanya Burnell staring at Andy. She moved toward Andy, tugged at his sleeve, and said, "Why are you so big, Andy?"

He and others smiled at her curiosity and forthrightness. He answered, "Partly genetics—the inner code of characteristics that gets passed along—and partly because I ate like a king during my early life."

"Yes, tell us about that...what did you eat?" Anya liked the topic of food; they had had so little during the Tribulation, and she didn't want to be out-done by her older sister, Tanya. She had the right to ask questions, too.

John chuckled at a question he had wanted to ask but thought it prying in nature. He'd had a fascination with Native Americans since a teenager, when he had turned up arrowheads on his ag machine. He had read copiously about them during his time in paradise and had tried to speak with every Native American while in his temporary home. Somehow, he had missed Andy and his family.

"My people lived by that river, and we ate from that river." He pointed toward the Susquehanna. "Eels going to the ocean in the fall. Caught in our rock lairs, which were shaped like a *V* and led them into woven baskets or nets. Fresh eels, smoked eels. In late spring, the shad came up the river and, by drying or smoking, could last many months. Sturgeons were plentiful, and they, too, spawned. The geese and the ducks left us eggs to be gathered in the spring. We would only take one egg per nest and mark the nest with woven grass so others knew no more could be taken. We guarded the nesting grounds from predators. The boys shot the foxes that would eat till there was no more to eat, for the foxes had young ones. Those ducks and geese were easy prey to hunt when in the water. Fish, plenty of fish to be speared or trapped. You could even kill them with stones when the waters were low in the summer—catfish, largemouth bass, walleyes. Trout in the streams and pike. Squash, beans, corn grew in the rich soils by the river. Our women and girls tended those. In the fall, the bears, their flesh oozing with fat, were eaten. Deer, racoons, possum, woodchucks all year. For a time, we hunted elk from the west branch of the river, and even buffalo, till stronger tribes claimed the hunting grounds as their own."

"How did it fall apart, Andy?" John asked, knowing the general theme through his readings but wishing to hear a personal account.

"Diseases unknown to our bodies, brought from Europe. We became hooked on the economy of trade. We supplied beaver pelts, deerskins, furs from many animals, for Europe. White men's history books called the time the Beaver Wars. We couldn't live without painted beads, European blankets, steel tools, pots and pans, and guns. Tribes competed for the riches of the forest. Killing your competition or stealing their harvest of furs was fair in our culture. Alcohol came to drown out our despair and poverty and to aid in cheating us. In paradise, after my earthly life, I studied the past. Learned to read, interviewed the few Native Americans who came my way, and learned the depth of our sorrows."

"How did you find out about Jesus?" asked Tanya.

"Many people came to us: foreign tribesmen, Catholic priests, Moravian missionaries, Presbyterians, Quakers. They made us aware of another way, other than our own. But personally, a friend of my father, a Lenni-Lenape, our name, or Delaware, to the settlers, knew of Christ from a trader who was fair in his dealings, who sold no liquor and seemed to care about the people he traded with. Our Delaware friend told me of the miracles of Jesus, that I should seek peace with all peoples, that I should make Jesus the king of my life. This friend died a martyr's death." Andy stopped as he searched his mind for the proper words. His audience saw a deep hurt furrow his brow. "I will not go into details at this time, but I will say I was tired of killing the enemies of my people, and tired of them seeking me out, hunting me down to kill me. And not only me, but my family. I knew what David knew when the enemies of the Lord sought his life. At different points in time, it seemed the Susquehannock could not find allies. Then the diseases ravaged us. The European settlers to our east took the land of the Delaware. The Delaware flooded across our ravished land. My wife, Leaf, is a Delaware I took pity on."

Leaf, a quiet woman, grinned broadly at her husband's nonsense talk of pity. The boys began to laugh. "Tell them why her name is Leaf. Tell them, Dad." Tuck's voice was excited with glee.

"Tell us," said Tanya.

"No secret there. I wanted my own name for her, as we were starting a new life together as one. I thought of Fallen Leaf as a name. It was the beginning of October; the leaves were falling, and in the first stew she cooked for me, a leaf had fallen. Of more significance, the eels were returning down the river to the great water, the Chesapeake Bay, twisting, turning over each other's backs in the weirs, corrals. I faced a great dilemma: name her Leaf…" Andy's large hand fell gently, wafting to the earth like a leaf. "Or name her Squirming Eel. My people had an eel dance. I will demonstrate." With a sudden vigor, Andy was twisting like a trapped eel within a weir. Leaf began a rhythmic chant, and his face became an eel face; his eyes canny yet stonelike, his cheeks inflating and deflating, his head connected stiffly to his elongated body. The startled onlookers gasped then laughed as he eventually fell to an outspread blanket Leaf had cast beside her, gyrating in his antics. Many had never seen an eel but knew they were looking upon that creature. Tanya, Anya, and Flo were mesmerized. The boys, tapping into past times of delight, began to snort and chuckle. Andy had ended his display with his head on Leaf's lap. She fondly stroked his hair. He slowly stood. "I decided Leaf was a better name." The audience laughed and clapped their approval.

"Now, gathered conquerors—not survivors; we are conquerors—I need to make my rounds. I suggest you turn in early. Tomorrow will be long, and we will start the day before the sun rises." Andy walked toward John and Diana and addressed them. "Would you two like to come along? I want to make a pitch to you, and to Mat as well." Andy turned and called, "Mat!" waving his arm in an inclusive gathering.

Mat approached. "What can I do for you, Andy?"

"Come along. I have a pitch to make." Andy kept eye contact with his companions as he began walking. "You three are mature of mind and young in body. Two of you are resurrected, and Mat is, of course, mortal. Each condition has inherent strengths. The pace of life will begin to pick up in the next hundred years. The saved mortals will be producing children, and the already-born younger children will be marrying as well.

"Though Satan is gone from Earth, two forces of contention still remain: the world, the system that imperfect humans devise when they turn away from Christ and live in themselves; and the flesh, the seat of personal passion and rebellion. The resurrected will not feel these forces, nor will the Tribulation saints. But the mortals born during the millennium will. They will have the choice to live in their sin nature or within the Spirit of God.

"Police officers—part emergency medical, part counselor, part psychologist—will be needed to keep order. The list of skills may increase—this is all new ground, never experienced by humanity. Our resurrected citizens might have problems coping with miscreants. Mortals born during the millennium may have a greater susceptibility to accidents and need emergency care, all will eventually die in these thousand years, to then be resurrected, if deserving, at the end of the age. Citizens may, at times, have differences of opinions with each other. Tempers may flare, and you may take the role of judge, with access to the right conduct and rules for the situation via the Jerusalem hotline. All three of you have been considered good officer material. Mat, for your military service and devotion to truth and order. John and Diana, for displaying the same devotion in your lives, as well as for your military service, John; and for the deductive reasoning skills you showed in uncovering the satanic bible, Diana. Get in early from the foundation and have a career. If you find it isn't for you, then there is plenty of time to make a career change. If you have any questions, I will answer them now, or come to me at any time."

Andy called out to the first circular grouping. "Sleep time! Rising before sunrise!" They walked to the second group in silence. The three candidates, pleased at being chosen, had looked beyond to the future risks and rewards of the position. Mat liked having his hand on the pulse of future conflict. His entire earthly life had been conflict, and he developed the need to be proactive because that is how he had survived. John, too, was drawn to the knowing, the being prepared and having access to the knowledge and skills of survival. Both men knew, from bible prophecy, that war was coming at the end of the thousand years, and wars usually had festering root causes that churned and simmered for years before being revealed. Diana wanted to help those in need, however inconsequential the need. She, too, knew of the end prophecy, and determined that consistent attention to the disturbed human heart could prolong peace and order. Andy sounded the call to sleep and an early rising to this group. "Not one question?" The silence of the sleeping was the reply.

"Us?" asked Mat, thinking Andy may have been addressing his entourage and not the last group.

Andy whispered kindly, "Yes; you too."

Mat spoke. "I intend to marry Barb; you are familiar with her. She wants to have a large family. And she wants to be a teacher."

Andy recognized the barrier. "The roads and rail lines projects will be started this week, so you can enjoy country living and work in the city that will soon sprout and grow. Personal electric or steam vehicles will be available to all commuters. The chances of you dying on the job are slim to none. Scheduling and leave time are always conformed to personal lives. We no longer need to worry about people abusing work time—that was of the age past."

"What about Dan, Barb's brother? He's my age and trained as a soldier," asked Mat.

"He has a deeper skill set in electronics, and his heart lies there. He was considered." Andy smiled; Mat was a kid who looked out for others, a good trait. Andy studied John and Diana and said, "Okay, the pitch was given. You may continue the rounds with me or head for the cots and covers."

"I have to talk to Barb. I'll give you an answer tomorrow," promised Mat.

"Good enough. If she has any questions, have her come to me," said Andy.

"Are you to be the new police chief?" Diana asked.

"Yes."

"We're in," John said with an eagerness in his voice.

***

Tom Burnell was two-thirds of the way done. Tanya and Anya had delivered their prayers to the Lord, they had talked to their daddy for advice about the little things in life; he had kissed their foreheads, a temperature reading as well as a gesture of his heartfelt affection, and moved to Flo, the youngest. He was thanking God for his kids and the knees that no longer hurt when he kneeled and the muscular strength that coursed through his legs when he arose. He felt seventeen, but his mind was sharper than it was at seventeen, because by that age, drugs had already seized the workings of his mind. Though not resurrected, he certainly had received a regeneration. His mind slipped into a memory.

The Lord had brought his family back from death that day He came with his angelic legions. Tom's family had been lying in the corner of an abandoned house with half a roof intact. They had eaten their last bit of food—a can of beans and some stale bread. They had drunk their last liquid, a single gulp of warm water for each. He had no strength left to search for food. His family was wanted by authorities for not complying with the mandate—the mark of the beast, an invisible number upon their foreheads. They would have died before giving up their loyalty and faithfulness to the Lord. They had been dying. They were faithful! He remembered the anguish in his soul for his failure to provide the most basic necessities of life for his family. He had failed as a daddy. He had stared at his beloved family: into the closed, pasty eyes; the faces with the cracked, swollen lips and dirty skin. Their black skin was ashen; bodies of bones draped in hanging flesh and rags. Only hours separated them from death. He had begun to sob, trying with all his strength to be silent. *Lord, Lord, Lord* had been all he could utter.

The Lord heard! The Lord knew where the Burnell family was! The Lord knew the Burnell family needed to be rescued, and the Lord's presence overwhelmed the little corner of the derelict house. Life welled up within them all. They saw angels coming right through the walls, and they scooped up his little family in their strong arms, and instantly at the touch of those heavenly beings, strength of mind and body washed through the emaciated bodies and minds. They smelled the clean, white robes scented with herbs and balms, so soft to their dry, ashy skin as they were carried to that place of safety where the multitudes of the redeemed rejoiced. Unceasing tears came to Tom's eyes.

Daddy bent down to kiss Flo; he didn't want to wait for the end of her prayers to give her a kiss. She whispered, "Daddy, you're all wet."

"Forgive me," he kindly petitioned.

"I do," she said insistently. (What else would she do?) "Now, listen to me pray."

"Okay," he whispered as the little voice began. He heard her plea for God's attention and His blessings, even for her sisters, though they had been mean to her and ignored her, and then there was the amen.

In a soft voice, Daddy spoke. "Maybe Tanya and Anya just got caught up in themselves and really didn't wish to ignore you…I'm sure you've done that to them. I have done that to your mother. Find in your heart forgiveness, and we will see what that medicine does for you and them."

"Okay." She thought that doable and pleasing to Jesus. "And Daddy?"

"Yes, honey?"

"Your breath has germs."

He smiled, *germs* their euphemism for *smells bad*. "Thank you for your honesty. I will brush my teeth." He pressed his lips to the soft skin of Flo's cheek and held them in place, not expelling breath, with a smile on his face. God had been so good to him. He returned to his cot, found a toothbrush in his toiletries. The brush had residual toothpaste upon it, he brushed. That was the last sound Flo heard as she fell into slumber. She thought what a good daddy she had; he not only listened to her but did what he had promised—he had brushed his teeth. Could she ever do less for him?

The air was warm; one blanket was all that was needed—just as Andy had promised them. Tom lay on his cot beside Tish's cot. He saw the sky of thick stars beyond the canopy. The air was clean, and he could smell vegetation. All these people, millions of them, all over the world, from their first gathering in Israel to this night, sleeping as a community, with no fear of their fellow pilgrims. No rapists, no child molesters, no murderers, no thieves roaming about, no locked doors, no weapons for protection. Full stomachs and above-perfect health. Minds filled with dreams of the new life, the new beginning, God's promises fulfilled: the patient and enduring, the meek, had inherited the earth. All minds attuned to their Lord, soaking up the wisdom of the Spirit every waking hour. The Lord leading them as surely as the people of Israel from the bondage of Egypt. Here they were, in the promised land.

He reached over and touched Tish's shoulder as he nudged himself as close as possible to her body. He spoke softly, knowing she was asleep. "Good night, my beloved." He had never before used the word *beloved*, but he meant it, this man who had once lived a life devoid of any good or complimentary comments.

No response: Tish was soundly asleep. Thomas Burnell spoke again. "Good night, Lord, and thank you." He meant that too, and in the time it takes to blink an eye, he knew, with a supernatural awareness, that God loved *him*, had always loved him.

***

Tim studied the face of Mary. Their cots were side by side, she faced him, and she was soundly asleep, with her sleeping grin on her face. What a pixie. Maybe Hope was turning; maybe Hope was lost in thoughts; maybe unborn children could communicate with their mothers. The Creator God was awesome in everything. Thank God the Lord had smashed into Tim Johnson's self-righteousness and ego to claim him as His own. What an adventure lay before them. These thousand years were just the first adventure. What was a thousand years in the course of eternity?

They were going to make this land prosper. They would be taught incredible things. He knew the primary goal was to teach repentance and salvation to the newly born mortals, and with wisdom and practice, secure them in Christ before Satan was let out for one last rage of depraved deception. These thousand years were a time to glory in God's faithfulness, yes; and Tim Johnson planned to do just that. But there was important work, too. He had to make sure the grandkids and great-grandkids to come wanted Christ more than anything else in life. *Love God with all your heart, soul, mind, and strength; and then love your neighbor as you love yourself.*

Mat had told him that Barb said yes to the marriage proposal. Katie…he had to be searching for a godly man for her. Eventually Hope would need a partner. In the old world, he had been tied in knots trying to think of what kind of partners could be found for his kids. There seemed to have been no one. How could you choose? They were all alike: selfish, animal in spirit. They had lacked character, compassion, and all virtue. He clearly saw now: they had lacked Jesus, the fruit of the Spirit. Only in clinging to Christ did people become human. Only then could they develop character.

Now his problem was that every kid seemed to have Jesus, seemed to have character. What work would Katie and Hope do? Maybe just wait till they were in their chosen fields, then the right guy might be stumbled upon. Ah, there was no stumbling in the life of a believer. Just a time that had been known long ago by Daddy God.

He was vaguely aware of Mat returning to camp. Andy had told him beforehand what he would present to Mat and John and Diana. Mat and John did have the temperament, but now police work would be on a different plane of knowledge and skills, a psychological field of play. Well, they had those skills, too. They really could do anything they set their minds to.

***

As Katie snuggled into her blankets, she looked upon Emily. Emily would need her more as Mother became absorbed in Hope. Certainly, Emily could learn mothering through Mom. That was an important skill set to learn; Emily needed a career, a direction for her life, and maybe by Emily taking an interest in her big sister's search, she would be better prepared for her own career search. What did Ms. Katherine Elizabeth Johnson want to do? She wanted people to know her Jesus, she wanted to help people. Seemed everyone knew Jesus now—the Holy Spirit was coursing through the minds of everyone, dispensing wisdom, friendship, showing them the character of God. The Holy Spirit had taken her job! She laughed to herself, partly at her own bold conceit and mostly at her stupidity. Jesus loved her. The great I Am loved her, her Daddy God. All would be well. It was said that the new children coming from mortal-but-saved parents would have struggles. Maybe that is whom she was destined to help. She loved that name *I Am*. Holiness was the attribute of God that really knocked her for a loop. He was an awesome God.

***

Andy returned to his little family. The boys were soundly asleep—they lived and played at breakneck speeds of intensity, and sleep was a deep and powerful world to them. Leaf was sound asleep. He wished double cots had been ordered. He enjoyed her scent and her warmth. It was good to be on Earth again with important work to do. Why had the Lord chosen him? This resurrection body was really top-of-the line quality. In paradise, the new body was good. But back on Earth, the upgrades were highlighted, and they were amazing. He was excited about learning to transport over the earth, to fly like an eagle or a hawk.

He had good people under his wings—what one would expect of the redeemed, resurrected, and saved mortals. The beginnings of future problems would start in 150 years, when the first generation of children born within the millennium would be ready to marry. These children would have no experience with the old world and the Tribulation. The experts thought an additional 150 years would be needed for a social system—a world system—of nonbelievers to form. He would study them, live with them, learn. It would be a psychological game; they could appear to be compliant, to believe in the truths, but they could be turning away, seeking their own paths. There were no "own paths." The gate was small, and the road was straight and narrow. Personalities, skills, the unique walk of every believer was good. But the gate was small and the path, narrow on the walk with Jesus. It seemed a conundrum, and yet it was not. Andy was not anxious. He had learned to enjoy the present. Even life with responsibility was good when the Lord was by his side and within his mind.

This work was a far cry from leading bands of broken people—alcoholics, women and men diseased from debauchery, diseased from smallpox and yellow fever and a host of other maladies; people who had lost their land, their rhythm of life, who had lost the knots in the rope that marked the seasons and forgotten the tribal dances that marked the milestones and all of the interpersonal rules of manners. The men who had hunted for food had been in the jug or in the grave. Or had been killed by other tribes, including the European tribe. This new life was easier than being hunted every day for personal vendettas.

It was God's hand that had allowed him to die at the age of eighty-five in a log dwelling, far from his beloved Susquehanna River, with a European bed as his bier, and Leaf beside him. His boys had died years earlier at the hands of a brutish Iroquois warrior. Leaf had died a month after him from a broken heart. In paradise he had met again the clergyman who had provided the bed and had allowed Leaf to remain with his family. Prior to his death, he had tortured and killed the Iroquois warrior who had killed his sons, and when that man's pain and suffering did not fill his heart with satisfaction and peace, he had turned to Jesus completely. Before, he had raised his family in the faith, taking only what he understood and ignoring what he did not wish to comprehend.

Enough of the past; that had been settled in paradise. Andy reviewed the qualities of his immediate charges at his camp—all were sound. Emily and Dan remained on his mind. Both had been severely traumatized. Emily, by her parents' death and her abuse; Dan, by witnessing his father's death and his own death. No one knew that Dan Sr. had physically abused his son. Andy thought of Emily and Dan because, although resurrected, their quietness and apartness was not typical. Yet, it had to be wholesome and perhaps intellectually deep because God had saved them, healed them, and placed them here. He must explore a different part of his mind to know Emily and Dan.

CHAPTER 4

The first year of Jubilee, after the cleansing of Earth and forty-nine years of rebuilding, came with palpable joy, satisfaction, and peace upon the world. For a year there would be no rebuilding. The reality was the citizens of the millennium had worked so diligently, with joyous focus, with minds and bodies a delight to work with, that truly there was little left to do. Many of the traditional reasons for the Jubilee year had vanished. There was no property to return. No citizen had debt—money was freely given by banks. If a citizen wished, through the bank, he could tithe a percentage of his profit (if an enterprise had been created) to the Church. Money was freely given for building projects, vehicles, and homes, and many citizens wanted to pay interest to the Church, and this was allowed, at whatever time, whatever rate they decided. The small family farmsteads had smoked, aired, sun-dried, salted, and freeze-dried meats; dried, ground, and canned countless nuts, berries, and vegetables; and turned countless grains to flour through the years so that food could be given freely during the Jubilee year. The large agricultural operations, which had used perfect regenerating fertilizers, natural weed control, and crop rotation had no insects or mold issues, had produced bumper crops for forty-nine years, and all excess had been preserved. The agricultural producers took the year off or went part time.

This was a year to give thanks to God for the salvation offered by Christ. This was a year to rest in the arms of a Providing God. This coming year, it would be a time of outdoor breakfasts, brunches, and dinners—picnics, grilling, open-fire barbecuing, campfires—with gatherings of family and friends, Church and community organizations. Planned activities were raft, canoe, tubing, kayak excursions down clean and sparkling waterways; horseback, bicycle, motorcycle, and boat tours; hikes, walks, athletic games, and contests.

The normal activities of everyday life would continue—meals cooked, clothes washed, gardens weeded and harvested—because these activities were fun and rewarding and produced the joy of thankfulness. "The sweat of your brow" reality to life had gone when Satan was locked away. Work was accomplished, and pay received; school was attended, and grades were given; and all was seen as secondary in value to honoring God. The tempo of life slowed, the urgency of increasing commitments to material productivity faded away. This was a time to rest in what had been achieved and to dream of the future. The Creator was honored and thanked, the Spirit of God coursed through the people in dance, song, and music. Artists and craftsmen displayed their homage to their Lord through countless indoor and outdoor venues.

The people of Tim's original first-night camp circle had gathered at Tim's homestead that Jubilee summer. The acreage allotments were popular with the resurrected of the preindustrial age. Although many "back to the earth" adherents had been found within the industrial and postindustrial eras, few had made the Lord the center of their lives, and so now they lived in Hades. Many Tribulation survivors had yearned for land. They wanted that security in seeing their food as it grew. The owners of acreage wished to make the land produce and found peace and satisfaction in doing so. "Homestead," "plantation," "farm," "farmstead," "land," and "holdings" were popular names for the acreage, proceeded by a surname, a prominent feature of the land, or a biblical reference. Katie's Cottage Homestead, Katie Johnson. New Canaan, Mat and Barb's acreage. River View Plantation, Tim's place. Burnells' Beulah Land, Tom Burnell. Andy's Acres, you guessed it. John and Diana opted for mountaintop acreage, as did Dan and Emily—both couples wanted to live high with a view.

Tim preferred the word "plantation." A term from the mouths of the earliest settlers, north and south, of the 1600s: a settlement in a new country. The name implied purposeful action—to plant not only crops, but a family. Fruit and nut trees and trees for lumber were arranged in orderly rows and cultivated. Gardens of vegetables and berries grew, and fields of grains spread to the farthest perimeters. Every home had a barnlike structure where crops were processed and tools, stored. Solar smokehouses were common and presses for juices. Dogs, cats, horses, sheep, goats, llamas, cattle, chickens, and tens of other domesticated animals could be found according to the likes and preferences of the residents. Ponds had been dug and streams dammed and stocked with fish. Windmills pumped water and solar-panel roofs created electricity. These miniature gardens of Eden were the fulfillment of many dreams, yearnings. There were some settlers, perched in tree house homes, or elevated stilt homes, who just liked to keep their holdings wild, delighting in the plants and animals and drama of nature.

The holdings of the people, once established, took only hours a day of their weekday time, and sometimes all of their weekends, if they were enthusiasts. All had other interests and work for which they were paid in true gold and silver coin if they wished. Some worked from home, some worked the ag lands as field hands or managers. Some took the daily commuter bus to the newly revived Harrisburg and worked in offices, stores, warehouses. Agricultural and livestock enterprises owned by groups of citizens and considered income-producing also flourished.

The government was, of course, a theocracy. The living Christ, Jesus, sat upon His throne in Jerusalem—He had an office with a desk and computer. He talked, advised, reached consensus, had working lunches, and loved to walk His city. Anyone upon Earth could come to Jerusalem and have an audience. Electrascreen meetings were popular as well. The Lord enjoyed visiting every nation of His realm, arriving without warning and leaving to the voices of praise. A beloved leader whom all wished to serve with a fervent desire and steady hands and minds. An executive branch and a legislative branch existed, as well as judicial. The laws produced dealt with infrastructure and the balancing of the great resources. Moral law was written into every heart, confirmed by the Holy Spirit within. Omnipotent God picked His leadership from those whose hearts He knew, those who had achieved for Him in the old world, who had had kept their faith, lived their principles, and conquered. In forty-nine years, His leaders had proven His selection as excellent—all were competent and beloved by the citizenry. Issues did arise concerning civil matters of property, land management, and business enterprises and were settled peacefully, without the hint of rancor, by frank talk and accurate information. No citizen was marginalized or unloved; everyone had people—relatives, friends, Church family—who cared deeply; and all wanted to please their Father God.

A national armed force did not exist in the United States, nor anywhere in the world. Unknown to the world, in Jerusalem, Christ kept a think tank of military officers whose sole focus was the return of Satan in a thousand years. Border guards and maintainers monitored travel across borders, both incoming and outgoing, logged itineraries and destinations, offered practical advice, and knew emergency medical procedures. No one needed to leave his or her home nation, for all had peace, economic security, vibrant cultural and social lives, clean water, and plentiful food. Many did seek the vast empty lands for the challenge of pioneer life—making new land produce and establishing large families. The people of a nation never lacked hospitality for new citizens, all were in Christ, and opportunity was unlimited. A well-staffed coast guard patrolled oceans, seas, bays, large rivers, and lakes. An air force monitored weather and could handle all emergencies involving aircraft, airports, or ships in peril. A national guard existed and had received training in crowd control—of nonhostile, both peaceful and confused and agitated—and mass-casualty situations, as well as policing. Laser weapons and a very few rapid-fire, revolving-barrel cannons existed for possible use in extreme emergency situations, where objects of peril might need destruction. They had been used in practice against avalanche snowfields and rockslides and in debris destruction in raging floodwaters. They had yet to see real action in true emergency situations. These arms were kept in vaults. No training was offered in military tactics.

The economy was Christian capitalism. Capitalism had always needed Christianity for a moral trellis—an elevating framework. Otherwise capitalism would devolve, through carnal desires, into a clever form of banditry. That era was gone. Supply and demand issues could never be used to destroy competition—no one thought to do so. Competition was absorbed or rerouted and only disappeared simply because no one needed the product or service. No capitalist had the desire or need to be the biggest supplier or the only supplier. The greed for money was nonexistent. The quality of the product, balanced with cost, was the goal. Common sense in addressing all the competing factors of production was used to determine a reasonable profit. Labor relations were based on the moral and ethical principles of a father and his family. Production standards were high, but time on and off work was flexible. The farmstead enterprises, offering peace and sanctuary, were for fun—intellectual stimulation, exercise; to appreciate the seasons, the plants and animals of the Creator's world; to provide wholesome food. The excess produce was used as a good excuse to keep in touch with neighbors through sharing and bartering.

Yet, many small businesses began on the farmsteads and created produce and products of unique and high quality and wages for many. Inventions were born in the backyard garages and barns. Economic policy encouraged the small-scale businessperson, the individual factory owner, the small workforce of multitalented workers. It was the antithesis of past communist and socialist governments of the world's systems, where economic blackmail created obedience and stupidity, and lack and want at equal levels; history taught that when bureaucrats controlled production, the human will died. The Lord loved His people's independence and creativity, their drive, their wish to serve and excel. All knew that the joy of freedom produced the best of everything.

Every county of Pennsylvania had sufficient paved roads and rail commuter lines. Every county had a quality hospital, usually empty; an emergency service, police counselors; schools that offered every branch of knowledge from theoretical to applied; vocational training stressed innovation, invention, and discovery. Tuition was minimal, and parents could pick their schools, though all the teachers were the very best. Most citizens used their local schools, so that most commutes were due to the individual family's schedules and convenience needs. Every child went to a place of learning—even the home computer—alert, healthy, with an excitement to learn and respect for the vast knowledge that teachers possessed. To learn was to explore the nature and mind of God.

A myriad of clean-energy sources brought light and power to communities, from wind and water to solar and even clean coal-burning units, as well as natural gas. Littering and dumping were unknown, and nothing harmful entered the land, water, or air.

***

Tim's River View Plantation consisted of a single-level main house built of volcanic ash (produced from the geologic turbulence of the Tribulation) compressed into large blocks. The flat roof was used as a patio; chairs, umbrellas, a grill, weights, one stationary bike, and three telescopes littered the space; the telescopes targeted the mountain, the river, and the sky. Comfortable, wide, cushioned chaise lounges provided night sleeping with starry heavens and falling stars. Porches, patios, piazzas, and decks surrounded the home as well as bamboo, pines, spruces, and flowerings vines of humming birds' delight. In his barn, a steam tractor sat—two quarts of water made her purr—and all tools necessary to make the land produce. He had a smoker. He had an inground pool and hot tub. His acreage was situated on a plateau by the Susquehanna's bank—a plateau that rose as it neared the bank, so as to greatly enhance the view of the broad river, whose wooded islands seemed sailing ships upon the water. The plateau sloped away from the river into the crease where a quiet creek meandered. Behind the creek a mountain rose, a long ridge with a symmetrical slope already covered in new trees of various heights and density of growth.

By the edge of the plateau, near the steep bank and the stone steps to the river, Tim and Andy sat on their newly bought Jerusalem chairs, John on an Adirondack, leisurely watching the river scene; Puck and Tuck fished live crayfish with rods and reels through the deep water behind exposed sedimentary-rock ledges. The air was warm, so shorts and a cotton shirt were the attire. The sunlight was bright, almost directly overhead, but not enough for a hat. Shoes were only necessary if descending the bank to the river. Tim sighed as a hummingbird hovered in front of his face, wondering if nostrils held nectar. A beautiful creature, he thought; a beautiful view as deer came out from the nearest island to graze on river-edge vegetation and stand in and sip the clear water. Bass jumped at various locations on the calm waters. Wildflowers were in bloom, and their scent filled the senses.

"What was it like when you first roamed this riverbank, Andy?" asked Tim. Andy had mentioned his "roamings" when the holdings were first chosen, bits and pieces of knowledge that had been increased over the years. Tim hoped more stories could be pried loose. Andy's Acres was two holdings down the river. Beside Tim's River View Plantation was Mat and Barb's plot, New Canaan, with their three little ones, then Andy's sons' holdings, which had not been built upon yet. To Tim's upriver side, Katie had her Katie's Cottage Homestead, a small cottage and acreage where she lived, when in the area. Emily moved between Katie's cottage and Tim's home. Emily had a great love for little Hope.

Little, because Hope was five years old in body development, though she had lived fifty millennial years. The mind did not correspond to the new formula of a "body time" of ten millennial years equaling one old Earth year. Hope's mind—all minds—were on a higher plane. By four months of age, a child had a vocabulary and created sentences. By eighteen months, a child had the potential for the logic and common sense that characterized an adult mind in premillennial times. The potential had to be exercised to reach fruition. How much knowledge a person accrued was still dependent on how much knowledge was absorbed. When Hope had lived one hundred millennial years, her body appearance would be that of a ten-year-old of old Earth time. By 150 millennial years, Hope's physiology would be ready for marriage, if she wished—her fifteen-year-old appearance hiding the physical dexterity, bodily control, muscular development of a mature woman of old Earth time.

In short, the body's aging process had elongated to ten years of millennial life for one year of premillennial body growth and subsequent aging. This metric was near perfect, as the new Earth environment of air, minerals, water, soil, food, and sun quality were enhanced. Gravity, magnetic forces, Earth's core temperature—all unseen cosmic forces that bound Earth to the interstellar world—had changed by degree and ratio to the salubrious pre-Satan levels. Harmful bacteria and viruses affecting the body were now gone. Even many genetic flaws had been destroyed or subdued when man reentered God's kingdom. This realigning of creation would have a great effect on longevity and quality of life.

Andy thoughtfully answered, "I fished where my boys are now fishing. The riverbank was not as steep or as high—the height added at the great quake. Same with the thousand-foot increase in the mountain behind us. You lived it."

Tim replied nostalgically, "Yes, a monumental event that told us the Tribulation was upon us."

Andy continued his narration. "There was one long island before us that hid two-thirds of the width of the river to the west. In the spring through fall, many camped along the island's bank. Our gardens and fields were on the island. To eat our crops, the deer had to wade the river, and not many evaded the arrow. A larger, permanent village was where we now sit. More fields were planted on the land you now reside upon. I slept here, on the riverbank. Every morning before sunrise, I would move slowly around the encampment, widening my circle, searching for enemies; bow and arrows in hand, war club over my back, knife in my belt. If I could get off a good shot at a deer, I took it. When light came and the young men were awake, one younger warrior always asked what I had seen—he was my replacement—then he would walk the perimeter. I would go down to the river to my big, flat rock, weapons still in hand. I would place my head under the water, sit upon the rock, and pray till I was empty of me and one with the creation and the Creator. Only then would I gather up my kill and return to our fire pit."

"Was it as peaceful and plentiful as now?" John knew that it was not.

"No, it was not. My vision of my Creator was clouded and incomplete. I did not know Jesus or the Holy Spirit. I had body aches and pains from past physical confrontations, bad sinuses from inhaling woodsmoke, viruses, and infections. My head hurt from searching for the next killer or killers lurking. White-oak–bark tea and willow tea were consumed weekly—the medicine of the times. Those I killed tormented me with their deaths in bad dreams. All those things are gone now. Praise to our God."

"Yes, praise to our God." Tim remembered the stress of living during the Tribulation—the constant fear of physical violence, the carrying of guns, knives. He had told Andy of the Tribulation in past conversations.

John remembered his war experiences and his hand-to-hand combat with Cain, the psychopathic killer for hire of the World Church.

"What does our natural-resources chief have going on?" Andy asked, wishing to move the subject to happier times. Tim's geology background had been expanded to encompass all resources for the region.

"Solar is going well. Wind is stabilizing. Our wind turbine on the mountain behind us has much more capacity—perhaps, for another fifty years of growth. Then another turbine would need to be added. The huge volcanic-ash field deposited far north is being systematically processed into building bricks and block, and at present rates will produce for another fifty years.

"We've been experimenting with unobtrusive water turbines on the river—safe to wildlife and noiseless, except for a slight thumping sound,"

Tim said. "Coal deposits are being tapped for home consumption; the new clean technology is 99 percent efficient. No environmental impact. Steam engines are being perfected. The big news, but of slight importance for long-term growth, is the downed forest we found under ten feet of soil and volcanic ash. An entire mountainside collapsed at the first major earthquake, burying living trees. It pays to uncover the wood and process it for furniture. Also, small deposits of gold and silver have been discovered, as well as rare earths."

Emily and Hope had appeared. Hope went directly to her father and was picked up and seated on his thigh. Emily stood, in perfect easy demeanor, before Tim. Tim noticed the Tribulation fears were gone completely. "What's the news, Emily?"

"Time to eat." She smiled, happy to deliver her message.

Andy stood and called to the boys. John sprang from his chair and stretched, breathing deeply of the scented air. The country life had always appealed to him, and his mountain-ridge home, with its view, was all the entertainment he needed. Still, being close to the river had an allure. But there was nothing to top holding Diana's hand and stepping off the deck at two thousand feet, looking southward, becoming buoyant, and transporting to work in Harrisburg.

Tim gathered up Hope as he stood, placed her between himself and Emily, and began the saunter over the thick, green grass to his home. Hope held tightly to the little finger of Emily's hand. He heard laughter from the pool, saw the chickens hunting across the expanse of yard for seeds and insects.

No fences anywhere. The wild beasts of the land did not harm the domesticated animals or crops. Scientists were attempting to discover how that phenomenon was produced. Some said a naturally produced hormone made domesticated animals unpalatable; others said it was the scent of humans. Still others thought it was a force field from God, though this latter interpretation begged the question of how. It was not uncommon to find wild foxes and chickens together on the lawns, the young ones playing chase with each other. On the lands outside the domain of humanity, the natural laws of predator and prey still ruled. But studies suggested the predator animals were eating more fish, insects, tubers, berries, nuts, and grains and that they were limiting their prey to land animals that died naturally or had debilitating injuries. Humanity could still hunt wild game, and the game animals fled, but no one would hunt within a farmstead's domain of peace. The same question of how was being asked as tornadoes and high winds still occurred, but none of humanity's endeavors were damaged or destroyed, and people were never touched.

Puck and Tuck had already raced ahead, kicking a found, weathered soccer ball between them. Tim never needed a report on Andy's work, as no one thought to break the law. Besides, Andy would volunteer any incident of note. Mat and John and Diana had joined the sleepy, small-city police force made sleepier by a citizenry of fully well-balanced minds and a zeal in caring for their fellow citizens. Their hours of active duty had been cut, but they were still on call and attending every seminar available on the theories of the new generations coming, who likely would be influenced by the negative forces of the world and the flesh. Free time was easily absorbed in the hands-on building of their plantations, and Mat and Barb's growing family, as well as Katie's coming and goings. John and Diana spent much time with the children. Tim had invented a mineral detector that could find flint or chert arrowheads and catlinite pipe bowls. Mat and John were carving out a dugout canoe with Andy's guidance. Tuck, Puck, and Dan were domesticating a wild crow and teaching her tricks. Many citizens simply explored the free hours away. History and genealogy, natural history, plate tectonics, geology, psychology, knowledge of the cosmos, all knowledge asked for was given by the Creator to a knowledge-thirsting public.

Tom Burnell and his wife were at the pool, watching the girls play. Tish and Tom had produced a son, a few months younger than Hope. Little Tom was poolside, playing in a sand pile.

Emily inhaled deeply of the sweet fragranced air. All the people she loved were here, and the green grass beneath her feet felt good, and the green mountain before her—each tree seen individually—was such proof of her Lord's power. She liked to write poetry in her time between duty with little Hope and helping Mary and tagging along with Katie. Hope still held tightly to one finger of Emily's right hand as she watched the kids in the pool. Emily sensed Hope's thoughts, and said, "We must eat first. The girls will be eating, too." Emily knew Hope had almost an adult mind and wondered why she still enjoyed holding hands. Evidently, there was a divide between Hope's intellectual capabilities and her emotional needs. Emily enjoyed the holding of hands, too. Emily thought, *Maybe adults should hold hands.*

Mary and Leaf were at the patio table, arranging the food items that Mat ferried from the kitchen. Katie appeared out of the woods from the vicinity of her cottage with her contribution to the dinner. With her free hand, she pointed to the southern sky, downriver. An object coming their way, lower than the mountain face that had been cut by the river. She saw John and Diana's roof on the mountain ridge.

"Here comes Diana," said Emily. "Look, Hope…in the sky."

Hope followed Emily's pointing arm. "Di Di. " *Diana* had become *Di Di* at Hope's birth, and although Hope's speech was perfect in enunciation, she still preferred *Di Di*. Diana touched the green lawn with legs already poised in the first step position. "You smelled the food. That's what brought you," said John, who was first to approach, wearing a whimsical smile. His partner had decided to sleep in due to late-evening work on their holdings. Emily doubted that claim by John about smelling the food, but then, she could smell flowers in the wind at incredible distances. Tish's family was leaving the pool; the girls laughed and raced toward Tuck and Puck. Emily knew *Puck* and *Tuck* were names from William Shakespeare's plays. She had begun to read Shakespeare and loved the entangled thickness of his word meanings, his mastery of language.

Everyone, in unspoken unison, had collected at the food table. "Where's Dan?" asked John of Mat and Barb. Barb spoke. "He's coming up from Washington after some early morning business. He plans to follow the river, transporting in free flight." As if on cue, a red-winged Dan came from high in the blue sky and, in a wide corkscrew pattern, descended upon the lawn. He hadn't needed the lightweight wings, but they did increase maneuverability, as well as his visibility to any other transporters.

"Where are the old timers?" Dan's eyes scanned the grounds. He knew Tim had invited all settlers of the immediate surroundings to join the party—in time-period groups, if they wished, wearing the clothes of their period and bringing the published sermons or tracts of their day and books, pamphlets concerning their faith. First Native Americans, then the settlers of the 1600s, and on through time.

"I wanted us to eat first so we could serve them and not be distracted," said Tim.

"What about all the good food they're bringing? The recipes from the past, like Leaf's hominy," said Katie, who, busy with her songs and arrangements in the past weeks, had little knowledge of the celebration.

"A little here and little there, through the course of the day. That's my strategy," Mat said.

"The main meal for our guests will be around four or five. Our early lunch will be our dinner. Let's eat. They'll be arriving in half an hour," Tim bellowed in his pretend drill-sergeant's voice.

Andy appreciated being a guest and not in charge. The majority of citizens were up an hour before sunrise and found themselves eating a main meal somewhere between noon and midafternoon. Most remained alert and busy through the evening hours. Their new bodies were enlivened to live fully, and it was natural to follow the ancient rhythm of the day. Four hours of sleep was enough for a normal body. Many people had learned that four hours taken in hour-long naps during a twenty-four-hour day was just as effective. No sluggish minds during the day, and no sleepless minds at night.

Diana lined up behind Katie in that secretive, girlish posture that promised good news and said, "Got some prospects for you. Interested?"

"Yes, still searching," Katie said in a hopeful but weary tone. Both concentrated on the food offerings and filled their plates. Katie continued to be amazed at her regenerated body and the food she could pile on a plate without gaining weight. "This resurrected body likes the food I see," she said in a jesting tone.

Diana chuckled. "Yes, they are really a pleasure to live within."

"To think humanity was duped out of this health by the deceptions of a snaky fallen angel," Katie said in disbelief.

"We were born gullible," Diana said, looking ahead. "Let's sit by that table under the tree."

Katie began walking and noticed the size of the table. "Room for only two. We will have our privacy. But let's eat first. Silence!" Katie's tone was severe, and she brought her hand down sharply in a chopping motion, then laughed, sat, and began to eat.

Mat grabbed a heaping plateful of food. He was to eat, then take over the care of his boys, Jedediah, four years old; Jeremiah, three years old; and Jeriah, two years old, who were currently under the watchful eyes of Barb. He sat hurriedly at the first picnic table available and began shoveling in turkey and ham, both raised on the plantation, and a grouping of side dishes that were melding together. He looked up to see Tom, with a crowded plate, looking for a seat. Mat raised his hand. "Over here." Tom approached.

"Dad, sit a spell," said Mat to Tom Sr.—*Dad* being a common form of address in the millennium for a man older than oneself, whether a father or not. "Are you intending to eat quickly then relieve Tish of little Tom?"

"It seems you're familiar with the plan, three times over," said Tom.

Mat laughed. "I'm engaged in it as we speak." He paused, organizing his thoughts. "When there is free time, I would like to have a sit-down with you about your pre-Jesus life, if that's okay. I might be overly worried about the future and the children who may leave the faith of their parents—kids deceived by their flesh and the world their generation will create and pull them toward. You might have insights you don't know you have."

"Stop in some afternoon. I'm usually puttering around the plantation. It'll be an excuse to sit, sip some herbal tea, have a few of Tish's cornmeal cakes, and watch the river go by."

"You're enjoying country living?" Mat saw Tom infrequently since his work in community relations, once known as law enforcement, had begun, and each family had concentrated on house building and their acres. Dad and Tom, both seeming semi-retired, now that the pace of life was so effortless, were always hopping back and forth between each other's homes, engaged in one project or another.

"Had I known how good it is…." Tom's thoughts ended with a bite into his ham sandwich.

Mat began on his hummus, honey, flatbread, and bean soup.

Katie and Diana had attracted the Burnell girls, Tanya, fourteen years old; Anya, twelve years old; and Flo, ten years old; and the Johnson's Emily, thirteen. These were their ages in old Earth years (OEY) and appearance, even though all had lived forty-nine years in the millennium, where each old Earth year stretched for ten millennial years. The marriageable years were approaching, and the girls gravitated to older women, who were contemplating marriage. Oddly a compulsion to marry had been created by societal aspirations and a defined time limit, one thousand years. A heightened sense of urgency prevailed for the creation of familial dynasties. Spiritual citizens and theologists wondered if this compulsion was the new beginning, a philosophy of a world order, that in time would oppose God. Children of the Spirit refused to rush. They searched for the partner chosen by God, supported by the new regenerated bodies that allowed children to be born later in life. Career choices and settling into a new environment could delay marriages, but not the desire to marry.

Katie and Diana, once their meals had been finished, were sitting beneath a shade tree. The flock of younger women sat on the lawn, near their table, seemingly unaware of their desire to learn and bond with Katie and Diana. Per new world rules, insects and bugs avoided humans. Mosquitoes that once preyed on humans were extinct or had adapted to undomesticated animals. Having full stomachs and being in the presence of ladies, the girls upped their behavior and gentility of spirit. Diana, studying the entourage, said quietly, "Let them learn from us."

"Yes, let them," Katie replied.

Diana straightened her posture in a businesslike way. "The first prospect is a few years older than you, a native of this region. He likes cardiovascular workouts, hiking, running, and his sport is soccer. He is currently a wildlife biologist. He is quiet but can produce some well-crafted one-liners. His humor shows kindness. He thinks on deeper levels of Christ and the past world and this current world. He is fascinated with the New Jerusalem coming. He wants a big family and, though he likes children in and of themselves, it is not lost on him they come with a purpose."

"Okay, his quietness could be the counter to my exuberance. And his depth could take me places I might not have explored. Next!" Katie called out in her store-clerk tone.

"Only one more. I went for quality, not quantity. This guy is always exploring the past—history. He's trying to trace humanity's interaction with God, through Christianity. The human reactions to forces placed upon us at any particular point in history. What was humanity looking for from God? Was it even the right search? It is really deep and complex, and I might not be doing it justice. But he is passionate in describing his quest."

"Was candidate number one passionate?" inquired Katie.

"More scientific passion…reason and logic," Diana said, after a pause.

"Passion is sometimes just emotion—a whim of the mind. Okay, my life isn't so busy I can't meet with them both. Does the second guy have hobbies?"

"He fishes, hikes, bikes. He currently works at the Library Project downtown."

"Give me their contact info. Are they aware I might reach out?"

"Yes, they are aware."

"Okay, thanks. Keep up the good work. Your credit will be on your account. Or do you want gold coin now?"

Diana chuckled. "Just invite me to the wedding."

Across the lawn, Mat was cleaning up the few crumbs on his plate. "I want to know the generational connection to your former gang, Tom," he said.

"The forces that gave it cohesion and purpose. See if you can define it as a group within a group and yet separate."

"I gotcha. My mind will be working till we have our talk. This week," said Tom.

"Yes, Thursday works." Mat saw the boys, Jedediah, Jeremiah, and Jeriah, intending to bolt from Barb's presence. Emily, usually with the boys, had disappeared, and Tish was distracted by Tom Jr. Mat added, "Duty calls."

CHAPTER 5

Thursday morning dawned with fog along the river's banks; droplets of water floated in the cool air, the fog was dense above Mat's head, the light was dark gray and foreshadowed rain. His lightweight athletic walking shoes were wet. He sauntered along the riverbank trail, passing through Tuck's and Puck's holdings, then Andy's homestead grounds. The deer he saw had separated into groups of bucks with velvety antlers and does with under one-year-old offspring. The forest litter was tracked and crossed, and he heard the sounds of sprightly turkey amblings and scurries. The woods gave forth their verdure, and the wide river gave the sweetness of flowering weed beds on sand and pebbly rock bars. He could hear fish breaking the plane of water and their subsequent slapping splashes as their thick bodies went home. A rose-breasted grosbeak, down from the mountain, called from a treetop.

Tom's property was entered. A sign, posted upon a thick tree, said, "All are Welcome." The path had been leveled and cleared of roots and rocks; the bare, sandy soil was soft underfoot. It appeared Tom had spent some time on his tractor, improving his part of the informal river trail. Perhaps someday a formal river trail would be upgraded and known to all. At least one equestrian had found the trail by evidence of the heavy hoof prints. A shower began, and Mat put on the wispy rain jacket carried on his hip belt. He straightened the upturned brim of his hat to protect his face and neck from the rain. The brim had been upturned to allow greater light into his eyes.

He came to a thinning in the trees and spacious lawns with cut grass; benches and chairs overlooked the still fogged-in river. He turned inland, could smell woodsmoke. Yes, a good morning for a fire inside. He could see above the fog the ridge top of the mountain coming toward the river. He was unaccustomed to seeing the mountain so near and looming. On his property slightly north, the mountain seemed distant and aloof. A nice morning for conversation of import—the fog, the rain closed in a man's thoughts, so that being within his thoughts held more fascination than the outer world. There was Tom's home, gleaming white, of the same volcanic-ash blocks as Dad's home and many homes along the river. Behind, he saw the outbuildings, garages, work areas, the gardens, the fruit trees, the play areas of the Burnell girls and little Tom. He noticed a jacket that hadn't been taken inside, and a soggy, half-eaten sandwich and a cup.

Out, away from the home, under a spreading chestnut tree, was Tom, draped in a poncho and rain pants, sitting in a chair. Mat saw the line of walk from the house to the tree, darker than the surrounding grass, as the footfalls had dispersed the water upon the grass. Tom was facing the forest but heard his guest approaching, through the use of his sound-detection hearing device. Nifty little gadget. Mat knew of the device, knew it was in place by the slight movement of Tom's head at the faint sounds of his footfalls.

"Mat approaching," whispered Mat—quietness, for Tom may have had a purpose to his sentinel.

Without looking, Tom waved him in with the slightest of movements. Mat stood beside him. Tom whispered, "A black bear and four cubs. Four!" He held up his fingers. Then he rose from the chair, faced Mat. Mat saw the gleam in his eyes, the utter delight in his sighting of the cubs. Four cubs to one mother was rarer than not, though one cub could be lost before the year ended. The whispering continued. "They came right up to the tree, looking for chestnuts. But my scavenging girls had cleaned them all up. Leaf had recipes of all types—ground, powdered, boiled in soups."

Mat could see the evidence of the story, the bear tracks leading from the forest, spreading out before the tree. "Did she respond to your presence?" he asked.

"Like a pet. The little ones flocked to me, sniffing and touching. Until she said, 'Leave him alone. Where are your manners?'"

Mat smiled widely. "What a wonderful world it is."

"Praise our God," Tom reached out to Mat's shoulder, slid his grip to Mat's upper arm. "Come in out of the rain." He and Mat turned toward the home. Tom spoke with passion. "Can you believe I'm here? Can I believe I'm here? It's just so impossible. The end of humanity's world order, our stupidity. A new world! As prophesied! God telling men the future, and as ludicrous and unbelievable as it all seemed, it darned well happened! What a reversal. It's like one of those sporting events, where the underdog is so far behind he couldn't possibly win. Then, undaunted, he comes back in the final seconds—the final play that decides it all. Victory."

Mat's tears streamed. Tom's enthusiasm, born of the Spirit, had taken hold. God was incredible, God was overwhelming. Life was never too hopeless, a person never too defeated for the Lord to bring His victory. The darned sports analogy, just like his dad and mom had always used. Just like he had always trained for in all his sports as a kid, just like he had faced combat, just as he had survived the Tribulation.

Tom continued, "These thoughts are all fresh in my mind due to your request. I decided to think back on the individuals I knew from my criminal days—my fellow gang members. Maybe one had repented and is here on this new Earth…or maybe two…and we, together, could have talked to you. I found the rolls of my gang. Over two thousand members in Harrisburg, and their families numbered maybe ten thousand people. Not one other soul from those twelve thousand people—not *one* knew to repent or wished to repent. Me. I was the only one! New waves of thankfulness washed over me, and unworthiness. There were good people in the gang—or perhaps, people who did good, perhaps for their own egos or political purposes. Doing good isn't the road to salvation. Knowing you are evil isn't the road to salvation. It is knowing that your evil is an affront to God, and this God you offend is the only good in the world. When you hurt God and are ashamed of your hurting Him, then you are at the threshold."

"Yes, Tom, I see it." Mat did see it, the essence that hurting God shamed a man or woman. That was essential, for it meant that person knew—*absolutely knew*—God lived, and God loved. This type of shame was that emotion that came from returning evil for good. Shame identified that you, alone, were the bad guy, the problem, the kink in the plan. *Tom Jr. ought to know the depth of his father's love of God,* Mat thought. And this wisdom just spoken had eternal value. This observation would be entered into the Tom Burnell journal Mat had created. His own dad had rated a journal as well. Mat added to the journals when something those men said struck deep, had significance beyond the present. In time, when Tom Sr. was in paradise, Mat would send the journal to Tish and the kids.

From the silence, Tom spoke. "Then, in deep shame, you ask for forgiveness."

"They could not visualize, believe in an entity—a God—to ask?" Mat asked.

Tom nodded. "And/or they could not admit there was a force greater than themselves or was greater than themselves and loved them." He paused and reflected on his thought. "I need to tease that thought out." His voice lessened, trailed again into thought.

Tom opened the door of the main entrance. The small foyer of hooks and hangers was strewn with clothing, and the floor, with children's shoes. Plates, cups, crumbs were stacked in a corner. At the sight, Tom smiled in domestic contentment; even the messes of his kids were beautiful and a sign of God's love. "It's a place to start our discussion on the power of the gang. People so deep in their flesh that, really, they thought they were God and could not imagine an outside entity that would love them more than they loved themselves. Strong wills or strong appetites for those props that made them feel godlike, superior to others; and drug experiences that confirmed their deity—sexual mastery and physical mastery over others. Or material objects—clothes, vehicles, homes above the ordinary."

They moved down a hallway, past the kitchen, into the spacious, high-ceilinged living room, before the window that spread across a wall and a cluster of sofas, recliners; the fireplace gave off its heat and light.

Tom said, "Take your shoes off, Moses."

"I'm Mat."

"Yes, I know. Your sister sings an old hymn called, 'Take Your Shoes off, Moses; You're on Holy Ground.' When we are born, we are on Holy Ground and created by a Holy God. The people not with us now never knew it." Tom sighed in regret.

Mat smiled. "I understand your meaning now, but I thought you were slipping."

"The first person of the millennia with dementia," said Tom. They laughed. Tom continued his conversation. "Speaking of slipping, try these slippers from the guy who raises sheep, back toward the mountain. The farmer from the late 1700s—Abraham is his name. Take your jacket off; hang it by the fire." Tom moved to the fireplace, used the fire poker to expose hot coals, then placed a three-quarter piece of trunk wood upon the coals. "What do you want to eat? Something bready or corn-meal texture? Eggs and sausage gravy over biscuits, pancakes?" Through the great window, Mat saw lawns and vegetable gardens soaking up the now steady rain, even as the fog was lifting.

"Some pancakes—three if they're fat—maple syrup and a coffee, two sugars and cream. Please, if you could." A wry smile still played on Mat's face from Tom's "slipping to slippers" remark.

"I'll call for my waitress." Tom ambled back to the kitchen. Mat felt the quiet in the house, the kids still asleep; the fire snapped and popped. He placed his shoes and socks near the fire. He slipped into the sheep-skin slippers with a wool-cotton mix lining. The warmth upon his feet was delightful. Tom had brought up some valuable points. Not only had new trails opened for identifying the ungodly, but for converting them, which had been forgotten in all previous discussions of the future. The troublemakers needed to be identified, and they needed to be saved, if possible.

Within two minutes Tom returned with a pot of coffee, cream, sugar, and the pancakes. "Eat. I'm going to make some toast for myself. Then we will begin."

***

Later that day, Mat sat contentedly on the rock ledge jutting from the river, halfway between Tom's riverbank holdings and the first river island. His skin, still wet from his river soak in swirling whirlpools along the rock ledge, dried under the midafternoon summer sun and gentle breezes. The morning rain and fog had lifted and disappeared hours ago. His swim shorts, made from a wicking material, had already dried. Puck, fifteen OEY, and Tuck, thirteen, OEY, were to his right, toward the island. They had been working diligently all morning under Andy's order to build an eel corral. The heavy river stones had certainly made their arm and chest muscles pop; fun work that would pay dividends in the fall for firewood splitting and hauling. Even though in a young man's body at twenty-two in old Earth years, Mat wistfully remembered the coming alive of his own musculature fifty-five years ago as a youth during the Tribulation. The thoughts of sports hero or soldier or firefighter, protector of the weak and innocent, came with the muscle. In the trials of the Tribulation, he had needed all of his natural strength and the Lord's supernatural strength as well.

His eyes parted from the broad vista to his south, of the wide river and numerous islands and the mountain crags to his left where the river had eaten the high and uniform mountain ridge. He glanced studiously at Puck and Tuck, who were cooperating in moving a massive boulder beneath the water. They were learning teamwork. He was bemused by their concentration and seriousness and had a momentary glimpse into their adult future when they would need to cooperate. Mat glanced to the left, in the expansive shallows, only inches deep, where Tanya, Anya, Flo, and Tom Jr., played. Emily stood by little Hope and kept an eye on Tom Jr., who was also five. Tom Sr., who was in the swirling whirlpools at Mat's feet, rose, his eyes locked upon the children, and backed onto the same rock as Mat.

Tom, facing downriver, studied the wide river, the looming mountain ridge that ended at the river. Bare rock crowned the top of the mountain at its terminus. Vultures circled in the strong wind currents at the top. Not a cloud in the sky, he noted. "I can see the beauty in vultures, now that the Tribulation is gone."

"Yes, they are noble birds when riding the air currents," said Mat in a tone of reflection, as he faced downriver.

"As opposed to picking at a human carcass," said Tom.

"Exactly," said Mat. Mat ran his thoughts through their earlier conversation on gang-related topics and Tom's experiences. "What would your summary on gangs be, if you were presenting to an audience or a board?"

Tom took a breath inward, his eyes stared into his mind as he spoke. "A gang is a group of people bound by a common objective, such as protection, material needs, political power. Social bonding provides a rationale to life, identity, self-worth, stability. The strongest, most persistent person or people become the leaders; order and brute force, bringing others into compliance by any means, is the overriding goal." Tom reflected on his summation. "I sound intelligent." He laughed heartily.

Mat chuckled. "You are intelligent."

"Gotcha fooled." Tom laughed heartily again. The Spirit of God laughed, as He had worked into every facet and cranny of Tom's old self and uprooted the lies upon lies seeded by Satan to destroy this man's self-esteem and self-worth. The laughter spoke of victory. The presence of the Spirit was upon the two men.

Mat's gaze went to the riverbank. "Tish is signaling from the bank. One arm straight up, and the other to the side straight out. Seems my dad is with her," said Mat, squinting from the sun reflecting off the water.

"That's an *L* for lunch," Tom stated. "We have a sign language." The heads and bodies of the children playing in the water snapped to the direction of the shore and the figures upon it. Time to eat. In playful, histrionic eagerness, Anya began a wild dash to the shore. The others matched her attitude and flailed arms as they lifted their feet high from the water in their awkward haste.

Mat called to Tuck and Puck and pointed at the bank. He knew they had seen the figures on the bank, but recognized they were so absorbed in their work they might choose to override their hunger.

Mat stood and called out, "Lunch! The rocks aren't going anywhere."

"In a minute," Tuck called back.

No need to answer. No harm would be done if they stayed, and they wouldn't; hunger would eventually win. Mat saw Tom moving toward Tom Jr. It was good for one adult to stay close to the kids, even in a near-perfect world and only inches of water and with Emily watching Hope and Tom Jr.

Mat stepped down from his rock perch, began pushing his feet through the deep water by the rocks, delighting in the hard, rock-cobbled bed and the clear water. Schools of darting minnows and the dark, blurred shadows of lightning-fast bass fled from his surging feet.

Mat, Tim, Tom sat at the picnic table with their plates of food, bare backs to the sun, and eyes toward the children eating at their own picnic tables. Mary, who had accompanied her husband, and Tish had prepared the food—chicken-corn soup and freshly baked bread. Andy's two boys came running at full sprint to the food table. Andy was working in Harrisburg, and Leaf was at her church, teaching handicrafts of the Susquehannock to those interested in native American crafts.

"Those boys run everywhere and with abandon," Mat said admiringly.

"Do you know why?" Tim asked soberly.

"A joy for life." Mat's tone was confident.

"A joy made greater because at birth, they were cripples," said Tim, his voice low and sober. "They were despised by their tribe, mocked and belittled, hectored, pranked and pushed, tripped and beaten. Their hobbling walks and walking sticks were parodied." His disgust at their treatment was evident in his scathing tone.

Tim whispered, but his anger burned the air. "Andy shut their mouths by the force of his arms—actual slaps, punches, and beatings. But there were always outsiders searching for the cripples; it was so good to hate, to lift yourself up by beating someone down with words and sticks and fists. Then, Andy would need to fight again. That's when he realized he had to teach them why it was wrong. Only the God of Christ had the truth to tell."

"I had no idea." Mat shook his head in disgust—remembered when he had been beaten, urinated upon, threatened with dismemberment when he was captured by soldiers of the "beast" during the Tribulation.

Tom took up the story. "A warrior from another tribe, an Iroquois, despised the boys. He killed them and taunted Andy with their dead bodies grasped in his hands, held high. Andy subdued him and methodically broke every bone in the man's body, then slowly cut him to pieces as he threw the flesh into a fire. He ate the flesh as the man watched."

"Dad and I came upon a scene like that during the Tribulation." Mat remembered the incident, the day after the first full day of combat. He and Dad had tracked enemy soldiers to a group of hostages, waiting to be tortured; a soldier with no eyelids, no lips, no ears, crying out for mercy and in pain, had led them to the scene.

Tim stared softly into his son's eyes. "I thank God for your courage in ending that scene."

"The Lord moved me." Mat's words softened in humility.

Tom chose not to ask what had occurred—in the future, maybe, when hearts were calm. The men sank into their thoughts, imagined the internal pain of Andy. Tom was the first to come out of the depths of thought and prayer. He looked deeply into Mat's eyes and then into Tim's gaze. "The Spirit arranged this time for me to tell you what deeply disturbs my mind as to the future and the end of this millennium."

"Speak, Tom. Speak your heart," encouraged Tim with a soft, determined fervency of voice.

Tom took a measured breadth. "The mortals born in this perfect world will have no remembrance, no personal remembrance of what is evil, what evil does to men and women—to humanity. The boys run with such glee and happiness because they knew the utter pain of physical immobility; they suffered lack—being less than those around them. They experienced hate, loathing from those who should have loved, encouraged, and comforted them. Andy, blessed with strength, found that strength alone could not heal his boys or even save them from the hatred of the world. Andy learned about love—who had created love and who had given it and, of course, who could not love and why. Can humanity know good without evil? Isn't this why God allowed evil—evil brought upon ourselves by ourselves? These mortals being born now, how will they ever appreciate life and love God before all else? Only knowing history can they even remotely, intellectually, know what Jesus's sacrifice means, and what they have."

Tim answered. "I have thought these same thoughts, Tom, and I agree with everything you have said. We must teach history. The resurrected must make their personal stories known, and the mortals of the Tribulation must tell their stories. This must be our life's work for this millennium."

Mat spoke in a sober tone. "That is why Satan will be unleashed for a brief moment at the end—the mortals must experience a life of choices, good and evil. They must learn to recognize what is of God and what is not, and through their actions, they must declare their love of God and their devotion. The last gathering up of the tares of the field of harvest will occur."

Tom spoke determinedly. "We need to make damn sure that there is little to burn."

"Amen," came from Tim and Mat simultaneously

***

Mat saw Katie moving down the river trail, through the grove of trees before the clearing. Paul was with her, her friend, business partner, now, and perhaps her future fiancé. Diana's dating leads had withered away. Paul had been found by accident. Paul was the boy at the mountaintop restaurant whom they had noticed before the Tribulation. *There are no accidents in God's world*, thought Mat, who wished his sister the happiness of companionship and children.

She came directly to the table of men. "Here's Paul again, my producer, don't ya know. Such solemn thoughts are an aura upon you, Gentlemen! Give praise to God. He's got it all under control, even as we think of how to serve Him." Katie walked away toward the girls, then ran, as if to pounce on the gathered children. Paul had begun to trail behind her when Mat called out, "Stay here with us, Paul."

Paul turned. "Sure." He wanted to know these men, for they knew different facets of Katie, and he wished to know all there was to know about her.

Mat was smiling at Katie's faithful optimism and in happiness at Paul's addition to the known thoughts and faces of his family and friends. Tim was remembering his long bunker stay with his daughter during the Tribulation.

Never had Katie's faith failed. Tom smiled upon Katie's appearance; she was so much like the angels of rescue who came to his family on that glorious day of Christ's return. Her voice was like celestial music. To think the God of the universe had saved him to live among such good and wise people. He was unaware that he was a good and wise person in the sight of God and his friends.

Mat spoke. "Dad, catch us up on what's happening in the world." He looked toward Paul, made eye contact and said, "He watches all the global electrascreen news; has his friends, Carl, in Southeast Asia; and Ling, a former Chinese soldier, give him news."

Tim said, "Carl sends his love to everyone. He's opening businesses, specializing in bamboo housing construction for the global market as well as providing community infrastructure for his workers. He's slowing down. Remember, he was in his late seventies, in old Earth years, when last we saw him. Ling has established many churches. China and the Siberian lands need people—the harvest of souls was so poor in that region that there is no one to take advantage of this thousand years. The cold is gone, the soil is fertile, the rain is plentiful and consistent. The resources are vast.

"A worldwide migration is taking place of the mortal redeemed from Europe and from the Middle East and their offspring—large families. Africa is the hotspot for growth, followed by northern Asia. All the inhibitors are gone—the extreme weather, germs and viruses, man-eating animals, human animals. The harvest of native souls in Africa and Asia was huge at the very end, during the Tribulation, proportionally, even though the population was small. Australia is booming, as well. With sufficient and predictable rain and flat, expansive fields, the huge ag machines are turning in bumper crops. The herds of grazing animals are beyond description, and mineral deposits are vast in size. Europe had the highest resurrected population, due to the long history of Christianity there. South and Central America's populations of resurrected and redeemed mortals were modest, but their industriousness is noteworthy."

"What do you think, Paul?" asked Tom, curious to know this man so close to Katie.

"Encouraging news. I search globally for music, songs, and artists. Katie has really been interested in early Judaic folk songs and dances and even in the music of the Byzantine Empire. I talk to many around the world, and they are praising His name, and life is good," Paul said. "The hard work of rebuilding is not given thought, but only met with thankfulness."

"What of the future? The end of the millennium?" inquired Mat.

"Everyone is living for now. This is a time for celebration. Everyone trusts God with the future now that they have such strong evidence. Christ came back—God's kingdom reigns, and in no time at all, we will see the foolish and evil of this age meet their final unresting place."

"Here, here. Praise our Lord," said Tim, as Mat and Tom gave amens. They had spiritual plans for the future; they were thinking ahead. With dutifulness, they could prepare for the worst and enjoy the present as God intended. In God they trusted.

CHAPTER 6

Tom Sr. looked out the floor-to-ceiling picture windows of his south-facing living room, at his gardens planted in potatoes, turnips, beets, and onions. The trees were bare of leaves, but the grass was thick and green. The cold rain was turning to sleet. His fireplace had three logs upon it—the maximum. The one month of what passed as winter was upon the region. Snow was rare; temperatures barely slid below freezing. His rows were covered in plastic sheeting. The mountain loomed before him; most of the trees leafless and the bare earth showing the strewn leaves lying over rock ledges and boulders. The pines, hemlocks, spruces, cedars, and bamboo hybrids held their green, and their canopies and tangled branches provided refuge for birds and other wildlife. He had a telescope aimed high on the mountain, where he had last spotted a herd of deer, probably a mile away. He spent hours with his telescope, studying the mountain, searching for animals. A month ago, the black bears were thick, the black of their bodies riveting to naked eyes scanning the vast slope. One cinnamon-colored bear had passed through, never to be seen again. The bears were snoozing now, but they would be back in action within a month. A month of fall, a month of winter, a month of spring. Just the way he liked it.

He sat near the fire, coffee in hand. It was just good to sit, to think, allowing the day to unwind on its own accord. Soon he would need to visit the kitchen and prepare a light breakfast. For now, thought and coffee were pleasing enough. One hundred and fifty years. The third Jubilee year had begun in the fall. Life, in this winter month, was just as good as it had been on day one of the millennium. Physically, at fifty-two years of life, measured in old Earth years and physical appearance, he felt he was holding his own: bodily strength still the same and mental abilities the same, meaning both were still a delight and still astonishing him. Tish, also fifty-two years of age, was in perfect health. They had both entered the millennium at thirty-seven years of age. She was the perfect mother and wife.

His daughter Tanya was a happy twenty-four-year-old, OEY, in physical appearance, married to Tobe, a good guy, deep in Christ, born in Africa to an African pastor and his wife. Tanya and Tobe had three kids and lived on an African holding of thousands of acres. Anya, twenty-two in OEY, had remained in the United States. She taught school in California and was married to Keith, whose family had Chicago roots dating to the days of slavery. They had one child so far, a boy only a year old. Flo, eighteen OEY, was still at home. She was a blessing, attending the university, receiving above-average grades; active in Church, with many friends both male and female, and with a one-day-a-week job for spending money. Tom Jr., fifteen OEY, was at home and had taken to making the farmstead run. He was good with tools, had an inventive mind, and was always tinkering in the barn. He liked solving problems, was good at math.

Tom was aware this was the year that the unsaved children of the millennium could begin to marry and produce offspring. Tom Jr. was such a child of this generation. He had been conceived after the beginning of the millennium. Legally and by the maturity standards of the millennium, he was ready for marriage if he desired. It was unknown if male children under thirteen and female children under twelve who had entered the millennium were indeed saved, though in a ceremony of baptism, all had declared as such. He felt secure in his first three, even though they had entered the millennium at the ages of nine, seven, and five, respectively. All that came forth from them spoke of the fruit of the Spirit, the salvation of Christ, the glory of God. Tom Jr. was more difficult to understand. Yes, he was male, and, yes, he was fifteen in body development; those were difficulties enough. He had been blessed with an ability of deep analytical concentration and, yes, math was easy to him. No one on either side of the family was noted for math. Did the math gene have a negative side? Tom had always thought "math people's" differences from the rest of mankind were noticeable and quirky, as if their brains were wired differently across the spectrum of thought. He should celebrate that difference; really, that is where success was located, in business, science, math.

The front door opened; he heard the bell attached to the door tinkle a bucolic, cows-grazing-contentedly ring. A male voice resounded. "Tom Sr., where are you hiding?" and just as suddenly, someone was seen in the yard, coming around the house from the front—a stocky Asian man, waving happily, quickly with short, muscular arms and a massive smile on his face. "Ling," Tom said to himself. That meant the voice at the front door was Carl Stasic's. Tim had told him the two were coming to the state capital on a commerce and trade mission and were also interested in purchasing farm and lumber machinery for their Far East endeavors. Hopefully, Tish had heard their arrival; they were early for visiting, and Tish was still in the bedroom, probably asleep. He had no idea if Tom Jr. was in his bedroom or out in the barn.

He was never disconcerted or offended by unannounced quests. Besides these men were more than visitors, having been to the homestead and conversed with Tom on the electrascreen many times. Their praise for Tom Jr.'s inventive work with machines, plant genetics, was always evident. They were family.

Tom opened a side door rarely used, and Ling, in all his exuberance, tumbled in, as the door sill was raised, and tripping was commonplace. Had to fix that problem, he told himself—again. Carl entered the room from the kitchen, simultaneously with Ling, with his arms outstretched, a bag in his hand. "We came with breakfast. Found a doughnut shop open in Harrisburg."

"Good. Everyone want coffee?" Tom asked. Ling and Carl both nodded their heads in affirmation.

"Hey, we came for your son," said Carl.

"We will spirit him away before you miss him," added Ling.

"Why? Is this a good thing?" Tom bemusedly wondered aloud.

"Don't you read his articles online?" asked Carl. "The kid is an inventor of the highest order. A hands-on guy. We need him for our operations, from washing facilities to the assembly line, where he'd invent cost-cutting machines for production. We need him for marketing products and for bamboo-development ideas."

"We will pay him well," added Ling. Ling heard coffee perking and wondered how. He peeked into the kitchen, and there was Tish, who had slipped in just as Carl had passed through. "Clever lady, very hospitable," Ling said to Tish.

"You're the clever one, bringing doughnuts to the Burnell household—the one bribe that always works."

A somewhat pudgy Ling laughed. "I took notes at the last party held here while standing by the dessert table."

Tish laughed in admiration at the untrue story but played along. "You are observant." Her tone changed. "So you want to take my son away? That's between you, Tom, and Tom Jr." She had no worries; Carl and Ling were good men and would treat her boy as their own. She knew her son had extraordinary talents. Everyone he would meet in China would be good people too—the trash of the world was currently in Hades.

She felt a lightness of mind and body that was real. The evil people of the world had literally sucked life from the people of God as real as an infection, a cancer, a virus. Once there had been anxiety and distress in meeting people, she remembered, and now there was delight at treasures found: everyone thinking the thoughts of God, positive, affirming, wishing the best. Carl and Ling had become good friends over the years, and when not visiting, they were talking on the electrascreen.

"Any black ladies of marriageable age?" she asked unaffectedly. She and Tom hoped their son would choose within their race. Their race was beautiful, their race had been created by God—by design—as had all races. Clearly, He liked His races, and clearly, He wished to see them flourish, and clearly the physical differences between men and women, differences in personality, were the only differences needed to make a marriage work. All other differences were distractions leading to disharmony. This view of race was prevalent in the millennium and accepted by all; it sprang from every person independent of philosophical thought or shared conversations.

"Yes, many fine women, more than you would expect in a region once totally Chinese. Economic opportunity is plentiful, and everyone from across the globe wants the challenge." Ling's tone was enthusiastic.

Tish remembered Ling's conversion testimony from their first meeting: He was raised as an atheistic communist in a high-ranking family. He had entered the People's Liberation Army ready, willing, and able to destroy all who were not of his type, and he was actively engaged in that process as China devoured Indonesia. One night, he took refuge in the rubble of a bookstore in an artsy section of a cosmopolitan tourist town that had been devastated by fighting. He lay on a pile of books, rearranging them to make comfortable his then-bony rump, and he pulled one book out. Here was the problem, it was smaller than the rest, allowing an inequity in weight distribution. Title? *The Normal Christian Life*. The author was a Watchman Nee, a Chinese man of antiquity. *Ridiculous name*, thought Ling. *What was he watching for?*

Between the soldier's life of death and destruction, he read the book, and the man named Ling, which in Chinese meant spirit and soul, realized he knew nothing about a man's soul. From the words of a dead man named Nee, a deadened Ling assumed a new Spirit, not his own, but powerful and real—the Holy Spirit. The new reborn Ling found no acceptance or respect in the People's Liberation Army and descended to the lowest of ranks. On the plains of Megiddo, at the battlefield of Armageddon, he and a federation soldier named Mat Johnson raised their hands in praise to the Living God. Amazing! Ling, having no Christian family, knowing no Christians, was at a loss as to where to go. The Lord, who was never at a loss, had Ling accompany Mat to Mat's family and friends, which included Carl.

"Tom, where is Tom Jr.? Let's get him in here," Tish called across the room.

"I'm eating doughnuts. Let them find him and give their pitch," he said sweetly.

Tom Jr. had reached full adult logic and maturity at the age of ten. She knew Tom Sr. was trying to aggravate her, because he thought she would think this event too serious for a mere boy of fifteen to decide. Odd how appearances fooled the premillennial generations, her included. She knew that Tom Sr. would know that she saw through his nonchalance, but he liked the attempt at disturbing her equilibrium.

"Well, pass the doughnuts over here, gentlemen. Check his bedroom or the barn." Her tone was possessive when talking of the doughnuts and flat when mentioning her son. Would she cause Tom Sr. to squirm? She hoped so and inwardly laughed as she watched his eyebrows rise as he processed her remark.

***

Within days, their boy was gone. He had spent the entire time with Carl and Ling, buying hardware, tools, electronics, and listening to recruitment pitches listing all the perks of the company. He had returned home briefly for his personal Bible, marked with numerous notes in various-colored inks, and his journals and computer. All his clothes would be bought at his new location. His parents had never seen him so enthused, so alive—his eyes were gleaming like lasers. When they had kissed and hugged, given the last of their sound advice, shaken the hands of a tired-looking Carl and a bubbling Ling, they said good-bye to their Thomas Brown Burnell Jr., a one-of-a-kind guy in love with life and with God.

They sat quietly in their living room, upon the couch, holding hands. The day was rainy, the fireplace pulsing heat and yellow, flickering light. Tish spoke first. "As always and forever, our child is in the Lord's hands."

"Amen, partner." Tom sighed, emotionally weary from the high of their son being wanted for his ability and the departure of their son from their immediate thoughts and home, where he had lived for 150 years. The emotional weariness caused a physical tiredness. His proverbial right hand had been taken from him, the energy, strength, passion of youth; the clear-thinking kid who could solve every daily arising problem on the plantation. Tom Sr. knew he could never have accomplished an iota of what his son had done, never would have had the confidence to go to a new country. He had raised his son up higher than himself and his girls. No, the Lord had done it. God deserved His glory. The hateful street punk—aka Pukie, for his negative attitude—had done nothing but submit to the goodness of God in the raising of his son. Tom spoke. "Carl looks worn, but Ling seems energized." He loved running his observations past Tish. Having someone to disagree or agree or add insight and nuance to his thoughts enhanced his life.

"Carl was twenty years older than you at the Tribulation end, and his life pre-Tribulation in the old world was no picnic."

"Yes, the state orphanage, the marines, starting his business with hand tools, explosives, and sweat. The World Church knocked him down at least once to give his success to another. I suppose he'll be the first of our friends to take their temporary absence," Tom said sadly.

"You and I will probably be next in line," Tish surmised.

"Me, not you. You've gotta remain on the scene as long as you can—keep the Burnell line running straight and true."

"It is already in capable hands," Tish said. "I want to continue with you," she seemingly petitioned.

Tom was silent; he really did want her company in paradise, and she was probably right about the capable hands.

***

Diana studied the panoramic vistas of the earth surrounding her mountain-top home. John had insisted on a wraparound deck. Directly to the west, the mountain ridge dropped quickly to the cliff face that fell to the broad river below. From the river westward were mountain ridges and rolling hills, with tilting plateaus between them, as far as the eye could see. The greens of evergreens; the brown, leaf-strewn earth of rock and ledge, deciduous trees; the green fields of winter crops, the brown fields of waiting soils absorbed into her mind and memory. This time of year had once depressed her, but now the presence of the Living God nestled in her soul and filled her with expectations and happiness.

Homesteads dotted the land, few and far between, tucked into ravines or boldly sitting upon hilltops. Below her, the river islands floated like battle-weary frigates of the past, missing their sails—brown and bare masts fallen and standing raggedly. The sedimentary ridges of the mountain's foundations were clearly seen under the clear waters. She saw buzzards circling below her, playing in the wind, sometimes rising up to view her with a turn of their heads, then sliding away. South of her, a valley, then another mountain ridge, she saw the road of the commuter and the rails for trains. A bright-red commuter railcar moved north; only a handful of family vehicles were on the road. To the north were jumbled hills, some of great height, near the river. She caught the glint of windows in a chalet-type home on the highest hill and facing south. She had been to the home and knew that the view south, catching the broad river on its southern turn, choked with islands, was magnificent. Good and friendly people, a family, lived within the home.

She saw movement within her home. Emily and Dan, who had arrived half an hour ago, were baking and making coffee and tea for a midmorning snack. She would provide lunch. The weekly gathering of the resurrected friends. Tuck and Puck soon would be arriving. She enjoyed this moment and remembered when she could not enjoy the moment, fleeing from the continent with John, searching for the satanic bible, being pursued by forces of evil, hiding in the desert until her death. She remembered the breakfast with John and Gramps, at his farmhouse home, and afterward the Bible had been opened. She remembered with a fluttering heart when Gramps had told her the Holy Spirit was upon her. That was the beginning of her walk. To have ended up here, in eternal life—they should have called it eternal adventure. She laughed in joy at her good fortune and thanked her God who had chosen her. He protected her. She would live eternally. If times of trouble came, they would only be seconds in the river of time.

The wind upon her face was clean, carrying the scent of bare woodlands and fields; the air seemed to sparkle. Winter was leaving, and spring was patiently unfolding the newness of life. The sun, which had been hidden the past couple of days, was shining brightly. She felt the warmth enlivening her face and hands. She saw a speck over the river to the south, even with the distant southern mountain chain that stopped at the river. She saw flashes from the speck. John's reflective vest. He had had a nightshift in Harrisburg and now was returning. She considered stepping off the deck and meeting him in the air, but he would soon be on the deck, where it was easier to talk and hug. She couldn't be close enough to John, and she knew he felt the same way toward her.

She could scarcely wait to tell him she had found Miss Ames, the American, her teacher at the state school back before the Tribulation. Miss Ames had been resurrected. Miss Ames had been Christ's follower during that secret time when "Enslaver" was the term for a true believer—one who knew the new birth and the indwelling spirit. She had been difficult to find, because her nationality had been listed as French during the Tribulation, to hide her identity. The first and only woman to show her the spirit of Christ in a world dead to love. John had been the only man to show her Christ. She ran with John to Christ as they ran from the world and the killer Cain.

John opened his arms like wings, separated his legs in a scissors move, right leg forward; his wind cap was tight on his head, and his goggles were clear. He pulled his head and upper shoulders back ever so slightly to break his speed and set down. As she was hugging him through his cold jacket, she noticed his eyes fixed on something behind her. She half turned, and there were Puck and Tuck alighting on the deck.

"Perfect timing," Tuck said with a laugh. As they all moved to the home of apple pie and biscuit scents and steaming coffee and log-fire warmth, they realized with thankfulness that they were in the company of truest friends, whose words were supportive or challenging, who had vast stores of interesting knowledge as they lived life to the fullest, searching and exploring God's creation as never had been done before. These were friends who always had your back—to your deepest thought—even though it was a world in which everyone, in a civil sense, had your back. All the time, they marveled and wondered at the great love of God who had placed them in the eternal adventure, as Diana called it, of life unending.

The morning flowed with food and talk of their hopes and dreams, the condition of the world, and that far-distant future time when Satan would have one last showing. The Bible was studied, and the vast new knowledge absorbed from the principal participants, from Adam and Eve, Moses, Joshua, Elijah, Elisha—all had written their autobiographies. All the disciples, save for Judas, and all the New Testament souls, men and women now walking Earth, gave their stories. Those who had miracles done to them or family members by Christ had written their accounts; even the servants who had filled the vats with water that became wine had written. Voluminous readings through thousands of years, making the times, the cultures, everyday life vividly detailed—and so real. Readers participated in mind voyages no earthly drug had ever given nor could give.

Each member had hobbies and interests to share. John's current endeavor was the study of the American frontier and the interface with Native Americans. He. He'd compiled a list of the resurrected of this time period and read their journals, and in turn, began a study of the American character and how it differed from those of other nations. Because of his closeness to Mat, he began a study of the Middle Eastern campaigns ending in Armageddon. Diana became interested in the history of education from ancient Israel to the present. She talked to or read the accounts of teachers from every methodology of teaching and students from every period of history among the resurrected. Dan turned to science and invention. Emily took an interest in the Old Testament, the laws, morals, and world view of that ancient time. Tuck's sole interest was interstellar exploration, the nature of the universe thrown across the night sky. He was certain God intended His people to find and explore new worlds.

Puck studied Native American civilizations through genetics and the migrations of Siberians to the new world. He maintained contact with current Native Americans. He also enjoyed picking up random autobiographies from every age in history. You didn't need to be important in history for Puck to read your story; you didn't need to have a life story of success—even those who succumbed under the burden of hatred from the world were read. The journals of victims of polio, starvation, disease, industrial accidents, of those beaten and killed by their parents or others—all were read. All writers were worthy. All had eternal life. Puck searched their books for their thoughts, for he wanted to know the mind of their great God who had deemed them worthy; who had suffered with them and patiently waited for the day He had saved them.

These friends conjectured upon and even anticipated the coming judgment of the dead, when those residents of Hades would likely give a defense or explanation for their sins. All courts transcribed proceedings. Why did Joseph Smith ignore the clearly stated words of Christ that a man married one woman, not *women*. Or why did Hitler think he had the authority to cancel the holy words of God when God said, "Salvation is from the Jews." On and on through the course of history, when humanity was tested and did not seek the wisdom of God, the friends asked why. No obscurity existed now, when living in the wisdom of God, and the current times had been ordered, birthed by the Lord on His throne. Yet, in the future, some would leave their God.

In time, when minds had crumbled in weariness, and apple pie and biscuits had stolen the efforts of the brain and they needed a change from the wood-smoke scent, they went to the decks. The breeze had died, the sun's heat had increased, and they explored their ability to transport and soar in the sky. Tuck spoke to Puck. "Remember our days as cripples, when we looked to the hawks and eagles overhead, the great buzzards circling?"

Puck laughed. "Don't forget the owls. Remember the owl that dove at my head?" Puck looked into Emily's eyes. "We had a hiding place on the mountain-cliff face, where we could lie behind a downed, sunbaked, and debarked tree trunk and watch the birds soar. How we wished to be free of our crippled legs and soar like the great birds of the air. Oh, to free our father and mother of their burden of protection. Only one grandmotherly woman in the entire village had kindness for us. To soar like a bird was as impossible as walking like a healthy man. Now we are both—walking and soaring—and healthy."

Emily, studying the brother's joyous eyes, answered softly, "Yes, let us concentrate on the dreams fulfilled. The goodness of our Lord." Emily remembered the beatings she had received as a child and the day Carl Stasic came and saved her. Like an angel, he had descended from the personnel carrier and placed her within the Johnson family. She had met Dan Jr. and learned of his terrible childhood. Together they had shared deeply of those awful times that was their bond, and it was why they liked the company of the brothers. Most of the resurrected had lived tortured lives upon Earth when Satan reigned.

"Now we can fly!" Tuck said as he leapt off the deck and caught a wind stream and an electromagnetic force moving upward and toward the river. The wind stream was not needed to fly, but it added speed and direction, and Tuck merely needed to follow its leanings. Emily laughed and then stepped up into space—she wasn't the leaping type. Dan calmly took a step into the air. Most of his free time had been used exploring this gift of flight. They had been taught to fly in paradise, as well as to pass through material objects and to disappear. It was not a magical teaching; there were no heavenly incantations to understand the science behind these gifts and then match the science to the subtle senses and feelings of the body and mind. Flight, for instance, was simply a matter of understanding the forces from space striking the earth and rebounding and the forces emanating from the earth into space. Quantifying the inner workings of the mind was difficult to do and had needed a new vocabulary in human speak.

John sat and watched. His workday and flight home from Harrisburg had momentarily satisfied his desire for movement. Diana sat beside him. He spoke. "What should we offer for lunch?"

"Let's allow them to decide. We have plenty of smoked meats and bread. I have many soups already made. Still have plenty of salad materials. Let's just rest and enjoy."

"Yes," he said, with a peace and contentedness of heart.

"I took a drive down memory lane—back to Gramp's farmhouse and our meeting with him," Diana said, gauging his possible interest in hearing of Miss Ames.

He took her hand. "I stumbled across Borelli today," he said dryly and absent-mindedly, not hearing the new subject of interest she had presented, as was his way.

Diana tensed with joy. "There's a name that brings back memories. What a noble man—to give two love-sick fugitives a chance at life. He knows the Lord! Did he know Him when he freed us?"

"No, but as he told me today, the Holy Spirit was working mightily within him—the reason he gave that second chance to us. Minutes before his death, lying in that parking lot, he asked the Lord for forgiveness of his sins. He was quite surprised when the angels came and carried him to paradise. He said he was accustomed to an organization of red tape and foul-ups and couldn't believe it only took seconds for God to communicate to His angels, 'That man has eternal life.' He was glad to have died in the parking lot. He knew someone else would have gunned him down had he lived."

She heard John struggle to convey his last few words. She said, "He is probably correct, but had he survived, he would have had only a few months more of earthly life before the Rapture would have collected him." She saw deep emotion welling up within John and knew a flood of memories were breaking his stoic bearing.

"Borelli's death moved me," John said. "The Spirit of God was upon us both. He was the only man I knew who had died for Christ, for me, for you. He, Borelli, had loved us. I had only seen men die in their pursuit of glory, pay, the satisfaction of dominating another, to better their earthly lives. He died unselfishly. I'm so glad he has eternal life. I was afraid to look for him."

She thought back to that time, the parking lot of an interstate rest station crowded with cars, the restaurant packed with travelers crossing the great lava-ash desert of the plains states. She and John had been caught in their flight by Hanson, the World Church's man. "Don't hide your emotions from me John. Share with me." She kissed him and wiped away his tears with her scarf. "How did you two cross paths?"

"A call from Maine. He lives there and is working as a detective. He saw my name, and yours, listed as police officers in Central Pennsylvania. Just a random perusal of mundane info passing through his computer."

"*Mon cheri*, you know I love you." She hugged him, she kissed his face, his lips. He smiled thoughtfully as the France years surfaced in her speech. She remembered the excitement, the fear, the striving to know and follow God in those early years. It was an adventure of growing.

"Never saw a girl take to Jesus like you did," John said. "Loyal and true to Him and to me. I love you with all that I am."

She replied softly, "All that I am loves you, for eternity." She would tell him of Miss Ames another time.

CHAPTER 7

Tom Jr., Ling, and Carl sipped nonalcoholic drinks of local teas, sweetened by berry concentrate, and partook of a colorful tray of native fruits on the wide, stone veranda of the corporate house of TLC Unlimited. Alcohol still existed as a cleaner or solvent. Medicinally, wine sometimes found use for stomach ailments. No one in God's kingdom felt the need for drunkenness or a high, and all knew alcohol could never give them the peace they felt with the Holy Spirit within. The hilltop view was unlimited, and the vast sea sparkled in the distance—forever, it seemed. The transoceanic shipping lanes far on the horizon were as busy as a two-lane highway at rush hour. Many ships were solar sailed, and many were rigid sailed—the air- and solar-catchers colored the brightest of yellows, blues, greens, reds, oranges, indigos. From the continuous line of ships some branched off, headed for the nearby docking facilities of the town. The green, rolling hills around the port town below, Ling Town, China, spoke of the perfect combination of soil, sun, rain found in the region. The *TLC* in the corporate name stood for Tom, Ling, Carl, and tender loving care is what they gave their company, their workers, and, especially, their customers.

This was the sixth millennial Jubilee year. Three hundred years of the millennial reign, and the beginning of the 150th year of Tom Jr.'s business association with Ling and Carl and his stay in China. This was the day of Tom's thirty-first birthday. On his thirtieth birthday, he had reached maturity, when his physical body and appearance maxed. A slow decline, almost infinitesimal, had begun, till at some point in time, likely in the eight-hundredth or nine-hundredth year, an underlying genetic weakness would peak, and he would proceed to paradise. This was life for the generations born within the millennium.

Carl winked at Ling. "Should we have a birthday cake? It seems appropriate, but it is a shame there aren't more people here."

Tom Jr. said nothing. He vaguely wondered why they were at the corporate home as the greater part of his mind was mulling the efficacy of a new invention he was building piece by piece within the scaffolds and braces of his mind. Ling answered, "Why not have cake? We are here, and we like cake." Ling raised his hand to the waitstaff at the entrance to the main house. Instantly, a man disappeared into the main dining area of the home and then reappeared, a tray between his hands, evidently heavy, by the straining neck and shoulder muscles. An entourage accompanied the man, their trays carried coffee pots, cups, plates, silverware, napkins. Tom's wife, Lana, and their five children, and Lana's parents, brothers, and sisters; Tom's sister Flo, who had recently arrived to begin employment in the company, was in the throng. Ling's wife and five children followed. Many were tooting party-favor horns. Perplexed, Tom Jr. wondered if the world had gone mad.

Carl and Ling watched Tom's expression of surprise turn to mirth and just plain happiness as the waitstaff surrounded the table, setting the scene of service. The heavy silver lid was removed from the server's tray to reveal a wide and tall chocolate cake adorned with thirty-one candles, which were quickly lit. Family surrounded Tom, his kids upon his lap and at his side, excited and anxious for the cake soon to be in their mouths. Ling's family settled in behind Tom's family. The birthday song began.

"Success, buddy," Carl said to Ling, with both thumbs up. "Complete secret, complete surprise." That Tom was a better reader of data than facial expressions and mannerisms had helped. Carl and Ling stood and sang as cake was added to their plates, as well as a dab of vanilla ice cream. They slowly disengaged to watch and just be guests at their friend's celebration. Tom had been the driving force in projecting their company to worldwide profits and recognition. TLC Unlimited was a model story on how to care for and empower employees and be good stewards of the earth, sky, and water. Tom was loved by his employees—from the planters and loggers, who wrestled in the heat, humidity, rain, mud of the jungle forests as well as the orderly rows of plantation trees; to the sawmill workers laboring within the noise and humidity of the high-ceilinged buildings; or the assembly workers making prefab homes, trusses, rafters, and furniture; or the office people of billing, packing, and shipping.

It is really Tom's show now and time to retire, reaffirmed Carl to himself. Ling had agreed with Carl's assessment, presented weeks ago. Ling wanted to relax with his family and find a new mission in life, even if just another company making life better for God's people. Carl noticed he was the oldest man at the party—108 in old Earth years at three hundred years into the millennium. He was the most worn looking, without a doubt. He did not notice that he was the only one of European descent, nor did anyone else notice; they were all just family. He knew he would soon be called to paradise for his resurrection body—and he was okay with that. At 108, his mind was still alert and quick, and his body like that of a thirty-year-old. He was thankful to God and understood that he had entered the millennium as an oldster, and even though body parts and processes had been revived, they could not always be replaced. He would be transitioning on a high note—a successful company established and prospering.

He should go back to Harrisburg, say hello to Tim and Mary, Mat and Katie, and his little Emily, whom he had rescued. Go back and remember the days of the Tribulation, when he had desperately attempted to save his country—his red, white, and blue sovereign nation—where anything was possible, and men once were called to achieve. Then, he had suspected but did not know that it was Holy God who had carried his nation so far above the others. It was the Holy God who had lifted Carl Stasic from his sin-infected body and given him a second chance that lasted forever. A tear came to Carl's eye. He would make plans to park his body in a Harrisburg cemetery. Maybe, in paradise they could wait together for their return home.

Ling watched the gaiety, the eating of the cake, the kids wanting seconds on ice cream. The inevitable dropping of a child's plate or the subtle drooping that slid cake and ice cream onto the patio stone; the hurried cleanup, and the new serving arriving before the tears could flow. He was aware his family were the only native Chinese at the gathering. Had it not been for Watchman Nee, there would be no Ling and no Chinese presence. It dawned on him that Watchman Nee was somewhere on Earth, a resurrected man. Why had they not met? A new priority one on his retirement agenda: find and meet Watchman Nee. The communists had killed Watchman very early in the new China's history. What a band of criminals, those communists—fools, who, by silencing Christ, had doomed billions not only upon Earth but in the afterlife. His animosity had nowhere to go, no outlet. The deed had been done.

Carl was beside Ling. Carl tugged at his sleeve. Ling bent his head; Carl spoke into his ear. "Come with me to Harrisburg for a visit. Bring your family. I might be staying. I'm sure Tom and Tish or Tim and Mary, someone on the river, will put you up."

"Perhaps a good idea. Let me poll my family and see if I can get a consensus." Ling studied Carl's face and sensed Carl's time was soon for paradise. Seven hundred years without Carl—that would be tough. Someone should be around to see him off; Carl's friends were everything, since all his wives and children had died without Christ. That was a burden of pain in and of itself. Ling made a decision and said, "Even if they can't make the trip, I will go for a vacation—two weeks." Carl deserved not to be alone.

Carl's countenance revived; the tired eyes sparkled with thankfulness. "Good. Glad to have your company."

***

Tim, Katie, Carl, DC Jones, Ling, and ten-year-old Pete, Mat's grandchild from his first born, Jedediah, stood on the unimproved road on the heights overlooking the ever-expanding Harrisburg. The first mountain ridge was behind them, lush and green with trees; the uppermost ridgeline was rock strewn, with stunted trees and grasses. Wind turbines, three in number, churned slowly. Below them, the city streets were laid out north to south, aimed at them. Buildings decreased toward the north ends of the streets, before the gathering, till finally the last ten blocks were barren. Carl and Ling noticed the skyscrapers were in greater clusters than they'd been upon their last visit 150 years earlier. (When they had come for their prodigy, Tom Jr.) The heights the gathered stood upon were the location where Tim and Katie had had their underground shelter during the Tribulation. All structures had been cleansed by fire, and the heights had yet to find a new population.

Mary and Mat had separated from the tour. They had never lived in the underground shelter—Mat had been at war in the Middle East, and Mary, in Pittsburgh and environs, running like Jonah from her God. They had left the party after walking the grounds of their tent home in the encampment, and their apartment home in the warehouse district. One of Mat's younger grandkids was in a play at his school, and Mat and Mary had gone to support his efforts. Barb was already at the school, a teacher there. Hope, an administrator at the school, had duties as the stage manager—the reason for her absence from the tour. Resurrected DC Jones had returned to Harrisburg at Carl's invitation. Pete was along because he liked history and enjoyed hearing of Great-aunt Katie and Great-grandpa Tim's experiences.

"Right about here?" Pete asked Katie.

"Yes, you can still see the depression in the earth," said Katie.

Pete scrutinized the depression and walked over it, hoping he would fall into the underground chamber and find some artifact from Aunt Katie's past. Ling studied the ground, took a panoramic view, 360 degrees around the location.

Tim spoke. "And Carl, we could see the government center plainly, usually at night, and in detail with ocular devices, but didn't know you lived there till near the end...and we had completely lost track of DC Jones."

Katie added, "We even walked the city once before the walls went up."

DC Jones laughed.

"Whaaat?" asked Katie, bemused and puzzled.

DC Jones spoke. "I saw you and your dad that day. You came from the river, entered my cameras. I picked you up again at the hologram monument. My security computer was signaling, "Enslavers."

"Whatya do?" asked Pete excitedly.

"I thermalized the system—cooked it with a heat bomb." She had added the explanation to answer his puzzled expression. "Then, I went to the roof, a break area. Tried to witness to a lady in the elevator. On the roof, I looked at that high mountain ridge behind us, and wind turbines were there then. Gosh, it was hot that day."

"They were all hot," confirmed Tim.

Pete determined DC Jones had melted the system so no one would know Great-granddad and Great-aunt Katie were in the city.

Jones continued, "Saw security coming. Took my killer poison capsule, met my angelic friends, and upward I went!" She remembered the dastardly act of the security guards upon her dead body. Tears were streaming from Jones's eyes at the remembrance of leaving the filth of the world behind. "Oh glory, what a Savior," she said.

Katie, knowing the unspoken part of the story—the rape of DC Jones's dead body—rushed to DC Jones. Jones, at one point in her life, had sinned many times in her flesh, and a dead guilt could enliven to accuse. Katie hugged her long and hard. "Let that river flow, girl…It is the river of our God, and it came for your cleansing. It is flowing for your salvation, and His love has washed our sins away."

Pete had begun to cry. He didn't normally cry, but he felt the Holy Spirit, a breeze caressed them, promised salvation; He sensed the price that was paid and the courage it took to stand for Jesus, and this was a grown woman—two of them and two men crying in gratitude and praise. Miss Jones had killed herself! He had never known anyone who killed their selves. Everyone seemed to agree it had been the right thing to do. His flesh rose as if an arctic wind had blown upon him, and he wanted that day when *he* would do something important and heroic for his God, who had given him his Jesus—the only one who loved him through and through, even after seeing all the dumb and disgusting things he had thought and done.

Tim, Carl, and Ling joined the hug and the tears. Pete was invited into the circle. Tim spoke clearly, strongly. "Listen to the times DC Jones had saved my family: She never told authorities of my brother, John, whom she had pursued in Poland, thus keeping the Enslaver title from sticking to my family. She never told authorities of the killing I committed in the tent city. She never told of the killings Mat and I had committed against agents of the beast: Hoagland and Simmons and the storm troopers, when they came to put the mark upon us. Now, this final act that she had never revealed until this time."

"Amen for DC Jones. For knowing and acting on the heart of God," said Carl, his voice wavering, and the amens came, and even greater tears were shed.

When there was silence, and they looked upon each other's tear-streaked faces and clearing eyes, Carl said, "You were on the other side, Jones, during the rebellion." That detail was for little Pete's understanding. "Where did we go wrong?"

"You didn't go wrong, Carl. You had a snitch—there is always a snitch. Judas concocted a reason to salve his conscience as he earned his silver. Our side knew what you were doing before your lower ranks did."

"Who?" asked Tim.

"No one even offered a conjecture during bull sessions, which was very strange. It was utter fear, I think, to even guess. Had to be someone in your inner circle—a liaison between each local uprising and the head of the national effort, or even a linking official between your planning committee and the ranks or your supply chain or security forces."

"It doesn't matter now. God saw his evil, and he is gone from this Earth," Carl said with a peace in his tone.

"What if he repented?" asked Pete.

"Very good question—very deep," Katie said approvingly, "Judas tried to repent. He felt remorse and wanted to return the silver. But clearly it was too late. No one allowed him to reverse his actions, and he committed suicide."

"Could God have stopped the suicide?" asked Pete.

Carl picked up the logic and answered, "For free will to exist, God won't make a man do anything. A man is responsible for his actions. Judas's actions were against the physical body of God. It was murder. To deliberately lie about the nature and motivations of God and place Him in the hands of murderers, the penalty must be death."

Katie joined the debate. "Still, David murdered from lust—or was it self-importance?—and he is living in Jerusalem now. He is the kindliest, most gentle man, a sweetheart." Katie rethought her position in the light of free will and spoke. "David, under his free will, made a wrong decision.... He should have inquired of the Lord. God would have answered and given the strength and will to do right. Uriah could have lived." Katie was unafraid of contradicting her position of seconds before. She added, "We should ask the Jerusalem hotline for an answer." She referred to Christ's handpicked people who clarified biblical history, stated the motives and actions of the participants, and revealed the solid and unchanging logic and laws of God.

"You know how to get the intellectual mind working, Pete. We need that—always," said Tim. "Uriah is in Jerusalem, too, living. He and David are the best of friends. Judas is in Hades. Our snitch is probably dead and likely in Hades. God is sovereign and knows the inner motivations and workings of the human mind...and who is truly repentant and salvageable and who is not. God can do anything, but many times He chooses not to do, because it isn't in line with His character or His immediate purposes— mankind's free will. Life belonged to us, and we had to live it." Tim placed his hand on Pete's bony shoulder and squeezed reassuringly. "God likes questions, Pete. Never forget, you can talk to Him, and no subject is out of bounds."

Ling began walking down the gentle slope, hoping to draw the group away from their inner musings and because he saw something sticking out of the hard-baked, vegetation-resistant soil of the area. He pulled his straight-blade knife from the belt sheath that conveniently fit into his pants pocket. *Once a soldier, always a soldier*, thought Tim, who was watching Ling. Ling began to scrape away dirt. The others had gathered around him. Tim would have stopped him if the outline of an explosive device had been identified. Once he had dug a perimeter, he reached in with the blade and pried upward.

Tim spoke before the object was even out of the ground. "Dented night-vision goggles."

Katie gasped in astonished remembrance. "From the man who had his face blown off!"

"What's the story?" asked Ling.

Katie answered. "Two men had come to our tunnel-hole door, always booby trapped when we were out and about. It was the night of the rebellion in the city, Carl. The day before the exodus to see the man called 'the Prophet.'" She refused to identify the Prophet as Pastor Dave, thinking she could avoid triggering her father's bad memories of the man.

Carl smiled sadly at the memories that flooded his mind; the mayor and the high priest—two fallen angels who had bedeviled him—and the rebellion in the streets, the brutal killings.

Tim picked up the story as Katie paused and her brow furrowed. "The first man wore those goggles, and the grenade caught him in the head, blowing the goggles back into the face of the second man. The first was dead. We let the second go...." Tim's voice trailed off, and Katie picked up the story.

"After he told us what was occurring in the city, he promised to leave and never come back. But Dad caught him circling around. The liar had found a piece of debris that made a nice club." She stopped.

Tim finished the story. "I escorted him home."

"Where'd he live, Grampa?" Pete said innocently. Carl and Ling smiled, bemused and pensive.

Katie bent down to Pete as DC Jones placed her hands on his shoulders. "That was a gentle way to say the man died, Pete. Lots of people like to soften their memories of death and give the death of others, those going to hell, a gentleness."

"But he deserved it." Petey stated determinedly.

"Yes, he did," said DC Jones, who had stooped to a squat, grasping Pete's arms for balance as she lowered herself to face him. "That's why we have no bad memories of those we killed. But we are sad for him and happy for ourselves that God showed us mercy, and yet others cannot grasp that eternal gift." She pushed his hair from his eyes to his forehead as she rose.

"I got it," said Pete, not the least dismayed that he had to learn another lesson they knew, and he did not.

They walked back to the location of the tent city where DC Jones had first met the Johnson family, then back up to where the warehouse corner apartment had once stood. Mat and Mary rejoined the tour, as they walked to the location of the high-rises where Mat and Tim had become separated in combat. The lots were vacant, and the cement foundations were still just barely visible beneath the earth. Grandpa Mat and Great-grandpa Tim hugged there and cried because Great-grandpa Tim had thought he'd never find his son again, but God was good to them and heard their prayers. Then they got into the van and traveled to "the Camp" where Carl had the headquarters to the real American army and where the Johnson men had trained for war and GG Mary had had a real home. The land now held naturally kept lakes and ponds, as well as swimming-designated lakes, along with public kayaks, sailboats, two golf courses, skeet and target ranges, and a first-class restaurant. On the mountain, biking and hiking trails, and artificial ski runs that operated independently of winter cold or artificial cold could be seen. Carl found the spot on the mountain ridgetop where he had determined to die. He even found a piece of his vehicle.

Then they traveled to Gramps's old farmhouse, rebuilt and restored. It was a national historic place due to the importance of Gramps's discovery and search for the satanic bible, which had led to the split of the World Church and the beast's rise. Gramps, John, and Diana were prominently mentioned on the historical marker and even GG Tim and family had a line. Aunt Katie said the upstate-New York seminary also had a national historic place designation.

Finally, they went to that place on the river where the last national outdoor baptism ceremony was performed, and the last roving Christian band captured. Tim and Katie indirectly were mentioned as escapees of the roundup and stalwart holdouts from the regime of the beast.

As they rode home, Tim driving, Tim asked, "What do you think, Carl?"

"It was good to see those memorable sights and how the land is returning to use and the population increasing. It is good to revive my memories—how I appreciate my Savior more. But I know a thousand years from now, my memory will be as real and deep as it was on the days when I first walked that ground."

"How so?" asked Ling.

"Our memory capacity is so much greater and sharper in our new world, and the resurrected tell me our minds are even sharper when in the resurrected state. I think our God designed it so from the beginning, knowing we need the memory of the bad times, the times of drama and even trauma to appreciate what is good."

"Yes, I see that need," said Ling, "but what really gets me is the overwhelming totality of suffering that the world knew. Your personal stories were like the stories of my family and friends. Except there was no Christ to hold onto, no concept of the suffering leading to something. Many people died simply from despair—no hope, even within our army. The idea of faith and hope kept your nation at a degree of civility that ours never attained. We were just constantly warring factions hellbent to wrest water and food for a few days or weeks more of life. When people have hope in the Lord, they can endure and even conquer."

"What do you think, Pete?" DC Jones looked across the seat at Pete, eating a cookie provided by Katie.

"It's too big for me. Overwhelming! It will take longer to digest than this cookie. Get back to me in a hundred years."

"That's a deep mind," said Katie, laughing.

***

Thirty-one-year-old and single, Hope returned to her father's home just as dusk was settling. She had been disappointed that she had not been able to take the tour of the Johnson past with her family. But she had been the only person at the school play who could make the production happen. What she owed the kids and their parents was greater than her sentimental attachments. Dad had drilled that into her—duty, first; self, second. William had been a godsend, an uncle to one of the children, who had volunteered his time. He was kind, attentive, and seemed to know how to manage kids and adults. He had lifted quite a few cares and worries from her, so much so, that she had actually enjoyed the excitement of the day. He seemed happy for her when the day was done and the play had gone off flawlessly.

Maybe, he was the one.

Her phone rang.

"This is Bill. I enjoyed working with you. I think I would enjoy talking to you."

She heard a shy guy rushing to the point without the common amenities, and that was okay in her book. She answered, "About what? Sorry, that sounded rude. We will find plenty—you seem a man interested in life. Yes, let's talk." She could hear his sigh of relief.

Bill spoke, "Tomorrow, perhaps." He wondered if that request was presented in a begging tone.

"Yes, tomorrow. Name your time, Bill."

And so began the courtship of Hope, a child conceived one day before the beginning of the millennium.

***

Tim and Carl sat in their Adirondack chairs as the sun was moving to the western horizon over the river. Ling and Mat were fishing the river, now cooling with the shade of the islands and the sun's indirect rays. They could see pools, eddies, quiet water smooth behind rock ledges, and the myriad insects and bugs lingering in the air or floating on the water shining in the slanting sun's yellow light. The katydids were sounding their grating, rubbing songs that seemed as statements. The tree frogs were chirping. On the lawns the crickets sounded. The bass were jumping, rods were bending, and reels cranking continuously.

"Thanks for the ride today, Tim, and the nostalgia. Do I look like I'm due in paradise?" asked Carl sheepishly.

"You always did get to the point." Tim laughed. "One of the reasons I like you."

"Yes. Gruff businessman, always thinking ahead." Carl looked inward and said, "I think I'm near my time for a seven-hundred-year visit to paradise, and I would like my body to be waiting in Harrisburg."

"How about here? We intend to establish a graveyard between our homes, Tom and I."

"Thanks for the offer, but Harrisburg might be better for the countless others who knew me and might want to visit, if passing through. I don't think there will be many, but you never know. They are not at our level of friendship, but I was a public figure. I don't especially take pride in that."

"You should. You helped many. You were just a man, Carl; you made mistakes. But as for your earthly legacy, the good you did was far greater than the mistakes."

"Thanks, Tim. I appreciate that."

Tim studied Carl's expression and then said, "Here are a few thoughts you should explore. Don't let them go to your head. I compiled a list, and not a week goes by that I don't think of at least one of these." Tim paused to clear his throat and to add effect. "You bolstered my self-esteem when I was down and out. You found me a job with housing when I had none. You backed out of bidding against me for supplies. You offered me entrance into an organization that provided housing, training, and weapons. That home meant everything to Mary and Katie and Emily. There you go: you gave us Emily. You saved us from the tent city and gave us a sense of worth. You offered earthly hope that we could win our country back. You gave us food and clothing. And in the end, you gave me my life back that night at the Prophet's encampment.

"I know you feel guilty about Mat entering the army and being at Armageddon, but it just made him stronger. Who knows what torturous end he could have met had he remained in Harrisburg? And he brought Ling with him. And you two have created a miracle in China. Was it a coincidence to God that Tom Jr. lived nearby?"

Carl's eyes ran with tears. He was about to mention Joshua and his followers to Tim. He had been responsible for their capture and so their torturous deaths. Every one of his friends forgot that sin.

"Carl, you are one of the good guys. I know you have regrets about your wives and your children and, perhaps, the unsuccessful rebellion. But you are here! Proof that God loves you. In time, I—and Mary—will join you in paradise, and probably Mat and Katie as well. Then we'll all come back together.

"We have eternal life and minds that will remember it all. A life of no regrets. Think of it: a million years from now, our God will have us somewhere serving Him, which means making life better for someone, some thing. Only God knows what worlds are out there, what the possibilities are, what the unknown knowledge is."

Carl spoke. "I'm a man of regrets."

"Just because we have eternal life doesn't mean we're perfect yet. The resurrected seem nearer to that mark. There is a question I've never asked them."

"How close to perfect they are? I suppose we will never be God, so we will always be imperfect," said Carl. "And I'm content with that. I also know that God doesn't love me more or less for the good works I accomplished through Him on this Earth. He just loves us, pure and simple, because we are His kids—His creation."

The simplicity of Carl's words was so profound and true that Tim had no words in response. He found only one word. "Amen." Tim noticed Ling and Mat returning. They had fished all the way to the island and were moving quickly back across the water, casting as they waded. He looked at Carl and wished to speak of the returning fishermen, but he did not. He didn't know why, until he glanced at the tear-filled eyes of Carl. The presence of the Lord surrounded him. Holy, holy, holy is the Comforter.

That evening Tom and Tish, Flo and her husband, Rick, as well as their twin boys, Talon and Amare, came over to Tim's home. An impromptu dinner was cooked, the outdoor fire pit cast light and heat. Flo and Rick took the twins to the heated outdoor pool. Tom and Tish told stories of their son and grandkids in China, and Ling added his knowledge, as well as Carl. Katie, Mat, and Barb heard the party and came over and sang, accompanied by Emily on a guitar, as an added gift. Paul, Katie's producer, watched and listened. The young ones chased and caught fireflies. Mary found jars, made breathing holes in the lids, and helped the children place the creatures within. Barb took her children to the pool to swim.

Carl was happy, watching it all. He was watching this reality as he had watched one of Mat's grandkids in a school play the other day. He understood for the first time that God had choreographed life—and the glitches, missed lines, missteps in the script were, in reality, the hidden gems that spoke of God's love. It was humankind's show, but He made it all come out right at the end.

Before he entered the guest bedroom in Tim's home, he looked deeply into the eyes of Tim and said, "Don't respond to what I say; just accept it. Thanks, Tim, for being who you are: a good daddy, a patriot, a trusted friend. Most importantly, a man who learned to love God with all his heart, all his soul, all his mind and strength."

Tim smiled and shook Carl's hand, the strong hand that had once torn down buildings. Tim turned to leave, an emotional smile upon his face. He would miss Carl for that length of time only God knew. He hoped Carl would not see the tears. He escaped down the hall, wiping his face with his hands, and entered his bedroom. Mary was already under the sheets. He lay beside her and held her tight. She did not know the reason why, but he had done it in times past from what she thought was appreciation for her and loneliness in himself. She just accepted his need; he would tell her when he was ready.

The next morning, Carl did not respond to the breakfast summons. Tim found the body of Carl in bed, with hands folded and a relaxed smile upon his face. Mat came into the room to keep Dad company; a call to the coroner had been placed. Mat studied the face and said, "Remember where I first met him?"

Tim immediately answered, "In the high-rise where we went to buy survival supplies from the drug-addicted ex-soldier."

"Yes, and Carl and I carried most of them to the elevator, the lobby, and to his car. Our first trip to the Camp followed. What exciting times for a kid."

"We had no idea where those times would lead," Tim said as he bowed his head in thought and prayers of thankfulness.

"To a failed revolution and the end of time as we, the world, knew it." Mat's memory filled with the times of trial and heartache. The entire seven years had seemed like unrelenting heartache and challenge, and yet living it, he had found times of goodness—all directly involving his family, his Savior, and his God. Always, always his God—every moment, sleeping or waking, seeing life through the eyes of Christ. What a privilege to know Him. Mat looked into his father's eyes and spoke. "No, we had no idea where those times would lead, but our Lord did."

"This eternal time is good," said Tim.

Mat thought of this man whom others knew as Tim; Mat's dad…his daddy, a good earthly dad. He had been blessed with a good earthly dad. He had been blessed with a Father God—the Daddy who had given him his earthly dad. He thought upon mankind and all the religions of the world men had invented, but none could invent I AM, the God of creation who loved humankind as His children. Mat said, "I love you, Dad."

Tim smiled broadly. "I love you even more."

Mat answered, "Amen."

Tim, still smiling, said, "And amen to Carl in paradise."

"Amen and amen," said Mat as he hugged his daddy.

***

Katie was with her producer, Paul, in a studio, recording, when her dad called with the news that Carl had died. Carl's last visit, just last night, was vivid in her mind—his worn countenance still wearing the trademark optimism, that *anything is possible* spirit, now firmly rooted in what Christ could do, through man, imbued with the Holy Spirit of God. Carl, angel-like, hopping off the personnel carrier and, with a visage of determination and ferocity, claiming the Johnson family as his; saving her family and herself from their awful life in the tent city. To a young girl, knowing there was someone outside her family—especially other than her father and brother—who cared about them and was willing to risk his life for them told her that Christ cared. For Christ had brought Carl to them at a time when no one cared about anyone. She began to tear up and knew she wouldn't be able to hold back the river that was coming. She quickly left the studio, a converted barn on a friend's holdings, and sought green lawn, trees, a free wind. Paul followed her.

When she looked at his face, she saw his pain for her, and it seemed tears would soon be upon his face. She spoke decidedly. "Don't you cry for me, you stinker. I want someone to remain happy."

He spoke apologetically. "I've been working with you day in and day out for months now. We've explored deep and meaningful lyrics and tunes that can lift and crush souls and every emotion in between. I know who you really are—and I love who you are. When you hurt, I hurt."

"Okay, I understand," she said, businesslike. He deserved to know. "Carl passed away. I know he'll be back at the end of the millennium and forever after, so I don't hurt as a nonbeliever used to hurt at someone's death. But Carl saved my family. He saved *me* from distressing times. He wasn't perfect, and under the pressure of the times, he placed Mat in the army. And he had a part in the rounding up of Josh and his band. But that didn't take away from the good he did that day and in the months afterward, when we had food and security in the Camp. His Camp."

Paul was holding her hands. He'd never done that before. He shouldn't be doing that. He spoke. "Katie, I do understand…I understand because I want to protect you, save you from emotional stress. I want you to excel in your gift given to you by God. You are so good, so pure, so in love with our God, with Jesus—I want to protect that in you. When you hurt, I hurt." He said it again.

"Stop it, Paul. You are my producer. My goodness. What's gotten into you?" He was hugging her. Tears were in his eyes. He hugged her tightly, and she hugged him—evidently, his loyalty needed to be rewarded. Did he really care about her? Did he really like her? Her emotions, her character, her walk with the Lord?

"Marry me, Katie. Say yes."

"You're the restaurant boy, right? The young man I saw in the mountaintop restaurant with his family, before the big quake."

She knew he was; they had talked about the coincidence of their surviving and meeting at his interview for the producer position. He answered, "Yes, the Lord had a plan—it was no accident. Let's fulfill God's plan like we were meant to do. Will you marry me, Katie Johnson?"

He was looking into her eyes. What a love-sick puppy. "Give me the night. I don't want this decision to be emotion driven. Tomorrow morning."

"Yes, I will wait," he said confidently.

"You're not worried?" she asked.

"No. You will consult with the Lord, and He will confirm I am the one."

Katie did consult with her Lord. The next morning, Katie said, "Yes."

CHAPTER 8

Tom and Tish sat on the steps leading into their swimming pool, in this four-hundredth year of the millennium, submerged to the waist, each with a twin within eyesight and upon their mind. Tom had taught himself to swim with the building of his pool. Tish had been a proficient swimmer since she was a teenager. Per a past agreement, established at the birth of Flo's twins, Tom watched Talon, and Tish observed Amare. Ten-year-old boys needed someone secretly watching every minute. Although they were mature intellectually, emotionally and experientially there were some blank spots, which was common among their age group. Talon was shinnying up the pole to the supporting crossbar that secured the chains to hanging swings.

True to his name, Talon had a strong grip. Tom knew the supporting crossbar was hot from the morning sun and wet hands slid easily over the painted metal surface. The hands slipping and Talon falling would be a good teaching moment, if he didn't reach the hanging chains that could entangle him on the downward fall. Tom was not alone; other caregivers were present. Talon had an angel watching and the Holy Spirit within. Suddenly, Tom bellowed, "Don't touch the chains!" as he saw Talon reaching his foot out for the chain. Talon's leg swung back to his body, breaking his grip, and he fell into the pool with a look of bewilderment on his face. Tom laughed; a safe lesson learned.

Tish wasn't as certain. "That was close," she said, wondering why Tom had waited to warn the boy.

Tom sensed she didn't understand his waiting. "Some lessons need to be experienced, and the shock on his face as he hit the water stated the lesson was learned. Me *telling* him what could have happened would have been a weak deterrence for the future."

Tish smiled. "A Father God lesson, there."

Tom noted Tish's answer but did not respond, as his memory kaleidoscoped through his life, the utter lostness and agony of living in his flesh, confused and emotionally bruised. He had not had the gift of obedience or of finding truth, and so he had paid the price. Some lessons needed to be experienced. The entire time of his "lostness," God had been pleading to take control, to teach him, to give him a good life of meaning and accomplishment.

The ten o'clock sun was warm, and Flo, thankful for a rest from the twins, enjoyed just sitting, sunning, smelling the country air of Pennsylvania. She remembered the humidity of the Chinese rain forests gladly left behind decades ago. The boring work of the plantations was not missed. She just wasn't cut out for work that seemed a grind to the spirit and the mind. She did understand why others could like the security and the sameness. A dose of humility was good medicine for the soul, and she appreciated those people who could do the work. God's love was not dependent on your work. He didn't rank work—all was necessary—and you didn't gain favor with a job title.

With that attitude, she had had a great work experience as a preschool teacher. That had been rewarding work. God had a place for everyone. Jobs were like clothes shopping. You kept trying garments on till one fit right, and God approved the look, and you knew deep in your heart that He wished you to be in that position. Once the twins were responsibly self-managing, and that time was soon, she might take the schooling necessary to be a certified teacher. Rick was doing well at his new job at Harrisburg International as an air-traffic controller trainee, which was about troubleshooting and overwatching the actual devices that kept the orderly flow of aircraft for arrivals and departures.

She had her family's future to think upon in this four-hundredth year of millennial life. Twins were enough for her, but she wished to please Rick, or Rickee, as he was known to his family. He talked about more children. What a blessing it had been to find him ten years ago. He was down to earth, spoke only kindness and peace, appreciated the little, subtle shifts in mood, saw humor and pathos, and had a deep, deep love of Creation and the Creator God. To think his mother was a thirteen-year-old from the deepest, darkest ghetto of New York City, who left the city on the advice of a Bible passage spray-painted on a wall, and so missed the leveling of the city in the great Tribulation quake. This girl had no mom or dad, no daddy for her child, no family, and no understanding of God, except that He would see her through. Two years after Rickee's birth, a street assault left her with an arm so cut up and mangled that the surgeon didn't want to waste resources or time, and it was amputated. Years later she died. Apparently, her faith had withered away, or she would be on Earth now.

Flo stopped the remembrances. She wished her half-brother, Tom Jr., would call Dad—he was never her stepdad; he had earned the title *Dad*, and she loved him. His birthday was yesterday. All the neighbors came over—the Johnsons, Andy's family, Emily and Dan Jr., and Ling and his family. He had spent two weeks with Dad and was leaving tomorrow. Her sisters had called Dad, unable to break away from their lives in California and Africa.

Flo heard the sliding door of a supersized van close. Her eyes went to the source of the sound, and there, across the front yard, were a host of warm and loving, dark-skinned people. Tanya and Tobe—and their three kids? The kids were men now, and very tall, thin, and healthy. Three little ones, boys, burst out from the pack and ran to their Aunt Flo, whom they had never met. *Each of Tanya's sons has brought a son,* thought Flo. Flo caught a glimpse of Anya and Keith. And their little boy? He looked to be in his mid-twenties, tall but wide, muscles all over him. Anya's little girl was a twenty-something woman, with a seven-year-old girl in her arms. Anya's stomach appeared to be close to delivery. A little girl stood beside Anya, her most recent, the baby who had been in the womb at their last meeting eleven years ago. Where had time gone? Their arriving was totally unexpected! No forewarning, but positively good.

She flew up from her lounge chair and ran across the lawn even as Tanya's three grandchildren were running toward her, with Anya's eleven-year-old girl sheepishly trailing behind, holding the hand of her seven-year-old niece. Flo dropped to her knees, and first contact was made. She began with the boys. She hugged those little bodies, grabbing their ears and shaking their heads, and the widest grins of the whitest teeth flashed the children's inestimable delight at being hugged by Aunt Flo for the first time. Flo reached out and grabbed Anya's shy girl, Angie, and smothered her neck and cheeks with kisses. The seven-year-old girl shook with anticipation as Flo smothered her with kisses. Then Flo rose and hugged her sisters and their husbands. Her father and mother, smiling widely, were eagerly approaching. Talon and Amare, with pleasure and excitement in their eyes, trailed behind shyly.

Flo became the greeter. "Get your bathing suits on, men—and young men—in that little house by the pool. Plenty of suits; find one that fits. Girls, we have suits in the guest bathroom inside. Any of you guys hungry? Thirsty? What can I feed them, moms and dads? What could you eat?" Flo knew that Mom and Dad needed to enjoy the kids, not play host; and her sisters and their husbands needed to unwind from their flights, and they belonged with Mom and Dad.

"My girls will help you," said Anya. "Tanya, stay with your family. I got this." She made eye contact with Tanya, who answered, "Thanks." Anya turned to her twenty-five-year-old daughter, and said, "Take these young ones to the guest bathroom, please, and find them suits. Mom needs your help." Her daughter beamed, "I got it, Mom."

Anya turned back to Flo. "We have already discussed what we could eat—sandwiches, lunch meats, any soups leftover? Chips, cheeses, water, juices, that homemade root beer." She broke off her conversation and hugged her dad and mom, planting ten kisses on each, then said, "I'm going to help Flo. I'll be back to you two."

Flo took Angie's hands as Anya grabbed her travel bag from the van. "Any word from Tom Jr.?" Anya asked.

"Not yet," said Flo.

"I called him to remind him a week ago," Anya said. "Tanya and I think there's something amiss in China."

"What?" Flo asked worriedly.

"Either work or family," Anya stated, as the two women moved into the house and made for the kitchen.

***

Tom Jr. sat in the spacious, quiet living room of his hilltop home in China. A breeze came through the tall but narrow ceiling-to-floor windows. The long-bladed ceiling fan hummed. He was only aware of the computer screen before him. He had to call his dad and wish him a happy birthday. Lana and the kids were gone, and Dad and Mom would wonder where Lana and the kids were. They would wonder why they heard no background noises. Lana and the kids were gone because he had been unfaithful—so unfaithful that he hadn't had the time or energy to watch over his business empire. His corporation was in dire straits. He might lose it all.

He had to lie—at least this one time—till he could find a solution to these problems and be the successful son with the beautiful family again. He dialed; the screen popped on. He studied his own face and made the necessary adjustments to the downturned mouth and shifting eyes. There was Dad on the screen.

"Happy birthday, Dad. So, you're how young?" He saw Mom in the background, listening.

"Oh, so good to see your face and hear your voice. Seventy-seven, like your mother. I have a few years left in me for this millennium. Where have you been? We used to get weekly Sunday screen time. Where are Lana and the kids?"

"They're at a Church event but plan to call later in the week. They wish you their best. I've been so swamped with work. I can't find people with the knowledge of Carl and Ling."

Tom Sr. spoke in an affirmative tone. "Pray about it. The people are there. You just need that divine discernment. He'll bring you through if you cast your burden upon Him." Tom Sr. knew Tom Jr. wasn't listening. Tom Sr. could tell by the set of Tommy's eyes, the dullness within the eyes, that he was in trouble of some sort and was hiding it. He knew that to ask about or to search for the problem would lead to alienation. He would pretend that he suspected nothing and exit as soon as possible. Then, he would call Ling, make contacts in China, find the real truth and find solutions.

"I'll do that, Dad…I'll do that." *What worthless advice,* thought Tommy, as his conscience added, *"He's trying to help."*

"Well, we have Tanya, Anya, Flo, spouses, and kids here now. We miss you, Son. Wish you were here, but we know how busy you are. Call with the family when things quiet down. And Son…"

"Yes, Dad?"

"I love you and always will."

Tish called out from the background, "I love you too, Son."

"Okay. Love you also."

The call was done.

Tom and Tish rose from the quiet study, where they had gone to take the call. Tish sought out Tom's hand and grasped it firmly. "Tommy's in trouble," she said.

"I know," said Tom. "Likely a woman. He's too analytical to be in financial trouble. I'll call Ling and ask his opinion on how to proceed."

"He's at some event with his family tonight. Just leave a message on his phone for a talk tomorrow, before he catches his flight back," said Tish.

"Okay," said Tom. "And of course, no mention of this to the girls till we know what's what."

"Of course," said Tish.

***

Tom and Tish hosted their girls' families for a week and a half. The young boys never tired of the pool, river wading and fishing, sandbar and island exploring, outdoor meals and fires at night. Their father's, being nearly mature men, had interest in historic sites, trail repair, and the sturgeon project. They took a deep interest in archeological digs organized by Native Americans and early settlers, who knew where the villages, forts, grist mills were located. When they discovered there were few gold and silver coins, they grew less interested.

The bones of the evil people whose souls were currently in Hades fascinated all of Flo's nieces and nephews. The realization that the bones would find their way to the proper owners before the great white throne of judgment and would be cast into the lake of fire held a fascination. Tim and Mary hosted a pool party at their home. This was a big success, as they had more and different floaties and a diving board and soft trapeze swings as well as ice cream sandwiches, which were new to the children from Africa. Mat, Katie, and Hope brought their kids—some were now adults—and grandkids, as well. Tim and Mary helped Tom and Tish during the family visit and even provided a historical tour of Harrisburg and environs for the entire group. The resurrected—Andy's clan, John and Diana, Emily and Dan—contributed their presence and help, too.

***

Ling did speak to Tom Sr. while on his flight back to China. He began his study of the corporation's profits and losses and of the men in charge as soon as he reached home. Nothing was hidden from him, as he was a major stockholder in the company. Besides, he knew how to find hidden files. Ling identified the problems. His and Carl's replacement needed some coaching and courses in management—but the immediate bottleneck could be broken by a few directives. Tom Jr. had not realized the bottlenecks existed. Tom Jr., although a math whiz, was principally an inventor; as a hardware- and manpower-problem solver, he did not have the expertise, time, or interest for complex management systems. An overall general manager was needed. All of this, Ling conveyed to Tom Jr. and to Tom Sr. Of Lana and the children, the affair, he said nothing to Tom Sr. To Tom Jr., he poured out his heart as a brother in Christ on obedience, repentance, the truly great wife Lana was, and the blessing his kids were. He reminded Tom Jr. of the trauma and lasting negative effects a divorce would have on his children.

Back in Pennsylvania, Tom and Tish watched Tanya and family board the flight to Nairobi; they watched Anya's family board a flight to Los Angeles. They said good-bye to Flo, as her family went home to their well-built and well-managed apartment complex in Harrisburg. Then Tom and Tish drove home to their holdings along the Susquehanna River, where they cleaned the house, washed all towels and bedding; Tom cleaned up the pool area and collected the clutter strewn about the lawn, shrubs, and trees. They weeded the garden and picked overlooked vegetables, and in the evening, sat together by their outdoor fire. They marveled at the stars in the heavens and gave thanks to their Lord for their wonderful lives, the husbands of their daughters, their grandchildren, and great-grandchildren. They retired early, kneeling by their bed, holding hands, and praying for God to open the eyes of their son.

One night, a week later, Tom Sr. awoke and could not return to sleep. Something felt odd within, yet he had peace of mind. Tish awoke and made him a glass of bicarbonate of soda, thinking it was something he had eaten. She was thinking in old Earth standards. She told the Lord that if Tom was going to paradise, she wanted to be there with him. Her girls were fine; their families were fine. God was faithful, and soon Tom Jr. would have his company in order and this would soothe the family dynamics-the unease that was apparently in play. Even though she loved her family dearly, it was Tom Sr. who needed her, and more importantly, she needed him. And so it was, in the morning, when Tim came over to borrow a mattock, and the garage had not yet been opened and the house was quiet, he called Flo to ask if Tom and Tish were at home. He entered their home, entered the bedroom, and Tom and Tish were holding hands, upright in bed, contented smiles upon their faces.

Another temporary emptiness crept into Tim's life. When Tim told his family of Tom's and Tish's deaths, Mat remembered his Tom Burnell Sr. journal. He chose to share Tom's musings from "the gang talks." He thought Tom Jr. would appreciate more the wisdom and walk his dad had had with the Lord now that he would be absent for some time. His sent an electronic note immediately to Tom Jr.

Tim had notified Flo first, and her first contacts were with Tanya and Anya. The girls supported each other through the loss and made peace with the temporary absence of their parents. Though temporary, the absence would certainly bring a sense of lack. It was not until late afternoon of that day that Flo found that Tom Jr. had yet to be notified. When Tom Jr. received the call from Flo, he was in bed with his sleeping lover girl. He acknowledged the news and said good-bye softly. Flo thought nothing was amiss (not knowing that lover girl existed) for that was Tom's personality; he was unemotional, and his thoughts were hidden deeply. He needed time to process.

Tom wished to cry but he wouldn't, as his lover would think that weak, and although having met his dad and mom incognito—as a secretary—he sensed she did not like them or his sisters. Lana loved his family, and his kids, of course, loved them. It would be his kids' first experience of the death of someone close to them, and he wondered how they would react. His analytical math brain failed him; what do you do with grief, analytical math brain? What do you do? *Does not compute*, the brain says. Dad had been his best friend, his biggest supporter. Living at the homestead, helping Dad and Mom with the daily running of their little operation; working in the garage, with the garage door open, the wildlife parading across the lawn, the birds chirping in the trees or winging for speed through the air. The slap of falling fish on the peaceful waters of the river, the flower, hay, woods scents. He and his dad engaged in debate as to the solving of some mechanical problem, finding a solution. Success. He saw his dad smiling. The perfect life with his truly good and wonderful parents. What would *his* children know of good parents? Parents they could respect? This tart beside him only wanted his prestige, his money, his body—not him, not the boy who loved his mommy and daddy and his sisters and loved God's creation and wanted to treat everyone with care and respect. What was he doing here in this place? Why had he run from everything that made his life worth living?

He sat in silence. In the silence, his phone hummed. A message from Mat Johnson. He supposed many messages might come. He wished to ignore this message and all those to follow. But Mat was a good guy, a friend, who had always been quick to help with projects around the homestead, had always loved his family, and who knew God as a friend. Knowing God was common for the time, but Tom Jr. had the sense that God considered Mat a friend. He opened Mat's message and read:

Your mom and dad were the sweetest, gentlest, kindest couple I have ever known. They were the first true neighbors I have known in my life; prior experiences of neighbors were strangers who lived beside us and usually were rude, uncaring, or simply unknown. Your dad's walk with the Lord was deep and satisfying to behold, and in his presence, such wisdom came forth that

I always felt blessed for knowing him. In fact, I have a thick journal, begun years ago, of Burnellian musings. I will just share one such musing, given to me when we discussed his gang experience. We had gotten together to explore his former gang life, as I wished to know what the future of the new mortals would be—those within whom the carnal body and their own world system might be pulled away from Christ. During this talk, your dad said, "It is knowing that your evil is an affront to God, and that this God you affront is the only good in the world. When you hurt God and are ashamed of your hurting Him, then you are at the threshold." He was referring to salvation as the threshold, of course. And, of course, we cannot hurt God—or I should say our attempts do not shake Him or perturb His being; it is all part of the plan. I will keep in contact, and you know if there is anything you need, I am here for you. Always keep in the forefront that your parents' absence is only temporary, and so remain deeply in the Lord. May the Holy Spirit be noticed within and around you. Your neighbor and friend, Mat.

PS: Love the Lord your God with all your heart, soul, mind, and strength. I will have the journal printed and give you all copies.

Tom slipped into his clothes. For the first time in his life, he felt shame. He was a carnal man. He had been pulled away from Christ and all that had been good in his life. He wrote his bedmate a note and placed it on the empty table. That seemed cowardly. He shook her awake gently, and when her eyes were three-quarters open, he said, "This is not pleasing to my Lord and Savior. I'm sorry I involved you in my sin. I hope you will find it in your heart to forgive me. I will deposit money into your account for an easier transition away from me. The best of luck to you." He was just one in a long line of fools; she would find another. As he closed the door, he heard her say, "F--- you."

His mind acknowledged that he deserved her venom. It was his sin, he owned it, he would repent, he would return to his loving Father and never leave.

***

Tom Jr. sat on the veranda of his tasteful, yet modest home on a hilltop on the outskirts of Ling Town, China. The morning air had a dampness, but the wonderful breakfast that Lana had prepared for him brought a warmth to his body. She had forgiven him one day after he had asked for a second chance. She had been a saint—never a cross word, no venom—just forgiveness. He had never been tempted again. The sun, still low on the horizon, gained heat from its reflection off the wide expanse of the Pacific Ocean before him. He saw the personally owned commercial fishing boats working a mile beyond the swelling waves in a loosely organized formation, aligning for a sweep. The boats were able to call in the species of fish wanted, sometimes by size and weight, through sound waves, electronic signaling, scents. Beyond the fishing boats, he saw four ocean vessels loaded with containers, hulls deep in the waters. Two were leaving for the United States with products from his factories in their holds, and two were coming in from the States with needed products. Beyond these ships, the great ocean highway was an ribbon of colorful, evenly spaced ships, traffic as heavy moving north as flowing south. He received the port manifests daily and greatly enjoyed knowing what the distant ships held. He also had the catch orders and manifests of the fishing boats and knew what went to the local fish market. The salt in the air mixed with the verdure of the surrounding lush forests.

He took his tea mug from the circular warmer it sat on. To be with his Lana, to have his kids right inside the house sleeping peacefully filled him with the greatest peace. They were all teenagers and for self-esteem and direction needed Mom and Dad as much as when they had been children. He anticipated looking in on them sleeping under their warm covers, and perhaps waking them with an "I love you" and a tousling of their hair, or playful, insistent slaps on both cheeks simultaneously. When they were young, he had given them a kiss, or placed a warm hand in their hand and said, "What are your plans today?" To hear little children's self-planned schedules as to what was fun to do on a free day with no school was a deep window into their souls. He knew that the reason he was here, thinking these thoughts, was because the Lord had put it all back together. The Lord had asked Lana and his kids to forgive, and Lana and the kids had obeyed. This forgiveness brought tears to Tom Jr.'s eyes.

His sense of unworthiness was strengthened as he read the past narratives of the TLC accounts, the directives issued by Ling when the company had been struggling. Ling was a genius! Ling had singlehandedly saved the company. From the volume of Ling's page turning and exploration of the problem—he had spent hundreds of hours in research to reach the right conclusions and course of action. Ling had done this to save the company and to save pupil Tom Jr. He had told no one; he had asked for no compensation, wanted no accolades. Tom thought back on the encouraging letters Ling had sent to him, urging him to repent, to heal his family, to rely on Jesus. Tom

Jr. realized that Tom Jr. had had a huge ego—that he had been the star of radiance within the company, that he had been all, everything—and now he saw he was just a boy who had inherited through God's creative processes a particular bent of mind, of invention. There was no star here, just a dab of light within a Milky Way of light.

Tom Jr. laughed at himself; he was not bitter that he wasn't the all-in-all, nor was he jealous of Ling. Laughter welled up and was heard across the lawn, into the kitchen, where Lana was prepping the kids' breakfasts. Oh, to laugh at himself, the fool. That was what men were without Christ—just fools full of self-delusion, self-love. God had known it from the beginning, and God had offered a solution, a piece of Himself, His Son.

Lana came from the kitchen at a quick walk, her robe tied tight, a worried or a grave look upon her face. Tom thought he had frightened her with his laughter. Or was one of the kids in trouble? No, she would have brought that child along.

"Ling has passed to paradise," she said, as she approached from behind, nuzzling her head against his, as she wrapped her arms around her sitting husband.

"What?" Tom answered in complete surprise and shock.

"Ling has passed to paradise," she stated calmly, as she rubbed his shoulders and neck.

He remained silent; reality was askew. Lana would not lie. He had been to the Ling home just a week ago. Hundreds had been in attendance for Ling's birthday, and Ling had been sharp of mind, agile in movement. The life of a combat soldier—those seven years of the Tribulation—must have taken their toll. He was consoled that soon Ling would be returned, along with his dad and mom and all the others, for continuation of eternal life in their resurrected bodies. God had opened Tom Jr.'s eyes at the perfect moment—Tom's awareness of Ling's goodness, as a memorial to Ling, the God-loving man who had founded a company with friends, who was patriarch of thousands, who worked hard, and who had loved deeply. This was the pathway to life and happiness. Looking at Ling's life, Tom Jr. saw that Ling was a man whose curiosity had brought him spiritual rest, a man with a satisfied soul. How clever were the workings of God's intent.

CHAPTER 9

On the very first day of the twelfth Jubilee year, millennial year 600, the old mortal friends, most if not all their offspring, and the resurrected friends gathered upon the spacious lawn of Tim Johnson's River View Plantation. The weather was—as almost every day—exceptional: clear blue skies marked by circling buzzards, hawks, eagles, and a few wispy, white clouds. The transporting resurrected had followed the river, while mortal hang gliders played in the updrafts by the mountain slopes. The first day of a Jubilee year had always been a time to recount those lost in the previous fifty-year period. Six-hundred-forty-two-year-old Tim (102 years old in old Earth years) sat on his handmade, double Adirondack chair, holding the hand of Mary, his faithful companion, who was now 640 years old (100 OEY). Mat, 617 years old (77 OEY), Katie, 615 years old (75 OEY), Hope, 600 years old (60 OEY) had just presented their parents with an ancient device: a "living picture" of 6 by 9 inches, the original device from the pre-Tribulation era, refitted with new wiring, battery, and screen. The scene captured Tim gently rocking his newborn Katie in his arms; Katie cooed, Tim's eyes beamed, his lips pursed, and he cooed in return. Mary led Mat into the scene, and Mat kissed Katie on the forehead, then attempted to leave his sister to return to play. He and Katie had been the best of friends from that time forward.

Tim rose from his seat—an Adirondack demanded strength to rise. Mary noticed her husband's vigor, strength; it was no less in power than when at its peak at twenty-five. He had known he was expected to speak, and his voice came strong and clear.

"I welcome all here to our gathering and to view our 'living picture.' It was of great value during the Tribulation period. The picture of our youth gave us a perspective, a history of when times were good, and therefore a hope for the future." He handed the ideograph to Mat to begin the chain of viewing among the guests. He looked over the audience—the mortals like himself, having been born pre-Tribulation, were few; those mortals born after the Tribulation, in the full glory of the millennium, outnumbered the "pretriburs" (tribur, the new slang for those who lived through the Tribulation) and the resurrected. "In those hazy days, when the World Church was corrupt, when the Lord wasn't our life, and we worshipped physical life and the world system of achievement for status, we really didn't know what eternal life was. Or rather, we kind of assumed it…as if it was our birthright for belonging to humanity's concept of God." His eyes fell to the earth and looked inward; emotion trembled in the eyes. "The Tribulation taught us that our Lord is everything. All else is superficial—even life—if not lived for the Creator, Yahweh, God, the I AM, our Daddy God, for we cried out to Him incessantly, and we cried for His presence; we cried for His love. He gave us love, and we endured.

"You mortals here must remember this: you must love God with all your heart, soul, mind, and strength. You must know Him, talk to Him, meditate upon His words, upon His character. You must quicken to His words, to His touch, and you must love those around you as you love your very self. Never love Him solely for what He provides—those things are just tangible gifts of His being, His character. Do not allow the gifts to become your God, or they will ruin you. Love God Himself; you are the form of what He is. He made you in His image. Live up to that promise. Love God for His love, His joy, His peace, and patience. Love Him for His kindness, goodness, His faithfulness. Love Him for His gentleness and self-control. Give Him free access to all that you are. He delights in you. That is all—and yet it is everything. Nothing worth having exists outside of this. Nothing, nothing, *nothing* worth having. Without Him, we are simply scoops of dirt; our spirits are the spirits of demented, hateful, demon-possessed subhumans.

"I see by the faces looking at me that you think that is rough, over the top, and the old patriarch is soon to be no more in this millennium. I know the overwhelming majority of you were born in these good times—the millennium. I know Satan is bound. You say the old creeds, the old prayers; you take the Lord's communion, and all seems right. You listen to the Spirit of God within you—within all of us—ever streaming, teaching, and correcting with ease, so much so that many will believe that it is *their* minds that produce such harmony." Tim held up an old, leather-bound Bible. "Here is where peace begins. You must search it out and meditate upon it. This is where truth begins—not in that happy place within the mind. Self-contentment and self-righteousness isn't loving God for who He is.

"You new generations, I beg of you: don't create your own world. Don't live within yourselves. Talk to the resurrected ones. Read or view their life stories in the internet libraries. Talk to the remaining members of the Tribulation period. History is your strength. See what happens to humanity when they do not seek the God of truth and love. Imagine the hateful world we, survivors, lived in—Satan's kingdom.

"Tom and Tish Burnell are no longer with us. Two hundred years ago, they entered paradise, and they will return at the end of this age. Tom and Tish had committed their life stories to print. Tom and I, unknown to each other prior to the 'Great Quake,' one day fought upon a subway train. The Lord God brought us back together again as friends. He was, and is, a good friend. Look up Carl Stasic in the library—he, too, is gone for the moment. As is Ling, a Chinese soldier straight from the battle of Armageddon, whom the Lord found in the most inhospitable of lands to Christ. Read Ling's story. It's a nail biter, a miracle.

"They are gone, but only for moments in the unending river of life. Among you mortals are certainly those who will spend eternity in the lake of fire of hell, if you do not heed my words."

Tim smiled as he surveyed the vast crowd stretching all the way to the wood line. "Sorry if I brought you down, but I've given you plenty of time to recover in the truth, the life, the way that is for eternity."

The resurrected, Andy and Leaf and Tuck and Puck, John and Diana, Emily and Dan, a visiting DC Jones, Gramps, and Great-grandfather Jeremiah spoke solemn amens. Katie and her husband, Paul, and their eight children, Mat and Barb and their eight children, Hope and William and their three kids; the Burnells—Tanya, Anya, Flo, Tom Jr.—and their spouses, all who had commuted far, save for Flo and Rickee, who lived in Harrisburg, swelled with hallelujahs and amens. The children of the triburs and their children's children clapped or remained in solemn, reflective silence.

"Enjoy the presence of your God within the camaraderie of this gathering," Tim said. He paused for a moment. "That is all I have to say." Tim turned to face Mary. He offered her his hand, and she accepted. He pulled her to her feet as if she were a child. He pulled her into himself, looked into her eyes, and kissed her upon her lips. He pressed his fingers into her arms, feeling her musculature, softness, and warmth, then his hands were upon her waist.

He spoke in a low and private tone, nearly a whisper. "The most endearing and resilient woman in the world. After we're resurrected, we will hang out together, for certain." He smiled; a deep reverence welled within his soul for his wife.

She pulled him close and said, "Yes, there will be a brief interval. I can feel my body ebbing."

Tim spoke, almost in a whisper as his cheek remained upon her cheek. "The life in the old world and the Tribulation were sure to tax our longevity. I feel it too, loving wife, mother of my children."

Katie grabbed her dad's arm. "Hey, there is a party around you." Katie's husband, Paul, held a little girl of the fourth generation of millennials as he faced Tim and Mary. Tim studied the happy, contented face of Paul. Tim had noticed that Paul always seemed to travel in an aura of contentment. Tim took Paul's semifree hand and shook playfully. "You're the kid from the mountain restaurant."

"Yes, I am." Paul played straight man.

"That is how I will always think of you. I remember that meal as if it happened yesterday, but not you." Tim laughed heartily, as did Paul.

Mary said, "Katie remembers it even better, I'm sure."

"Yes, I do. I thought, *That is a kind-looking young man. I wonder if he knows Jesus.* That was it. Now let's go sit in a quiet place, with a plate of food. Perhaps the river overlook," said Katie.

"The river," declared Tim.

Paul spoke. "I'll pick up some lighting, courtesy of Dan, the man." Dan Smith had invented thin-shelled spheres of floating gases that illuminated a twenty-foot radius. The spheres were held by a tether, a thin string. He had become rich through the patent. Ninety percent of his money, a willing offering, went into the funds of the Lord Jesus, sitting on His throne in Jerusalem. Jesus never had to impose a tax; all His people loved Him much.

Katie had both her mom and dad in hand when she said, "Where do you two want to be interred when you pass into paradise?" She remembered how she had held her mom's hand that day on the outskirts of Harrisburg, after Dad's supposed death, as Mom had stumbled over the dry earth, searching for her family. At the food table, Katie loaded up their plates. Mat was standing beside her, seemingly coming out of nowhere. She placed the plates on his tray.

"Mary and I believe any of the local mausoleums in Harrisburg are acceptable. We'd like to be with Carl, if possible. Glad I never followed through with the home-cemetery idea. Nothing to be gained by it. Heck, if we were to go tomorrow, we'd be resurrected in only four hundred years. We may make another Jubilee year or two. I'm only 102 and Mary, 100, in old Earth years. The Lord promised a span of 120. Eighteen Earth years… that's 180 millennium years. I could see the beginnings of another generation of your offspring."

"And ours," volunteered Mat.

"Yes, yours too. Where the heck did you come from?" said Tim jokingly.

"I'm always here when you need me." The words held emotion as Mat remembered the day of rebellion when he and dad went to war together. The Lord had guided him, preserved their lives. The quest for liberty had failed, but the righteousness of their God had not failed. "Dad, I need a computer spreadsheet to keep track of my great-grandkids and beyond."

Tim addressed his hope to Mat. "Now, with the Lord's help, you and Katie and Hope must ensure that as many of our descendants as possible cling to our God, love Him, so that we may live with them into eternity."

Mat answered, "Tomorrow, Dad, we will sit outside again, by the river, and we will make plans to see to that happen. Name by name—there are over a thousand names—we will assess each family member, strengthen what may be lacking."

Tim chose the collection of benches and chairs by the river bluff's edge and sat. Katie distributed the plates. Fading sunlight, at the moment; the yellow orb would soon kiss the western sky beyond the river. *That Dan Jr. is a wiz. Balloons of light*, thought Tim. *A shame Dan's dad can't see his son now. Dan Sr. just did not get it. Dead, totally dead, to Christ.*

Between mouthfuls of food delivered by fork and spoon, Tim looked at, studied his kids, and Paul, William, Barb, and Mary. He needed to talk to Mat and Katie. He needed their forgiveness for an old sin. A second thought intruded, and he said, "We must not forget the Burnells. I promised Tom Sr. to overwatch their affairs. None should be lost. He would have done the same for me. I must pass that obligation to another in our family, so that when I go—"

Katie spoke up. "Tom Jr. is a capable man. He's watching his family." Then she changed the subject. "We've eaten half our food and said not one word of thanks. Think back on those Tribulation days when starvation was a constant companion." Her eyes moistened.

Paul said, "Katie just recorded a new song. An old, old song from the past, called 'Hard Times Come Again No More' written by a man named Foster. It was quite popular in his time. He was a hymn writer as well."

Tim said, "When I first laid eyes on that plate of food, my mind went immediately to those days of trouble. Always, every time I eat, no matter when or where. The Lord has etched it into my heart. I remember His goodness, for even though I had nothing, I had enough. I had Him. How do we teach that to kids who have never known want?"

"What happened to fasting and praying?" asked Paul.

"What happened to our faith, the words of the Bible admonishing us to fast and pray, to experience hunger?" said Katie.

"Remember when we worried about a career for Katie?" Mary searched Tim's eyes. "Now our little girl is a worship leader and a renowned singer—all by the hand of our God. And she married a man, her producer, who believed in her when she was just a skinny kid full of passion for her Savior."

"What about me? I'm somebody." Mat laughed, taking up the old sibling rivalry that had died before it started. He only needed the Lord's approbation, and He gave it daily, by the minute, the second.

Tim spoke up for his son. "Paul. Bill. Mat has saved this family times innumerable. He saved us from the prying of state inspectors—as a kid, mind you. He saved me in combat. He rescued scores of our soldiers from torture and death. He saved our family from receiving the beast's mark. He saved Katie and me at the river baptism. He saved little Emily with the Holy Spirit's touch and his love."

All these things Paul and Bill knew, had been told to them by Katie and Hope. They never tired of the retelling.

"Now I must talk to Mat and Katie alone. Mary, you may remain of you wish. I don't exclude anyone because you are not trusted but simply because I want Mat and Katie to know what I say is for them and because I get somewhat embarrassed when I cry before people—even the most trusted people."

Paul and William rose, put hands on Tim's shoulders. "It's okay," said Paul.

"We love you, Tim, and it is okay," said Bill.

Hope's touch lingered on her dad's shoulder as she followed Bill.

Mary took Tim's hand and Mat and Katie moved in closer with their chairs. "You better not make me cry, Daddy," scolded Katie.

"Here's a hint. Hope is not here," said Tim.

"I caught that fact and know where this is going," Mat answered.

"Yes, it is going back to when Hope had yet to be born. When Tim Johnson lived for himself—and because he lived for himself, he walked his family into seven years of hell on Earth."

Dad could barely finish his sentence, before his shame and remorse welled up in his throat, into his eyes, and he sobbed. "Please forgive me. Please. I'm so sorry."

Katie and Mat closed in upon their daddy, smelled his hair, his aftershave, the scents of their childhood when he wrestled them, tickled and hugged them, when he carried them in his arms when they were tired little kids; the scent that came when he bent down over their tucked-in forms in their beds and kissed them good-night. Their daddy, who had put his own life on the line time and time again, who had sacrificed for them, struggling to make his wrong right. "I just couldn't see Jesus, so wrapped up in me, my career. Such a selfish man, such conceit."

Katie said, "You had help—Satan, the flesh, the world system. Few escaped, and none escaped without our Lord, Daddy. It's what we are born: sinners."

Mat spoke determinedly, assuredly. "Dad, we forgive you. You turned it around, brought us victory, brought us Christ, kept us alive. You didn't quit. You were preaching that in our lives before the troubles came—never give up, endure to the end. It was a rough time, the worst the world has seen. Because it was so ugly, we know Jesus so much better." Mat hugged his dad, and Katie ran her hand over and over his shoulders and back. Mary had both her hands in his, and she sobbed as she kissed his hands.

"Dad, you are forgiven," said Mat. "Forgiven for being deceived by a world that didn't wish to know Christ; forgiven for being deceived by the allures of the flesh, which the world said was life itself; forgiven for being ensnared by the deceits of the most cunning foe, a being of powers beyond a man. No man or woman has the power to find our God, Dad. Why should you be different? The Lord chose you. He saw your love for your family, and He knew He wanted you."

Mat's words burst into Tim's consciousness. The slobbering regret was that Tim Johnson *still* had the conceit that he had greater insights, greater willpower, greater intelligence than any being created, and he had just not used these powers. He should have known because he was so superior! Tim inwardly chuckled at Mat's wisdom and his own stubborn conceit. The Lord crushed his self-pity—that is all this outburst was. Tim accepted the fact, and his burden of shame lifted.

"I too forgive you, Daddy." Katie understood her brother's statement. His children knew he needed to hear those words, though they didn't think he had anything to be forgiven for.

"You were the best daddy a girl could ever have," Katie declared.

"And the best dad to a son," added Mat.

Mary spoke. "Now let's hold hands and think of the God who brought us through, of His faithfulness for eternity. Let us rest and enjoy this evening."

***

The evening passed as the bats cut through the dusk; as the bent, thin-winged nighthawks glided, chirping their plaintive calls; as the river coolness rose into the air, and the fish jumped and flopped back into security; as the deer snorted in alarm at the people gathered on the bluff; the tree frogs chirped; the bullfrogs croaked; and the katydids and crickets competed for attention as the muskrats roiled the water and splashed. The wildcats called their throaty ode to life far up on the mountain, and in the meadows, the coyotes howled. The stars thickened the sky. Laughter and talk were heard from those gathered at the house and in numerous groups on the lawn and bluff. Dan Smith's floating balls of light gave off a star quality, as if the heavens had gathered. The smell of woodsmoke scented the air. The children of the Lord absorbed their Creator's world. He had defeated Satan, taken back His good world, and to everyone but Him, it was a miracle. But all knew it was Victory. One thousand years of celebration of living life as it should have been lived from the beginning, the children adoring their Father, and the Father loving His children.

Tim and Mary retired to their bedroom, showered together, washed each other's backs, toweled each other dry, slipped into their soft-fabric gym shorts. Mary moved toward the bed, and Tim diverted to the open, broad window that faced the tree line along the river. He could see the water shimmering between the sparse trees. A moon had been uncovered from a misty band of clouds. The few remaining partyers were on the lawn, facing east toward the mountain behind their bedroom. He breathed in deeply of the river, the trees, the freshly mown grass; heard the tree frogs; saw the lightning bugs. Mary joined him, she held his hand.

She spoke. "You think it's beautiful. You know how fortunate you are, as am I, to have lived beyond the Tribulation on Earth. To have experienced six hundred years of near-perfect life after the nightmare of forty-two years in your own flesh—and forty years for me."

He kissed her and said, "You know everything about me. I am glad my children forgive me. I have a deep peace." Tears welled up as his emotion spoke to him: *You should have died in your sin, ignorant to the life and to yourself, a failure of a husband and father, a dead body on the battlefield of life. And here you are a winner, victorious, with a loving wife, son, and daughters. You, a child of your creator God.* "What an incredible God we have, Mary, to save us, the worthless and self-deluded."

She squeezed his hand. "The only good within us was that we knew we had none."

A knock sounded at their door. Mary quickly found her robe, tied it, and answered the door.

Their daughter, Hope, born in the first year of the millennium and now six hundred years old or sixty old Earth years, stood before them holding her five-year-old great-granddaughter, Mary and Tim's great-great-granddaughter, Patience.

"Sorry to bother you. I saw your light still on. Patience wants to say thank you for the party and good-night."

Tim and Mary each held a hand of Patience. Tim spoke. "What is it. Patience? What do you have to say?"

"Thank you for the swim and the cake and hamburgers." She paused for a breath. "I love you." She reached out, and Tim drew close for the hug. "We love you too, honey." Tim kissed the tiny cheek. Mary hugged Patience, and another kiss found Patience's cheek. Tim, with eyes of mirth and love, studied the eyes of his little girl, Hope, fully grown. "How beautiful your spirit is. Thanks for bringing her. The perfect close to a beautiful day. I love you intensely, Hope. You are a good daughter, and you are raising our descendants well. And in a short time, we will see you again."

"Okay, Dad. I love you, too. And you too, Mom." Hope kissed Daddy, then her mom. The door closed as Patience waved, and Mary waved back. Tim and Mary returned to bed. Tim whispered to Mary, "You did a good job in raising Hope."

"I didn't do it alone." She thought back to Diana and the last day of the marriage feast, six hundred years ago, when they had discussed raising children. "All our kids turned out just fine, with the Lord as our guide."

"Yes, they did. They are raising their kids even better than we raised them. God willing, the future is secure."

"God is always willing," answered Mary, "when we ask and patiently work."

The light went out. As Hope walked down the hall and out to the waiting vehicle for the short ride home, where her kids were staying for the night, she was happy that she had followed her sister's advice to see their parents. They had needed a boost, and little Patience had come through. Hope glowed in her dad's remark about her own spirit. "Beautiful," he had called it. Hope thought on Dad's last words, "And in a short time, we will see you again."

As Mary and Tim entered a deep sleep, an angel of the Lord awakened them for the very short and easy ride to paradise.

***

Andy had been standing alone on the river bluff of his homestead, unwinding from the party, and had just turned around to view the long ridge of mountain in the moonlight, when he noticed a whitish, translucent dash of subdued light depart upward from the location of Tim's home. He was only puzzled for a second, for he had seen such lights many times before.

A band of angels had escorted someone to paradise. You needed a spirit-focused mind to see this, though the new Earth environment enhanced the image. *Tim* and *Mary* were the names the Holy Spirit presented to his mind. With deep sadness he waved good-bye. The parting would be short in the time of eternity, but they were good friends, and he had drawn strength from knowing them.

The tree frogs were chirping, and the amphibious frogs were croaking, and he thought at least one racoon was working the shoreline for crayfish. The hazy moonglow, the scents of summer, and the temporary loss of friends took him back in time to his childhood, when life still maintained a small hold on goodness. The deluge of foreigners had yet to come; only a few traders were known. All neighboring tribes were at peace—or not actively at war. A kid with a bow had nothing to do but roam the river, creeks, and mountains, studying the ways of the animals.

Why had God been so good to him? Eternal life with Leaf and his boys, when so few tribespeople were called. He had killed so many men, beaten more, and yet he had been forgiven. Jesus had said the gate to life was small, and the path so narrow that those who found it were few. All would be revealed in its proper time. All would be revealed.

***

Tom Jr. and Lana, Tanya and Tobe, Anya and Keith, and Flo and Rickee had walked back from Tim's homestead by way of the river trail to Beulah Land. Tom Jr. paid for the upkeep of the home and acreage and welcomed all family members to visit and vacation there whenever possible. The insect and amphibious life created a cacophony of sound that had entered their nervous systems and hummed along the spinal column into the mind. Flo could hear nighthawks above in their deep, raspy chirping. Her dad had taught her about nighthawks; he had identified other birds by their calls and songs. He had loved his holdings and soon would be back. They were all tired, Tanya, Anya, and Tom Jr.'s families more so from their flights from Kenya, California, and China. Flo and Rickee could have driven back to Harrisburg but wanted to remain with family as long as possible. All their children were grown, and all had started their own families. As much as she missed them, it was good to be with her sisters, like it was in the Tribulation days, before their tagalong little brother was born.

She blurted a question to whomever wished to respond. “Remember when Dad came home with a can of beef stew that a ‘Mr. Johnson’ had given to him?”

“Girl! You remember that?” Tanya challenged laughingly.

“What a memory!” mused Anya. “What were you, three years old?”

“Maybe four,” guessed Flo. “Every life experience was burned into my memory—the times were so tough, and we had only each other and our God.”

“Jesus was on our lips every waking minute; that is truth,” said Tanya, adding, “Yes, that seven years is burned into my mind as well. Especially the last three and a half years.”

“And the name of Jesus, too…and even now He’s our first thought when we rise,” Tobe said.

“For all eternity,” said Keith, as amens came from the throng of grateful hearts.

“Remember eating that chicken that was all dark meat?” Flo’s tone held a puzzlement.

“When was that, child?” asked a bewildered Tanya.

“I think she means the four-footed chicken,” Anya said sheepishly.

Tanya began to laugh, as did Anya. The men laughed just because the laughter was contagious, and two of them had also eaten four-footed chickens.

Keith was still laughing when he asked, “Did that chicken have whiskers?”

“Tell me!” Flo demanded in bewilderment, as Keith’s comment frightened her.

“That was rat meat, girlie, savory and greasy…,” said Tanya, pretending to be lost in fond memories of a good meal eaten.

"But highly nutritious," Anya interjected. "I can't believe that in the last six hundred years, this never came up."

"Dad hid it even from me till the millennium. Right down there, by the river, we saw a river rat, and he told me the story," Tanya said.

"Tim told me the Johnsons ate one only once," Anya said, "and the waiting to get sick, even though they didn't, wasn't worth the eating."

They left the trail and walked across the mown lawn, minds deep in thought. Tom Jr. and Lana, holding hands, contentedly listened. Tom thanked his Lord that he had the money to keep Dad's home maintained. Here, on these grounds that Dad loved so much, his memory would live till he again was with them.

"Do you remember when the angels came for us?" Flo shouted, in her excitement of that time.

"Daddy's face was covered in tears, and we ate the last spoonful of beans, the last piece of bread, and had the last sip of water," Tanya interjected.

"We were dying, honey; a dying family," Anya added.

"Dying from starvation, and Mom was just skin and bones." Flo spoke quickly and determinedly. "But we would not give in to Satan. We woulda rather died than kiss the ring of the beast."

Voices ceased. Holiness surrounded their thoughts and embraced them. The silence of voices was consumed by nature's life sounds. Tom took the lead and held open the door to the main house, then flicked on a light, threw kindling and a log on the fireplace embers. The couples spread around the fireplace on the comfortable, worn chairs and sofas. Tanya stood up, her back to the fire, facing those she loved, and said, "Sisters, we are getting old. The years in Tribulation times and six hundred millennium years, they take a toll. We will be going to distant homes and may not see each other before we pass on to paradise. But we will surely meet again for eternity. I just want to say how much I love you, how much I need you, how blessed I am to have such a family." She looked at the floor. "I know you all feel the same way. So come here and hug me, including little brother and wife, then stand beside me and receive the hugs from the others."

The newly added wood burst into flames and lit the room. The family stood as one, and each hugged Tanya deeply. Each in turn was hugged, and tears flowed, and smiles were exchanged, and kind and good words were shared, and the Spirit of the Lord embraced them all.

CHAPTER 10

Tom Jr. awoke suddenly, panic and desolation in his heart. His sense of lostness dispersed as he listened to the cacophony of insect and frog life outside his China home. He sat up in bed. Lana lay peacefully beside him, with a contented smile on her face. A sense of purposelessness clung to him, as if his life had meant nothing, as if Satan had stolen it all away. He was seven hundred years old, head of one of the richest companies in the world, with almost half a million employees. His sons, Bongani and Chuks, and the girls, Deka, Ebele, and Imani, had all prospered; and Bongani, the oldest son, his name meaning *the grateful one*, had a son, Michael, who was about to marry. The attacks to his sleep had been almost constant for two weeks now. Were these attacks inspired by demons? Or was it his God, his Savior, warning him of Satan's wiles? His God would have spoken to him directly through the Word or through other people of God's Spirit. God was not mute. If they were demons attacking him, what were they after? His death from lack of sleep? Or through worry and anxiety? How could demons attack when Satan was bound in Hades? A subconscious battle was taking place; the subconscious, the wastebasket of the past, the rotting remains of the once-living, carnal man.

He had repented heartily of his affair, and Lana had forgiven him. This current unease had no connection to his past stupidity. He had simply lost sight of what was good in life, and the flesh had subtly stolen his heart from God and replaced it with the allures of the flesh—empty allures that now disgusted him. His stupidity and weaknesses disgusted him. How good and clean he felt within his marriage with the only earthly being who truly understood him and cared for him. How could he influence this new subconscious battle? Play Bible verses at night while he slept? Read scripture in a formulaic schedule daily? Pray five times a day, every three hours? Somehow, he just had to hold on to the Love of God. He had only faith and the record of God's goodness in his life.

In fewer than three hundred years, the millennium would be complete. Technically, he could live three hundred more years, but all millennials would need to face death by the end or soon after, in order to receive their immortal resurrected bodies. He knew of no scriptural reference to mortal bodies continuing past the millennium. Methuselah had lived to be 969 in a world not fully gripped in Satan's control. Perhaps the final release of Satan three hundred years from now would be Tom Jr.'s end; maybe he would die in war. His plan, then, in the intervening time, would be to keep the business going and prospering for his workers and their families.

Tom noticed the time—4:30 a.m. He heard the birds beginning to chatter. He rose to the broad, open window overlooking the bay. He saw the rose tint staining the eastern horizon of the sea; the wispy clouds caught the colors. Another perfect day was beginning. He gave thanks to the Lord, and he remained confident in his Lord to provide an answer to his subconscious battle.

***

Mat hopped off the commuter trolley directly before his place of work, the expansive, three-story building of the Bureau of Rapid Response. At seven hundred years into the millennium, he was eighty-seven years old OEY, but his mind and body were as healthy as that of an old-world twenty-year-old.

No, his health was better than a twenty-year-old's. His mind could easily run three or four streams of consciousness concurrently; his muscular strength was that of a weightlifter, his quickness that of a soccer attacker, his stamina that of a long-distance runner. No head colds, no viruses, no harmful bacteria, nothing to impede health.

The trolley ride from his river home had been scenic vistas of the river and mountains—lush greenness from trees and fields, fields of grain, wild meadows of deer, elk, buffalo, pastures of cattle, sheep, llamas. Beautiful, quaint, and novel homes were scattered about, and children waved at the passing trolley as family pets wagged their tails wildly and barked hellos. Not one unhappy face among the commuters; many with bags and boxes of fresh produce to sell in the city to coworkers or the general public. One young man onboard, appearing to be in his twenties, was waving and laughing at the people outside their homes, in villages, at crossroads, working in fields or barns, or at small industrial sites.

Something remained in Mat's mind from the young man's laughter. He buried the thought. The good life lay ahead, and that is where he was focused. Mat believed that his own body could make it through the end of the millennium into that time when Satan would return and gather up his own of the mortal millennialists. Mat wanted to live that long, till Satan's final return, and fight humanity's foe into eternal impotence and tortured captivity.

Coworkers and friends passed him as he entered his workplace. The bays of the emergency-response vehicles were full; land-, water-, and air-capable platforms waited. The first responders sat at their communal table, shooting the breeze. They were all resurrected and therefore could transport to an emergency quickly without vehicles if the emergency was nearby. However, vehicles might be needed for extra equipment or transportation of incapacitated patients. Or for lengthy trips, where vehicles could out-speed transporters.

Mat bounded up the stairs to the third floor. A stream of consciousness hit Mat hard. The young man's laugh. Some quality, some tone that wasn't right. Jedediah, his first child of eight, was already in the office of Police Services. The entire top floor consisted of broad sheets of clear plexiglass—not really plexiglass, but the old name had stuck. Not one fleecy white cloud in the sky. He was drawn to the window and usually began his day just gazing at his city. Harrisburg sprawled before him, growing rapidly, as most millennials preferred city life—they preferred people; perhaps the country lacked stimulation. Or was it because the negatives—crime, social unrest, the mentally ill, poverty—were gone, and everyone was united in the quest to live well and true, faithful to a community spirit, the inner code of "love they neighbor as thyself?" Andy had the day off, as did Uncle John and Diana.

Mat studied his son's face—mostly a Johnson face, but Jed had a trace of the honey-blond gene that was found on his mother's side, the Smith genes. Dan Jr., Barb's brother, had the same trace of dark blond within the brown. Jed was 699 millennial years old, or sixty-nine OEY. Jed's line had already produced three generations of Johnsons. Although Mat's mind was keen, he had resorted to keeping a genealogical map of his progeny within his handheld-phone computer. Birthdays, parents, siblings, likes and dislikes, appearance, including pictures, and what Mat thought were dominant traits that might have bearing on future employment were in the phone.

He greeted his son, Jed, with a hand squeeze to the shoulder. Then, his subconscious stream of thought coalesced. The young man on the commuter. The laughter of the young man, the body posture, the waves spoke of contempt and mockery. He had been laughing at the people, not laughing in delight for the goodness of life displayed. Mat's mind had brought this forth when the incident had combined with memories of the first meeting of the Smiths, that day Carl Stasic had taken the Johnsons from the bondage of the tent city. The day the Smith family and the Johnsons had been saved from their personal hell and entered the carrier for the ride to freedom. The enemy at the checkpoints had waved—they had waved like the young man on the morning commute, with contempt, hatred, and mockery expressed in words, posture, facial expressions.

In this perfect world, what had created the contempt, the mockery? Jed noticed his dad's deep concentration—he was oblivious to the distractions of the office. "What's up, Dad? You seem in a different place."

"I am. I was back in the dark days of the revolution, riding in a personnel carrier. That day, Carl freed our family, and we rode through the city, eventually picking up your mother's family."

"I remember the stories, Dad, from my youth. You were the best storyteller. All eight of us agree. It's the reason I was a history major when I first entered college. That oral tradition—telling us where we came from and what you and Mom believed when the world around you just wanted you to live a lie, believe a lie. The struggle to know Christ in Satan's kingdom." Jed floated away into the little-boy world of comforters and soft couches and brothers and sisters curled up, limbs touching limbs. The fire low in the fireplace, and Dad and Mom just retelling one heart-wrenching story after another. He loved his dad and mom—all of his brothers and sisters did—for teaching them what they had now and what they had left behind. They loved their God who had stood with Mom and Dad and brought them through. Jed spoke. "Why were you thinking of that day?"

"I saw a young man on the commuter this morning. He was waving at the people we were passing, the neighbors and friends of us all. He had an oddness of expression and posture, which, at first, I couldn't place. Then, I remembered that day in the past. I had seen the same posture, the same expression on the faces of the enemy as our personnel carrier passed through checkpoints. Loathing, mockery, hatred. The commuter today, this child born in the kingdom of God, free of Satan, free of want, free of disease and violence, his mind streaming the goodness of God, valued none of what he had."

Jed responded pensively, "To the pure, all things are pure, but to those who are corrupted and do not believe, nothing is pure. Their minds and consciences are corrupted, says the holy book. Titus, I believe."

"But why do they not believe? Why are they corrupted?" Mat challenged.

Jed smiled; he loved these debates—"searchings," his family called them. He had had these with his dad since he was a boy. The finding of truth with the man he admired. Points of view were never mocked. You could think aloud not knowing what would come from your mouth, foolishness, or wisdom, without fear of belittlement or castigation. Just kindness and openness in the pursuit of truth. "I think there are many factors working in this situation. One: he had never been in contact with the older ones, never read a history book, didn't have parents like you and Mom who freely communicated with him. Satan's biggest gambit while he ruled was to destroy the history of his deceit and lies and place it upon Christ. The horrors of the world governed by Satan were never made real to this child. He has no reference point. That's what history gives us, and the more brutal the history, the better. Satan's reality is brutal, for he is brutal," Jed said.

"The second point is this young man was born in the flesh. He has wished to be a god from birth. He wished to have parents who attended to his every need, as if he were a king. He wanted no siblings to share his glory. He wanted no one to correct his actions. All his thoughts were superior. He wanted to be surrounded by people who thought as he thought. We know there will be one last battle after these thousand years. It will happen because of those mortals still living in the carnal self, the flesh. They will just need an ignition source to their tinder, Satan."

Mat was awed and pleased at his son's wisdom. Jed sensed the utter malignancy of Satan without ever having experienced his rule. Mat answered, "You're correct. I know these things. It was just a shock to see such hatred risen again. We need a strategy to counteract this. We need to preach the gospel of salvation again. Tom Sr. said this to me well before his death when this problem first felt real. I interviewed him, and this is what he said: "When you hurt God and are ashamed of your hurting Him, then you are at the threshold." The threshold of salvation and new birth. We must teach the law and the perfect love of God. We should teach that the shame produced by the betrayal of God and His righteous kingdom is a warning state of mind. The lack of this shame means the love of God is no longer valued. We cannot let this love of self take our loved ones from us in this perfect millennium."

In a businesslike tone, Jed said, "We are informed of the latest trends, sociological studies, psychological studies. People, through the wisdom of God, are working on this. As citizens, we have the right to inquire. As officers, we can check his biography. Encourage courses of action that would lead to positive results. He maintains his freedom to accept or not. It is still the same as it has always been: people can think what they want; it is their actions that come into conflict with the law. We only have three hundred more years to go."

Mat said, "The Lord is sitting on his throne in Jerusalem. He is aware. I just need to stop worrying."

"That's right. Don't worry, but it is right to take an interest and maybe delineate a role for yourself. In fact, with that in mind, why don't you talk to my Peter, your grandson. He was at the Jubilee celebration. At age fifty OEY, he knows these newer generations better than we do, and he is paying attention to this very phenomenon. He wrote his master's degree paper on this subject."

"I remember that now. I believe he told me when he thanked me for his graduation gift. Yes, I'll make the connection. Pete and I go way back. I especially remember being with him on the tour of the Tribulation sites. Tell him I'll be in contact," said Mat.

***

The river was wide, sparkling in the midmorning summer sun. A gentle breeze blew southerly, pushing against the bare skin of Mat's back, which acted as a sail; the current was steady. He had planned this trip for a weekday he was not scheduled to work; took the commuter all the way to the village of Sunbury with his kayak and computer and a few snacks. Vultures were in the air, circling high overhead. He had remembrances of the vultures of the Tribulation. These vultures were benign, artists with wing-tip feathers brushing the air for subtle changes in movement. He had a longing for his resurrection body, in which he, too, would fly. Andy said the resurrected could see the fish below the water's surface. He scanned the shoreline; waters had receded, leaving a light-brown discoloration on the vegetation two feet up the bank. River birches shaded the bank; some had fallen down the bank or leaned over and dipped their leaves into the water. He could smell rotting fish, mud. Occasionally, beavers would slap the water with their tails. Muskrats were scurrying about, collecting young shoots of green. The shoreline mud was heavily dappled with animal tracks.

Time slowed to the rhythm of the occasional paddle. Mat scanned sky, river shore, mountain's heights, islands. He would like to have seen this view as Andy had once seen it, with tribal villages along the shore, native cornfields of bean and squash intermixed. In time, he approached the acreage and home of his grandson, Peter. Peter had yet to marry, and the acreage had just been purchased through the hiring incentive of his employer, a think tank in Washington, DC. He saw a square object against the bank. This was probably the pontoon float used as a summer porch. The home had been built somewhere back and up from the river on the wooded and rather steep sides of a bluff. Peter had an American flag flying from the pontoon deck. Nationalism had really taken hold during the millennium, after the judgment of the nations, when the United States, with all her corruption, selfishness, apostasy, groveling, and begging to the godless Federation, still had outshone all other nations in her basic kindness and sharing with the saints of the Tribulation. Empathy, mercy, kindness had been found among the dirty faces of the masses known as Americans. Mat remembered that Tribulation meal of beef stew cooked near Gramps's farmhouse for Josh and his band of missionaries. Dad had offered that freely, even when his own family was starving, and supplies were measured.

Salty tears mingled with the salt of his sweating skin. How close they had walked with death each day. Eating nothing but the word of God, living on nothing but His love and their love of each other. Every second of life was a gift from their Lord, with nothing but faith to even hint of enduring to the end. Here, this day, was the fruit of endurance: a thousand years of Christ as king upon Earth, and a world—a life—so full and beautiful that a man could scarcely comprehend his Creator. Here, in the land with the red, white, and blue flag proudly flying. How his dad always cried when he saw it waving. His dad had believed before the Tribulation; his dad and he had answered the call to native sons, sons not of land possession, martial strength, or blood and heredity, but believers in the spirit imbued by God into the founders' words. He and Dad, Dan Jr., and even Dan Sr., had answered the call and began a revolution they had not won. God was true to the sacrifice, though many men were not, and the flag waved again. Mat thought of that ancient Christian truism, "When God is in it, little is much." Persistent, unyielding, uncompromising Jehovah always had His way. The lowliest, smallest, most insignificant man or woman, if loyal, would be used by God to do great things.

"Ho there, Peter!" Mat tracked the kayak toward the platform only a few feet above the river. "Give your gramps a helping hand." Strange to call himself *Gramps* when his own Gramps still lived. He didn't feel like a gramps.

Peter, coming from the back of the platform, was beside the kayak in an instant. "I'll hold it steady," he said to Gramps. He called over his shoulder, "Grace, grab Grandpa's hand." Like a spirit, Grace was by the kayak with her right hand outstretched and her left firmly grasping the frame of a two-by-four structure. *Smart girl*, thought Mat. S*he has done this before*. The hand was small, but every finger strong; the palm and forearm, strong. Mat was upon the platform. Mat sensed a bathing suit beneath the baggy shorts and T-shirt; the faint smell of sunscreen was present.

He sensed she was the one, and his happiness for Peter sat deeply in his soul. Barb was the best gift God had given him, other than life itself. Peter had built a small ramp into the deck and slid the craft out of the water, grabbing Mat's belongings from the kayak well and placing them on a nearby chair. "Sit, Gramps, and get you bearings. Want something to eat?"

"What have you got?" inquired a smiling Mat.

"How about some fish fillets fresh from the river? Grace has them warming on the grill."

"I thought I smelled fish. Smallmouth bass."

"Yes," answered Pete.

"You can identify the fish by smell?" Grace's expression held amazement.

"No, just a lucky guess." Mat laughed as did Grace, as he continued his thoughts. "You know, smallmouth were not native to the Susquehanna drainage. Found that out from my boss, Andy, a Native American of the Susquehannock tribe."

"Just largemouth?" Peter questioned.

"Yes, they were native to this watershed," said Mat.

"Sun or shade, Mr. Johnson?" Grace offered chairs in either location. The term *gramps* seemed too old but using *Mr. Johnson* seemed too formal.

"Dad will sit in the shade awhile," said Mat, who sensed the predicament.

Grace smiled. "Okay, Dad," Her tone held triumph and satisfaction with the new term. *Dad* was a common title for any older man and convenient to the times with so many generations present. Mat nodded his head in approval and joined in a laugh, as he said, "Success. The simple victories are sometimes the most pleasurable."

Grace liked Dad, and she sensed he liked her. He and Peter shared that family trait of ease, love, and calm. She wondered if Peter would want to tell him.

Grace served Dad the fish with fried potatoes and iced tea. Heard the kind, "Thank you," and sat beside Peter.

Mat addressed Peter as he ate. "Your dad says you have thoughts on the new generations of mortals and even wrote a paper on the topic. I had a revelation one day on a commute into work."

Peter said, "Yes, Dad told me. The ungodly behavior that indicated a problem in thinking, if not a problem with the soul."

"Exactly. In everyday terms, speak to this. Let your mind ramble freely; we can pick up loose ends in my thinking as we go or at the end. This was the subject of your master's dissertation." Tim thought a concrete point was needed before the ramble.

"Yes. I have been noticing such behavior for years. I think I saw it because I had been born into a family that freely discussed the old world and the Tribulation. I had a mind-set born out of those times, and I think this was greatly reinforced by my father's memory of the stories you would tell him and his siblings as they grew. I read all the autobiographies—yours, Great-granddad's, and those of all our relatives and family friends. Most millennial households lost that key generational link—most people of your generation never passed on their memories in a clear, consistent, or maybe indelible and insistent way.

"I have that fact—that the Tribulation has been forgotten or the topic, avoided—supported by data. Many have thought that the Tribulation, in which the last hope of Satan was destroyed, meant an end to carnal life. The millennium has only rewards for people, and the pervasive spirit is that all people only want to do good. But now those who live without penalties for false thoughts and actions personally do not think these negatives exist, and so when they stop pursuing Christ, they fall into a deadening malaise, where they are prone to creating the world in their image and concentrate on pleasing their flesh.

"Man was not created for the flesh or carnality, for man was not designed to be or to function as an animal. Is God, in whose image we were created, an animal? He placed us in an animal-like body, but His presence within our lives pulled us to Him, His likeness, and His power. Adam and Eve, before the introduction of Satan, automatically were pulled into God's will and spirit. God's presence negated the power of the animal body.

"The fall of man—that act of disobedience that cast humanity into bondage to the physical, the flesh," Peter said. "The carnal man who only thought of food, shelter, clothing, dominance of others, sexual pleasure. That was Satan pulling his first fast one: the flesh is everything. You must meet the needs of the flesh before all else. Christ said to forget your earthly needs and seek God, and the needs of the body would be met. The flesh was never meant to dominate the soul. Some within humanity realized the truth. Satan had to destroy the truth and those who knew the truth. His second fast one, and why he is called *the deceiver, the adversary*, was the concept that the flesh, the body, were evil and must be trained into subservience through punishment. This was only slightly corrected during the great reformation of the 1500s.

"The great truth is that a child always innately wishes to love and please his parents. The great lie is unless there is nothing—or something not enough—in it for him. Here is the problem in the millennium: humans, not feeling the hand of an active Satan, cannot perceive the love of an active God. They cannot see the love of people who are always there to help and encourage in a world without physical harm or want. The reality of Christ's reign loses its vitality, its allure, and its rewards. It becomes mundane, commonplace, and the small amount of energy and desire that is required to activate life is swallowed up in boredom and ennui. That environment is perfect for the carnal human and the world that is created from it. They have defaulted to the power of the flesh."

"Is there no sense of guilt?" asked Mat. The potatoes had been eaten. The fish fillets were next.

"Little, when you take your eyes from your Creator," said Peter. "Even though the Holy Spirit streams through their minds and the perfect world surrounds them, they are dead to Him. It is like background noise to them, and it is ignored for the stronger song of the flesh. And if that isn't enough, they bond together in their generations and create a world system that is dead to Him. Their mangled view is strengthened by others; they share bonding techniques, words, phrases, gestures, body postures, clothes, jewelry, hair styles that are codes of reinforcement to those of their world. Then God's perfect world is the enemy world, and their world of the flesh is the better world."

"Would I be able to tell between the godly and ungodly? By sight or by behavior?" Mat ate the last fish fillet.

"If you are skilled, I can promise you a 75 percent detection rate. But we can't say for certain that these will be the ones who rebel; just that they show the indicators. Only God knows, when the final choice is made, whom they will have chosen—themselves or their God." Peter looked at Gramps, saw some tiredness. "Let's tour my property, stretch our legs, work off the sluggishness of midmorning and the increasing warmth of this day. Allow your mind to digest the information as well as the stomach, your midmorning meal. Maybe in an hour, a light lunch—salad from the garden, freshly picked."

"Sounds good, Pete. Are you coming along, Grace?" Mat said as he rose. Touring a person's holdings was the etiquette of the millennium, as all landowners wished to show their cleverness and industriousness and God's bounty.

Grace took Pete's outstretched hand and bounced sprightly to her feet. "Wouldn't be left behind." Pete had come so alive in talking to Gramps. The Holy Spirit was thick upon the two, and she liked being in that aura of God. To be in the presence of the Lord was everything.

Mat followed Pete. He'd noticed, while on the river, stone steps from the pontoon to the first bank and an insertion loop, likely for cables to pull the pontoon onto the bank, probably for winter storage. He noticed a water pump attached to the refrigeration unit in the kitchen area of the pontoon and the solar panels, with auto control, making a slight shift to the new location of the sun. A water-purification unit sucked river water into a five-gallon holding tank. The deck held chaise lounges large enough to sleep upon, and a bureau, no doubt holding clothes. Plenty of fishing tackle was strewn about. He noticed a fire pan and firewood. Mat said, "You basically spend days here and even sleep here in the summer. You pull the pontoon up in the winter?"

Pete, happily pleased at the observations, said, "Yes and yes. This is our home-away-from-home during the warm summer months, and yes, we will pull up the pontoon." They were upon a level bank that once held a road or railroad tracks. "Haven't done it yet. Built it just this year. But we plan to drag it to that newly carved-out flat spot on the slope." Pete cast his arm toward the base of the bluff, and Mat saw the clearing and inquired, "All this is yours?"

"The bluff before us is ours, as well as land on the plateau above. Our land ends at the riverbank. See the two former erosion gullies on the slope? Both have springs at the top, and we have controlled the flow." Pete was smiling as he finished talking. Mat heard in Pete's tone his deep appreciation for his holdings and the delight owning land brought to him.

"This flat area?" asked Mat, pointing to the ground they stood upon.

"Once held a railroad line. Too much rocky fill to have a garden here. But as you see, blueberries do nicely."

Grace began picking and placing berries in a container, and with a sideways glance, said, "Perhaps some short cake and berries would be good."

"I like the way you think," said Mat. The summer sun was hot on the shadeless railbed. They entered the trees of the slope. The well-used trail, with some stones and logs for erosion management, paralleled and crossed small man-made ponds and pools and small waterfalls. A band of cedar waxwings dove and stalled, picking off large insects that had swarmed above the pools. Mat saw brown trout in the clear waters. He heard the splashing and fallings of a larger waterfall, then caught a glimpse through the trees of a ten-foot drop into the largest of the pools.

Peter stopped, made the hand motion for silence. They paused. Mat heard the gobbles, the calls. A flock of twenty to thirty wild turkeys came through the slope of the ravine like an invading army on a search-and-destroy mission, eating spiders, ants, bugs, earthworms, garter snakes, frogs, newts. When they had passed, Peter said, "When they're on a mission through our gardens at the top of the bluff, they never eat a beneficial insect, never touch the plants."

"First thing I noticed when the animals began to come back to my plantation," affirmed Mat.

At the top of the bluff was a cottage built on thick concrete stilts, and with a few key trees cut down, an excellent view of the river had been produced—fluffy islands, sparkling waters, the far western shore of trees, fields, plantations, and commercial ag lands. The breeze was gentle and delightful with the scents of flowers, hay, wild cherry trees in bloom. Mat followed

Grace into the garden behind the cottage. She had picked up a large wicker basket from the steps of her cottage. Cucumbers, peppers, onions, a cauliflower head, a head of lettuce were placed in the basket. Pete took the basket and made for the kitchen. Grace led Mat on a guided tour of the plantings of fruit and nut trees and the gardens of corn, beans, grains. Wheat was the commercial crop that would be sold to a local mill, the mill owner harvesting the wheat as well. Bluebirds lived in every bluebird house. The view to the east was magnificent, rolling farmland, and untamed meadows, with deer, elk, and buffalo darkening the green fields.

They returned to the kitchen, where Peter was mixing a salad dressing. A bowl of chopped egg whites, sprinkled with garlic pepper, sat on the counter. "Sit out on the deck if you wish. The breeze and the sun will make good companions till we arrive with the salad. How about a few slices of buffalo heart with horseradish, and a tea to drink?"

"Yes, exactly what I desire," Mat said cheerfully, delighting in the graciousness of his hosts. Pete was examining Grace's eyes, hoping she would pick up the work of the additions to the meal. She went to the refrigeration unit for the heart. Mat watched and pleasantly confirmed their marriage; they were a team—no orders, no talk was needed. He had been watching every little detail of their interactions since stepping out of his kayak. They had a reverence for each other, a delight and peace. "I'll be on the deck." He grabbed his computer from his baggage.

He rested his body, leaning on his forearms against the safety railing, watching the cloud shadows play against the wide and open eastern lands. He saw to the south a long mountain ridge popping with fluffy trees that were so crowded together, no earth or rock was visible. He had to thank Yahweh, the Creator. The beauty of creation. Being in a healthy, vibrant body, with all senses attuned to ever-increasing degrees. Being with descendants whom he admired and even liked. They would be with him on this journey for eternity. He thought of the little boy who had prayed while kneeling beside his bed, asking God to show him the way for the sake of his sister, Katie. Prayer fulfilled. To think he once wondered if God could forget the needs and hopes of a little boy.

He wished to sing. By the name of the Lord Jesus, sitting on His throne in Jerusalem, why should he not? The words of thanks and praise came without effort, the tune without thought.

Grace, within the kitchen, took the hand of Peter and whispered, "He is singing! Singing praises."

"Yes, he is." Peter felt the small wrist, the warm forearm, and the scent of Grace entered his mind as she pressed against him. "That generation went through much, and so they love much. You have yet to hear his sister, Katie, sing."

"And we reap the rewards of their past struggles and efforts," she said humbly.

"Our time will come, Gracie, my girl, when we will give Him all, and we will count our sufferings for Christ as our greatest moments." Peter embraced his pal, his friend, the other half of himself, his loving woman, his wife, and felt her melt within him.

***

Mat munched happily on the last of his salad as he readied his computer for audio and the actual interview. He cleared his throat of the last vinegar tang and spoke. "Peter, give a synopsis of where God's kingdom stands with the new generations of mortals who profess salvation."

Pete began. "Many of these, I can't give a percentage, do truly understand salvation; the Spirit of God has made it real to their hearts and souls. They have eternal life. They have had an easier time in coming to this realization than previous generations did, as the Holy Spirit is overwhelming in His presence as a teacher. Intellectually, the autobiographies of the saints and Christ's clarifications from His throne in Jerusalem give a complete picture. No deceit is added to the truth, as Satan is bound. Since this world is now God's kingdom, there is no outward evidence of enticement to the flesh—no prostitutes, no porno shops, no salacious programming or dress. There is no art—no plays, no poetry, no written word in any form, no lyrics—that entices, or glorifies the darkness in humanity. There is no growing of illegal drugs or making of harmful pharmaceuticals. No thievery, no violence.

"However, evidence shows there is also a vast number who go through the motions of belonging to Christ, while protecting their rebellious status deceitfully and willingly. There are few who go through the motions and are *honestly* duped by lack of knowledge or self-awareness. This is almost impossible because all have the Holy Spirit streaming through their thought processes. To not hear the mind of God takes deliberate action—a choosing."

Mat heard Pete's voice trail into silence and, realizing Pete had no more to say pertaining to the first question, presented a new question. "Why is there no outward rebellion? I know the answer; this is for the record. And a follow-up question: Are these people in communication with one another? Or how do they hide what is truly in their hearts?"

Pete took a deep breath. "There are levels to the first question. Having a theocracy led by an omniscient God, the criminal has no refuge between thinking lawless acts and initiating a lawless action and discovery and punishment of the same. If a man plots murder within his mind, murder is immediately known by the Godhead; and the man, if initiating action on his intent, is immediately removed from Earth. God needs no police force, no jury, no judge. A thousand-year reign of peace was declared by God as reward for the faithful, and crime cannot be tolerated. Even a lie is cause enough to remove a person from the millennial kingdom if that lie is to be acted upon and would cause injury or death to someone else. Temptation is still not a sin. It is the willful acquiescence to act upon temptation that would result in bodily injury, death, slander, or theft to an individual or the Godhead that will bring instant justice. Some people resist temptation, and some embrace it.

"On the other hand, God is a God of mercy, and He is determined to save whom He can—really, those who wish to admit their need. Spiritual education, correction, reproof is offered to those whose planned offenses have not reached the action stage, brought bodily harm to others, or shaken the peace of the kingdom. We have people in perfect health, who have never experienced sickness or bodily injury at the hands of another, or never experienced the famine of war, or the loss of loved ones, and sometimes they have difficulty imagining the effects of the sin they would like to initiate. We have classes, really history lessons, where the range of human emotions associated with Satan's kingdom and human rebellion are experienced. But never to the point of physical or emotional damage. I think that is a sufficient answer to the first question."

Mat spoke. "Yes, proceed." As a police officer, Mat knew of the removal of undesirables. He knew that correctional-educational classes included controlled experiences that could induce anger, rage, feelings of injustice, loss, and helplessness.

Peter continued, "There exists among the general population of mortals a core of organized and committed God haters. The scripture has warned they exist and will rebel when Satan returns for his final appearance. If it were not for the prophetic warning of scripture, it is doubtful anyone would be searching for them. Their tactics and communications are deep and subtle; their type legion yet diffused."

Peter paused, took a long sip of the homemade root beer bartered from a neighbor. He glanced out over his grassy acreage. "The turkeys are back."

Mat turned, and Grace went to the railing. A hundred turkeys in a long line swept through the lawn and gardens. Behind them came foxes, who then settled into the grass as the turkeys continued through. "This phenomenon always gets me," Mat said. "It's like the foxes have honor, and they respect the landowners' wishes by not attacking here but waiting for the turkeys to wander off our holdings. Though, in reality, they won't automatically pounce on the turkeys after they leave our sanctuary."

"They only eat the wounded and aged turkeys," said a smiling Grace. "Continue your explanation, Peter. Every time you tell it, you add something I haven't heard before."

"I know how to keep an admirer," Pete said to Mat, lifting his eyebrows.

Grace rolled her eyes. Mat noted the intensity and depth of their love.

Peter continued, "The bad guys have different motivations. All are bored with the good life. They want excitement that, to them, is truly exciting and not the wholesome excitement of rock climbing, kayaking, windsurfing, hang gliding, competitive sports—those types of fun. Even acting, or a comedy routine, or narrative readings before an audience. The flesh cries out to them, and they would horde riches, if that wouldn't give them away. They would become gluttons, if the new metabolism, created by the new plant and animal life, allowed it. They would have harems, if possible.

"They are left with controlling people, creating a dependency upon themselves, a slavish obedience to themselves. They like physically dominating and mentally controlling others. Wrapped up in that goal is sexual freedom, which to them means to indulge with whatever gender or age, in whatever manner. The breaking of the sexual order is perhaps the zenith of their hierarchy of achievement. Minor crimes are theft, slander, gossip, or communicating deceits about Christ and His kingdom, which usually is done through graffiti or published tracts, even scribbled notes. The most interesting forms of rebellion—long missing from Western civilization—are the forms of baiting. Look up *badger*, *heckle*, *hector*, *chivy*, *hound*. These terms have made a comeback, and computers and mobile-phone systems are the perfect tools. Like the guy in the commuter, pretending to embrace goodness while engaging in mockery…playing with reality affords them great pleasure. The worst are those who hate God and His order, tapering down to those who just want to break a law for the thrill of it—the sensation of fear, dread of capture, the exhilaration of getting away with it."

Mat shook his head. "Same worldly motivations as in the old world, except being in the majority and in charge is not a tangible goal now."

"That's their frustration, though many would find, if their kingdom were established, there would be no excitement; just actions leading to the death of the soul and life," said Peter.

"Certainly, God knows of those offenses you just mentioned. Does He act on any of the offenses? I know you mentioned some." Mat asked the question for the record.

"In the sexual realm, He only acts on those contemplating sex acts with children or abusing corpses, and He protects the feeble or infirm, and the immature or damaged mind being enticed by a mature mind. These people disappear to await their final judgment. He removes them immediately, before they even act. He does not overlook same-sex perversions or adultery, but He sometimes postpones judgment, hoping for awareness and repentance. Consenting unmarried adults who keep quiet as to their sin are unhindered at the moment...in hopes they will repent.

"In the nonsexual realm, theft, graffiti, or any public display mocking the kingdom is dealt with by removal. Physical and mental attempts at domination, deceits about Christ or uncharitable speech, and the unmarried boasting of sex are infractions for the police to deal with, though there has been a rise in the number of people who just disappear for baiting and related forms of belittlement or domination. God will not allow the tender hearts of His people to be destroyed. Words do hurt. They do damage. They malign the reputations of God's people. God doesn't have to prove anything in a court of law with tangible evidence; He sees the soul of humanity."

Mat was astounded at the undercurrents within society that had been hidden from his daily observations. "You can take me into a crowd and show me these unsaved and rebellious people? Pick them out?"

"Easily—at least the less crafty ones; the intelligent ones wait patiently. The waiting increases their pleasure and their drive to succeed. As this is an individual's game, most evil is between two or three people." Pete's mind and his voice were devoid of pride in his knowledge and ability.

"When do we go?" asked Mat.

"Stay the night. I will accompany you down the river to your plantation, then we'll take the commuter into Harrisburg."

"Good plan. It's settled. By the way, congratulations on your marriage. Grace is a lovely soul. And Grace, Pete is a lovely soul, also."

"Thanks. I knew you'd catch on," complimented Pete.

Grace beamed and blushed. "Thank you."

***

Tom Jr. smiled at his grandson, Michael, and his fiancée, Amy, and wondered if they could read his thoughts. He wasn't much of an actor, but Lana had taught him how to keep smiling whatever he was thinking, and it had seemed to work in the past. Michael and Amy had invited him to lunch to personally announce their wedding date. He could tell by Amy's eyes, when she looked at Michael, that she was asking him, *Do you think Granddad knows we are a couple?* Meaning, having sex. Michael's eyes laughed back, *No, the old man doesn't know*. There seemed to be a mocking in this hidden conversation.

From the moment he had walked onto the seaside restaurant's ocean-facing deck, they had said the right words; the story of their first meeting, their courtship, their hopes and dreams. Michael recounted the interactions as a boy with Granddad and Granddad's sisters and their families. Michael gave him an invitation to the wedding, a year from the current date. Tom suddenly realized Michael and Amy had never, in their back story, mentioned their employment. He deduced they were here, in part, to ask for employment. Likely, it was the reason they had invited him to lunch. This did not bother Tom; he wanted to find people work. Under the tutorship of Carl, he had learned to appreciate what work meant to men and women—back when he was just a nerdy boy with big ideas and was learning his first job. He would save Michael the embarrassment that might exist in asking, and he said, "Do you two need employment, real jobs with the potential for growth?"

Then with lightning-bolt clarity, he understood that his sleepless nights, with the desolating subconscious dream, had begun the day he had learned of Michael's engagement. He hadn't made the connection because he only had fond thoughts of Michael.

"Where do you think I'd fit, Grandpa?" Michael's voice held an innocence that seemed real.

Tom spoke. "Do you want to work outside, hands on, either in production or assessing new leads, enterprises? Or office work—scanning charts, figures, developing ideas? It's all there. The company will give the tests, three or more, that pinpoint your abilities and then mesh them with your personality and life goals. The tests are fun if you are relaxed and open to all possibilities. People who think they know the job they want feel the most pressure."

"That won't be me," Michael answered unaffectedly.

Tom smiled. "Good." Now he would ask *the question*—the question he asked all potential employees. A question, Carl and Ling had told him, that had once been banned in the hiring process before the Tribulation.

"Tell me about your walk with the Lord." Tom saw a momentary break in Michael's thought processes, a stunned look; for he had never supposed in all his wildest planning of their meeting that this topic would arise. In that instant, Tom sensed a failing, for evidently this grandson had never heard him speak of his walk with the Lord. His heart was for the Lord, he was committed, all his thoughts revolved around the Creator and what He wanted for His world, and yet this had never been real to at least one person in his family. Tom filled the silence. "Michael, the Lord is everything—we have our very being through Him. He has a plan for our lives. He wants good things for us. You are living in the millennium, the greatest period of peace, prosperity, and self-fulfillment that humankind has ever known. Jesus sits on His earthly throne, and the Holy Spirit is streaming through all humankind's collective conscience and personal consciences as well." Tom stopped; he could have gone on, but it appeared Michael wanted to speak.

"Yes, I go to church. I love to sing His praises. I love the people of the church. I am aware I am fortunate…even more fortunate than others. I don't know who I am, but I want to succeed. I want to marry Amy and have kids and raise them right."

Is that all Michael could say? Or was he asking too much from this young adult? You had to walk with the Lord to know Him, and the longer the walk, the deeper the rapport. You had to be denied things, make crucial choices that had consequences. You had to fail and allow the Lord to teach you lessons and remold your heart. But there was a break in continuity here. Michael did not understand the millennium and what it signified in humanity's history. God proclaimed the future; God proclaimed His victory before it appeared upon the world. The millennium was the "I promised. I delivered." Michael had no sense of history, of where he was in the continuum of time. He only saw the beginning of his career.

"What about you, Amy? Are you onboard with that dream?"

"Yes, and I would like to work too."

"Then you shall take the tests as well." He would not tell them that he knew of their sexual liaison. That was a temptation every young person faced, and though they had failed, they realized marriage was the place for their creative desires. What bothered him more was their delight in fooling him. They took happiness in that, not circumspection, sober thought. It seemed they enjoyed lying, and that worried him greatly. Or was he imagining it all?

Tom smiled. "Okay, I am ravenous. Let's order and eat."

Michael looked at Amy with a big smile and the look of *We got it done. We fooled Gramps*.

CHAPTER 11

Mat and Pete left Mat's New Canaan at the same hour and on the same weekday as the day he'd experienced the hateful twenty-year-old on the commuter to Harrisburg the previous week. A humid ground haze clung to the wet land; it had rained the night before. Stepping onto the commuter, he noticed the face staring at him with laughing eyes and a huge grin of clenched teeth. The clenched teeth promised violence, an attempt to intimidate. Mat had seen too much in the Tribulation for this wimp of a young man to create fear. He would have pulled the boy/man's head down over the backrest edge of the seat and choked him to submission in seconds. He felt a sadness at his descent into the mindset of the Tribulation and, at the same time, thankfulness for a body that was as strong as it was—stronger and quicker than in his youth. The sadness left as God reminded him that evil still lurked in the minds of men and to have a plan for victory was no sin.

Mat met the gaze with unwavering eyes of confidence and said, "This is the day the Lord has made. We will rejoice and be glad in it." Psalm 118:24 had come spontaneously to his thoughts.

The man did not answer but continued his grin. The laughing eyes held a dread and a panicked violence barely suppressed.

Mat spoke in kindness. "Is there a hurt behind the happy exterior? Unburden yourself. Sometimes I give advice to my children that works." The hateful man never expected concern borne of care and kindness. Mat saw confusion in the eyes. Perhaps he had been wrong about this young man and the motivations of his heart. Mat slid into the seat beside the young man, and Pete, into the seat behind.

The man stammered. "My name is Dylan. Both my parents had a rare genetic disorder. I am their only offspring. They died, and now I will die. I'm going to the hospital now. I go every day. Watching life from the commuter sometimes is too much. Everyone else has health and a long life, and I do not." The stammer and the lies came so easily that it was difficult for Dylan to keep a sober face.

"But you do have eternal life. It will seem but a short while until you and your family are reunited, in perfect health and resurrected bodies," Mat said. He sensed the story was a lie, but the story was plausible, and jealousy for the lives of others with less complicated circumstances could lead to a hardness of heart. Pete seemed content to analyze and not advise.

"Money would help. I just want to experience this earthly life now before I leave. A few good meals, a few trips. I'd like to see Niagara Falls and Washington, DC."

"There is money for people in your situation—any bank can help. Free money, not loans." Mat knew that every citizen was aware of these benefits.

"It wasn't enough. That is why I have a bitterness within my heart. Can you give me money? If not, please leave." The young man admired himself for his fast escape from a dead end to his scheme.

"I can give you money, but I will not. You can earn money by attending reeducation classes. Your lack of money is not your problem. Your lack of trust in the Lord is—and it really could affect your eternal life." Mat's fleeting hope had been dashed—the boy/man was a con man.

The clenched teeth of the commuter were apparent as he spoke. "Stiff upper lip, think my way out of my depression and die?" The words were heavy with biting sarcasm and had an honest tone.

Mat knew the tone was dishonest but true to the con. He said, "Melodramatic. You will leave your body and live in paradise until the close of this age. Then a new body and life eternal." Mat continued the appearance of belief in Dylan's lies. What would he do with the insult of *melodramatic*?

The young man looked away, his body tensed, his eyes hardened. Mat watched for the bodily clues that portended violence or anger. No emotion boiled up; the dead calm remained. Mat placed a few gold coins in the young man's hand and stood as he watched the eyes. He saw a glimmer of arrogance. Now, he had an emotion to work with. Mat spoke harshly, demandingly. "The common phrase used is, 'Thank you.' You'd better use it."

"Or what?" Dylan spit the words.

"Or your genetic disorder might flare up," Mat said calmly.

"Thank you," said Dylan, wondering if he had elaborated on the disorder or there was a hidden threat in the man's comment.

Mat touched Pete on the shoulder as he said, "Your welcome," and moved down the aisle to different seats.

Pete whispered, "He played you well. A real pro. You were just taken by one of the more popular scams."

"I played him. I wanted him to think he won. I was evaluating him. I found his conceit has a home—in his doggedness, his determination to pull others into his falsehoods. He enjoys the manipulation and will even make his need or desire for violence subservient to it. We will follow him, see if we can get a name or place of address. Then we will devise our own plan and bring charges: lying, misrepresentation of need. Or a reeducation course. What would he spend his money on? Sex? Drugs?"

"You play a good game," Pete said admiringly, finally understanding the judo-like repartee.

Mat spoke without emotion. "The Tribulation was my playing field—seven years of people like the so-called Dylan."

"You are a champion, for sure. And about where the money will be spent, maybe on both. Did you notice the one small tattoo at the top of his forehead, near the hairline?" asked Peter.

"No," Mat said incredulously.

"Don't beat yourself up. It was the size of a printed period. Could have passed for a mole. It is the beginning of the snake bite. Who came down and tempted Adam and Eve? When another dot appears beside the existing one, a person is declaring that his mind belongs to the snake. Whether Satan is actually real to him—or them—is unknown. There is great risk in that second dot. That's an open challenge to Christ's kingdom. Since God knows the thoughts of every mind, if the person is identifying with Satan, he is removed. Those who believe they are just rebelling in a general way against the status quo or who belong to a group of others as a social group of friends will live. The population of believers would have no fear. However, if this tattoo should ever be identified by the general public and associated with Satan—and, more importantly, if that causes worry or fear, then the person will be removed. God is undeniably in control of His kingdom, and no evil, however small, will be allowed to interfere with His perfect reign."

"The Lord is showing them and him mercy," stated Mat.

"Yes, the chance to reject the sin of self and the world and have a new birth in Christ. Jesus just wants one more harvest of believers."

Mat offered his thoughts. "Satan is the clueless precipitate—the refining agent that collects, gathers up the valueless chaff for hell's fires."

"I agree. By the way, the snake bite can be found on hands, feet, genitals, and in the heart region as well—anyplace the recipient has dedicated," whispered Pete.

"Any other physical tells?" Mat asked, searching his memory of known miscreants, hoping to remember a sign upon them.

Pete answered, "Sometimes along the hairline at neck or near the ears is a small braid or gathered strands almost unseen. Clothing varies and changes with the whims of the times. A mark on shoes or shoelaces, a row of stitches of the same color as the fabric upon the pockets. The stitches represent acts of rebellion performed. The braided strands of hair mark verbal rebellion."

The commuter entered Harrisburg by the river as opposed to Harrisburg on the flat or Harrisburg on the bluff. A change in the normal routing. The majority of the mortals born of the millennium preferred city living in apartments or condos but could tolerate suburban/urban, as it was called: single-family homes with small yards, built around a small nexus of schools, a church, and public playgrounds, and surrounded by a greenbelt of trails. The commuter usually went directly to Harrisburg on the flat—the commercial and governmental center. Dylan seemed irritated by the change, and he exited by the river walk. Mat was about to speak when Pete countered the thought that was formulating. "Don't worry. I tagged him."

Mat smiled at Pete's sleight of hand. He had not seen the tracker placed. With clarity, Mat realized that Peter had a position within law enforcement that had been hidden from the family. Tracking was allowed only by a select few. Pete's think-tank job based in Washington had always remained ambiguous. Mat concluded that people high up were preparing for the future.

Mat loved the river route, a place of so many memories. He compared his memory of the old city with the new city. New bridges had been built, a small dam stretched across the water for recreational boating, with fish ladders along the shore and scattered over the expanse. Unobtrusive generators were incorporated into the architecture of the dam at regular intervals. Flowerbeds were everywhere, and wide, spreading shade trees. Ducks and geese waddled on the courses of green grasses. People walked, jogged, ran, biked, or just sauntered. Street vendors sold meals, snacks. A new hospital had been built in the location of the old. The memories tugged with the new buildings, structures, and roads as he attempted to find the route they had taken to the hospital among the earthquake's ruins—that place the pervert had tried to attack him. With Christ in Jerusalem, perverts had disappeared. He remembered his dad retrieving the medical device that healed Katie's leg. Dad had been soaked with sweat, drenched was the word, from moving the heavy machine in a high rise without air conditioning. A guy named Anthony had helped Dad, and he was probably in Hades, as suggested by his lewd eyes upon Mat's mother. Then, the long trip home through the debris of a city. He turned his head suddenly to attempt a sighting at the mountain behind them. He wished to see the high mountain ground where the warehouse apartment had once been located.

"All the memories coming back, Granddad?"

"Yes, Peter. Do you know the stories, the memories? Have I shared them adequately?"

"Yes."

"Do you remember the story of the pedophile?"

"Tell it again. It's not coming through clearly." Peter did remember but hoped for some new detail scraped loose by the vagaries of memory.

"The first day we arrived, carrying Katie on a litter, I went to a work crew, and a man took a perverse liking to me. Nothing happened. He tried to get my pants down, but I reported it to my dad. Dad confronted him, and the man was so bold in his perversity. Not till I read my dad's book did I realize how dad had struggled with taking the law into his own hands—which speaks to my dad's moral compass but also to the time that was thrust upon our morals. And I tell this story to you not to arouse hatred in those who do wrong and think wrongly. But for you to have no doubts for your actions, no wavering of faith when confusion comes to the world. You will be forced to kill in the times coming."

Was Granddad slipping a little? He said, *will be forced*. Or was this a prophetic statement from a man who was holy, who knew the Lord. Had God spoken of the future through Granddad? All believed the only violence in the final rebellion would be in the Middle East, around Israel or in surrounding areas, and perhaps in Europe.

"I understand," said Pete. Mat heard the resolution and was satisfied his point had been taken.

The commuter arrived before the Bureau of Rapid Response building. Mat bounded out, anxious for the police computers that would track where the young man had gone. Pete felt his granddad's excitement but began to worry that he had revealed classified information and not warned his granddad.

"Gramps, hold up a minute."

Mat stopped instantly, faced his grandson expectantly, and said, "Keep quiet about the snake-bite tattoo and the other oddities?"

"Yes, until I check to see what the protocol is. No use worrying the general public." Granddad's mind could still connect the dots. An unintentional pun. Pete smiled wryly.

Mat, reading body language, knew the words were finished, and he turned, entered the building, and bounded up the stairs, as was his habit in any building, to the third floor. His son Jed stood looking out the window toward the west.

"Where are John and Diana?" asked Mat, as he stood beside Jed and studied the city before them.

"Hello, Dad. They're out at a school, giving a presentation on emergency procedures and also on career paths in emergency management." Pete trailed into the office and waved at his dad, Jed.

Jed said, "Hello, Son. What can I do for you two?"

Pete answered. "I tagged a suspect. He hit up Gramps for some cash."

"The same guy you told me about?" Jed asked his father.

"The very same," said Mat.

Jed proceeded to an electrascreen and activated, through the keyboard, the wall map for easier viewing. Without being asked, Pete gave a number, which Jed placed into the electrascreen computer. The computer located the tag Peter had placed on the unknown man, then backtracked his route since receiving the tag, pulling footage from surveillance cameras on the route. "Is that the man?" Jed asked.

Peter and Mat studied the photo and answered, "That's him."

Jed initiated a facial profile. Mat and Pete went closer to the wall screen.

Mat read aloud, "Our Dylan is Andreas Hahn, twenty-six. Agricultural science degree, works on genetic applications to increase yield and hardiness of root-based crops. Not married; father, mother, older sister in Germany. All are mortals born within the millennium. Lives in an apartment in a downtown high-rise. Attendance spotty at his local church."

Pete was reviewing the course of travel since Andreas had been tagged. He had visited a coffee shop on the corner opposite the agricultural research building. He came out with a bag and a large drink, crossed to his work building. He remained in the agricultural building; he was there now. The human resources departments of large work sites maintained personal records of employees. Counselors spoke with employees, who wished to speak, on a weekly or biweekly schedule. Citizens who were self-employed had regular meetings with counselors through the church of their choice. No citizen of the kingdom ever lacked people who cared and were concerned about their individual lives. A twenty-four/seven hotline was available to all, but it was rarely used—so much so that the employees were allowed other secondary employment. All individuals were encouraged to maintain contact with their biological families, with church and business friends and social groups of hobbyists. Reports, if any were generated, remained with the company or church and could only be accessed through direct human-to-human contact with the group. Anyone could report someone who seemed headed for danger. The individual was always informed of any concerns and who had reported the concerns. Nothing was kept secret.

"Let's make contact with human resources and his assigned church. Per law, the tag will be cancelled at the end of twenty-four hours," Jed said.

"What shall we do in the meantime?" asked Mat of Pete.

"Let's hit the downtown concert series in the river park. Watch the crowds, study dress and deportment. Maybe I can pick out some possible dissenters."

***

They crossed the wide, pontoon footbridge that had been designed to rise thirty feet with floodwaters, though the average rise was six feet. Millennial experience had proven that devastating floods were no longer occurring, as the natural world was fully under God's control. The Lord allowed reasonable flooding—the fluctuations were harmless to mankind with proper zoning laws, but beneficial to agriculture and wildlife. The river park was located on the man-made island constructed during the millennial reign to replace the island scoured away by the lava waters of the Tribulation flood. Mat could see far north to the furthest mountain range, where the last baptism of the Tribulation had been held. He remembered the lava waters, their trip across the river on their makeshift boat, working as a team, and the subsequent death of Emily.

Mat and Pete walked the river trail south for an hour, passing a revitalized steel-producing plant by a town appropriately named Steelton, and they stopped when they saw jetliners descending for landing and ascending for flights. Harrisburg International was beyond the tree line. Returning, the few people using the trail were in recreation clothes and provided no tells that would identify their rebellion status. The two took a midmorning brunch at a café with outside tables as they watched the broad river. Gone was the canal channel within the river of Mat's youth. They left the café when they heard, from City Island, musical instruments sounding warmup notes and riffs.

Mat saw the stage from a distance and heard an ensemble playing classical music. The wind from the north was gentle. People were gathering quickly, the scheduled start time fast approaching. Buses from schools filled the parking area. Mat and Pete leaned up against a two-tiered railing of metal, placed a foot on the bottom rung. Pete spoke without turning his head. "There is Andreas Hahn. He's standing close to three people. By their stances, they are friends attempting to pretend they don't know each other."

"Why?"

"They evidently believe they have secrets between themselves that are criminal in nature. Here." Pete handed Mat a pair of ear sound receptors. "I'll aim my pen-like device at them, and you listen." Pete liked his secret-agent gadgets, even though he found humor in his liking them.

Mat listened for a few minutes before taking the earbuds out. "They're discussing the ladies. Too much graphic sexual detail. Physical dominance and mental control seem to be the themes. What ever happened to noting a well-cared for figure and positive qualities of deportment and bearing, including clothing style and appropriateness? I wouldn't let a young woman in my family near them. My girls would be wise enough to avoid them."

Pete answered, "Most of the rawness and outright filth was to establish rank among the other three. The same base need that leads to gang rape. Yes, no evidence of the Holy Spirit within them. I know of the other three—they've been on the watch list for some time. Interesting to note that the three have the same style shoe, a lightweight high-top hiking shoe with a strong toe guard and indestructible sole. They dye these different colors in an attempt to hide their sameness and military connotations, not from style concerns."

Mat took up the thread of conversation. "So that's the uniform, and the shoes would be good for kicking, stomping, and destroying objects, no doubt." A strand of his thought was upon the past, when his Tribulation duty was to protect his little sister, Katie, from rape by a lone male or a group or even by women.

"The high-tops leave room for objects of concealment—small knives, for example." Pete was scanning the crowd for other likely candidates when he noticed the first singer was upon the stage and the grounds packed with an audience. "Hey, that's our Katie on the stage!"

Mat wondered if his eyes had seen Katie, and her presence had registered in his subconscious thought processes before his conscious mind recognized her. That would account for the Tribulation memory of his sister. "Yes," he answered in agreement. He watched her searching the crowd. The search was part of her routine. She said God often pointed out individuals to her who needed help, encouragement. Words often came to her, and she spoke them to the person and to the audience. He knew her routine had started hours earlier in prayer for her performance and for the people in the audience. Even her pre-performance meals were specially chosen. She wanted enough food to feel strong but not enough to affect her diaphragm, and she wanted to feel hungry at the end—everything used up, every bit of her being.

He began waving both arms in the air just to see if, at this great distance, he could have her recognize him. Pete stepped back and away and formed himself into a group of strangers to his right on the offhand chance that Andreas and his crew would search the crowd, see the waving arms, and identify him or Mat.

Katie, scanning the farthest reaches of the crowd, saw waving hands, and she stared. Mat sensed an awareness enter her. There was a slight delay, then she erupted in happiness, elation. She pointed at her brother, clapped her hands in celebration above her head. Her arms remained raised as the Spirit of the Lord encompassed her. Her hands slowly fell to her sides. She addressed the audience.

"My brother is here. He was my guide to the Lord, my protector during those times called the Tribulation. Soon, in time eternal, Satan will come again, and you, good people…," she said, pointing slowly across the great gathering, "will understand, for a very short time, what the saints endured. So, today, at this moment, in this time of song, fortify your heart, soul, mind, and strength with the ever-flowing goodness and power of our I AM, our Creator, Our Dad, our unfathomable God Jehovah, Yahweh!" The crowd erupted in shouts of acclamation; the roar rolled over the waters of the river and into the heart of Harrisburg.

She continued, "Jesus is our ever-flowing strength and everlasting power. Abide in Him and conquer!"

Off mic, Katie spoke to Paul. Instantaneously, Mat's phone rang; Paul calling. "Hey, Mat. If you can, meet us around five for supper at Katie's cottage. Bring Barb and whoever else." Mat, contentedly pleased with his sister's esteem for him, answered, "Barb and I will be there."

From the hush that settled upon the crowd, a celestial voice began—a voice of great range and power, smoothness and rawness, passion, and sensitivity. The people of the audience laughed in wonder at His love, cried in their thankfulness and unworthiness, gave praise to their Lord in adoration, felt deep peace and a conquering spirit of no compromise. Pete and Mat focused on the four, who, in the beginning, had made snide comments, but in the end were immersed in peace.

Andreas Hahn laughed bemusedly to himself as the singer began. She was some old bitch from the Tribulation times. But she did have charm, even as she spouted lies. And she did honestly believe her lies. He took great delight in watching the crowd—nothing but emotion-filled, wimpy fools. Sheep. He would gladly dine on them. Lamb chops on the grill, or sliced for gyros, a preferred sandwich. He laughed to himself. If only they could hear his thoughts. He searched for the most vulnerable and attractive young women, preferably alone or with disinterested friends. He would choose none with men, though the challenge was tempting. Few men could match his bulging crotch. He only found one prospect. He decided she wasn't worth the effort. Her raised arms, her tears…she was a true believer. Too much work. He didn't have the patience to listen to her Jesus BS. He walked away from his mesmerized friends. He had a pocketful of money, duped from a self-righteous fool in the morning. He'd put in a few more hours at work, then in the evening, eat a fine meal in a downtown eatery, courtesy of the fool.

***

Katie, Paul, Mat, Barb, Hope, and William sat outside of Katie's cottage. The meal, finished, gave a physical contentedness to body and mind. The air had turned a degree or two cooler, though the sun was bright and warm, and a sweater was not yet necessary.

"It's a shame Pete and Grace could not be here; a church commitment," stated Mat.

"Yes, I saw Pete was with you this afternoon. Or I thought it was Pete. He was standing closer to another group," said Paul.

Mat spoke. "He didn't want to be associated with me." Paul's eyebrows lifted as understanding came of Pete's shadowy life. What exactly did he do for a living? Mat resumed conversation. "He's teaching me more about these rebellious ones hiding in our midst. Pete will likely be here on Earth when Satan comes again. An advantage for our side. I pray every day that I may see that day, remain for that time."

Katie spoke. "Better to be gone, brother. You have done your work on Earth, during the Tribulation. Our family and I especially owe our survival to you, and in turn, Hope and her children, and all the offspring of the men and women you saved from death, as well as they themselves."

"That's a goodly number of people," Paul said, as the accounts of Mat's legacy played through his mind. "Countless fellow soldiers and citizens."

Mat shook his head as a disagreement contested in his mind. "I only did what the Lord wished. Maybe I should sit this next one out in paradise. Maybe it's only ego, but I just want to be useful one more time…want to serve Him when everything is on the line."

Katie thought her brother was not framing his uncertainty correctly. "But it is not on the line, in the sense that we know the Lord will win. We have that certainty verified through the events post-Tribulation," she said. "During the Tribulation, we had faith there was eternal life, a heaven, but we really didn't know. Now we know for certain—every resurrected citizen proclaims eternal life by their presence. There would be no test of faith for you now. And you know you can't die in the eternal sense. It's time for the millennial mortals to find *their* faith." Katie's words were convincing.

Paul added, "The Lord will provide you opportunities in the future—the eternal future, might I remind you. We will be serving Him forever."

Hope entered the conversation. "Don't you wonder if there are other worlds out there, and will we have work on those other worlds, maybe sharing the gospel message?" Hope inserted her longing so quietly. All of the living had thought these thoughts and dreamed of future worlds.

William, seeing an advantage in Hope's words, decided to steer, if the guests were willing, the talk into the future and away from the Tribulation past. "Let's think upon the future, beyond Satan's feeble return," he said. "Why puff him up with the mention of his name?"

"Well spoken, Bill. He cringes and dies when the saints shun his name," affirmed Barb.

And so, they talked past the setting of the sun, the dusk, till the stars came, imagining the beauty and challenges that the future might hold. Only at the end did Mat and Barb and Katie and Paul remember the love that was born of the Tribulation. Their devotion to mothers and fathers, brothers and sisters, the acts of kindness and sacrifice, the prayers of yearning for those they loved, and God's deliverance.

Hope and William returned to River View; they were living in Tim and Mary's home until their return. Mat and Barb returned to New Canaan, showered, settled themselves into bed. Barb pulled up the heavier bespread, as the air had turned cooler.

Katie and Paul, at home, tidied up the kitchen, showered, and as they had done since their marriage, bent their bodies before their bed, with hand holding hand as their arms rested on the mattress. They prayed their hearts' yearnings, longings to their God. They thanked Him for His past faithfulness, so thick within the Tribulation. Each wiped the tears from the other's eyes and hugged as their bodies melted into each other. Paul pulled the covers over them. "I love you, Katie Elizabeth Johnson. And she answered, "I love you Paul…my dearest Pauly," as they snuggled into sleep.

At three-thirty in the morning, the presence of the Spirit prompted Katie to leave her warm bed, walk outside to her patio. The Milky Way covered the heavens. She looked over at New Canaan and saw a whitish light rise from the roof and streak into the heavens. She knew Mat had gone to paradise. She had known the time was near, since looking upon him from the stage that afternoon. The Lord had made it known. She had been given time to send him off without regrets for missing the last testing upon the earth. How could a girl have been born with a better brother? He had guided her, searched the scriptures as just a kid, prayed with her without really knowing how, both on bent knees before their beds, not knowing if their mom and dad even knew what they were doing, whether they even understood God and Jesus's sacrifice. Mat had killed for her; she knew it now, in hindsight, now with an adult understanding; those times he left the home, serious and calm, on some errand he could not share with her. In the next day or two, someone on the periphery of their lives was found dead or just never reappeared. He had carried her on the litter to the hospital that day of the great quake—carried her miles over debris, doing a man's work as a child. He had killed the beast's men when they came to take her into captivity. He had saved her and Dad in that moment of escape from the water baptism on the river, by pulling them from the force field. He saved them again when he became the willing decoy to free her from the manhunt. He had suffered long and hard in the Middle East as a result. The stories he would tell of harsh deaths, punishment for the slightest infractions, the half-animal–minded soldiers he fought beside, the constant bombardments, and whizzing projectiles just over his head.

"Good brother, I will see you soon." She kissed her palm and extended her arm toward the heavens. She returned to bed, cuddled up close to Paul. They would be going soon, together or alone? She realized she had forgotten Barb. She began to rise, and the Spirit of God stayed her and told her that Barb wished to remain alone, and that the Comforter was with her.

Hope turned to Bill in the early morning hours and took his hand. He was fast asleep. Her brother was gone. The Spirit was telling her this. The Spirit, He was within her heart and within the room. Mat had been like an uncle or second father. When he was near, she always felt protected, like a warm blanket over her shoulders on a cold winter's morning. By God's grace, she would live without him for a very short time.

***

Katie and Paul continued to write lyrics, create, and recreate songs; they gathered and assembled the music of the ages with the resurrected musicians and singers of the past and produced a musical encyclopedia for the ages past and present and eternal future. This great work was done within ten years. As with all Tribulation survivors, their bodies bore the toll of near-starvation diets for seven years, the bacteriological and viral diseases of the time, the abnormal stress levels, and trauma to bones, joints, muscle tissue. These stresses countered the positive physical gains of the millennium—the miraculous regeneration of the body (truly, the absence of Satan) caused by enlightened genetic procedures, medicine, diet, water, air, earth quality, mental health. Like all Tribulation survivors, they had a sense of their bodies' coming expiration dates.

When Barb, her best friend, her sister-in-law, her worship buddy at Carl's Camp, passed on to paradise to receive her immortal body, Katie longed to go along—to reunite with brother, Mat, and with Dad and Mom. The transition would be painless and the time in paradise short before she would return to Earth. Paul knew, of course, that no mortal upon Earth could avoid death. (Enoch and Elijah left Earth alive and received their immortal bodies simultaneously as their earthly bodies exited, according to their autobiographies.) But certainly, Paul's time was coming soon also, for Katie was indispensable to his happiness, his joy for life.

***

On a bright-skied, clear spring morning favoring summer's warmth over spring's chill, Katie and Pauly sat on their red-white-and-blue-flag–draped deck on the riverbank. The Memorial Day holiday had been established a year after the Civil War, when the bones and blood of soldiers still moldered and soaked American soil, fertilizing a united nation in theory and intent, where God-given rights and freedom were extended to every man and woman. The resurrected Civil War veterans remembered most vividly, and their homes were strewn most boldly with old glory. Flags lined the main streets. The cemeteries were covered in flags of red, white, and blue. The Southern veterans remembered Satan's great deceit and praised God for His forgiveness of their sin. The black and white veterans of opposing sides hugged and cried, and both thanked God for this second chance at freedom. All the nation remembered their patriots from every war, from Native American skirmishes to the failed Tribulation rebellion. Andy, who had fought against settlers and fought for settlers, who had fought against Native Americans and for Native Americans, who had fought the French and the English, received honor. He had never killed women, children, the aged, or the surrendered combatant, but only resisting warriors. He had never fought for the possession of land but only for the side that wanted peace and fought war with honor.

On that glorious late-spring day, at midmorning, in the millennium year of 852, Katie and Paul sat on comfortable chairs and watched kayakers, canoeists, wading anglers move down the muddy but not-too-high waters of the Susquehanna River. They said hello to walkers, joggers, bicyclists, equestrians on the River Trail Path. They anticipated the coming of Emily and Dan and sipped their black tea spiced with sassafras root, taking bites from a bacon, egg, and cheese concoction wrapped in something akin to a croissant or knish dough. They waved to whomever waved at them—a sharing of the goodness of the weather, the beauty of the river, and the thankfulness for men and women who had given their lives to maintain the goodness that was still upon the land. In the final reasoning, they waved, and all the other citizens waved because they appreciated their neighbors and because God was good. They felt a sadness for those who had died never belonging to their Lord, who would have saved them for eternal life.

Without warning, before their eyes, stood four angels. "Oh, your wings are so white. Snow-white wings," Katie said in amazement, remembering the lyrics of a song.

Paul added, "Come 'round us and stand. There is our Jordan River." He pointed to the Susquehanna. "Did you gentlemen ever hear the song, 'Angel Band'? The lady beside me recorded it ten years ago."

Katie blurted resolutely to Paul, "But we aren't dead yet!" Still, she wondered in astonishment, realizing the likely reason they had come.

The angels had gathered around; they exuded a warmth of emotion and thought that soothed her. She sensed they were gentle beings with nothing but good thoughts, supportive and caring. The lead angel bent his tall frame, took her hands, and spoke in a distinctive, melodious voice—but a human voice, nonetheless.

The angel declared joyously, "You *are* dead to this world."

"I don't remember that happening. Is Pauly dead too?"

"Yes, the both of you," replied the angel.

"Shouldn't there have been a last gasp?" she asked sheepishly.

"Sometimes there is," said the lead angel.

Another angel spoke. "You and Paul were at rest, drawing your peace and life from the Spirit of God, and you have such gentle spirits that you passed into our world without a hiccup, so to speak."

The lead angel continued, "This is a rare phenomenon—to be so at peace, so one with the Father. We congratulate you."

"Thank you," said Paul, his emotion soothed in the praise.

"Should I leave a note for Emily and Dan?" Katie asked. "We love them dearly, and they will be here soon. And for our kids?"

A third angel spoke. "Remember, your earthly physical bodies will remain behind. Your friends will understand, and your children are mature adults."

"Well, then. Won't we disturb passing citizens?" inquired Paul.

"They will think you two are napping," said the third angel.

"Then, decidedly, bear us away on those snow-white wings to our immortal bodies," Pauly said.

"Yes, immortal bodies—they are our immortal homes. Paul, isn't this wonderful that we could go together?" Elation was in Katie's voice.

"Yes, it is." His prayer had been fulfilled.

The angels took them arm in arm, delighted for their guests that they left the world before Satan's return and the last harvest.

CHAPTER 12

Tom sat with his laptop before him on a small outdoor table. The veranda was tastefully arranged with outdoor furniture, chairs, tables, foot rests, umbrellas. The view of the bay, the many ships, the docks, the quaint homes could be mind-absorbing to the casual observer. The day was warm, breakfast had been eaten. He did not regret moving to a half-day schedule soon after Michael and Amy joined the company. They had been the impetus—or rather, their spiritual condition had been. He understood that his priorities had needed to change, that people knowing and living from Christ was now of greater importance than employment, or housing, or even food. The newer generations like Michael and Amy were sadly lacking, and even though Satan was gone, the flesh and the world were enough to steal away hearts and minds. A flock of trolling sea gulls looked down upon him in their swoops. Vines were flowering and smelled sweet. Lana sat nearby on a chaise lounge, reading a book. The sun gave just the right amount of heat, the breeze was pleasantly mild—just enough to bring the fragrant scents.

Millennial year 852. Most of the mortal old-timers were gone. Mat and Barb, Katie and Paul, Tanya, Anya, Flo were gone. No doubt their Tribulation years had taken a hidden toll on their longevity. Still, they'd had good full lives in the millennium and would return soon, at the millennium's end. Of his own line—Bongani, Chuks, Deka, Ebele, and Imani lived and had produced myriad offspring. Michael, son of Bongani, had produced, with his wife, Amy, three children—sons Robert, Edward, and Samuel. Tom sensed he would likely be gone from Earth in the next fifty years. Hope Johnson, too. Methuselah had reached the age of 969 in the world before Christ and before the effects of sin had affected longevity. He saw God's plan: to have none of those who had experienced the Tribulation or known a Tribulation survivor be on Earth when Satan returned. The new generations of mortals had to undergo a testing of their faith, suffering mentally and perhaps physically, through the return of the embodiment of evil, Satan.

Nostalgically, he brought up the personnel files of Michael and Amy, both of whom had risen quickly in the company. It read so sweetly, their test scores, high; their personality leanings, so normal; their placement within the company, perfect. Comments by peers and bosses, stellar. Their lives, as sweet and warm as the day. He mentally began to applaud them, his company, and even himself. Then someone slapped him across the side of his face. He bolted upright, fists raised, pivoting, knocking his chair to the ground. Lana jumped up, responding to the rapid, violent movement of her husband. Dazed, alarmed, she scanned her surroundings.

Tom looked around. There was no assailant. Had a passing bird struck him and flown away, or did he receive a potent sting from a wasp, or had a random muscle spasm occurred?

"Did you doze off, my imperturbable man?" That was her favorite adjective—that was Tom. God had known Tom would be born and then introduced the word, *imperturbable*, into the English language. Now *imperturbable* did not fit.

Tom rubbed the side of his face—no swelling, no brush burn. He spoke happily. "I think the Spirit spoke to me in language even I could understand."

Lana was puzzled by his face massaging, probably an involuntary muscle spasm or a tic. "Someone or something got your attention—and mine. Want to share?" She knew what he would say: he had to prove it out. That was his standard, ubiquitous phrase. He didn't want to speak a falsehood, and that's all that guesses and suppositions and assumptions were. She sat down, the unexplained danger gone.

“No, not quite yet. I must prove it out,” he said, already absorbed in thought on the perfection of Michael and Amy’s work history. He would stretch before sitting, was her guess.

He stretched, waved his arms, walked around the perimeter of the yard of short-cropped sand grass, took a drink of his iced tea, and sat back down before the computer. He found redacted material in both Michael’s and Amy’s files, always interviews and with the same interviewer. The department manager was always the same; he allowed material to be redacted. One copy of the interviews, the official version, showed nothing. Only in interpersonal e-mails did the redacted copies show, and these were seen by a department head, Malcom.

Tom was familiar with him; they had had daily contact. He then reviewed Malcom’s personnel file; and knowing the tricks of subfiles to the fourth level, he began to explore the machinations of an obsessed, driven, ambitious man of few scruples, if any. A personality hidden by the veneer of righteousness and Christian principles espoused; in short, he talked the talk but didn’t walk the walk, and he did this consistently.

The bottom line of the extensive exploration was that Michael and Amy had gone higher, faster than their production output warranted. Why was Malcom pushing them upward? What plan had he created, and where was it going? He had to get into Malcom’s personal computer—evidence might exist, though a totally meticulous man would have used word of mouth, where there was no danger unless recorded. All employees signed a waiver of their privacy rights on personal computers, communication devices, or any company writings, if just cause was found to examine them. Just cause had been found. A five-member board must be unanimous in the just cause. Now he had to explore Michael’s and Amy’s files—perhaps they were a part of whatever Malcom’s plan was. Maybe Malcom just wanted to make his boss happy? Or were incompetent Michael and Amy hostages or bargaining chips for blackmail?

He looked up, and Lana’s face was beside his. “Do you want some food?” Her voice held such sweetness and concern.

“Already? Didn’t you ask that before?” He was puzzled.

“Yes, at lunchtime. You ate some cashews. Now it is dinnertime, four hours later.” Tom was known for becoming “absorbed.”

He shook his head. "Lost myself in these files. Yes, food please. Forgive me if I appeared annoyed at you. I am annoyed at someone else." He spoke distractedly as he kissed her lips. A glance at the bay showed the light was weakening; hard cumulous clouds of dark gray had piled up. He turned on the keyboard light. He realized he had apologized in a distracted manner. He grabbed Lana's hand before she could leave. He stood, held her arms, and kissed her as if time had no meaning. "I love you," he said.

She answered, "And I, you," as she pulled away, smiling happily.

He faced an ethics decision: Should he ignore the unanimous, five-person-board requirement and enter Malcom's deepest personal keyboard strokes and files on his own? Or should he convene the board, which might include confederates of Malcom? How many days of probing would be needed to confirm the integrity of the board members, and would that possible finding of integrity be 100 percent? If he actually found a smoking gun, could he even use it to initiate action, as it had been uncovered illegally? He did have a clause in the corporation's charter that gave him complete control over all information. He knew Malcom was clever and intuitive. Malcom might destroy documents at the merest hint of file penetration.

His dad had always said, *Never make a decision when tired*. But his dad had also said, *Strike when the iron is hot*. He had used that last phrase for the first time while working in the garage at their thrown-together forge. An old bolt needed to be straightened for reuse on the canal boat found within the river. Tom's tired mind moved into the pleasant reverie of that time, just a child, being with his dad—his partner—learning new skills. Learning history: that canal boat had dated from the 1830s. The bolt and sundry iron items had been preserved by a heavy industrial grease, part of the cargo, which had spilled. He longed for the day that his dad and mom returned.

He decided the iron was hot. In a few hours, the files he wished to see could be destroyed or moved. He took his hands off the keyboard, straightened his hunched-over back, gazed into the glorious heavens beaming above with untold stars and planets, and uttered a simple request and prayer. "God, your will be done." Common sense said *wait*, but Malcom is an uncommon man, and he definitely does not esteem Your ways, said Tom's argument. Tom waited. A shooting star flashed, looking like a spark from a piece of hot metal at the forge. He opened the files.

***

Three weeks after Tom's discovery, Malcom walked tentatively into the private study of Tom's private residence, the home overlooking the bay. He had never had a personal, one-on-one meeting with his boss, anywhere. He thought the odds of some or all of his Machiavellian schemes being known at 50 percent. He could have been summoned to discuss an advancement, or perhaps Tom esteemed his knowledge and needed guidance or advice.

Tom noticed the shy walk; not a modest or self-deprecating walk; no, it held timidity. Perhaps this was the animus of this man's diabolical evil—a deep insecurity, fear that his moral weakness and lack of physical boldness would be uncovered. He compensated for his weakness with cunning and cleverness, an understanding of the base side of humanity's being; and with little confrontation, he could bring those superior to him to their knees.

"Have this seat, Malcom, right before my desk. Very comfortable chair and the same height as my chair. I never speak down to people; don't like those subtle games, props, for dominance. I like straight talk—of course, with love, understanding, and without malice."

Malcom smiled weakly, but clearly, the boss wasn't rattled. Still, he held the upper hand. "Could I have a glass of water?" Malcom looked at the clear glass pitcher of water at the corner of the desk.

"Certainly. That's why it's here." *He doesn't need water. He just wants to test his voice and set his tone and his stance*, thought Tom. Tom poured Malcom water and handed him the glass.

Malcom noticed Tom's hand was steady; Tom was confident, Malcom concluded. Tom's voice was strong as he spoke, "I'll move past a narrative of why and how I know. You've carved out a sphere of influence within the company that is not good for the company—works against our ethics, our purpose, and at a very human level, it shows your disdain for Christ and all

His precepts. Remember the first tenant of our company: *Love God with all your heart, soul, mind, and strength, and your fellow employees, and customers as yourself.*"

"That certainly is harsh. But I know you wouldn't say it if you didn't think it was true." Malcom's voice was clear and strong with no trace of volatility.

"I know it is true, and further I know you know it is true," said Tom unabashedly.

"What do you intend to do?" said Malcolm with a broad smile of self-congratulation. Tommy wasn't going to reveal anything. Smart move—keeping his opponent off balance and worried.

"As of three weeks ago, all access to files have been tracked and all communications monitored and recorded. Your position was terminated three weeks ago, and nothing you ordered done or requested was carried out in your name. All the sites you created to release your poison have been shut down. Depositions have been taken, charges filed, and the police are outside the door, waiting for this meeting to end."

Malcom smiled as his mind raced. He leaned back in his chair, realizing he had begun to hunch forward. Clever strategy, if true. Boss was forcing him to reveal his hand. The only means of escape was to play the blackmail cards—the pictures and movie-set actions of graphic detail of lover boy with his girlfriend. A woman meticulously chosen from an illegal dating service by his very own analysis of Tom Jr.'s personality. Tom Jr. might back down if his precious name might be besmirched. Of course, Boss would need to fire him; but no jail time, and blackmail payments instead of a pension. It hinged on whether the police were outside the door, with an arrest warrant in hand. Had the police truly been called? Had Tom discovered all the sites? There was the advantage.

"Are you sure you found all the sites of your personal pictures?" Malcom wished to see a flinch, inner-eye movement, searching, guessing what "personal" meant.

"Yes, I have all of your porn blackmail." Tom's eyes burned with hatred as he remembered the torment those items had caused for the last three weeks.

A forlornness that his life's work would be washed away, his good name—his life in Christ—annulled, a life lived that would no longer have meaning or purpose. The subconscious dreams that had begun 152 years ago and re-awakened him had been a foretelling not from Christ, but from an absent Satan, embedded in the flesh, rooting like a hog within Tom's grounded and good mind.

"What if you missed one?" Malcom's smile became a subdued chuckle.

"I'm sure I didn't. But even so, destroying you would be worth whatever penalty I receive from public opinion."

"What of personal opinion?" queried Malcom.

"The key player has known for years and loves me still, as I love her. The kids are adults, and all family members will love me just as Father, Son, and Holy Spirit still love me."

Malcom thought on God on His throne. "Do you think that Holy Trinity loves me?"

"They always have, and they always will. Ready to forgive and bring you into the family."

"Fuck them. Bring in my warrant and let them take me away." He spoke boldly, thinking he was calling Tom's bluff.

The police entered without a spoken word. They had been listening to it all.

***

Two weeks later, Tom brought Amy and Michael into his office. Tom studied the faces of Michael and Amy. He had seated them on a couch. This had been done purposely, even as his seat, a single comfortable upholstered chair with accompanying side table a few feet from the center of the couch, had purpose. He wished to see their choices. Would they sit side by side, holding hands, or would they choose the opposite sides of the couch, distancing themselves from the corrupting influence that had brought their lives to ruin.

Malcom's corrupting influence had been exposed, hundreds more had been exposed, including Michael and Amy. Everyone in the company knew the details. The major news outlets would not spread the story worldwide in salacious, hurtful detail. The men and women who had been entrusted with running news organizations knew the destructive power of words, and they abhorred destruction unleashed for the sake of destruction. Mistakes were not news, and innocent failings were given no attention among the populace. Many people within the company would experience prison and counseling time. Michael and Amy had chosen to sit side by side, but neither touched the other.

Tom spoke. "I know you have both been reprimanded and suspended. You even have fines to pay and jail time ahead." Amy's eyes broke contact, and she buried her gaze in her lap. Michael looked beyond his grandfather, focusing on the far window, as if escape was possible. Tom continued, "I wasn't fully surprised by your actions, but I was shocked with the ease in which you lied to me, hid the destruction of my company from me. This doesn't speak well for your character."

Michael began to utter a word. Tom spoke. "Don't speak, Michael. Neither of you need to speak. Speaking will not help at this point. Only your willingness to comply with the present course of action will have merit.

"I love you both. I love your children. I have not given up on you. This is a learning period in your lives. No one is born perfect. Really, this incident should cause us to give thanks to the Lord. He has allowed you two to see how the world and the flesh can pull a person away from truth and righteousness. How can a person know God, if they don't know how utterly inferior they are to His standards—and I've seen my inferiority many times in life. My affair speaks for itself.

"Your incarceration time will be spent in reeducation, study, exploration of the sin nature in man in a general sense, and as revealed through your particular circumstances. You will have sound sleep; good food; exercise; simple, basic, furnished quarters. Your mind will not be reprogrammed with repetitious phrases.

"The court has given Lana and me custody of your children till the age of twenty-one. Lana and I have decided to take them back for an extended vacation at Dad's home along the Susquehanna River in Pennsylvania. What is good in life can be found there, in the way my sisters and I were raised. I hope I can be as good a man as my dad. Of course, when your reeducation ends and probation begins, you can initiate a court process to bring your children home to live with you.

"Dad once said, 'It is knowing your evil is an affront to God and this God you affront is the only good in the world. When you hurt God and are ashamed of your hurting Him, then you are at the threshold.'"

"The threshold of what?" Amy asked meekly.

"Repentance, salvation, the love of God poured out into your heart and soul. A new life."

Moisture came to Tom's eyes as he looked into Michael's eyes. "Success in life is loving God with all your heart, soul, mind, and with that strength that sometimes is hidden within you, with no worldly reward attached. Love people like you would like to be loved, Michael. Treat them as you would like to be treated."

Tom stood. "Stand up, Michael."

Michael stood, wondering if he was to be struck. Tom drew close and hugged him. Long and with love. Michael placed his arms around Grandpa; *What a sentimental old fool.* Amy was standing, waiting for her hug, and Tom wrapped his strong arms around her, and she wept tears of repentance.

***

Robert, known as Robbie, fifteen OEY; Edward, known as Jack, fourteen OEY; and Samuel, known as Sammie, thirteen OEY, walked out the door of their aircraft into the bright light of Harrisburg International Airport's vaulted terminal building of busy, moving people, intercom calls, flight boards, escalators. Their minds had had the logic and reasoning levels of adults since they reached age ten OEY. In the years after, experiences had multiplied their wisdom even as their facial and physical appearances were those of teenagers. Emotionally, they maintained traits of teenagers of old Earth time. They had only their flight bags with computers within and a few personal items.

Tom and Lana met them within the terminal, walked with them to Tom's rented van, and within minutes, they had fast-food meals in hand and were moving north, out of the city, as the eastern sky livened with an orange-hued sunrise. The morning was cool, and a dampness was upon the earth; trees were budding, spring flowers piercing mulch and earth, birds declaring territory, the fields showing freshly planted rows.

Lana leaned in upon Tom; he was one of those warm people who always had some to spare, as if he perpetually wore heated clothing. His eyes were tired, and he was reliving memories that he was sharing with his guests, as well as pointing out salient features: the river, the mountains, the farms, villages, the size and nature of the city of Harrisburg. He began to talk of his happy upbringing on his dad's plantation. Lana saw the happiness of the past and the understanding that the time was past. She knew he just wanted to give his great-grandsons the same memories—even as he knew they were flawed in their upbringing by not having his father as their father. Their father, Michael, had never drawn his life from life-giving Jesus. Their grandfather, Bongani, was not a bad father or grandfather, but not exceptional; for the Lord, to him, had just been a magic genie, not a living, vibrant source of wisdom and power. Bongani had worshipped the gifts bestowed upon him and forgotten the giver. Tom remembered the impassioned speech Tim Johnson had given in the year 600 at Jubilee. Perhaps that flaw in Bongani, which was passed to Michael, had been Tom's mistake—for not addressing that subtle shift that he saw in his son. Bongani had passed the flaw to his son, Michael, where it had multiplied, and now to these boys, already men.

"Are you up for this challenge?" Lana asked Tom in her whispering voice, which he loved most of all her tones, when he had fallen into silence. The boys had immediately placed their earphones in.

"You see I am an old man," he said with true humbleness, the quality she loved the best of all his qualities.

"Even with age, you've got what it takes. Just love them, delight in them, see the battle already won." She clenched his arm. She looked at the three, huddled and talking low or singing to themselves as they stared at the countryside until Peter's Mountain Tunnel became its own closed world till they emerged on the south side of Halifax, where the land leveled, and sunlight ruled again.

Such wisdom in her simple words. Tom knew that to most, it would have gone undetected. He could delight in his great-grandsons and love them when he kept his eyes on the new men they would become. To focus on what they were was defeat.

How would he know when the boys had accepted Christ into their lives as Lord? Was that even a realistic goal with the time he had left? Even if he could just bring their carnal minds to the brink, to the ideological cliff, where they could not go back down the rugged path but could only go forward, off the cliff face and into the waiting arms of Jesus. If they were stuck on the cliff till that motivating something happened, well, that was better than climbing back down into their sin. He could trust God that a push would happen. Moses had never lived in the Promised Land, but he had brought his charges to the River Jordan.

His own father, Tom Sr., had provided that cliff face and those words that pushed. Dad's thoughts and actions, concisely revealed in words relayed to him by Mat, so many years ago: "It is knowing your evil is an affront to God and this God you affront is the only good in the world. When you hurt God and are ashamed of your hurting Him, then you are at the threshold." They must see the incredible purity of goodness and love that is God, and then they would see their own lack of goodness. This was a realistic goal. Only the Spirit of God could make a man jump into His arms.

The van turned onto the gravel road at the little crossroads village, the same village where coal-fired steam engines once stopped with itinerant farm hands 1,500 years ago. The same place a village of Susquehannock tribesmen once called home.

CHAPTER 13

Tom noticed smoke coming from Dad's chimney. No one should be in the home of Beulah Land. Weeks ago, he had called his sisters' kids and his own to verify the home was not occupied. He owned the property and made it accessible to all family members, and all requests for time at the holdings went through him. He called Tim's River View home. Hope, the youngest child of Tim and Mary, now lived in the home. Hope was only a month older than he was—this was the bond of their friendship, their shared generation, their parents' friendship, their river homes. Tom spoke as he pulled over onto the lawn of the estate. "Hope, this is Tom...Tom Burnell Jr. I'm minutes from Dad's home, and there's smoke coming from the chimney. Anyone living there?" He listened.

"There shouldn't be, Tom. I'll call John and Diana—they're in Katie's cottage at the moment. Law enforcement officers, if you forgot. I'll have them call you if they can't come right over. Looking forward to meeting again after all these years."

"Thanks, Hope. I, as well." Hearing her voice anchored his soul and his return home. They were the first generation of millennials.

The boys had perked up at the call and had followed the conversation. Tom exited the van, his eyes staring intently at his childhood home. Technically, he was sneaking up on the house. The boys piled out, and Lana decided she'd tag along. Tom had his "pursuit" face on, the one he wore even if at the computer, pursuing an idea, a piece of knowledge; he was oblivious to her presence. Tom moved at a quick walk. The boys began to forge ahead, believing confrontation and adventure were in the home. Tom thought their boldness was rash or overly aggressive, their bodies riding the hormones of dauntless teens.

"Don't leave us old people behind." His step was as vigorous as theirs, his keenness of mind as sharp as theirs. His ability to command tense situations was superior. Better that they thought they were doing a favor to him and Lana.

The group slowed as they passed through the perimeter fence and main gate. He noticed shrubs, trees needed to be pruned, and some downed limbs and trees on the lawns needed to be removed. No gardens had been cleared and planted. Outdoor furniture had not been covered from the previous winter or taken into the garage. The pool cover was leaf-littered, a corner had doubled over, and a black mass of rotting vegetation was murky at the lowest depths. He tried the door by the living room with the full window. The door opened without the need for a key. No one in the room. He noticed the couch had been pulled close to the fireplace—warning, danger. A long-haired man bolted upright from behind the couch's concealing backrest.

"Who are you?" Tom's voice was stern, forthright, and bold. His entourage was lingering outside.

The man's eyes were dazed, his face blank. He answered, "Stan…I'm Stan, your Kenyan relative."

Tom's posture stiffened. "Stan, the Burnells are black folk, every last one of them. And you are white, Stan. Besides that, I'm the guy who books the guests, and you never contacted me."

Stan's face was contorted with flustered embarrassment. "I'm sorry. I thought it had cleared channels. I was told it was okay. I flew from Kenya just weeks ago. Should I leave now?"

Tom saw John and Diana outside on the veranda, talking to Lana and the great-grandsons, then all rapidly entered the door. John spoke. "Is this the guest?"

Stan, with innocence on his face, and peace, answered, "Yes." His buddy, Andreas, had said the owners would not be present and were no danger; no anger would be displayed and certainly no physical violence. He had had two months of free living. He had made money by selling a few small objects borrowed from the home. He was the winner in this transaction. He just needed to ease out and be on his way.

"So he says," said Tom.

Stan said nothing; he would listen and find an angle of escape.

John continued, "I've already searched through the surveillance footage. He's been living here a couple of months. Walked onto the property, broke in, living like a slob. He had a few pharmaceutical friends as company for a week, until some type of altercation took place, and they left."

The brothers, who had rushed into the room after John and Diana, had moved behind and around, very close to Stan, and were enjoying the confrontation. John searched their eyes. They had moved to within arm's length of the stranger. They liked the excitement. Might make good law officers if their hearts were thirsty for truth and loyal to Christ. "Hey, guys, if Stan is asked to leave and told he will be handcuffed as a matter of procedure, will he resist and flee or will he submit?"

They looked at each other and guffawed. "How could we know?" said Robert.

John continued speaking his thoughts. "His words and demeanor have already shown you the bent of his nature; you just can't see this because you weren't trained to look for it."

"What's he going to do?" Sammie asked John. Sammie came across as bolder than his brothers.

"Well, I can't tell you, because then he might respond in accordance with the dare. We would be influencing his behavior. I'll write my prediction down and place it in my pocket. Afterward, we'll look." John wrote rapidly but had no time to write the entire word.

Stan had listened placidly as he had been discussed. Now, Stan bolted for the rear door to the kitchen, the foyer, the front door. Diana moved to her right, a wireless taser produced from her pocket, a sudden jolt, and fleeing Stan dropped in the foyer.

John, with admiration in his tone, addressed the group. "She noticed that angle when we made our sweep around the building, looking in the front-door windows. That's called planning." Diana was already cautiously moving to the downed Stan and secured his hands.

The boys were chuckling in awe. "So, what's your paper say?" asked Jack.

John tore the slip of paper from his small notebook. "What does it say?"

He handed the slip to Jack. Jack read aloud, "Ru…. I suppose that's *run*," said Jack.

"How'd you know?" asked Sammie of John.

"He's an American East Coast product by clothes and speech; probably local, as he knew of the African connection to your family. Everyone in the vicinity knows that fact. Really had nothing to lose by attempting a run, but he could have gained his freedom. Caught, he'll be fed, housed, see a doctor, participate in educational classes, and secretly increase his network of like-minded people. No deterrent quality in these things."

"Is lawless behavior common here now?" asked Tom.

Diana spoke as she held the cuffs of her standing Stan. "Only 148 years from the millennium's end. Jerusalem says identity theft, con games, graffiti, and gambling will increase. The Lord will continue His hard line against fantasy and planned crimes of violence toward his saints and disrespect for the Church. Such people continue to disappear. He promised a thousand years of peace, and He will deliver. Even these petty crimes could be wiped out instantly, but they are within the tolerable limits of the process of spiritual growth. That's a lot of words by me to say, yes, lawless behavior is more common."

Diana prodded Stan out the door to await the police van already enroute. Tom and Lana were thankful and enjoying the lessons John and Diana were giving the brothers.

John spoke. "Do you want to stay with us tonight, Tom? In Tim's home, where Hope is staying. She would like your company. Rest up from the trip, sleep in clean sheets in a warm home, have a good breakfast tomorrow before cleaning up around here?"

"That is charitable and accepted. But let us take a quick walk through, so we can plan for tomorrow."

"Okay, good idea. We will walk through with you, give advice on what may be needed, and where to buy."

The prisoner transportation van had just pulled up to the house.

***

Within two days, Tom had confided in his Susquehanna River friends his reasons for bringing his great-grandsons to the country estate: the poor leadership and Christian walk of their parents, their own lack of drive and commitment to the Lord, their frivolous behaviors and attitudes concerned with materialism and status. Such things could be defeated within a normal cycle of millennium life, but now time was comparatively short. They would be in their early thirties when Satan returned with his demons and fallen angels, and though only three or four months of conflict was expected, death and destruction would walk the earth, and many were expected to follow Satan to Jerusalem and destruction. Temptations and trickery and deceit would be offered to the souls of humanity. How many would be duped and lose eternal life?

Tom led the reeducation efforts, beginning with hard manual labor on the grounds. He presented them with the written testimonies and autobiographies of Tom Sr. and Tish, Tanya, Anya, and Flo, all of whom had experienced the darkest days of Earth's history. Then the autobiographies of Tim and Mary, Mat and Barb, Katie and Paul, John and Diana, Dan Jr. and Emily, Andy and Leaf, Carl, Ling, and even DC Jones. DC Jones took the time to fly in, visit with the brothers. Those mentioned above who were living on Earth intended to meet the brothers and discuss their lives. No electrascreen, no wrist phones during the day or evening, unless history was involved. John and Diana spearheaded the training, as they had known the evil of the world prior to the Rapture. John had combat experience, had fought hand to hand with evil. John hiked the boys to the mountaintop for vistas of the river. They kayaked on the river and fished, hunted deer. He and Diana showed them the use of crossbow, long bow, cartridge weapons. They were taught hand-to-hand combat. The Spirit of God accompanied them as friend and teacher within it all. The wars, raids, battles of the Old Testament, the warriors of renown in Israel and their deeds were discussed, their autobiographies read. Samson's killing of a thousand warriors with a donkey's jawbone elicited the most wonder. The autobiographies and computer interviews of Christian soldiers were studied, and electrascreen question-and-answer interviews were conducted.

One evening at bedtime, Jack passed Sammie's room on the return from his oral hygiene in the bathroom. He heard a whimper coming through the closed door. He knocked lightly and entered without waiting for a reply. Sammie lay in bed upon his back, covered. He pretended to be asleep, but Jack saw the tear-stained face. Jack sat on the edge of the bed. "I know you are awake, Sammie. Tell me what's bothering you. Share with me; that always helps."

Sammie opened his eyes, a puzzled look on his face. He realized he had no desire to invent a story. "These people are better than us, Jack."

"They are older. We can become better," said Jack.

"No. They love us. We don't love anyone or anything but our dumbass, selfish lives. Great-granddad and Lana love us! All of the Johnsons love us. Especially John and Diana. Andy and his family love us. Dan and Emily love us. We don't deserve any of it. They lived through times when men and woman were hateful and cruel; all these people had faith and suffered. They know something we don't."

"They know God, Sammie. He is real to them. That's why they're so different. I know what you're saying to me, brother. I once thought it was a race thing, but Tom and Lana are as black as us. Ling, who loved Great-granddad, was Chinese; and Andy is Native American; and John and Diana are white. I thought it was a culture thing, but our Tom is one of the ten richest men in the world and has a kind and humble soul, and Andy's sons, Tuck and Puck, are just working men, and they all go to the same church, and all hear the same message preached. I realized on this visit. It's an awareness thing. They know things about themselves—about humanity—that we do not see clearly, but they do. They tapped into some force of life we don't have. I'm just a boy, trying to be a man. They aren't trying; they are living their God easily, without effort. They are Him." Jack's voice trailed into perplexity.

Sammie spoke softly. "I want God to love me, Jack. If He would only love me! I got nothin' to make Him love me. I'm so lonely."

Jack shook his head in his perplexity. "They say no one has anything to make Him love us. He just does because He made us, and that's who He is: love. Why don't we just believe that and live for Him? That's all we can do."

Jack began wiping the tears from Sammie's face, then he gripped the sides of Sammie's face with his two hands and tightened his grip. "I love you, Sammie, and Robbie loves you, and we're no better than you. Let's ask God to love us. I've been meaning to do that myself."

Jack slipped off the side of the bed to his knees. "Come down here beside me, Sammie. We gotta show God it is important to us."

Sammie threw off his covers and knelt beside his brother.

Jack spoke. "God, we know you are here. We know you sent your son to die for us and our sins, and if not for Him, we wouldn't even know that you are here, and we have a chance of knowing you. We are ashamed of our lives, what we think, what we have done with them. Forgive us and guide us, please. In the name of Holy Jesus upon the throne, send us your Spirit to teach and guide us."

Sammie said, "We've done this before—said such words."

"But now we want it with all of our being. We're on empty and want nothing but Him. That's the difference," said Jack as he rose and gave a hand to Sammie. "Let's get Robbie and pray over him."

***

The weeks passed, and Tom and the boys were often in the garage, repairing hand tools, making weapons, knives, swords, crude shotguns, pistols, rifles. John would come and give lessons on military subjects. Fields of fire were demarcated, and ranges. Firing positions dug, camouflaged, landscaped into the surrounding lay of the land. John did not believe armed conflict would be a reality in the United States—the violence would be in the Middle East. It had been decided Tom's home would be the rallying place, the place of refuge when and if they were attacked. On a warm day, in the morning, the sun bright, John paused from shoveling with his crew. The Spirit of the Lord spoke to him, sat him down on a nearby wrought-iron bench, and talked to his spirit. Jack, Sammie, and Robbie noticed their boss was sitting, and they stopped working. John looked at them and spoke. "Come, sit with me. I have things to say." The brothers pulled up their breaktime folding lawn chairs and sat. It felt good to sit; they had already worked up a sweat, and the muscular fatigue of the past days sat within their musculature and hummed a peaceful sound. The air carried sweet-smelling scents, and the river's currents, seen through the trees, seemed lazy on their southward flow.

John said, "You weren't brought here to learn to shovel, to construct, to shoot—all important and interesting to learn, because the future might come to violence, and you will be prepared. But you weren't brought here to be used, to be forced to be soldiers for a cause you don't understand. God's people have many capable resurrected veterans. No, you were brought here to grasp the goodness of God and His world of peace and beauty and His offer of eternal life. You are here to learn how to draw your life from His living waters, His flowing strength. Without Him, you can do nothing worthwhile, nothing of value and meaning. I know, because at one time in my life, I was just an animal, living from my flesh, distracted, with truths and half-truths and lies all jumbling in my head. Whatever good I did, I tore down; and whatever evil I did, I sometimes unsuccessfully tried to amend. The deceiver kept my mind reeling, tumbling, so the truth could never take hold."

Jack spoke. "You are talking about an awareness."

"Yes," John answered. "An awareness of such force that it can knock you off your feet and send you in another direction. But this force is within your ability to discern, and it compels you to go where you wouldn't have thought to go. The Holy Spirit will guide you into the ever-flowing river of life. That flowing power will carry you and provide all the necessities of life, food, shelter, clothing, and purpose. Christ said, 'I am the vine, you are the branches. Apart from me you can do nothing.'"

Where was he going with this? Was the Lord directing his words, or was he merely babbling? He stood. "Let's check out the river." He liked to stand by the river periodically during the course of a day and observe nature's story, partake of the beauty of life. The river attracted the wildlife, and just the other day, two long, sleek river otters had cruised by. A few days before, John had witnessed a submerged snapping turtle of immense size latch onto a water moccasin, slowly reeling it in at every mouthful. He loved watching God's creation, loved the vast openness of the river and the sky overhead. How old had that snapper been? What had he seen of life? Where had those river otters come from? New York, up at the beginnings of the Susquehanna. And where did they intend to go? To Chesapeake Bay?

They moved from the landscaped lawn to the river trees, moved down the bank onto the small beach of river stones. John was gazing at the distant island when Jack exclaimed, "Look at this!" He had in his hand a long river stone, a celt head, made before the local tribes traded for metal goods. The two ends were flaked. One end was rounded, but the striking surface was perfectly flat. The other end slimmed in size to reveal a flat, narrow, rectangular striking surface. Jack showed the stone to John and then carried it the river edge, where he cleaned it with water and his hands. His brothers gathered around him. John spoke. "Save that for Andy. Maybe he can tell us if it had a particular function."

John studied the river, the shoreline of the island. At the far end, a small group of deer raised their heads from the cool river water and watched the humans. At the estimated middle of the island shore, he saw the wild grape vines. Their large leaves and distinctive leaf color—the bottom side a pale, whitish-green—and the sheer length and height of the vines were eye catching. He had noticed them the very first summer of the millennial reign.

He pointed to the vines. "Wild grapes." The brothers followed his eyes and arm. "That cluster of big, light-green leaves." He saw Jack's eyes make the connection. John continued, "Andy said that island had grapes back when he was a kid."

"Are they ready to eat?" asked Robbie.

"Not till late summer or early fall, though the birds will eat them before we get the chance," John said unhappily.

Robbie's nose went into the air. "I smell smoke."

John, too, now smelled smoke. A slight breeze came from the north, but no scent of smoke. He saw tendrils of smoke under the trees to his south, surprisingly close, misdirected by an updraft under the trees. John began to walk south along the shore of mud and small river stones. The brothers trailed behind from curiosity. Soon John saw the figure of a man, sitting close to the bank, where a tree had toppled, and the root ball upheaval had created a sandy, muddy-earthed flatness. The man tending his small fire waved them in.

"Good morning," the man said amiably and with a confidence that spoke of trust. John took note of the wading sandals still wet and even the fringe of the cargo-pocketed shorts. The fishing rod leaned against the downed tree trunk. A wire roasting rack with a handle, balanced over coals, held four whole-bodied, gutted, descaled, smallmouth bass.

John was happy for the man's success. "Good morning. You've had success." Something about the dark-haired man was familiar.

The man spoke. "Cast the bait in the swift water that runs past the quiet pools behind the rock ledges. So simple, even I can be a success." The man laughed at himself. "Join me." His tone was earnest. He rummaged in his nearby rucksack, pulled out a package of flat bread. "Come, sit. I desire company." He motioned them to sit.

A thick tree branch from the fallen oak beckoned them, and they sat. John picked up the bread package that was tossed at his feet. "Galilee Bakery" was printed on the package, as well as an Israeli address for the company. John took half a piece and passed the package to Jack.

The man studied the faces of the Burnell brothers simply in friendly inclusion. He noticed and addressed John's thoughts. "The Middle Eastern store in downtown Harrisburg carries this brand." John knew the stranger was a resurrected man as their minds easily intertwined.

John smiled broadly in sudden recognition. "I haven't seen you in over... close to nine hundred years!"

"Yes, in Israel. I've visited here often over weekends, to fish and view the river. I haven't been far from your mind and your friends' minds, and that makes my heart glad."

John understood that Joshua meant all the people John knew and cherished, including the three brothers beside him. Joshua silently told John to present him to the brothers. Joshua turned the fish. "Soon they will be ready; deep inside, they are cooking."

John laughed deeply. "Are you talking about the fish or the brothers?"

Joshua was laughing and answered, "Of course, I'm a fisher of men. Both are nearly ready."

John turned to the line of brothers sitting on the branch, all looking perplexed. "This is Joshua. I last met him in Jerusalem on the seventy-fifth day after the end of Satan's kingdom. He suggested the banks of the Susquehanna as a place to live our millennial lives. You know him by the name of Jesus."

The brothers sat dumbly, even as their minds worked in overdrive. Jack spoke first. "Jesus as in Savoir of the world?"

"Yes, I am He. I have come to meet you because of your heartfelt prayers and for the many others who pray for you. I have come to bring clarity to your minds and to tell you I want you in my kingdom for eternity. You three—Jack, Robbie, Sammie—are important to me. The Holy Spirit has been working in you, and very soon He will reveal our presence with force and certitude. Do not turn back; endure, I say; endure to the end."

Silence. The four knew they were not to speak, just to meditate on the word given. Joshua pulled his fish from their resting place over the coals, examined the flesh. "They are done. One for each of you. I am satisfied with the bread." He returned the fish to the coals and rose. "Stay seated, men." Joshua went down the line, His right hand centered before each person's eyes, at the vertical, slightly cupped, rested individually upon their heads, as the impartation of the Holy Ghost was planted, and each felt power and prayer pierce his spirit. Their minds entered realms of discernment and prophesy they could not utter or truly comprehend. Peace and joy and overwhelming love brought them to their knees. A bubbling welling up overwhelmed their torsos like an internal and eternal fountain bringing refreshment. At some point, they realized He had gone, and they stood and laughed and felt such privilege that the peace and joy would course through their minds again and again. And even after they ate the fish caught by Jesus, the Savior of the world, cooked on a humble fire by the King of the Creation for them alone, and they sat in thought, the overwhelming joy would well up and bubble over them once again.

***

Tom and Lana arranged a gathering for the last night of their great-grandsons' visit. All had heard of the visitation of Christ and were overjoyed for the brothers. But it was a tempered joy, as they knew that for this visit by Christ, Satan would have a need to wrest their souls away. Christ's very words to the brothers, the emphasis on enduring to the end, was a warning for vigilance. Diana and John had come early to help and guide their charges, to organize the chairs, tables, plates; to gather firewood and build a fire. They had grown close and could freely talk to the young men as friends. Both were interested in this newest generation, its perceptions, interests, thoughts on Christ, but had never placed the boys within the context of their generation.

John addressed them as the last chore had been accomplished and all sat around the fire pit, the fire started while the sun shone. Coals would be used to roast ears of corn and, eventually, bison steaks or fish for the evening meal.

"We know who you are. We like you. But what of your generation? How are your friends like you and how are they different? What do they think of Christ?"

Uncharacteristically, Robbie spoke first. "They don't think of Christ. They occasionally hear His name on the news, linked to initiatives and rulings."

Jack picked up Robbie's theme. "He's the man in charge, but they don't seem to associate Him with the Jesus who came to Earth, suffered, and died for us."

Sammie smiled as he spoke. "We were the same…" He looked down at the earth, swallowed hard, and finished his sentence. "No better than anyone else." He looked at John. "You resurrected people taught us different, and I thank you. The Lord seeking us out, standing before us. Observing, looking, and seeing—*feeling*—His majesty made the whole story real and made it truth."

Robbie spoke reverently. "He entered into our minds, imparted His Spirit."

"Thank you for listening and taking it to heart," said Diana, who knew the feeble efforts of the resurrected had been surpassed by Christ's visitation, but their contribution had prepared the minds of the brothers for a rebirth.

Robbie said, "The stories of the past world, when Satan ruled, made us take it to heart. It was a brutal world. Bigotry and deceit, every person your enemy." Robbie recalled John's time in the army, the platoon of men he had fought with and against. Jack remained silent, thinking of Diana, deceived into a life of whoredom—a little girl just wanting to do good and be good.

Jack spoke. "Our generation has it too good. We don't know suffering or even striving against a force of evil. We don't see the evil within ourselves, our lust for recognition, the lusts of the flesh—food, drink, power over others. Just go to church, shut off your mind, and live for yourself. That's the new generation's attitude."

"How is that wrong?" challenged John.

"Because we belong to each other. That is…the body of Christ, the Church. We have to keep on that straight and narrow path," said Jack.

"And never forget our God. We need to love Him with all that we are," added Robbie.

"And those around us, so we don't go back to those dark days," Sammie said. He wondered if that is what he truly believed. Or was that just what the moment required? Sometimes he felt false and empty when he talked of God, but he knew that was a lie, and so he had the advantage.

"Our generation has so much sin, but it's within the mind, hidden. No one sees it, but it is there," said Jack.

"It will come to light as the millennium ends. Be ready for that time. Keep building yourself up in Christ. It is coming," said John.

Tom and Lana returned from the kitchen with Dan and Emily and Pete and Grace and their two children. Andy and Leaf transported in with their sons close behind. By the summer night's end, it appeared there was no more to teach Tom's great-grandsons. Robbie, Jack, and Sammie knew deep in their hearts what their God wanted from them. His goodness, His kindness was evident to them and appreciated. They appeared to love God with all their hearts, souls, minds, and strength; greater still was the miracle that they loved their neighbors as themselves.

***

Within a year, Amy had successfully completed her time and petitioned the court for the return of her children, as Michael's reeducation was still ongoing. The court granted her motion. Robbie, Jack, Sammie wished to return to China, just for a visit, they thought. But the pull of familiar surroundings, friends, and young marriageable women were found to be stronger than the new life they had begun on the banks of the Susquehanna River. Tom wondered if the seed had really germinated in their hearts. Had the soil been deep enough? Would the temptations of the world, offered through their friends, be resisted? He was skeptical, for ungodly friends had been much of the problem, and new believers were always forced to leave the temptations of the past life, if they were to grow. Had he taken them to the cliff's edge? He did not know.

In the year 920, Jack returned to Tom and Lana, who had remained on Tom Sr.'s original land grant. In the year 935, Tom and Lana passed to paradise, and an emptiness was felt by Jack and his neighbors, only to be allayed by the fact their beloved Tom and Lana would return soon. In the year 936, Jed and Catherine, the parents of Peter, passed. Hope, the last child of Tim and Mary, passed, as did her husband, William. Life continued as full, beautiful, and hopeful as the very first day of the millennium. The mortals born of this period well outnumbered the resurrected. The resurrected noticed a large percentage of their mortal brethren no longer sought their company. Perhaps the mortals were simply overwhelmed by the demands of the new births, the ever-mobile and expanding family ties, the pursuit of careers. Perhaps.

CHAPTER 14

Peter awoke to the April sun cresting over the forested mountain ridge to the east. The long valley had haze in the deep recesses of ravines and bottom lands. The thousand years of the millennium had ended last night at twelve o'clock. Good people did not commemorate the passing with celebrations, though they had loved the millennium dearly, and the millennium itself had been a thousand-year celebration. Church services had been scheduled this morning for remembrance, nostalgia, and prayers for the future. The good people knew a darkness—very limited in scope, but nonetheless, a darkness—was coming. People yearning to be free of the kingdom of God did celebrate with glee.

Pete had heard the fireworks last night; he had smelled smoke, had seen fires burning in abandoned buildings, sheds, garages, barns—even in forest land on the mountains. Street signs had been stolen, and large trees felled across roads and highways. Masked strangers collected fictitious tolls from passing vehicles and splattered slogans on vehicles, roadways, and the walls of buildings. Satan had wasted no time in collecting his own. Grace lay beside him, her face contented; her body curled up. They had only wanted two children: Peter Jr. and Gracie, who were grown, married, and had moved to Mediterranean Africa to begin the establishment of large families, taking advantage of the sparse native population—most of whom were resurrected from Christian/Roman times—and the fertile land. Pete and Grace had more than fifty descendants now, on this first day post millennium.

Everyone upon Earth had known Satan was coming. Everyone knew there were unsaved, unregenerate people born during the millennium—people of the flesh and of the world, waiting to bend life to their persuasion. It was written plainly in the Bible for all to read. It was written that the ungodly would fail and spend eternity in the lake of fire! And yet, the ungodly did not believe the holy book, did not believe God would do what He said He would do, when proof of His steadfastness and unyielding words surrounded them in the very existence of the post-Tribulation world. All of the mortal adults who had experienced the Tribulation period were gone, and none of the children of the Tribulation remained.

Pete and Grace were alone—all the familiar faces of their lives, from childhood through adulthood were gone; only their children remained, and their children's children. Maybe this emboldened the nonbelievers—the tangible, mortal proof of the Tribulation was no more. Not even the childish memories of a handful of witnesses remained. The resurrected of the Tribulation period had been few; Dan and Emily were examples, and their nonmortal status identified them as outsiders. The resurrected from Earth's past history, unable to produce children, seemed like ghosts—childless freaks who belonged in monasteries. Their radiant aura, once esteemed, now was the garishness of antiquity.

Strange times ahead, thought Pete. It was good to be on his little homestead of bounty and beauty. It was good to have Grace curled beside him. It was good he had resurrected friends who had sold themselves to Christ and who could not turn from their allegiance, had they wished such a foolish thing. It was good he had mortal family and friends whom he trusted. More importantly, he had, from his youth, studied the ungodly people of the flesh, the pride of life, and the hidden world order they had created. He had worked undercover among their so-called "clubs" and by long interactions was considered a trusted member of their community.

"Time to rise and shine, sleepyhead." Pete tousled Grace's auburn hair. Grace, without warning or even the appearance of wakefulness, bounded up out of bed and then hurled herself upon Pete, tousling his hair with great vigor. "How does it feel, Petey?" He felt her fingers roughly massaging his scalp. She burst out laughing at the bewildered, fearful countenance of her husband. "You're not ready for anything!" she taunted playfully.

He sank into the bed, holding his hand over his heart. "Certainly not a demon-possessed wife." He feigned delicacy, hoping to bring her into a remorseful state.

Grace's voice sounded deep, masculine, harsh. "Get with the plan, man. Deny you know Him and lust for sex, for material possessions, for power!" She could not sustain the act, and sarcasm overwhelmed her. "What fools. What utter fools. To leave our Lord and Savior for the emptiness of the worthless yearnings of the mind and body...worthless junk!"

"That's the problem. To them, it is not worthless junk. Because they have never recognized His love and Lordship. They have never known His presence. Worthless junk fills the emptiness in their souls," said Pete.

"Enough of these thoughts," Grace demanded, and then with a feminine charm, commanded, "Let's have a cup of coffee and breakfast from the bounty of our land. Prayers of thankfulness for knowing Him and for our kids and their kids knowing Him." Grace bounded out of bed again, grabbed Pete's arm, and began to pull.

"You convinced me," he said as he gained his feet and moved toward the kitchen. The electrascreen snapped on as Pete entered the living room. Must be a news alert for the screen to engage. Pete sat before it, knowing Grace would bring the coffee. "You're pretty spry for a thousand years old," he said blandly, as she walked by, knowing darned well she wasn't a thousand years old. He wondered what she would do with his remark.

"I'm a youthful eight-hundred years old and don't look a day over fifty, in old Earth years. How's that case of senility?" she said just as blandly. He laughed as she returned from the kitchen, sat close beside him, placing his coffee on the tree-trunk table crafted from their very own woods.

The face of a familiar news reporter filled the projected screen space. "Below-normal harvests are anticipated in all agricultural project zones. Possible food shortages in the fall." His voice trailed to silence and confusion, as he had never read bad news before—especially in an ag report. "Now to world events and the most crucial story of our time. It is reported that the great deceiver, the fallen angel known as Satan, has escaped his imprisonment. His whereabouts are unknown. But as you know, his likely destination is planet Earth. Report any knowledge of his whereabouts to the proper governmental authorities." The voice again trailed off in confusion.

Pete turned down the sound. "How that liar, Satan, managed to coerce the news stations is beyond me. They must be infiltrated at the highest levels."

"You mean the food shortages?"

Pete answered, "Yes. That's a lie. Pete Jr. and Gracie just recently told us they're looking at one of their best years. Besides, the Lord doesn't run out of food in His kingdom. The New Testament plainly shows that fishes and barley loaves will multiply when needed. That, as well as manna from heaven in the Old Testament, tells us this famine rumor is a lie. But it will spur a run on the existing food supplies and cause a shortage and perhaps violence. The sentence, 'He has escaped imprisonment,' is also a lie. He left imprisonment because he was allowed to leave. That is clearly stated in scripture."

"Appears he owns the news media, and we can expect lie after lie," Grace said as she went to the food-service door in the wall between kitchen and living room and pulled out breakfast—eggs Benedict and hashbrowns.

"All evil intents begin with controlling the dialogue," Pete said. "The first lies will be bombastic, big, incredible, and unending in their accusations and supposed veracity. Human nature always believes what it first hears and, in innocence, thinks it is true, because who would make destructive accusations without proof?"

"The king of deceit would," Grace said, with a determined affirmation in her voice.

Pete reached for his laptop as he spoke. "Wonder what he did to the internet?" He began exploring as he ate.

Grace sat quietly, eating as the keyboard sounded. She noticed Pete's homemade longbow and full quiver were leaning against the wall. She had noticed his crossbow by the front door. Andy had created the bow-making passion; a Christian soldier, a crossbowman from warring Europe in the fourteen hundreds, had inspired the crossbow. The cartridge pistol was on their nightstand, fully loaded. He had been issued the cartridge pistol just recently, in his government work capacity. He must have placed the bows last night after they turned in.

"Any trouble last night?" Her voice held concern.

"You didn't hear the explosions or smell the smoke?" He knew her to be a sound sleeper.

"No."

"Sounded like the Fourth of July, and people were burning any uninhabited structure they could find, as well as forest land. The bamboo groves were heavily hit. Had they been able to organize prior to Satan's return, they could have overrun the country."

Pete refocused on the laptop, and then, with an exasperated sigh, he said, "The internet has been fully corrupted. The names of countries, towns, cities, rivers, mountains, borders, governmental leaders, roads, and highways have all been changed or moved or distorted. Biblical information is absent or distorted, names changed. Climatic data has been changed. You couldn't build a birdhouse from the directions given. Even history has been changed. I wonder if we can communicate with anyone? Try to call Pete Jr. or Gracie."

Grace picked up her phone, punched in a phone number. "No service."

"Oh!...Oh!" Pete's voice trembled with emotion, a searing, painful groan underneath his exclamations. Whatever he had witnessed on his screen had torn his heart. Grace, in one quick motion bounced on the cushions, to his side. Seconds were needed for her eyes to comprehend the pictures before her. Resurrected people of both sexes, or with mixed sexual anatomy; dwarves, midgets, people with extra appendages or no appendages or supersized legs and arms or small heads or large heads; women with beards; deformities of every possible description. Then, bodies damaged from war, fire, accidents, or disease. Names underneath the pictures, addresses, photos of their current bodies. She saw Tuck and Puck with their crippled legs, their throats cut; Dan Jr. with his blown-apart head; Emily with her body crushed by a fallen boulder. All were in their death bodies.

She turned away in anger. "I guess I hadn't thought of the mind of Satan or the evil he's capable of." She held her anger and rage in check by the thinnest of margins. "The precamera representations totally made up—from what? Did he penetrate the vaults of life?" She referred to the vast, unending storage vaults of all that was and is.

"No doubt, the vaults. Angels are administrators of the vaults." Pete spoke in his questioning tone. "Perhaps some of the fallen angels?" Then he said, "The master of the flesh knows how to turn the flesh against itself. What's worse…anyone might be at risk. Christian men and women engaged in fictional poses of all kinds of filth by the power of the computer. Our resurrected saints belittled, mocked, ridiculed, embarrassed."

"Do you think God should have allowed this?" queried Grace.

"Ah, the reason it was produced, for that question will be asked by many. It's an aspersion upon God's character, reasoning, and power. To start the doubt on God's goodness and His love of His children."

"Yes, I see through it already," she said.

"Yet the resurrected will hold strong—they have already passed the test. It is the mortals, such as us, who may fail. Perfect strategy, though, to divide the resurrected from the mortals. For this strategy to sting, the rebellious mortals will need to personally hector and harass with words and printed photos the resurrected—in-your-face confrontations, with an audience of mortals in attendance."

"None of God's mortals would participate in that behavior." Grace's tone was defensive.

"Exactly why God allows it. He's saying to His children, 'See the evil in their hearts; see how they cling to the kingdom of the flesh and raise themselves up through the flesh, boasting of their own beauty, health, and perfection. The perfect plan to make real the difference between the kingdom of God and the kingdom of Satan—who discerns with the heart and soul of God, and who sees through the eyes of physical self-love and contempt?"

The cast-iron bell on the front porch clanged, and they heard an entrance, as they had taught their friends was proper protocol. "It's Tuck. Can I come in?"

"Yes, Tuck, we're in the living room." Grace's voice rose in volume with perfect clarity. They had been expecting Andy's family for lunch in the afternoon, along with John and Diana and Dan Jr. and Emily. Grace loved the resurrected—they glowed, they were always positive, they had a deep peace, knowing they were secure in Christ for eternity. Could Satan destroy this peace and security? She liked and needed close friends. Her family was rooted in California, and her remaining sister rarely made it to Pennsylvania. Even the members of Pete's family were somewhere else—mostly in Mexico and South America, managing their newly acquired farmsteads. Her kids and their offspring were in Mediterranean Africa, of course.

Tuck entered the room, his skin heavily tanned. Like all resurrected who had died as children, he appeared to have stopped physical development around the age of thirty. Emily proved that point, as well as Tuck's brother, Puck, alias Robin. Puck had decided on a name change now that he worked as a banker. Emily looked thirty and was an attractive woman. Grace was glad Emily and Dan had bonded deeply. Dan also proved the age-thirty rule.

Even the oldest resurrectionists never appeared to be over fifty, even if they had left Earth at ninety years of age—Gramps Johnson and Great-grandfather Jeremiah were proof of that reality. She thought of the two—deeply connected to the resurrected of their generation; she rarely saw them.

"Coffee, tea, breakfast, Tuck?" Grace asked. Pete found contentment in his wife's role as hostess. His mate was a sharing woman, who always presented the bounty of their home, compliments of their gracious Lord. He liked it when guests left their cottage with tummies full and delightful drinks lingering in their mouths and more of Jesus in their souls.

"I'll have coffee, and if you have any of those cornmeal cakes left over…," he said shyly. "By the way, obscene graphics now adorn your garage. Part of last night's festivities."

She always noticed Tuck's shining black hair, always tied. He had his father's size and still moved like a mountain lion. He loved his cornmeal muffins.

"We must expect such things with Satan's return," Grace said, her tone dismissive and buoyantly positive, though it worried her that evil had been so close to their home. "You're a dipper, Skipper Tuck." She, too, believed a cornmeal cake dipped in coffee, or taken with a swig of the same, was better than a doughnut. She had begun calling him *skipper* after seeing him on the river in his water-conservation boat, wearing the employer-issued hat that had the appearance of a civilian yacht captain's hat.

Tuck laughed. "A rhyming tongue never goes unsung."

"What's that mean?" she asked in mock annoyance.

"I always tell close friends about your newfound propensity to rhyme."

"Is that a crime—to rhyme?" Her face distorted, her body tense.

The histrionics broke Tuck's gravity, unleashing the chuckling laughter that was his trademark. "Please, I want to be serious."

Pete sat up; he heard a worrisome quiver in the tone that was real and painful. "Look at me, Tuck." Tuck looked into Pete's eyes as Pete asked, "What is it?"

Grace quickly retrieved the coffee and corn cakes. Such a distraction might be needed. Had Tuck seen the pictures?

"Dad received reports that Satan's attacks have already begun. I was transporting all night—putting out fires, sawing felled trees, comforting robbed commuters, and rounding up delinquents."

"I heard the fire crackers and saw the flames," Pete said.

Tuck continued, "Many of those explosions were firearms, and even bombs. We all know where this is heading. One account says that Christ wants pictures of all the resurrected in their former bodies, as Satan is stealing identities and producing clones of the resurrected."

"What are these evil clones supposed to accomplish?" Pete knew the answer. He had just seen a representation of Tuck and his brother, Puck, with crippled legs and their throats slit. The leg deformity had been present from birth and had made them despised and hated by their tribe, other tribes, and white settlers. Andy had been forced to fight daily to validate their right to life. Pete answered his own question. "Sow discord among the population, make everyone doubt God's sovereign powers, and separate the eternal resurrected from the mortal believers."

"God forbid," Tuck stated emphatically.

"It has already begun, Tuck, on the internet—taken over by Satan—photos and films of the resurrected that only the perverse would find amusing. The entire factual validity of all sites has been twisted into confusion and misinformation, as well."

"Come over here to Pete's laptop and look, Tuck," Grace said.

Tuck came over to Pete, who offered his seat. Tuck scrolled, saw himself and his brother in their crippled bodies. He muttered, "My…my…my God!"

Pete spoke. "We shouldn't discount the discord this will produce. Satan is dredging up the pain of the past with these images. To have your body or your loved ones' bodies shown in their former states…" Pete's emotions were being touched as his mind remembered. "In that state and many times because of that state, they were abused, tortured, held to public ridicule, and made to feel shame and disgust for their being. The deformed, the lepers, those mutilated in battle or by evil men, the so-called 'freaks' born without arms or legs or parts of bodies due to myriad reasons or the effects of syphilis at one time. People with mental diseases, syndromes of coordination and movement, atrophying diseases, nervous disorders, genetic flaws. Many of these are the people who loved the Lord most deeply, who sought refuge in His love and longed to see His kingdom come. Definitely, not fun to be hated as a loathsome beast not fully human."

Tuck gently reasserted himself. "Apostle Paul called us Christians 'the offscouring of the world.' My brother and I have peace with our deformed bodies, with the past treatment and our murders, and have no shame. The shame is on our persecutors—such fools to think that health and wholeness made them attractive in their Creator's eyes. The pride of life, the love of the flesh. My family has not seen even one of our tormentors in this millennium—not one's eyes were opened. Not one accepted salvation. The resurrected, all of them, know only to love; they know it is the spirit of God's children that He cherishes. God knew all along the flesh was to no avail. Our brothers will cheer those whom Satan would mock. In fact, we could quickly round up those mortals not in Christ simply by their arrogant bearing, the eyes burning with hatred and superiority, their pride in life and in their own self-delusional wholeness, which they think is a sign of their superiority."

Pete was reminded of the depth of Tuck's knowledge and emotion, which was easy to forget, as Tuck presented himself as a lighthearted woodsman. "Well said, Tuck. Yes, we will see their eyes aflame with conceit and superiority." How apt was Tuck's name: emotion and wisdom were hidden. His provision for life, secreted away, tucked into this man who had endured much. "But it is apparent to you the Lord did not author this pronouncement. He knows His own. Visual pictures are not needed. He does not hold up his children for mockery. Christ was mocked. He was held up by a tall cross on a high hill in a large city—bloodied; panting; deprived of skin, flesh, blood; naked for the world to laugh upon. His kingdom is upon the earth, not Satan's; and the Lord's Spirit still reigns."

Tuck spoke. "This evil of the past will be cast upon those who now appear whole of body and mind. Satan will slander and accuse all the saints, inventing ugly incidents, thoughts, actions to pin upon the redeemed. Invented witnesses and victims, and visual proof, to tarnish the upright."

Grace spoke. "Pete and I have discussed this reality. No one will be immune from attack...." Grace's words trailed as the scenarios of slander and false accusations filled her thoughts.

Tuck returned to his train of thought and said, "My dad has momentarily fallen into the trap of the past, and we must lift him from that pit. He went through great emotional torture to keep us alive as long as he could. Had he not, we would never have known Christ, would not be here today."

"He will be greatly affected by forces wishing to hurt his boys." Pete felt that searing pain in Andy and knew that hopelessness was attempting to steal his heart for depression's lair. God had answers, and the people of the Lord would watch the ungodly descend into the eternal lake of fire.

Grace inserted the corn muffins and coffee on the table by Tuck. "Eat. Drink. All this is in the hands of our Lord. It is just a prelude to victory."

As she finished her last word, the bell clanged, and a deep voice sounded. "Andy and family and Dan and Emily, John and Diana."

Grace smiled as she heard Andy's voice. She answered, "In the living room." Her tone was of pleasant surprise. Her guests were hours early. But they weren't guests; they were family. And seeing them sooner filled her with warmth. Extraordinary events had occurred. Jack Burnell needed to be called, now that the gathering had begun so early. She wondered at this early arrival. Had Satan cast a shadow of fear on her friends? Well then, what better time to gather and strengthen each other? For the entire length of the millennium, the only time she had experienced, it seemed as if all people were her family. She wondered if that concept was now dead, for there evidently was a sizeable group of people not under the lordship of Christ, people who wanted to do life their way, which was to say Satan's way, and who would force others to that way. When Pete discussed his work, he made these rebellious people seem harmless, and their numbers inconsequential. As their guests entered the living room, Grace and Pete were on their feet—Pete taking the drink requests, and Grace presenting the food choices. Hugs and handshakes were exchanged.

Andy spoke. "Sorry we're early. The electrascreen has created discomfort to our lives. Confusion." Grace saw on Andy's face and heard in Andy's voice that he was clearly rattled. Robin had said nothing—he had helped everyone with their food and drink order. He seemed to be enlivened underneath his quietness. She thought he wanted confrontation. Leaf was only disturbed because her husband was affected. "I came along to see what mischief the rascals have been up to," Leaf said. "They defiled your garage wall."

John and Diana appeared to have a soberness. They exhibited the greater calm within the group; Dan and Emily held a comforting steadiness. Grace addressed John. "Were you out last night?" She thought John and Diana, being law enforcement and looking slightly tired, had been on duty.

John spoke softly. "For a while. Smelled smoke. From the deck, saw fires scattered over the valleys, mountainsides—quite impressive. I knew no one's home was burning by my fire board—an electronic map collecting data from home heat sensors. Decided just to provide security for the homes of our little village. Somehow missed seeing the graffiti artist working on Pete's garage. Sat with my night scope till first light."

Emily picked up the conversation. "Dan was transporting in from Washington, and I was pacing my kitchen, weighing all the disinformation on the internet."

Dan interjected, "From the air, there was nothing but fires, evil people collecting by bonfires. Some even shot rockets at me."

Grace realized Jack was standing in the kitchen doorway. She spoke loudly to be heard over the hum of conversation. "Jack, your food and drink of choice?"

He smiled in the warmth of inclusion and said, "Whatever is handy."

Grace answered confidently, "That means you haven't eaten breakfast. Would coffee and sausage gravy over biscuits hit the spot?" Her statement, backed by past meals eaten in her home, made Jack's face light up with a smile. "Yes. Perfect." Grace moved quickly to the refrigerator, the gravy and biscuits already made, waiting inside.

Grace was humbled by the fact that all of her guests, save Jack, had seen Satan's kingdom, lived within it. She and Pete, like Jack, had only read accounts of his reign and heard the words of the survivors. She knew Pete was analyzing the states of mind of their guests and he saw what she saw. She could tell just by the look in his eyes and his mannerisms. She was correct in her belief, as she would find later. Pete knew Andy hurt the most, for he had been traumatized by the violence he had witnessed and the violence he had inflicted to give his disabled boys peace and safety within a world that despised them. Tuck and Robin had no fear and wished the waiting period was over; they wanted confrontation. John and Diana also knew the violence of Satan and the games of deception in a world of duality. They were patiently waiting for their time at bat. She sensed they desired the extra innings. Dan and Emily had lived in a time of complete chaos, the worst the world would ever see, and in surviving and in dying, they knew there was nothing to fear, for the Lord stood by His own.

As greetings and food and drink desires crossed between people, and words of intent for the day's activities were expressed, Pete looked into Andy's eyes and said, "This time of confusion won't last more than four months, and then it will be resolved. Satan will be gone to his lake of fire, and all the mortals who chose him will be dead and awaiting the white throne of judgment, along with all the inhabitants of Hades."

Leaf spoke for her husband. "We just wish for the end of it—the memories of the rebellious, their cruelty…"

Pete spoke reassuringly. "Only a hundred and twenty days at the most, Leaf, and the Lord won't give them the chance to rise to their full evil. This is the Lord's kingdom reigning now. Back then, it was Satan's kingdom—he was given an upper hand in those days."

Pete had a cup within everyone's reach, and Grace, a plate of food before every guest. Eating and drinking consumed the gathers, voices were few, and compliments on the food and drink the primary topic. Most went back for seconds, which delighted Grace. In the quiet that eventually came, Robin spoke. "There is talk of armies forming from the four corners of the earth and already moving toward Jerusalem."

"Huge armies," added Andy.

Dan recognized Andy's unease, uncharacteristic of him, and said, "As the Word prophesied, Revelation 20:8, 'They are like the sand on the seashore.'" Dan also recognized that Andy would be responsible for thousands if not millions of lives in the central Pennsylvania area.

John, too, understood Andy's state of mind and said, "Remember the army that came with Christ to Earth a thousand years ago? The sky was filled! Satan can't match that."

"Amen," said Diana.

Pete, who had yet to be born at the second coming, wondered why Andy, who had been a part of it, had lost his sense of awe at God's might. He cancelled the negative thought. Andy, who would likely be in charge of Harrisburg and the surrounding county, felt the weight of responsibility.

Andy was just a man and had felt Satan's hand personally in his life and his family's life. Pete resolved and prayed that he would encourage Andy, bind up his weaknesses, help him with the full force of his being during this time of stress.

To Grace, it was evident and natural that Robin had absorbed some of his father's foreboding. He had become a successful financier and banker, of all things. He wore his raven hair short. Stability and calculated moves had ingrained themselves in his expectations, and a hint of something other than those qualities raised alarms. She remembered Robin playing chess as a scrawny kid. He carried the chessboard everywhere, and whether he was in a bathing suit, school clothes, or pajamas, he was ready to play. She wondered if the banker's life had begun on the chessboard.

"The Bible clearly states they will lose," Dan said.

"We will need an army to oppose them." Andy knew the plans existed. "Our auxiliary police forces and national guard won't be enough."

John mused, "The scripture gives the impression our God will destroy Satan's armies personally. Fire from heaven when they reach Jerusalem. Maybe his people are just to watch them gather and go to their end."

"It wouldn't hurt to be ready, if that's not the case," Robin said.

"I agree," said Dan, who unconsciously rubbed his eye. "For Satan's recruits to gather, they will need to travel across the country to airports and seaports."

Pete caught the inference. "They may travel like the gangsters and thugs they are."

Tuck joined the discussion. "We have plenty of crossbows, bows and arrows, flintlock and percussion cap guns and bolt-action rifles." Lasers and assault rifles were no longer manufactured (except for police and military use), as there was no demand—no one had been buying them. Most of the mortals had chosen an urban lifestyle and had no interest in hunting. Mortals who lived in the country and hunted preferred weapons of antiquity. The resurrected preferred not to hunt, as they could easily talk an animal into approaching them, and if they wished, dispatch the animal. The resurrected could also capture hidden, unseen fish with their hands. Smiling, Tuck added, "Little is much when—"

"God is in it." Leaf finished the phrase.

"Or we could ramp up production of lasers or military-grade weapons," Robin suggested.

Pete shook his head. "It's going to happen too fast. Satan will move with incredible speed. Speed is his only hope."

"Then there is no hope for him. For who can outspeed the Creator of speed?" Robin laughed.

"I think we need to show ourselves united, even with only primitive weapons in our hands," said Andy. "We could begin a mobilization."

"Let us await the instructions of our Commander. Jesus is sitting on His throne in Jerusalem. None of this is unknown to Him," said John, who added, "That He did not send directions, orders, a month ago…that He did not ramp up productions of laser weapons may be telling us something."

"What?" Pete inquired softly to himself.

John, through his resurrected powers, heard Pete's self-questioning. John answered in a determined tone. "He just wants us to move these insurrectionists along—to Jerusalem, to our conquering God, just as the Bible has already stated. We don't need to hear from Him. Could we even verify the pronouncements that come from Jerusalem?"

"Are the emergency frequencies and internet sites compromised?" Grace asked.

Andy answered, "We believe they are, yes. No false messages yet. They are simply listening in."

Quietly yet forcefully, John said, "Before we settle into our communal friendships and conversations, I believe the time warrants a prayer, a supplication to our Lord Christ, who reigns in Jerusalem. His God is our God, and the times may demand much from us. Any takers?"

Robin raised his hand. The gathered assented and encouraged him. Robin rose, and as he rose, the gathered saw the Spirit of God envelope him. The voice of the Spirit was within the voice of Robin.

"Awesome God, Magnificent Creator who set the universe in motion, who established the rhythms of life and order within the world. Commander of angelic hosts, Keeper of knowledge and wisdom. Redeemer, Savoir, Blessed Counselor and friend, hear our prayer.

"The coming struggle will be fraught with tests of faith for your resurrected. For the unsaved mortals, eternal life in heaven or hell will be decided. Give all your people the will to endure and minds totally committed to victory. Never allow us to leave the fray or turn from our people in need. Allow us to represent You boldly and bravely and fulfill, through victory, the truth of Your Holy Words. Amen."

"Amen," said the assembled.

Jack, who had silently listened to it all, gleaning the wisdom of older adults, wondered about Robbie and Sammie, who were mortal and gullible. He shuddered and knew he had to bring them under his care. It was here. War!

CHAPTER 15

On the second day of Satan's return, before sunrise, Peter and Grace had kayaked (not knowing the safety of the roads) downriver to the collection of holdings of their friends to explore the idea of moving there for the "safety in numbers" factor. They met Jack Burnell, their only mortal buddy, and toured the farmsteads. The settlement had strong defensive lines, a population skilled in warfare, and a cohesive social fabric. They decided to return to their acreage upriver to secure property and the buildings, install surveillance cameras, gather up food and clothing and any equipment that might have worth in the months ahead, and return to the holdings of their friends and family. Jack desired to accompany them, as he feared for their safety. It was cautious and prudent to assume the enemy was lurking. Furthermore, the commuter trolley had not been seen on its hourly runs, and this was unusual. They took the old, four-wheel-drive, steam-powered utility vehicle that had been Tom Sr.'s joy. Jack drove, moving into an early morning fog that clung to the river valley and would be dispersed by the heat of the sun.

Not more than half a mile from where they had turned off their stone country lane to head north on the main road, they found the commuter trolley overturned and burning along the roadside. Jack stopped the vehicle a distance from the scene; they remained in their seats. The three mortals born within the millennium looked at the overturned bus with astonishment and wonder. Accidents had rarely occurred in the millennium. Jack whispered, his caution seeming appropriate, "Last time I saw an overturned vehicle burning was on the corporation's logging roads in China. A mudslide had knocked it off the road, and a battery had sparked a fire."

Peter said, "Us, never. Better take a pistol, Jack." Peter reached into a satchel wedged between them. "Just a quick perimeter check. Maybe someone's been thrown out and is wounded."

All quietly thought, *Or dead.*

Grace whispered, "I'll let Tuck know." Grace exited and stood behind their vehicle as she made the call. She wanted room to run, if necessary. Peter took a powder pistol and handed another to Jack. They exited; Jack threw his ruck upon his back—packed for combat and rescue. John and Diana, Andy, and Robin had decided to report for work in Harrisburg, even though Andy's emergency-management-team communications were not working, nor was Robin's bank number. Tuck had decided to remain at the holdings of his friends, with his mother, as his work schedule was flexible and the river accessible for any work-related calls. Emily and Dan Jr. had decided to transport to Dan's workplace in Washington, DC, for instructions and to pick up personal items.

The two men approached the bus, Pete to the left, Jack to the right. Jack raised his hand. They both could hear a sparking within the engine compartment and see and smell burning seat padding and the acrid-scented flames and smoke. The silence surrounding the bus held an eerie quality. Clearly, the raised hand meant wait. Pete's ears and eyes scanned the narrow band of woods to his left. The distant woods to his right, well back from the road, could just as likely hold an ambushing party. He had had training on the range of the old-time cartridge assault rifle as well as other firearms. Jack remembered his training under John and Diana to listen, surveil for movement or shapes in the surrounding area. An ambush would have already occurred—the fog had placed then in a vulnerable position; luckily, there was no one to capitalize on their failure to back away and hide. Jack whispered, "Stay close."

Jack crossed over Pete's projected path and moved directly into the tree line twenty feet from the road. Pete moved to the right and took Jack's old position. A scout or ambusher would be in the nearest trees for concealment. They moved north, searching the weeds between road and tree line. There was the body of the driver, the dark-blue uniform pulsed in their eyes. The body was facedown. The weeds had been crushed around the body—someone had looked upon his kill, maybe more than one person. Jack spoke, still in a whisper. "Pull the rope out of the outside right compartment of my ruck. Let's check for a booby trap."

Pete nodded his head, opened the compartment, unwound the tightly coiled rope. Jack gingerly tied an end upon the man's belt. They moved back into the woods and signaled Grace to get down. She understood. The rope was tugged hard, and just as Jack was pulling with both hands, a resounding whoomph sounded, the body lifting four feet from the earth. Shrapnel whizzed through the air and black, dense smoke and sod rose. Jack had fallen back to the ground once the rope lost tension.

"Who would have thought it?" Pete declared resolutely, as he knew the world had changed dramatically. He knew this change in the world would demand change in them. He extended his hand to Jack. This was no accident upon the road; it was murder! Murder hadn't been seen in a thousand years. Such men and women had been removed by a Holy God, who knew the thoughts of humanity. Nothing was hidden from Him, as the world was His kingdom and He had promised a thousand-year reign of peace. He had removed murderers before they could act. This mortal trolley man was now in paradise or Hades. Pete pulled Jack to his feet. Those who killed the man soon—very soon—would know the agony of eternal hell.

Grace approached her men. "Big noise. Wonder if our foes heard."

"They may be setting up an ambush farther up the road for us," said Jack.

"We can move to the unimproved river trail…the vehicle should have no problems," Pete's tone was pleased with his assessment.

"More places for ambush…crossing creeks and brooks, the trees thick, and the fog even thicker close to the water," Jack offered as a counterpoint.

Grace thought as she spoke. "Any evidence of people on the bus, commuters?" She moved quickly to the bus, as Pete trailed, and saw no suitcases or apparel left behind. She did not wish to leave potential prisoners or wounded people.

Pete spoke reflectively, calmly. "We can take Tuck's boat up the river. Load our gear in his boat and fill our own boat, if needed."

"Yeah, you're right. We don't need to be heroes, sneak up the river, a westerly route, hide behind the islands," said Jack.

"You already are a hero in our eyes," said Grace. "You took the wood line, where there was the most danger." They moved quickly to their vehicle, alert, eyes searching. In silence, they rode back to Beulah Land, thinking of the dead man, who, if found worthy, would soon be in his temporary body in paradise, and within months would be back on Earth experiencing earthly life in a new way. They thought of the unsaved who had killed him. They were more than stupid men; they were cruel men. Were these murderers, who had never seen a man killed by violence, shocked at their own evil? Were any of the killers suffering remorse? Pete, Grace, Jack could scarcely comprehend the scene they had witnessed. Christ had certainly pinned the right name to Satan—*the deceiver*. His kingdom was now upon Earth, and their duty was clearly to tramp it out, with violence and death as their weapons.

***

Returning to Tom's estate, they saw Andy, John, and Diana in full exoskeleton armor, which they hadn't known existed, upon air platforms. The platforms had their emergency systems packed away, and full military systems were apparent, bristling with gun barrels and loaded with ammo feeds and containers. The existence of gun systems was a shock to Pete, Grace, and Jack. They noticed Andy, John, and Diana carried powder assault rifles. Where were the lasers?

"What's up, Andy?" Pete said in surprise, his senses heightened.

"Tuck relayed the commuter-trolley incident by Morse code—a system so obsolete the enemy was likely unaware. Harrisburg and the suburbs are quiet. Most people remained at home, and the few who went to work returned home. With the internet jumbled, it's the best place for them. No malcontents on the street. We called up the auxiliary police forces to be a presence on the streets, especially by food stores. The media is pushing the idea of famine to create panic. I am arresting the liars. We're thinking this commuter killing is the beginning of an elaborate plan. Draw Dauphin County's emergency-response team to the hinterlands and wipe them out. That three or four of the top law-enforcement people—me, John, Pete, and even Dan—live in this area is an added plus to the enemy. Assures them of at least getting the leaders and thinkers in their first attack."

"Do you need us?" asked Jack. He now regretted not entering law enforcement. Maintaining highways and communication sites had paid well. He had planned to marry and raise kids, and a steady daytime job seemed important for the routine of raising children. A wife had not come his way.

"We want to help," volunteered Grace.

"Remain here in reserve, be ready. I have other officers in the area of the commuter ambush, transporting as lone operatives, armed with our few laser rifles. I also have a quick-reaction team of three more air platforms—armed—waiting on top of the mountain." Andy reached into a box upon his vehicle. "Come here."

Jack, Peter, Grace moved quickly to Andy. "These are smoke grenades—the black-colored ones are black smoke for hiding your movements." He pulled out red grenades. "These are for stunning and disrupting—loud sound, tear gas. You may be called for extraction purposes only."

Jack absorbed the information and volunteered a guess. "Do you think they want your weapons and machines more than they want you?"

"It's all the same," said Andy. "I'm sure that is part of the calculation. Good thinking on your part. Your mind is fully engaged."

The communications receiver on Andy's chest sounded a low grunt that vibrated through his skin. He answered, "Alpha 1," and listened in his earbud. He spoke. "Move all snipers to the coordinate. Snipers, engage for individual targeting *only* if combatants are identified. I repeat, *only if they are hostile combatants*. Mobile team remains in overwatch."

Andy surveyed his three friends. "We found a cluster of hostiles at the base of the mountain." Andy pointed at the swirling fog on the ridge top, then moved his hand north and down to give an approximate location. "Excuse me for a minute." Andy walked away slowly, immersed in thought. He had been raised as a child to think like a warrior; to think of the enemy as an individual warrior, and then as collections of two or three warriors, and then as groups of as many as the fingers on both hands, then as a band of warriors—fingers and toes—and then as a tribe. Different tactics for different numbers—combinations of strategies, wiles, ambushes, and full assaults through the fields, meadows, woodlands of Pennsylvania. A thousand years of peace had passed, and the knowledge was as vibrant and living as the day he left Earth in the year of his Lord 1765. What if the figures were hostages, not hostiles; and his men fired upon them, killing or wounding them? Then the ambush became a rescue mission. What if during the rescue mission, his men were attacked? He knew there were rock ledges and slit openings to caves that could hide men. He had taken bears from those dens during winters of starvation. Not mothers with cubs—single male bears. He remembered the rejoicing, the fat meat, barely roasted, sliding down, sprinkled with salt bartered in trade from a tribe further west.

This hostage ploy had been used by the Shawnees on the great Ohio River to lure unsuspecting river travelers from their boats, into shore and death. The lure, a white captive, coerced or adopted into the new culture, calling out to the boats for help. Today, it could be mortals of the rebellion pretending to be hostages, or lost, fleeing civilians.

He spoke into his mic. "This is Alpha 1. What is the status of the snipers?"

"They report these may be dispossessed friendlies."

"All forces hold. Remain in position, and do not fire. Caves in the area may be hiding combatants; hostages may be acting as friendlies. Bait to the trap."

Andy moved back to his friends. "Anyone ever explore the base of the mountain?"

Jack raised his hand. "My brothers and I did, back when we had free time on our hands."

"Did you see the rock outcrops, the slit openings?"

"Yeah. In some, you could hear running water."

"The enemy forces may be waiting, hiding there in ambush." Andy thought through possible plans. In a few months, Satan would be no more, and the second resurrection would have occurred. His air platforms could simply kill everyone, whether satanic forces or hostages or fleeing mortals. The old adage, "Kill them all and let God sort them out," had some merit, but though it was viable, it showed no consideration for the individual lives involved. He could wait for any forces within the caves to come out and do the same to them—ambush them.

Second option: His men could announce to the group of people that they were surrounded and order them to throw off their packs and step away from their equipment. His forces would need to approach and search the people as a second group of his men approached the caves from another direction. The resurrected, like himself, could not die; but if a bullet caught them while in the material body, a severe disruption in their being could take place before they could self-heal and participate. Head shots would lead to the most severe disruptions.

In the end, it was an easy call. Send Pete, John, Diana to the band of people at the base of the mountain. Pete knew how to pick out the Satan gang signs in dress, deportment, and language. He may even recognize individuals from his extensive undercover years. Pete's squad could simply retreat, and the air platforms perched on the mountaintop could take over, if the unknown group were all hostiles. In the meantime, the air platform with Jack attached could overwatch the cave area.

"Pete, John, and Diana, foot patrol into the camp. I'll accompany," said Andy as he studied Jack's face. Jack was hungry to belong, to see action. Andy addressed Jack. "Jack, you are to deploy with the air platforms that will overlook the cave area. Keep the enemy in the caves. Your platform will pick you up here. Be ready."

Grace said nothing. She knew it was best that she remained behind; Pete would be distracted by her presence, and she had no combat experience. She would remain and pray for them. Even as she knew God went with them, she worried. She had never worried in her life—a strange sensation, attempting to produce scenarios that she could not control, and her Lord could not foresee. She could not think of a time when the Lord had been found wanting, and He had never lost His omniscience, and so she emptied her mind of that emotion called worry.

***

As planned, Pete was in the lead, under the forest canopy, as they came into the vision of the gathered refugees, men and women, some teenagers, some middle-aged and older. Pete attempted to run his eyes over the group unobtrusively. He scanned clothing—no tells, just average, outdoor dress. But there were no children—this seemed unlikely if they had been dispossessed by the rebellious. No tells in hair style. He was worried; one woman seemed to be watching his eyes, and fear was building on her countenance—a tightening smile, eyebrows rising. Pete spoke loudly, looking directly at the woman. "Greetings, roaming people of the woods." His words seemed innocent, yet he had embedded terms the rebellious used: "roaming," in their parlance, signified discontent and searching, as the Christ was not enough for them. The word "people" followed by a description of nature—"woods"—was code. For Christians, *people of Christ*, *people of the Church* were common titles. The rebellious always mocked these greetings by using some earthly created thing as the object of people. As for "woods," the rebellious hungrily worshipped God's creation, although they rejected His authorship. Spirits, natures, forces lived in and gave meaning to the earth.

His phrases elicited no comment, no emotion in facial features. The gathering did not move. He came near to the woman; her face beamed blankly at him. John, behind Pete to his right and slightly higher on the sloping ground, was running his eyes through the gathered twenty-plus people. None had made a move to gather by the new arrivals; this told him they were the enemy. No citizen of Christ's empire had feared authority or others for the last thousand years. These people before him had been trained to keep their space for survivability when the rounds began zinging through the air. John noticed the woman's blank stare and saw the slow motion of facial muscles turning the corners of the mouth into a smile. She was laughing in joy at her own bravado and because her motives were invisible to the enemy before her. Evidently, Pete caught the smile and the failure to move, because he brought his left hand behind his back in a fist. The signal of danger. Diana casually walked higher on the slope than John, and Andy moved to Pete's left, down the slope. They were increasing their field of fire.

A movement came from within the crowd—something coming out of a jacket. The band of four reacted, and the silent, unmoving forms of the masquerade suddenly danced to the chatter of mechanical fire. The dancers belatedly pulled hidden weapons from their clothing, even as their arms, legs, heads separated from their bodies. Down the slope, farther north of this scene, the air platform's rapid-fire guns began the long unzipping of rounds against flesh, bone, ground, stone, and forest.

Stillness. The band of four walked through the downed bodies, searching for a living being. Pete had barely fired a shot from his pistol. These sensations were all new to him, only new to him—death, the smell of blood, and opened bodies. He saw a photo in the scattered debris near a woman's corpse. He picked it up—the photo of a man in his twenties. He handed it to Diana, and Diana handed it to John. Diana seemed only slightly moved by the chopped up corpses, though it was her first group combat. John smiled at the photo and said, "Andreas Hahn. Mat's old friend. Pete knows him. Must have had a girlfriend in this group."

Pete heard and answered, "Maybe he's in this group." Pete searched the male faces with diligence, as did the others.

"All units report. Alpha 1 has neutralized the threat," Andy said in a calm voice.

In a businesslike tone, a voice answered back. "Alpha 2 is in control. Possible survivors in caves, but entrances sealed."

Another voice said, "Alpha 3 reports two large enemy forces moving to sounds of battle from the north and from the east. Expect contact in minutes."

In a monotone voice, Andy said, "All units regroup at predesignated coordinate." He wasn't worried about survivors within the caves. They'd had their bells rung and would be worthless on the offensive. "Snipers, maintain positions if regrouping places you in danger. Fire only in self-defense." Andy clenched his teeth. He had seen this before, too, in the forest wars—an enemy with overpowering numbers dangling the temptation of victory before its victim's eyes. Must be high-quality fighters to be so stealthy and to cover ground so quickly. He had seen this near Fort Ticonderoga, in the years of his prime: marauding bands of hundreds swooping silently from the dark forest depths upon scouting squads of American citizen-soldiers.

He attempted communications with headquarters in Harrisburg; but as he silently predicted, no contact. Peter was now a hindrance, slowing the movement of his resurrected friends. The three of them could have transported out. Andy suspected, because of the number of enemies involved, Satan's men either wanted the air platforms for themselves or they wanted the air platforms destroyed. The platforms had already returned to Tom Burnell's place; they were parked in partially hidden, dug-in positions consisting of a center and flanks—a half circle, the river at their backs. He would keep the platforms silent until an enemy rush of the homestead. Then, their firepower would be effective. To send them into the air was to invite small-arms fire, rocket attacks through the canopy. He was certain the enemy had rockets. The platforms had no antimissile capabilities, other than wasting what few gun rounds they possessed. Once the platforms had used their ammunition, they would creep down to the river and head south, skimming the river to Harrisburg. Pete, Grace, Jack, and any other mortals could leave with them. Then all the resurrected forces left behind would become marauding snipers, able to disappear and transport. Where would the enemy go? To Harrisburg—at least two days of walking, all the while being picked off. What if they seized a home and forted up? Again, they would be surrounded by an unseen enemy and killed at leisure.

Satan's troops had only one strategy that would work: a sudden, overwhelming rush of the homestead with all forces. If they had rockets, the rockets would be used. Victory or defeat in one assault.

***

"All these positions you and your brothers created years ago still have worth," said Andy approvingly to Jack, "but who could have foreseen air platforms?" He had spoken as he heaved a shovelful of dirt. The heavy digging had been accomplished with one of Tom's tractors attached to a front-end loader. Jack was cutting up the heavy sod with an edging shovel. The sod rectangles were to cover the exposed dirt mounds created. Andy continued talking. "Remember, the platforms will fire till ammo is gone, then move back to the river, where you, Pete, Grace, and Leaf will board and exit with any severely wounded."

“I would like to stay,” Jack stated resolutely.

“You can’t disappear and transport like the rest of us. You’ve done well. There’s more fighting ahead; you’ll get your share. I need the three of you to find out what’s happening in the city—fighting might be occurring there now. Report back to me, unless communications allow a message. They’ve already caught onto my use of Morse code with headquarters.”

Jack listened and understood; leaving was best for all. “I will leave with the others,” Jack’s voice was flat.

Andy smiled benignly. Jack had displayed maturity; he had denied himself for the good of the many. Andy winked at Jack, and Jack felt the respect and value Andy had given him.

***

The fog was slowly lifting. The white light was shining above the fog. A flock of geese flew inland, low from the river, searching for safe fields to forage. Squirrels hopped on the dewy grass of the surrounding lawns, searching for nuts, and birds sang and chased, harassing the squirrels. A deep voice, hugging the ground, sounded through cupped hands. “They’re coming.” Digging stopped, soldiers jumped behind barricades and into trenches.

The enemy burst from the thick band of trees on the mountain slope, into the pasture land that ran along the far side of the main, north–south, two-lane highway. The enemy numbered into the hundreds, dressed in camo greens and browns, all armed, moving in platoons. Pete and Jack were shocked by the numbers, the speed and seeming coordination of the attack. The resurrected veterans clearly were not dismayed or frightened, noted Jack and Pete. Satan’s forces had already crossed the highway, flowed down the road embankment into trees, and emerged, running at a sprint across the wet grass up the ever-rising grade to Tom’s farmstead structures. Incendiary devices dropped from the sky onto the structures of the farmstead, their origin unknown. They were crude devices of no real military value but to create havoc. Sporadic fire came from the Christian forces, carefully picking targets—the most forward of the charging enemy. Jack and Pete were agitated by the speed of the attack. There was no time to carefully plan or even to think.

Then, the charging forces, en masse and in an orderly fashion, dropped to the ground and began crawling on all fours; they gained ground as the opposing riflemen lost the bead on their targets. From the base of the mountain a quarter mile away, where thick woodlands broke apart on grazing land, rockets came, streaking toward the Christian lines. The enemy rose immediately after the rockets had passed and ran toward their Christian foes as the rockets exploded upon the fortifications. The deception had gained fifty yards and saved casualties. Men, equipment, machinery, earth flew into the air. The guns of the air platforms, seeing the movement on the mountain slope, had switched rate of fire to full automatic. Gray clouds of gases escaped from the guns. The smell and smoke hung in the air. The distant mountain slope spewed up ground, equipment, body parts, tree limbs, bark. Whole trees fell. The sound overwhelmed all other sounds.

The enemy met the defenders' lines almost immediately after the rocket barrage. The line was breached. The center gun had exhausted all targets and was moving back to the river, with Pete, Grace, Jack, and Leaf cautiously moving behind. The flanking guns embedded in the woods that ran the length of the riverbank did not stop until the ammunition was gone. The retreating air platform saw enemy troops wading in the river and up the bank; the platform's guns riddled the ranks of the attacking forces. The waters of the river erupted in geysers of great height from the downward trajectory of the rounds. Andy's flanks had fallen back into one mass; a counterattack was needed. The woods had been chopped down to knee height, fifty yards into the once deeply forested riverbank. His men were veterans; some had fought with Cromwell and some against; some had fought Native Americans and the British in two wars; one man had been at Chapultepec; many were Civil War veterans. On through history from every previous conflict, soldiers fought.

Andy rose to full height and stood as if time had stopped. "Hand to hand! For Christ, our King!" he bellowed, his tone deadly serious, and his own words strengthened him, for he had dreamed of the day he would give back to his Lord, the Savior of his soul and his family's souls, the God who had redeemed them. He knew he could not die, nor any of his resurrected men. They could be taken out of effectiveness, could watch their bodies be hacked and shot, could feel the pain. They could lose the fray. They could know shame. They had to give the struggle all that they were. Jack and Pete were overwhelmed with emotion and found weapons—a steel bar, an axe. The resurrected fixed bayonets, grabbed combat knives, hatchets, axes, sickles, clubs of tree branches, rocks. In one rush, they went into the fallen trees and the chopped-up branches and sought the enemy. Quarter was given to those who begged and were unarmed; the remaining were killed.

***

Andy sat in the shade of one of the few undamaged trees on the riverbank. He saw the trees begin again at fifty yards, both north and south along the bank. His leaned up against the tree, feeling rivulets of sweat trickling down his face and chest. The day was hot; emotion and exertion had increased the natural heat. He saw a small tree frog, motionless, in the debris by his feet. How delicate and happy appeared the frog. They always looked happy—as if they possessed a grin and mirthful eyes. He was pleased with the outcome of the battle. The alacrity of the enemy forces amazed and puzzled him. To project such numbers and quality soldiers so soon after Satan's return spoke of planning. Why should it worry him? The enemy soldiers had trained, and they had lost. That they had trained was simply a warning to look deeper into his enemy's strategies, capabilities.

Pete and Grace sat quietly. Grace had dug positions, carried water, and run ammunition along the lines as Pete fought. They leaned against each other; backs supported by a landscape wall of mortarless stones. Their faces wore the tiredness of exertion and emotion. They sipped their drinks from kitchen coffee mugs, cold mint tea provided by Jack, as if it were medicine—except they savored every drop. Leaf, pitcher and cups in hand, was providing for all the fighters. One Revolutionary War soldier called her "Leafy Pitcher," as he laughed, in honor of a heroine of his time, Molly Pitcher. Jack and Tuck worked the kitchen, making coffee, providing juices, teas, fresh water, and platters of bread and sandwich meats. John and Diana had not rested; they were collecting bodies, fingerprints, DNA swabs, gathering weapons and ammunition strewn on the battlefield. They found restless men to help in their endeavors.

In time, John and Diana sat together on the same rock wall Pete and Grace were leaning against. John had handed Andy an old-fashioned slip of paper with a casualties report and weapons-collection figures. John and Diana both noticed the aura surrounding Pete and Grace—they were in a realm of shock, but the Comforter was upon them too. They had never seen violence—men killing men—had never seen blood flowing like water from a hose, had never seen pieces of human flesh appearing like butchered farm animals. Pete had never purposely tried to kill a living human being. Around them, the resurrected acted as if this were normal and appeared happy in this time of killing. Pete believed he killed two, with his pistol, in the initial slaughter of the of the first band. In the battle for the settlement, others, perhaps ten, had died because of his actions with pistol and ax.

Diana spoke. "The Comforter is upon you. He will teach you. I know it's rough and at complete odds with what we know is the way life should be."

John added, "You have witnessed the ultimate deception of Satan. He convinced these rebels that the taking of lives was necessary and even good—good to crush Christ and the perfect harmony of a loving God. For the past thousand years, you mortals knew only goodness. Mankind's ugliness was hidden from you—murdering, hateful people were removed before they could act. You understood that those who had rebellious attitudes or misunderstood God's intent could be brought back by conversation, by debate and arguments with words, and that everyone would surely accept the truth. Now, you face reality: some people don't want the truth, will never follow truth, will never allow the Lord within them. The only recourse that remains is death—eternal death."

Pete spoke. "Intellectually, spiritually, Grace and I both knew these truths you talk of. But seeing it, tasting, smelling, feeling it emotionally and physically certainly is a blow."

"We know. We were once mortals in the kingdom of Satan. Truly, the resurrected understand," said Diana.

Andy had followed the conversation. He saw no need to enter. John had given his report on paper because communications networks, computers systems were still not working. John had taken fingerprints and genetic swabs of all the enemy dead—it would be good to know where these fighters had originated. No one recognized them. Autopsies would be performed for evidence of gang signs, tattoos, and hair braids, and to learn if drugs were a part of their combat readiness. Maybe that information would cause the five wounded and semiconscious prisoners to see the light of Christ's presence and recant, saving further death. The five were on their way to Harrisburg hospitals, along with five wounded mortals he did not know were part of his forces. His forces had ten resurrected with ghastly wounds that would heal themselves in time. Three mortals had died and were certainly in paradise at this moment.

Jack appeared with a huge pitcher of mint tea, followed by Tuck with a food tray, offered to all. Jack sat among his friends; the combat adrenaline was decreasing noticeably. Tuck sat, he had a contented mind and body. He had, in a small way, righted the injustice done to him and his brother. The men he had killed were Satan's men; all were the same—they had the same daddy, and all shared the guilt of each other, even if separated by a thousand years or more. Tuck spoke. "So what did they gain?"

Andy answered. "Because they lost, they gained nothing, perhaps, but time—and diverting us from some other goal they are working on. I'm sure possessing or destroying the air platforms was their immediate goal."

Grace said, "Maybe when Dan returns today, we'll know more. He seems to be connected with the grand strategy area of operations."

"Maybe," said Tuck.

Andy studied his son's demeanor. His Tuck was happy, contented; he had had the chance to fight those bullies who had once tormented him. Satan's people—the same bloodlines, the same evil thoughts. Any one of those who died today would have found great delight in tormenting a crippled little boy—or the boy's friend, Christ upon the cross.

Andy felt a need to honor John's previous insights of days ago. "John was correct about Satan's strategy. He must move fast. He needs to get all his people to the Middle East as soon as possible to overwhelm and conquer Jerusalem and our Christ who reigns. Just like today, overwhelm us before we have time to react."

"Amen," spoke the gathered, who then settled into reflective quiet.

Grace was the first to break the silence. "Jack, want to return with us to the old Johnson place? John is hosting," said she teasingly, as she didn't know whether John had decided to leave his mountaintop perch. He had first rights to the river home, as brother to Tim; Pete, the great-grandson, had a lesser claim.

"My pleasure," offered John.

"We'd feel better with company," Diana said. "The mountaintop home is too exposed. We will eat supper by the river, in a nondestroyed environment, and see Dan and Emily return. Andy and Leaf, you're invited too, and Tuck."

Grace spoke. "Maybe tomorrow, Tuck can take Pete and me upriver to our home for supplies and clothes."

"That was today's plan, wasn't it?" Pete asked.

Jack entered the conversation. "Hard to remember. This day seems like a week. And yes, I'll be at the Johnsons' with John's nod."

John nodded his head. "Glad to have you."

Jack fell back into his silence. He had killed men; it had happened fast, instinctually; he felt no guilt, just a sadness for the unsaved dead. He held onto the lingering feeling of thankfulness—for surviving, for belonging to the Lord, for serving the right cause. Even though he had given such inconsequential service to the kingdom of God, he felt a deep satisfaction.

CHAPTER 16

Andreas Hahn awoke, noticed the gray paint on the cinder-block walls was the same paint on the low, cement ceiling. The scent of coffee and the sound of percolation were in the air. His arm was tingling; it had fallen over the side of the cot during his sleep. He sat up, began rubbing the arm back to life. Others were waking, putting on their black clothes, visiting the long table where the coffee perked and doughnuts, muffins, even pancakes could be had for breakfast. A far wall had computer operators, sitting at a long desk, staring at their screens. They surveilled the streets, searching for targets of opportunity—helpless citizens or motor vehicles. The narrow, rectangular windows were covered up, save one, where he could see the feet and legs (up to the knees) of pedestrians on the city street above. This early, no feet were seen. The weather appeared to be good; the street was dark, due to surrounding high buildings blocking sunlight till the afternoon. Another day to cause mayhem, feel excitement, draw life from the discomfort and fear emanating from the "good" people of the city.

He liked the people around him—his terror platoon; the women were willing to give sexual favors, and the males, his buddies, all strove to outdo each other in decadence and violence. They were loyal to each other and countless times had saved each other from imprisonment; all of them had his back, as the saying went. The camaraderie was excellent; they had skills—were trained fighters with martial arts experience and personal weapons knowledge; high school, college, semipro, and professional athletes were among them. Holding his own with athletes, professional fighters, made him feel powerful and elite. In time, he would surpass them all and be a leader. He just had to hide his sexual prowess or jealousies would destroy him.

The food deliveries came on time; the coffee was always fresh; any pharmaceutical he needed, available. The goals were clear-cut and achievable. They had a cause—the destruction of the old system—just because it was the old system and stifled a person's impulses and freedom, and someone had to pay for that. That was justice.

"Hahn, be ready in ten minutes. We're going to break some wills, make some people cringe, embarrass and belittle to tears and shock." His captain, by the coffee percolators, had spoken. He had used that phrase every morning for the past seven days, and those words captured the essence of their mission.

"Yes, sir." Andreas hurried his dressing, wolfed down two cinnamon croissants (real cinnamon being scarce with world trade interrupted), and gulped a cream-and-sugar coffee. He felt for the two sets of brass knuckles in his pockets, the weighted truncheon strapped to his forearm, the fixed-bladed dagger in his boots. A can of mace, he kept in his pants cargo pocket. He joined his platoon, forming at the side of the doorway and corridor leading up to the street. His body felt strong, and his mind alert. Life was good.

"Attention." The captain's deep voice addressed the platoon and echoed through the vast basement. "We will be headed for the Bureau of Rapid Response building, engaging targets of opportunity on either side of the street. Always move in your threes. No violence to children—yet. Women should be slapped, but words hurt them the most…*bitch, cunt.* Tell them what your pricks are going to do to them. Do not rip their clothes off; that is for the future.

"Preoccupy the so-called men with mass shovings, strikings, clothing tearing and removal, paint splashing, mace sprayings. Embarrass, demean, degrade them. If there is no one on the streets, try doors. Enter quickly and leave as quickly. We need to keep a momentum, a pace. All face masks on. Move out." The captain's tone ended satisfied, expectant, proud of his platoon.

The excitement mounted with each step upward. They stomped hard on the cement steps. Only the right foot stepped up. They created a cadence; a deep voice counted the steps. On the first day, there had been fear mixed with excitement, but hour after hour, confidence grew. No one could withstand the pack—not even three or four men. The overwhelming numbers always won, caused the hectored to retreat. Sometimes the victims were able to resist till police arrived, and then the pack would break apart and regather. The door was pushed open, the entire platoon shouted deeply, and they were on the streets.

A lone man in his thirties came from a side street, saw the pack, and began to run. They pursued, the designated sprinters racing ahead. The man outran the initial sprinters, but then another group, jogging behind, began sprinting as their comrades were waning. The second group of sprinters caught him, twisting and turning him as they cut and tore his clothes from his body. They were about to paint him when two men came from the building where the man had stopped. They swung baseball bats at the pack, and the man stumbled into their building.

The attacking civilians were maced in the eyes. One man, blinded, was grabbed by the ankle. He fell backward, his skull hitting the concrete; he lost consciousness. Bravely, the last man remained, swinging his bat. The man who had escaped came out of the building with a large, mace-filled cylinder. An iron bar was thrown at his head; it clipped his skull, he faltered. They were upon him, stripping him and snapping pictures with their phones. The pictures would become posters, hung and secured along the city streets. Somehow, he managed to unleash the high-pressure mace within the cannister. The pack backed away.

The captain approached in a run. "Move on to the Bureau of Rapid Response! Now!" The pack obeyed.

***

Pete stared out the third-floor windows of Andy's office in the Bureau of Rapid Response in downtown Harrisburg. One week had passed since the firefight on the mountain. It was clear, looking out the windows, what the greater objective of Satan's forces had been. Every citizen of Pennsylvania west of Harrisburg seemed to have arrived in the city, and particularly at the international airport. The migration had been sparked by false rumors of starvation due to supply-chain issues with food, marauding bands of criminally minded citizens, medical personnel being transferred to population centers. The rumors were a ruse to hide those feigning allegiance to God (but secretly people of Satan's persuasion) while they moved to an international airport, such as Harrisburg's, or a port city. Many continued on to Philadelphia, a major hub of trans-Atlantic travel by air and sea. The Middle East and Israel was the true destination. Among the migrants were confused and anxious believers who professed Christ. It seemed half the new arrivals into the city found shelter with family members or hosts of their own kind. The other half of the refugees had tents and flimsy shelters on streets, under bridges, or on athletic fields.

Most had no clear and verified reason for moving, just rumors. Confusion had become a reality. The stores were empty, as people had overbought and horded. Locals donated or sold foodstuffs from their holdings. Some charged high prices, and some were robbed as well. The black clothing, the chosen street wear of the common citizens of Satan's legions, outnumbered police, national guard, police reservists, conservation officers, federal investigative officers. Every county in the United States had been isolated, via internet and transportation services, and without the necessary knowledge or infrastructure to reorganize. Communications had not been restored. The internet specialized in falsehoods and slander of godly citizens. The electrascreen specialized in pornographic programming featuring high-status citizens (created by computer magic) and scenes of the vilest street violence.

No one wished to be on the streets. Impromptu sexual orgies or rapes were reported among the black-clothed citizens but had yet to be attempted upon a Christian. The black-clothed men and women blocked access to food stores and pharmacies. Stripping the clothes from Christians was common, as was capturing the event on phones for electrascreen viewings. The resurrected were hectored and harassed by mobs with reported photos of their bodies prior to resurrection. Women were being called whores and men, cowards as they were punched, prodded, soaked in water or urine. Feces was smeared on the unknowing Christian, as well as paints, oils. Embarrassment and ridicule were the weapons of the ungodly. Police patrols struggled to keep order, and mortals died every day—both the good and the evil.

Pete just shook his head in amazement and shock. He learned from Dan that the great Tribulation had had less social unrest simply because everyone was starving—hate took energy that no one had; a world ravaged by famines, quakes, and mass deaths left few to cause trouble. Although rape and sodomy had remained popular crimes in those times, none of those factors, except a scarcity of food, was present now. The people of the flesh, Satan's legions, were enlivened with hate and supposed superiority. Any Christian could tell who belonged to Satan just by the arrogant gleam in their eyes. Both Pete and John noticed in Satan's people a joy, a delight that had characteristic elements of sexual arousal. He knew what the biblical term "pride of life" truly meant. They just couldn't let go of their beings of perverse fantasy and domination. As someone noted, their god lived between their legs.

Satan's people directed their propaganda strategy upon the dormant procreative sexuality of the resurrected, though the resurrected had been and were clearly men and women, naturally living, thinking within the context of their genetic identity. They had been fathers and mothers, grandparents, great-grandparents; they loved children as God loved children. They had enjoyed marriage and the making of children. They were now portrayed as somehow dirty and unclean, foolish and weak, and their God, who denied human flesh—sex—was the greatest abomination of all. No thinking soul wanted eternal life if he or she couldn't have sex. What kind of a twisted God would make such a condition? Having sex forever was a right, not a privilege of a prescribed time.

The goodness and rightness of Christianity wavered on one sentence: "For in the resurrection they neither marry, nor are given in marriage, but are like angels in heaven" (Matt. 22:30). The military campaign against Jerusalem now became a protest march, a demonstration for eternal sexual rights. Christ would be petitioned. Supposed Christians left their faith in overwhelming numbers, many for the comforting theology of Islam, in which heaven was a sexual paradise. Satan had memorized the Koran and had it reproduced. (He had the Bible and all religious books and doctrines memorized.)

John and Diana had just entered the room and stood by the window, studying the empty streets for movement. Only the homeless camps had bodies moving on the streets. Pete stared over at his friends. "How quickly faith was abandoned."

John answered, "It was the same before the Rapture. The world *appeared* to have faith—never in God alone and His goodness, but a false faith, never tested. These mortals of the millennium had the true faith, the true character of God before them and within their minds, and they blindly mouthed the words, went to their church activities. They lived in their flesh and not the Spirit of the Lord. All it took was the presence of Satan and his demons to start the fire. I'm sure many now see their error but have too much fear to openly proclaim their doubts and desires to remain true to Christ."

Diana added, "It takes courage to fight against the overwhelming flood of the false world."

"That's why God freed Satan," said Pete.

John nodded. "Same story as the original story. He wants people not only to choose Him freely but to fight for the right of that choice."

Pete thought back to his combat experience. Pretty cheeky to walk into a group of hostile people who, at the time, he'd thought probably wanted to kill him. The Lord had given him the courage. No, he hadn't even believed death was a possibility. Although he knew that if he died, it would only be seconds before he entered paradise and only months before he walked Earth again, the thought of his flesh being ripped apart, his blood spilling to the earth could have paralyzed him with fear. The Spirit simply kept fear from surfacing into his conscious thoughts.

"Do the resurrected have fear of their flesh being mutilated?" Pete queried John.

John grunted a laugh. "I know I do. I don't want the hassle. I don't want to be removed from the fight when I could be helping others. I don't want a prolonged wait to return to full duty. But knowing life isn't ultimately over does instill a peace and calm, a steadiness the fearful don't have. They are in a rush, unless doped or drunk. That's why soldiers and athletes drank back in Andy's day. And even my day. Now, it's the pharmaceuticals."

"To slow the rush," Pete stated.

"An artificial means to achieve calm and purposeful action, yes," John said. "Many of our foe are under the influence."

***

Jack, Tuck, and his brother, Robin, came hurriedly into the room. They appeared agitated.

Andy, wearing his combat gear, burst into the office, striding purposely, his torso tightly aligning his hips and shoulders, his neck muscles bulging, his arms raised to his waist as if preparing to strike an enemy. He spoke loudly. "Just made a command decision, with info from Dan and Pete, which should have been made days ago, but I waited for consent from others, which never came. Today, we clear the streets of the ungodly. By whatever force it takes. Blood, gentlemen, blood will run! Because no retribution came to them for their insults, they grew bolder. They should have been crushed, ground into the dirt, the moment their depredations began. No compromise now. The homeless will be driven out of the city to a designated site. The food stores and pharmacies will be cleared of Satan's malingerers. Looters will be stopped by force. Anyone in black clothing will be detained and taken to an enclosed area, where they will be interrogated. No engaging in talk, no special privileges to any. All go. Verbal abuse, thrown objects, physical force can be met with lethal force. They will fear the God who made them!"

Andy strode to his interoffice phone, picked up the handset, and said, "Sound the sirens. All forces move." He looked at his gathered friends. The three days he had been distracted by the battle at the holdings had given a start to the street degradations. Then, a day to analyze the new problem and half a day to attempt to coordinate with a higher command. All the while being assaulted by pictures of his sons in their crippled state and taunts on his computer and on the streets. He had just viewed a simulated rape of Leaf. He had seen his law officers doused and tripped, pushed, shoved, beaten. John and Diana were strapping on protective gear from their lockers. With gear on, John unlocked their weapons from the wall rack. Diana found old military rifles, copies of bolt-action designs, and placed the weapons into the hands of Jack, Pete, and Robin.

Tuck had his service revolver. Andy spoke. "Stay near me. You are bodyguards, messengers, and fighters."

Down the three flights of stairs and onto the street, clogged with organized ranks of men on all four sides of the building. They moved. To the four corners of the city, down the center of the streets, they marched. Rescue and combat air-platforms hovered above, watching the movements of the masses. Civilians on the streets were swept up before the ranks; no one was allowed to fall behind. Whatever legitimate plans had been made by citizens that day were cancelled. Those who had homes were returning to those homes. Scuffles began to break out, curses spewed into the air; bottles, bricks, chunks of asphalt were thrown. Bullets were returned. The unruly, the slow to obey were subdued with force, cuffed and sometimes shackled, thrown onto stake-bed trucks, and chained.

***

Andreas, the leader of his platoon, ran at a trot, conserving energy and keeping his command from dissolving. Other platoons had coalesced on this main corridor to the Bureau of Rapid Response; they were behind Andreas. The captain, who seemed near the end of his stamina, had wisely slowed down to incorporate the trailing platoons. The captain saw the supermarket ahead on his left. He knew men were stationed there, and barricade rubble had been prepositioned. One of the black-clad of the supermarket contingent waved to the captain, called him over. "The major wants barricades erected. I'll show you the stockpiles. He wants the storefront barricaded and the street." The captain, worn, and with duties involving higher command and placement, yelled out, "Andreas Hahn!" Hahn was the most capable and savvy of his men; he would be put in charge.

***

The first supermarket Andy came upon was barricaded, the enemy stood behind the barricades and threw rocks, stones, arrows; crossbow bolts whizzed into the ranks of the auxiliary police and newly conscripted national guardsmen. The police snipers, with their few laser rifles, began the systematic killing of the enemy shooters. The air platform ahead warned of a massing of the enemy and a likely breakout attempt—not to flee but to target

Andy and his group of high-ranking men. Andy, in a clear voice, communicated into his mic, "Permission to fire."

The guns of the air platform made their zipping sound for ten seconds, a pile of bloody body parts formed, and the breakout never began.

Andreas ran for his life. He had watched the captain take rounds in the chest. Sergeants had been targeted and died, as they were initiators of actions. His platoon had been devastated by a burst from an air platform. He was incensed, enraged. It was open war now. He needed to get back to the dungeon hideout. They had weapons, cartridge arms hidden. His body felt exhilarated, he had good stamina, his youthful soccer training paying dividends. With the captain and the sergeants gone, advancement would be easy. He wanted a weapon badly. He wanted to kill.

When enemy snipers appeared in windows, snipers on air platforms ended their dreams of mayhem. The fleeing black-clad insurrectionists were shot as they ran. Buildings were set on fire, vehicles were pulsing smoke, corpses remained uncollected on the streets. High-rise apartment buildings were secured with hardening foam, until the streets were empty, and manpower was available for searches.

By the setting of the sun, the city streets were clear, the indigents were in their tent-city home, surrounded by impenetrable fencing, standing in lines for a hot meal. The black-clothed people, or those known to support an antiorthodox view, were in their own encampment, without tents, standing in lines for a bowl of soup and two pieces of bread. They would be interviewed through the night. The perpetrators of rapes, of strippings, of heaving liquids, of assaulting civilians and police personnel, were tried the same night. Those who were convicted of murder, rape, assaults were lined up before firing squads and sent to Hades. The God of justice gave His compassion, His love, to the victims of crime and the loved ones of the victims.

Order came to the city with force, as fear and respect returned to the minds of the ungodly. A will formed in the minds of the godly that was greater in power than the hate and the loathing of their enemies.

***

Emily, Dan, Jack, and Leaf sat under a spreading chestnut sapling. They were aware of the shade on their slightly damp skin, the soft, warm breeze carrying the scents of grass, flowering vines, flower beds. Jack's Beulah Land home had been restored to normalcy. The cutting of downed trees and limbs had been handled by Jack, Pete, Tuck, and Robin, who had returned from the city once the stabilization, the quashing of open anarchy, had been accomplished. Robin desired the hard manual labor; working in a bank had ruined his homestead physique and stamina, which further armed contention would test. Dan, too, had toiled in the forest debris field, clearing earnestly, before being pulled back to the city and to investigative intelligence work with Emily as his partner. Grace, who had kitchen duty that day, returned from the main house with pitchers of drinks. She said a silent prayer for Pete, who had gone back to the city to establish an undercover surveillance and information-gathering network. Dan would leave tomorrow to take Pete's place. She poured the desired drink for each guest, then sighed as she, too, sat. Two single-shot flintlock rifles and a cartridge pistol were stationed nearby.

Dan, who had purposely sat facing the east to view the main road and the open fields, spoke quietly. "Two men are coming down our road, almost to the dip where the creek passes through." All eyes moved to the location described.

"They're your brothers, Jack!" Emily's voice had risen in pitch from her surprise and happiness.

"Robbie and Sammie!" exclaimed Leaf.

Jack bounded to his feet and stared at the figures—did he need a weapon? He and his brothers hadn't parted as friends. He had told no one of this change in their relationship. He recognized their walks, Robbie with the smooth glide and Sammie with the little bob at the beginning of his stride when he extended heel upward before the push. Jack went toward them, empty handed; he was at peace. He had prayed for this moment. He began at a slow walk. He could see they were worn, they had lost weight, they appeared anxious. Worried that he would not wish to see them? Worried that he no longer loved them? But he did love them and would always love them. His walk became a jog.

He remembered that final argument many years ago, back in China, on the corporation's holdings, in his home. He had told them to live like Christian men, men who knew and loved Christ and obeyed Him. He had told them to stop their hateful assessments of people and see their good. He had told them to encourage people and nurture them, to bring out their best and treat them with respect. He had told them that women weren't objects for their pleasure, to be used and discarded. Climbing the ladder of success to live lazy and indulgent lives was not the purpose of life. He had reminded them they had been visited by Christ in the flesh that day by the river; the Holy Spirit had been given. He had cuffed both of his brothers hard, and they had struck back and then left in anger.

That day, he had left them behind permanently. He had realized that for years, they had consistently attempted to pull him from the narrow path. He would follow and obey Christ alone, if need be. He had and would always. Great-grandpa had said, *Love the lord your God with all your heart, soul, mind and strength and your neighbor as yourself.* That knowledge was the blessing of his life; while he lived it, finding the flowing strength in the vine called Jesus, he had peace. That he had never achieved wealth, position, or power, and not even a loving woman to give him worth and understanding, seemed of little importance to what he had: Christ within.

He was upon them, strong and healthy, and he saw them shrink back in their weakness and forlornness. He grabbed their faces in his rough, manual-labor hands and shook their heads till they bobbled on their necks; he hugged them and wept tears of joy. And they, in their exhaustion and bodily and spiritual starvation, clung to him. In thankfulness that their brother still loved them, they wept.

***

Andreas Hahn had moved quickly when he saw the foam hardening over the windows of the basement barracks and then over all doors and windows. He knew his forces needed to hide within the apartments above their basement headquarters. He found the occupancy data in the rental office, led the survivors to all the empty apartments in the building and assigned rooms. Then he backdated and added the new names to the occupancy list. He had organized a charity clothing drive within the building for dispossessed travelers. He had reclothed his ranks. The black clothes had been hidden. He had issued weapons and then had the weapons broken down into easily hidden parts. Afraid to contact higher command, suspecting a trap, he had decided to move his forces to the airport—or rather, to the wooded shore of the river right below the landing strips. He knew the area from a fishing trip with friends along that portion of the river. The land was uninhabited and rarely visited by hikers or shore fishermen—no one wished to camp or build in the area, due to the noise. The woods were a narrow band of wilderness whose trees even hid the runway workers from sight. Over the course of two weeks, he had dropped his people from a second-story window to the unlit streets of night. Satan's forces had temporarily cut off power to the electrical grid. The night he departed—the last man out—was the same day the building was searched by the enemy.

***

A transient and unstable pall settled over the city of Harrisburg and surrounding countryside. Communications with surrounding counties, states, or the nation were nonexistent. Dan made weekly trips to Washington, but little was learned. He transported, and on his last trips, he had been targeted with bullets and missiles. The resurrected citizens remained optimistic, with even a giddy confidence in God's overwhelming sovereignty. God's people were winning. The city, although tense, had a peace when citizens remained in their living quarters. All transients coming to the city had a proscribed route around the city to the tent city. A loyalty oath was administered to those who claimed Christ in their lives; those who renounced Him were sent to the international airport for a flight to a Middle Eastern country or loaded on buses and trains to Philadelphia and airports or ships for the same destination. Speed was of the essence; hand them a bag of foodstuffs and shove them aboard.

The rules agreed upon said a declaration of allegiance had to be heard by Christ's men and Satan's men. No Christian hostages could be taken overseas. In turn, none of Satan's people could be denied travel and sent to reeducation classes in Harrisburg. This was not a gentlemen's agreement, and big-bodied men with hidden weapons and not-so-hidden weapons were there to contest the choices made, only once. Overwhelming Christian forces of war-hardened, resurrected soldiers established physical and legal dominance and decided the issue.

Within the city, Pete and Dan's surveillance teams ferreted out the nonbelievers from the legally established residents and sent them to education classes for information and spirited verbal argument. No one was forced to believe, and if people wished it, they could join the many heading for the Middle East. In the countryside, Christians gathered in defensively strengthened, sturdy homes surrounded by barriers and stockades as roaming bands of Satan's men searched for wandering or weak bands of Christians to kidnap for the Middle East and war.

The resurrected soldiers, who had the ability of flight, of appearing and reappearing and passing through solid objects, roamed the woodlands and fields, corralling wandering bands of refugees to the main highways and to Harrisburg. Satan countered with his fallen angels, who had lost their ability to fly or dematerialize but nonetheless had well-tuned senses, strength, and hardiness. The Christian forces gathered into reactionary strike forces, when large bands of the enemy were located, and having airpower, were always overwhelmingly victorious. In the war of spirit beings, Christ's angels crushed the forces of fallen angels a day after the rebellion had begun.

Andy spent as little time at headquarters as possible. His first business of the day was to check on the combat readiness of his blocking units, those who shunted the arriving refugees around the city. He feared a hidden army in the mass that would overwhelm his forces and ravage the city. His second duty of the day was to make certain no one left for the Middle East who did not go voluntarily; he feared kidnapped Christians would be pressed into military service through extortion. He believed some of Satan's converts professed Christianity and were penetrating the city. His last concern was ensuring the food produced by the agricultural industry of the surrounding county poured into the greater metropolitan area. Price fixing had been necessary.

Pete and Dan spent most days at headquarters, directing the placement of surveillance cameras to form corridors of overlapping coverage. The two men began compiling a list of known and possible enemy agents, saboteurs, and soldiers. The enemy was identified by name through facial-recognition data that had been rescued from destruction by computer technicians and by agents on the streets and embedded within Satan's organizations. Emily had a skill in piecing together the fragments of people's lives, their interactions and associations seen on camera; and she partnered with Dan. Pete's long background in satanic organizations gave clarity and identified many players. Grace remained his helper, and like Emily, had a skill in identifying and deducing the everyday plans of the citizens of evil.

Andy's sons, Tuck and Robin, because of their size were stationed at the agreed-upon allegiance sites (along the corridor around the city and at terminal locations). Occasionally, Tuck assisted river patrols in routine work or rescue missions. Robin assisted in uncovering and destroying any banking schemes of the satanic forces. Leaf remained at the homesteads, tending gardens, cooking meals for all, and keeping her charges on their schedules of work in the city and duties on their off days.

Pete and Grace remained at the New Canaan homestead (Mat's land) and aided refugees with food on their free days. John and Diana remained at Tim's River View homestead and opened the home to Christian refugees. New Canaan became the new stockaded farmstead. Robbie, Jack, and Sammie rotated from a quick-reaction force in the city and county to stockade duty at the Johnson stockade, and they were coached and supported by John and Diana. Off duty, they continued with maintenance of the Beulah Land homestead.

***

Andreas Hahn lived in the woods, sleeping under plastic sheeting, with the ragtag survivors of his company. The captain was dead, and by vote, Andreas was the new captain. They trained in hand-to-hand combat and learned the use of the cartridge rifles in their possession. Stragglers were added to their numbers. Naïve women, who were gullible enough to love Andreas, found themselves passed down as perks to his men who showed leadership ability and influence. He knew that his position was known; satellites and air platforms with heat-signature devices could see through the night and the trees. As his men were out of the way and were never seen moving toward an objective, they were allowed to remain in stasis. Likely, the enemy believed they, too, just wished to depart for the Middle East.

CHAPTER 17

The mid-June evening was warm; later in the night and early morning, a jacket might be needed. The gathered neighbors, the dearest of friends, sat in darkness. A fire's smoke would mask the summer scents of flowers, shrubs, vines, the grasses of lawns. The looming mountain ridge to their east was a dark thing, delineated by the star-filled sky above. A fire would disturb the light breeze that caressed them; the fire would be seen from the north–south country road, where the commuter once traveled, uniting the once-numerous inhabitants of the Susquehanna River plain. When the breeze shifted, they could delight in the river smells of wetness, mud, weed beds, logjams of new and rotting stumps and branches. The bones and scales of rotting fish carcasses, the after-dinner remains of many a predator, added pungency. When the breeze shifted, the overwhelming sounds of insect life, of frogs, and nighthawks, tripled in intensity.

John and Diana had chosen this location on Jack's homestead for the view of the north–south road. Intelligence reports warned of something happening on July 4 in Harrisburg—something big, of great import to the cause of Satan's rebellion. Intelligence said Satan's people were on the move, collecting, gathering secretively, and headed somewhere. John, Diana, Jack, Robbie, and Sammie wore their combat gear; they were on home-guard duty. John and Diana carried laser rifles, the Burnell brothers were armed with cartridge rifles of a bolt-action model. Pete, Grace, Leaf, and her sons, Tuck and Robin, had the comfort of civilian wear. Pete and Grace were armed with cartridge pistols; Tuck, with a laser rifle; and Robin had a bolt-action cartridge rifle. Pete and Grace, Tuck and Robin savored their freedom and ease. Tomorrow, they had duty in Harrisburg, patrolling the streets.

The wind shushed in the trees. Bats aggressively worked the open sky above the fields. Leaf saw an owl swoop down from a massive oak onto the field. It was good to be with family, thought Grace, Diana, and Leaf. Leaf watched the owl pick and tear apart a baby rabbit. Leaf popped open the large container of homemade sugar cookies. All eyes went to the sound. No chocolate chips available anywhere—her first choice for a cookie. Chocolate had not been seen since Satan came to town. "I would have given you chocolate-chip cookies, but that rascal stopped me."

Diana laughed at the thought of Satan being a rascal. "You have a way with words, Leaf." Yes, what an insult to the deceiver to be seen as a weak disturber of the peace, an antics player instead of a killer.

"I was always known for my catchy phrases," Leaf deadpanned.

Grace and Diana and Pete all laughed, knowing Leaf was the most stoic person they knew—and the stingiest with words. John grunted in delight, and the Burnells shook their heads in wonder. Her self-aware humor was a treat.

Leaf passed the container on; to rise would create a silhouette to anyone on the road, watching. In the world she had been born into, she had learned of silhouettes as a four-year-old. John took a cookie as he watched the road. He had been absorbed in scenarios, always where he was, tactically—terrain, available firepower, probable threats. People were depending on him to make decisions that would keep them alive and further their cause. Diana, Robbie, Jack, and Sammie were attached to him. He considered Jack combat ready, based on past performances. Robbie and Sammie had only seen patrol duty in the city; they weren't afraid to tussle, but in the social context had yet to understand the subtle body postures, words, facial expressions that could forewarn of hostile intent. The player who shot first and accurately had the advantage. They had yet to face an environment of prolonged chaos, with bullets incessantly zipping by their ears. Perhaps there would be no prolonged chaos in the course of the hostilities.

John turned his head to them and spoke. "So, are you two newbies grounded in Christ? Still remember that day, when in the flesh, Jesus imparted the Spirit within you?" He couldn't teach them much about combat, as it was simple: keep your weapon aimed at a hostile target and shoot. He could remind them of Christ and of the Holy Spirit within them. He needed to know they were committed to the undertaking and would remain loyal when it might be easier to surrender.

"Sure," and "Yes sir," came two replies. Neither had surety in his tone.

John would not address the unsureness—what would be, would be—and Christ would win. He spoke. "I have a vibration-sensor alarm beam on the river trail north and west of us. I have antipersonnel mines placed. I have a surveillance camera there." John turned his wrist, pulled back his sleeve to reveal a three-by-five screen strapped on his arm. "I thought we might be hit first, before they roll down the north–south road with their main forces, bound for Harrisburg."

He looked over at Tuck, who had been listening, and spoke to him. "If that's the case, you might want to take Pete, Grace, and your brother and mother south to Harrisburg on your boat."

Tuck answered, "We could set up an ambush farther south."

"Or just notify our Halifax forces on your way to Harrisburg." John thought this the more prudent course.

Tuck was about to speak when John's wrist camera pulsed a quick red light. The camera showed men moving quickly, crouched, with weapons in hand. The timing of his talk seemed supernatural.

"Up we go, home guard. Hurry, hurry." John was already in the lead, watching time ticking from his stopwatch. At twenty seconds, he reached into his pocket, and explosions sounded through the still air. Hopefully, he had taken some motivation from the enemy with his antipersonnel devices. Trip wires no longer worked; scanning devices could detect straight lengths of any material or invisible beams. As he ran, his vision searched to his right and rear. Tuck's group of noncombatants moved cautiously toward Andy's farmstead to the north, keeping to a weedy, shrub-filled rivulet that ran north. Tuck's boat, their gear, was stashed in an outbuilding used for hand-tool storage.

Simultaneously, John saw movement on the main road. A column of wheeled vehicles, just emerging from the woodlands to the north, had inched into the open, treeless stretch of roadway and stopped. Perhaps they had received a report of the ambush along the river and feared the open stretch was mined. He needed them to speed south—he had counted on it. It was the smart thing to do. Not stop and help root out the resistance within the farmstead community. The column could easily annihilate his forces.

To his left, the Burnell brothers stretched out, in a jog, keeping combat distance, searching ahead. Diana was behind him, purposely lagging, watching their rear. The Burnell barn and garage offered cover before the dash over open ground to the large and sprawling home. They rested behind the barn for thirty seconds. They sprinted over the open ground. The sprint ended. Jack entered; he would clear the home. The main party would stay to the south side of the home, with Diana remaining at the corner to kill enemy forces exiting the home or coming to occupy the north side of the home. Jack exited at the riverside entrance as the squad met him there, and Diana was called forward.

John studied the river woods; no movement in the cleared area from the combat of almost two months ago. He looked north and saw the newly damaged and downed trees from the newly initiated antipersonnel mines. No movement. In a loud whisper, his orders came. "Down to the river. Watch both flanks and the river woods. Repressive grenades and five rounds of fire. Five and counting." They all knew the possible enemy forces to the south could be waiting for this move over the open lawn. Or could the enemy be to the north, recoiling from southward movement after the antipersonnel mines?

"Five, four, three, two…" Grenades were in hand, pins pulled. "One." Grenades arced ahead, and weapons were picked up and aimed even before the detonations. The bolt-action gunpowder rounds went out slowly. John and Diana stood and their lasers sent out an even stream of destruction. They thought they heard shallow whimpers and grunts within the downed trees and branches as they charged straight for the river. Rounds whizzed through their ranks from the north. No rounds came from the south. The enemy had recoiled and waited. The enemy had called for reinforcements from the road.

"Up the shore, quick time, crest the bank when you're even with them. Kill any way you can. Watch for Tuck and his people up top, moving north or coming to us." They all understood. He saw it in their eyes: they were playing out the same scenarios in their own minds. Everyone had a lucidity, no shock, no confusion.

***

Tuck and his group had moved north along the shrubby and high-grassed rivulet, moving between sightings of the main road strike force that was slowly adding to the fight centered on Tim's and Mat's homesteads, even as forces streamed south on the main road to Harrisburg. Tuck, Pete, Robin, Grace, and Leaf knew the situation was dire. The boat was on Tuck's farmstead, between Johnson land and his dad's holdings. They could easily be pulled into the fight when trying to reach it. Tuck believed they could possibly add their forces to John's forces, but they would need to fight their way in, and then what? They could fight, and the resurrected could disappear, leaving the mortals, Pete, Grace, and the Burnell brothers, to surrender. Surrender to be killed or tortured or to be treated humanely? No humane treatment by Satan's men. Or could the resurrected remain hidden and kill the mortal captors? These scenarios could be avoided by simply moving south, away from the fight—if they could secure his boat and make it to the river's edge. Attach the water-propulsion unit to the boat, place Pete and Grace and Leaf and Robin within, and watch them disappear into the river mist. Then he would go to the fight raging.

Tuck spoke to his crouching, tightly bunched group, hiding behind a rotting tree trunk. "I'll get the propulsion unit out of the garage. Just wait here." He bolted; they would quickly piece together his plan. The run to the building through the open field seemed like an eternity. Twice, he fell to the ground at the passing of enemy units on the not-too-distant dirt road to the river. He grabbed the lightweight, plastic propulsion unit. The battery had been checked earlier in the day. The other supplies would remain; too much weight and no time.

He caught a break on his trip back over the exposed ground; no enemy units seen on the road. The firing was intense by the river, and he wondered if the Burnell brothers were already wounded or dead. He called to his group, "Follow me. Hurry." He did not break his stride as he ran past them, headed back along the rivulet. He reached the outer eastern edge of his holdings, where his boat, covered by a camo tarp, sat in high weeds. The sound of firing to the north had decreased in volume. He heard no sound, saw no movement to the south on his dad's or the Burnell holdings, though he suspected enemy units were likely positioned in the vicinity, as another road connected the main road to Jack's Beulah Land.

He was within a crease of two swales, darkness; the earth swales absorbed sound, the group made for the boat in the weeds. Tuck pulled out an old, wooden, flat-bottomed boat from under the camo tarp. Robin flipped the boat deftly to force water from the floor, grabbed the motor from Tuck's hands, and began attaching the motor to the stern. Tuck quickly attached the water-intake and -expulsion hoses. Tuck stated, "I'll take the front. Pete and Robin, take the rear. Mom, Grace, carry our weapons and flank us, one on each side. Throw your lose gear and packs into the boat." He saw the gear going in. "Let's go."

***

The river's edge was upon them, and the men's forearms and hands ached with pain; they had not stopped in their hurried walk. They had held the boat waist high to give freedom of movement and speed to their strides. They had seen no activity on the river trail. On the bank, Tuck had almost fallen when momentum had gotten ahead of him, as Pete and Robin had forgotten to pull back against the force of gravity on the boat's downward trajectory. The boat was slipped into the water. Tuck flicked the battery switch to ON. The ON light lit. Tuck was about to speak; Robin felt his thoughts and grabbed his arm forcefully. "You go with them. You've gotta reach the protection of the island. That's two hundred yards of open water! You know they have men below us, waiting to shoot anything on the water. Get them to Harrisburg. I'll join the fight with the others."

Tuck gritted his teeth. "Why are you doing this to me?" He had more combat experience and training. He should be going to the fight. He wanted to go to the fight.

Robin pleaded, "Because it makes sense! You know every submerged rock and deep channel....Die to yourself, brother. Do what it isn't easy for the flesh to do. Take Pete and Grace out of the hand of death—they are needed in this final struggle in Harrisburg. And save your mother from being severely wounded and the drama and trauma that brings. You know the river. The rocks, currents, the choke points where the enemy might be hiding."

Tuck spoke angrily. "You heard Robin. Get in. I will be your pilot." *Die to self.* Tuck humphed. Robin knew their Jesus.

Grace smiled pensively and spoke softly. "Right call, Tuck." She could feel Tuck's pent-up desire to fight. Pete moved to the front of the boat to even out the weight and provide immediate fire on the downriver journey. Tuck helped his mother in. He lifted the rear of the boat just enough to slide it into deeper water, then climbed in himself, which lowered the boat to the muddy bottom. Robin gave a heave with both hands as his lower legs submerged. Someone put a piece of clothing over the lit ON switch as Tuck aimed the craft toward a secretive channel that cut the island in half. The soundless engine carried them away.

Robin regained the bank, his shoes squishing. He took his shoes off, stuffed them into his rucksack, left the socks on and moved south to provide supporting fire if any shore units would react to the boat. He heard the firefight to the north increase in volume. He could just make out the boat disappearing at the island's shore; they had slipped into the channel hidden from view. He moved with a celerity and yearning toward the sounds of violence.

Within fifty yards of the sounds of now-sporadic shooting, Robin realized his friends were surrounded within the belt of woodlands that ran the length of the riverbank. Even the river shore was being raked by enemy fire, both north and south. As the bank jutted into the river, the enemy's rounds continued into the river without hitting their own men stationed north and south. Robin, foregoing the time-consuming putting on of boots, stuffed the ruck under a downed tree limb and entered into invisibility. To avoid fire, he elevated and dropped into John and Diana's perimeter.

He remained invisible. All three Burnell brothers were wounded. Jack in his right calf—an in-and-out wound from a non-mushrooming round, probably an old target round. Robbie took a round in his upper left shoulder, another target round that had missed the lung. Sammie had the most grievous wounds. A round had passed through his thigh, and another into his torso, below his lungs. Robin thought the wound in the torso may have been a deflected round— perhaps the same one that hit the leg. John had already applied the clotting agents, and no blood flowed. John, Diana had wounds, but their resurrected-body hardiness and clotting agents kept them in the fight. They sensed Robin's presence, and then he was gone.

Robin elevated and toured the enemy lines. Numerous dead, perhaps fifty, and as many wounded. Clearly two hundred men were still engaged in the assault, diverted from the Harrisburg convoy. More units were being added. It was clear what the outcome would be: annihilation. It was clear the only course of action was the surrender of the Burnells and the disappearance of the resurrected. The Burnells would be immediately shot or tortured for days, only to succumb to their wounds. Days of torture were unthinkable. He knew the spirit imbued in John and Diana would be to fight to the end to save the Burnells. The Burnells could die, and they would return in resurrected bodies and live eternally. Dying wasn't a lark, but it was doable and had occurred to almost all flesh—save for two Old Testament prophets, Elijah and Enoch; and the living saints, like John Johnson, at the time of the Rapture.

He had wasted seconds in his scout. The fire pouring into his friends would eventually kill the Burnells. Shallow trenches had been dug in the soft and sandy ground, but the roots of trees offered resistance. The fallen tree they used as cover had been chewed away by rounds. An escape corridor could not be kept open, and even dragging the wounded left them exposed to more rounds. Robin entered into the circle of friends and manifested himself, prone, behind ground-hugging Jack. He whispered into the ear of Jack, "We are surrounded. If you surrender, you may be killed outright or tortured for days. You must speak for your brothers. It is unlikely we can break you free for an escape by the river." He saw bewilderment upon Jack's face.

Conflicting thoughts and emotions came so quickly that Jack's mind sank into a deadness.

Robin spoke from his own anguish for the brothers. "Quickly. We are all dying here."

Jack looked angrily at Robin. "They have offered no flag of truce. They wish us dead. Infiltrate to the command center….We will attack toward the carrier. Death has no sting."

Robin smiled at the bravado wrapped in that perfect faith. "Amen," he answered.

Jack rolled to Diana and John. They read his thoughts. *Attack. Fight to the end.*

The three were gone. In seconds, they appeared among the enemy lines. Grenades were exploding so rapidly it seemed like a mortar barrage. Then, the flash of lasers, the high-pitched humming of their mechanisms. Jack and Robbie stood, steadied their old-fashioned bolt actions against tree trunk after tree trunk, as they moved forward, firing. John and Diana had silenced the center, then each took a flank and circled behind, destroying the encircling enemy as Robin remained by the carrier, where the enemy attempted to rally.

Robin, Jack, Robbie, John, and Diana realized they stood in silence. Sammie only knew his pain. The enemy combatants lay upon the ground, dead or wounded so severely that only death throes and spasms moved the vegetation. Robin was staring at the massive wheels of the carrier, wondering if enemy troops were alive within, ready to burst from a turret or ramp door. He approached as Jack and Robbie went back for Sammie. He entered the carrier; no bodies, no blood. The steam-engine boiler held pressure. Dad had a steam tractor; their operation was easy. He heard the brothers return and exited the carrier; John and Diana were with them.

Robin spoke to John. "Let's put the Burnells on a boat; you could navigate. Diana and I could take this vehicle to Harrisburg, down the main road. Be there in no time. Probably will find Tuck's boat and come out and meet you."

John looked hard at Sammie, then at Jack and Robbie, and answered Robin. "An unarmed air platform has, in a rotating schedule, been stationed at my home on top of the mountain, for emergency rescues. Go now and bring it here." Robin was gone instantly.

***

The air platform lifted up. Jack saluted down to John and Robin. Diana, the least wounded, riding shotgun and accompanying the wounded, saluted the men on the earth. The two earthbound men watched the craft disappear to the south. John turned to Robin, placed his arm around Robin's shoulders.

"Well done, soldier of the Lord of Hosts, the God of Battles."

Robin smiled. "We all did well for our God."

"Yes, we did. Are you up for cleanup and burying the unsaved dead? We can use the front-end loader," John said.

Robin answered, "I've got lots of nervous energy coursing through my body. Better set some smoke grenades with movement detectors along the road. We don't need to get plunked off our vehicles while we work."

John laughed sheepishly. "No, that wouldn't be good."

Robin looked above, into the sky. "The mists are breaking up, the birds are singing. Another glorious day of eternal life."

"Amen," said John as he rearranged his bandages. Then he shed a tear as an overwhelming, silent, "*Thank you!*" burst from his soul.

CHAPTER 18

The day was hot in Harrisburg, the church almost empty on that Sunday prior to July 4. The majority of citizens were at home, or in their apartments, or in temporary housing of shipping containers, or within massive emergency-shelter buildings formerly used commercially, or within a tent, or under waterproof sheeting. The electrascreen functioned only when the satanic forces broadcast pornography, or footage of street attacks and the ensuing shame, or the pictures of the resurrected in their former flesh. Andy's headquarters marked the locations where the screens were not shut down and demented followers of Satan watched in delight. Video-capable drones were sent, and the enemy faces, recorded. In the rural areas, some churches in towns, villages, or at crossroads, held services. Armed parishioners stood guard. Some stockaded homes also held services.

The Sunday-afternoon picnics and catered gatherings once sponsored by Harrisburg churches and youth organizations had been cancelled. The Fourth of July weekend musical entertainment of every type of music, from rock to the folk music of every time period as represented by the resurrected, even Native American song and dance—had been cancelled. Before Satan's return, riverboats would give free rides, people would swim at sandy beaches within buoyed rectangles of safe water; the adventuresome would sunbathe and lounge on river rocks or wade as they fished. Athletic events had never occurred, as Sunday had been a day of rest, a day of peace and ease and fellowship, not competition. This day, as in the past, the flag of the United States flew everywhere, except in Satan's strongholds, for the good people knew the history of their republic. They knew that the Spirit of their Lord had guided men, the founding fathers, who were intelligent men to be sure, beyond their intelligence to that place of wisdom in the mind that only God's Spirit could touch.

Weeks before, a rumor had spread through central Pennsylvania that the last of Satan's followers would be leaving on this day. The great migration to the Middle East would be over, even as Satan armed and honed his army near the borders of Israel. Even as demonstration posters extolling the right to eternal procreation received their last sprays and dabs of paint before being posted. Regardless of Satan's possible plan, a credible report circulated: the Lord sat on His throne in Jerusalem, unperturbed, conducting mundane business, even as He managed the response to the insurrection.

Pete sat tall in a pew of the vaulted-ceilinged church downtown, as he meditated on these world events and the local situation. Grace's arm lay upon his lap. He felt her cool, tanned skin; the muscles of her forearm; and the narrow, dainty wrist. He focused his eyes on the left side of the sanctuary, where the rifles had been collected and locked. Keeping his good posture allowed him a clear sightline. He was security that day and would move to his weapon with alacrity if the red warning light pulsed above the weapons or undesignated parishioners moved toward that location.

He glanced at Grace; her mind was fully engaged in the sermon. She had earned a place on Andy's guard detail. Her shooting and target acquisition had been top of the class. The woman of nurturing kindness, innocent of the world of violence, had become a hardened soldier. The inside air temperature was comfortable—the air-conditioning system was clearly able to meet the demands of the heat wave that had enveloped the city for the past weeks. The oppressive heat seemed to have begun the day after he, Grace, and Leaf arrived on Tuck's boat from upcountry. Tuck had been hit by a grazing round shot from half a mile away. He had been struck by two rounds in the chest, fired by what he thought was a sniper from the same distance, but a fabric body armor had been enough to deaden the shock, and only sore ribcage muscle and bone were the result. John and Diana sat to his left, and Andy and Leaf to Grace's right. The wounds John and Diana had received in the river skirmish had healed. The injured Burnell brothers had recovered and were working this day, as were Tuck and Robin, Dan and Emily.

Andy's monitor hugged his ear securely. A nondescript ring on his left hand would pulse green for any incoming call of importance, giving him time to concentrate and focus. He was, in effect, the top man in Harrisburg and Dauphin County—all surveillance, all watching teams reported to the command center on the top floor of his office building and directly to him. He was given thirty seconds, and then the info was sent out to all teams. In those thirty seconds, he had time to make any decision he thought prudent, even the delaying of the transmission of information to all parties. The rumors begun weeks ago by Satan's forces—to heighten tension—were well known. Officially, the local militia, Pete included, knew only that there was an alert for today and tomorrow. John and Diana, being of the upper echelon, had equal knowledge with Andy. Intuition told him that the day the rumor mentioned would be this day, Sunday, the Lord's day. The timing was symbolic. Tomorrow was the nation's day—that was symbolic, too. Fighting would continue through the Fourth of July, the nation's day. Satan abhorred the United States, but he hated the Creator more.

All knew that Christ Jesus, the king of the world, had sent angelic couriers to His people in leadership positions. He kept the possible scenarios broad—from simple street demonstrations to actual destructive violence to property and even life. Satan's remaining people would be taking over airports and rail lines, ocean ports. They were to be allowed to depart unmolested, if they refrained from violence.

Andy's ring pulsed green. Although a sizable gap was between them, John and Diana felt Andy's alertness, as the resurrected had a sentience. Andy stood, moving in the narrow spacing between the pews to the outer aisle and the huge pillars that supported the roof. John and Diana had already gained the center aisle. As the three moved, they heard through their earbuds the reports of street demonstrations, of the bombing of statues, of random fires, of tear-gas discharges. Andy saw Pete and Grace rise quickly, and other men throughout the congregation, moving toward the gunrack, which pulsed red. He could now hear the explosions, shouting outside the church, and a commotion at the main doors of the church. At twenty-five seconds, he broke into the reports still streaming to him and ordered, "Ark

Angel Michael!" repeatedly. He had just ordered all auxiliary units to be armed and massed, all police units on duty to be deployed, and all off-duty support called to duty.

John and Diana were before him, his bodyguards, moving toward the heavy church doors, where the ushers kept watch. To Andy, the doors were the small gate, and the wide world beyond held the narrow path. Within Andy's mind, the ancient personal prayer that had carried him into countless savage melees came. "The Lord is my God, and there is no other. The Lord is my salvation. The Lord is my strength. I will not flinch. Victory is the Lord's."

At the approach of John and Diana, without a word being spoken, the ushers stepped away from the doors. John kicked the center of the joined doors; the doors burst open; a signal to the black-clothed combatants. From all directions, they began to coalesce at the opened doors and around the men coming out. All were dressed in black, with black face masks, black bandannas on their heads, rounded steel bars in their hands—or sharpened metal spears made from construction materials—and knives on their belts. Men, women, youth. Within the black garb of everyday wear were military uniforms of black. Andy knew the uniforms were the mark of the elite, those who had sold their souls to Satan. The enemy surged into the Christians exiting the church.

The Christian forces knew the enemy could only be met with overwhelming, unrelenting force. The butt ends of John's and Diana's rifles knocked into faces, stomachs; the standing bent or careened backward, falling to the ground. In a lingering daze, they groped and found their equilibrium. The enemy presented no firearms; this was purposeful, to create hesitation in the reactions of Christian forces. Satan's forces had come to hinder and distract, to compel the enemy to use lethal force first.

Andy had holstered his sidearm. He was reaching into the mass, pulling bodies into his body, tripping them, casting them onto the ground. Pete and Grace, near the end of the column, searched for firearms in the crowd and shot the holders dead. Between Pete and Grace and the head of the column, where John, Diana, and Andy fought, the police forces truncheoned, punched, and kicked the fallen rebels, then cuffed their hands and ankles. A volley of shots from the enemy ranks was heard, and a heart-piercing wail resounded. Shouts of mercy sounded. Andy knew that all his men and women knew these forces were a just distraction, buying time for some other sinister attack of deathly significance.

Many dressed in black, on the fringe of the rebel crowds, were jolted to a realization upon being struck or hearing the vulgar hatred of those around them. This was not a game. This was not entertainment, not a release from supposed boredom, stagnation in life. They had never thought this through…never realized that they had turned from their God, who had been so good to them. They had never read or talked to people from the past. Never learned of Satan's evil, of his control upon the world; never knew at what cost their good lives had been purchased—that good men and women and a suffering Christ had paid for their freedom. They had been duped, lulled to sleep by the lies of the discontented and the vicious and the small world they had created and lived within. These people saw their foolishness and repented with arms raised and knees bent. To the surrendering, their fellow citizens extended mercy, kindness. Words of encouragement were received; words of hope, forgiveness; words of approval for surrendering, for giving in to what was good.

The instigating, pressing mob of hardcore Satanists before the church had become subdued after the volley of shots. Many had melted into the crowd and retreated. Andy was receiving a constant stream of information through his earbuds. Having quelled a mob and rendered it useless, units moved to another point of conflict. Outnumbered units received reinforcements. Andy saw a kneeling prisoner, whom an auxiliary police officer was repeatedly striking as another officer looked on. Andy's open hand hit the striking officer on his solar plexus, and the man fell. He loomed over the officer. John and Diana had seen his decisive movements, followed, and stood by his side. Andy helped the victim up and then grabbed the two auxiliary police officers, the harsh grab melting into an inclusive touch of camaraderie. His voice came softly. "Give first aid to the prisoner and take all prisoners to be questioned. Christ showed you mercy; do as He did. Be wary; you can't read minds."

An urgent message sounded in Andy's ear. Unauthorized flights were leaving Harrisburg International—flights not checked by his men for abducted Christians. Trains were leaving for Philadelphia unchecked. As Andy received these messages, a convoy of buses and trucks passed by, flying the black flag of Satan. No doubt these, too, would empty, and the occupants would board planes or trains bound for Philadelphia. Andy replied to the new information given him. "Do not—I repeat, do not—fire on loaded vehicles of any kind, unless they are firing at you. If they can be stopped safely, you may do so." That, too, was the plan: give the rebels time to repent, to fragment, and the abducted, a chance to escape.

Andy searched the faces of those gathered near him. Behind his men sat prisoners, perhaps a hundred. Pete was before him, looking physically worn but mentally alert and holding back words. "Speak it, Peter. What have you to say?" ordered Andy.

"They have gathered at Reservoir Park. Hundreds if not thousands of them, and with trucks."

"Where did this intel come from?" Andy asked. He had heard nothing concerning Reservoir Park, named for a water-storage facility underground. It sat on the highest hilly overlook of the city, and therefore was a place of military significance. Fired from Reservoir Park, artillery, mortars, rockets could easily control movement within the city and surrounding river bridges and transportation routes.

"From my eyes, and from these prisoners." Pete began walking away, pointing, looking to the east, removing the blocking church from his vision of the horizon. Andy followed till he, too, could see the heights and the movement of men and equipment on its crest. Andy held up his hand, asking for a pause in movement and chatter. He said into his mic, "Reservoir Park update."

He turned the volume up and switched the sound to speaker mode. "Barrels are skyward," said a voice.

"Okay, lower the net," Andy said decisively.

"Roger," came the reply.

Andy pointed to the sky above the heights. A darkness seemed to descend from the sky like translucent black smoke.

"Mission accomplished," Andy announced to the gathered. "We knew that Reservoir Park, the highest, nearest ground overlooking the city, made a perfect bastion of final resistance and for the launching of rockets or mortar rounds on the city below. An electronic force field has temporarily neutralized the rebels." Andy looked into Pete's eyes. "What else do you have, Peter?"

"What do we do next?" Peter asked as his body sighed with the release of immediate tension.

"At Reservoir, clean up the pockets of resistance. Stress surrender. If we can keep the rebels surrounded and nonlethal, we can move the force field and take them peacefully. If they are spewing out fire, they must be destroyed."

"What was the point of this mess?" Grace asked, perplexed. She moved her extended arm over the scene of prisoners, wounded, and dead. He saw mild shock registering in her eyes and words. First combat fighting as a soldier. She had done well. He knew she knew the reason why—it was just the futility and the pain she couldn't grasp. He would retell the truth, and in the hearing, she would sort out her emotions.

"Satan knew he had no hope of or time to conquer nations; he had to go straight for his enemy, Christ in Jerusalem. This display was just a final farewell, a diversion, and a way to abduct Christians to convert or kill or use as hostages. Satan just wanted to inflict one final sting of the flagrum to the body of Christ. Satan's army will be destroyed by Christ, then the evil of this world will be judged." Andy felt satisfaction; the true end of this worldly age was soon to be complete. Men of the world, the flesh, and Satan would be eternally impotent.

"Pete and Grace, go up to Reservoir. See if you can separate the sheep from the goats among the prisoners. Find the Burnell brothers to help you and provide security. They are up there somewhere. Try as much as possible to keep them and yourselves out of harm's way. Our war is almost won." Andy paused, weighing his thoughts. "Leave your rifles here," he told Pete and Grace. "We'll have need of them. Keep your sidearms." His eyes moved to John and Diana. "John and Diana, find Dan and Emily and collectively see if you can do the same at the airport and train and bus stations. As for me, I'll collect my sons for bodyguards and head to the bus station. But don't count on that—the situation is still fluid."

John and Diana saluted. She had seen John salute for her entire millennium life, and it had rubbed off on her. And no one was more worthy of respect than Andy, the man who carried the weight of Satan's final rebellion.

***

Pete and Grace found the Burnell brothers intently peering from the windows of a lone structure, a farmhouse, which sat neglected, upon a vast pastureland east of the primary hill of Reservoir Park. They could not see the city, as its sight was blocked by the hill, nor could they see the enemy fortifications on the brow of the hill that overlooked the city. Pete had noticed that the pastureland soil was rocky, strewn with crumbled cement and occasional pipes. A suburb must have sat upon the land before the days of the Tribulation. The farmhouse's outbuildings had all been burned in the recent conflict, and the farmhouse itself had been the target of rockets and rifle fire.

The brothers were still smiling at the arrival of their company, for all three had, in private talks, agreed that Pete and Grace were top-of-the-line friends, full of the richest hospitality—in food, in accommodations, in genuine care and concern, with not a self-serving or hokey bone in their bodies. Pete and Grace had cared for them after their recent wounds and lifted their spirits through the setback of inaction as they healed.

Peter, smiling, announced, "Good news. You are to be our bodyguards and eyes and ears for a while. Andy wants us to interrogate those captives on the hill."

"That sounds like fun," said Jack without a trace of sarcasm. It would be enjoyable in a challenging way.

"But they're not captives yet," said Robbie.

"Why do you think they are?" asked Sammie of Pete.

Grace spoke. "Didn't you see the net drop down upon them?"

"A real net?" asked Jack.

"An electronic barrier," said Peter.

"We saw a gray cloud fall, and it kept falling, collapsing on that open ground before you," stated Robbie.

Peter grabbed Grace's arm. "Let's get out of here!" he said to all. They surely had been seen entering the farmhouse, and with no blocking net, one homemade mortar round would kill them all. Peter moved through the rooms to the doorway and past the broken-hinged door. Jack, alarmed at Pete's facial expression more so than his words, grabbed his ruck and weapon and followed. Robbie and Sammie caught the fear on their brother's face and ran toward the door with gear in hands, half draped on shoulders. All followed Pete as he ran east, keeping the farmhouse between himself and the crest of the hill. They heard ordinance falling to the west, in Harrisburg, and felt the ground rumbling. With no sound for warning, the farmhouse suddenly exploded into debris. Their supporting forces, a handful of men on the flanks of the farmhouse position, were see running east. From the crest of Reservoir Park, the enemy forces, men and women, began descending.

"They after us?" an alarmed Jack asked Peter.

"Probably going to swing around the base of the hill to the front and outflank our troops at the base," Pete explained as he slowed his run to a walk and crouched within an area of shrubby trees. The others settled in beside him. The enemy forces did circle the base of the hill and showed no interest in his group. A squad of the flanking Christian forces saw Pete's group and gathered with them. "What should we do?" asked the leader of the group of volunteer citizen-soldiers, all of whom were mortals.

"Let's leave this backdoor open for defectors. The hardcore forces are circling to the front of the hill. We will follow behind them. No shooting unless they shoot. This is the last hurrah; no reason to suffer a wound or endure the agony of death so close to peace. Agreed?" Pete asked.

"Agreed," came the replies, as Pete reharnessed the ruck and unholstered his sidearm. "Single file. Leave distance. Follow me."

***

"Pete! Pete!" Jack called with force and urgency in his voice. Pete, in turning to Jack, saw a lone enemy soldier waving a white flag, moving directly toward them at a quick pace, helped by the hill's incline. At the same time, sounds of explosions and small-arms fire came from the far side of Reservoir Park. The explosions increased in volume, the ground shook. People were dying on the far side of the heights. The thought chilled their hearts and pulled them to the sound, even as it repulsed and frightened them.

The man was before them—twenty-something, white skin, tall and lanky, bulletproof vest, full-automatic squad-cartridge weapon. An oddness was in the movement of his body, as if his joints had no fluidity. The Burnell brothers had their weapons trained on the man. Jack yelled, "Stop." The man stopped. The Burnells, Pete, and Grace knew the man was hardcore—vests and full auto guns were only given to the true believers. Even without the vest, the thin man seemed puffy through his midsection. Peter whispered to the man nearest him, "Pass it down: slowly move backward." Peter saw the man beside him turn and whisper. Slowly the word went down the line and movement began.

He watched the enemy's eyes, saw him recognize the unit was moving backward. Pete caught a twitch of movement in the man's leg. He began to raise his pistol when Jack's rifle recoiled, an ear-piercing crackling rent the still air. As the man was falling backward, his head exploded and his torso disappeared; head, shredded neck, and arms flew into space. Pieces of a leg skittered backward along the ground. A black liquid dispersed from the exploding body. Shrapnel that had been packed around his body shrieked through the air, over the heads of Pete's crouching unit. If not for the man falling backward ever so slightly, the unit would have received the full force of destruction.

Pete's ears were ringing as he ran down his line of men. The black mist was the blood of a demonic angel. Carl Stasic had told him of killing two in his time. Warnings as to their presence had been made by Andy's staff. Pete was physically shaking, he skipped checking Grace—she was smiling and okay. He hurriedly touched each man, searching for blood, a wound, shredded clothing. Coming back to the lead position, he noticed Grace was looking at him oddly as if asking what had happened. He saw the blood on the side of her face. Saw it coming up from the neck, saw it spurting as he placed his hand tight against the wound and searched his chest pocket for his coagulant packet. Found and bitten and torn open, he laid her down, then raised her to a sitting position, all the while pouring clotting powder into her wound, pressing his hand upon her neck. Jack, Robbie, Sammie had gathered by him. With a finger, she touched his forehead directly before her face. And then her eyes glazed, and she was gone, gone to paradise. He felt the presence of the angels beside her as her soul came out of her mortal body and went into the arms of the waiting angels, who carried her within the aura of heaven around them. Swiftly they were gone.

Jack, Robbie, Sammie fell to their knees in disbelief; they were open-mouthed and unbelieving but not panicked or dismayed at the absence of their good and precious friend. Oddly, to Peter, he was remembering a time when he and Grace had first met Grandfather Mat at their cottage on the bluff. It was a happy time; they were freshly married and in love with their Creator and each other. It was before the kids were born, when the millennium was new and fresh and God's glory was everywhere. They had watched Grandfather Mat singing praises to God on their deck. She had said, "And we reap the reward," referring to all the sufferings Grandfather Mat's generation had endured. Pete remembered saying, "Our time will come, Gracie, my girl, when we will give Him all and count our sufferings for Christ as our greatest moments."

Grace had suffered for Christ not only in her last moments but during this satanic rebellion. She had drawn closer to her Lord. It would only be a short separation, and she wasn't separated from God in paradise, receiving her immortal body. In eternity's vast stretch, this parting would seem like seconds. He searched the faces of his friends. Sammie wept, Jack had anger upon his face, and Robbie seemed to grieve in some unfathomable place in his heart. Peter, for all his intellectual knowledge of the Lord, felt a turning and twisting within his soul for the agony, the pain that Grace, his perfect wife, in that perfect fleshly body that had thrilled him intellectually, spiritually, physically and bound itself to him, had felt. For minutes, the pain had been upon her, and he knew her mind had left her body, and her mind had not felt the pain, and yet, still he hurt. He should have checked her first, and so he cried. Jack came to him and kissed him on the cheek and rubbed his shoulders, repeating over and other, "Jesus wept, Jesus wept, Jesus wept." Robbie came to him and wept beside him.

CHAPTER 19

The Spirit said the work of the harvest was not yet complete. Time was short; they would see their Grace again. Move to the battle with all speed. Pete looked at his brothers in Christ—in their pain, they would rest in Him. The tagalong squad had gone to their knees and were praying with open eyes. Pete spoke as he wiped his final tears away. "The Lord has need of us. Let us find the battle." The Comforter picked up His men, put them on their feet. Instantly, straps were tightened, belts secured, weapons checked, ammunition shifted for easy access; a slow walk began as eyes scanned. This was the way to the Cross; this was the way of duty. As their steps became a walk, then a trot, equipment moved upon their frames in cadence with their bodies. Eyes reached out, attempting to bend around the heights to their left, to the forward slope where the sounds of battle spoke of mayhem, carnage, and the animal struggle to maintain life. A quick glance to the right—desolate grazing fields and glimpses of the buildings of the city, smoke clouds hanging like ocean reefs, fires burning. Deep, dark clouds seeming to transform to asphalt the heavy sky upon their heads.

They turned the rounded corner of the hill, which now hung above and beside their left shoulders. As though stage curtains had been pulled aside, the sky now seemed limitless; the western lands stretched beyond the river. On the flat land to their front, before the drop-off to the river flood plain, they saw thousands of men—the Christian forces and the rebels—all shouting, it seemed, in pain, agony, and vehemence. Little antlike figures engaged in war. In the area nearest to their entry upon the scene, vast groups of black-clad rebels were sitting or kneeling upon one knee, with standing guards of Christian captors watching. Farther away, in the center, thousands of men fought. The mass moved, swayed with hand-to-hand skirmishes; contending, surging, and receding groups groped, punched, stabbed with knives, bludgeoned with bars of steel and wooden clubs, fired bolt-action rifles, plunged with bayonets. Smoke and dust hung above the figures—a stagnant cloud waiting to cover the dead with a shroud.

Jack's wide eyes looked into Pete's eyes, and Jack spoke. "Stay here with the prisoners. That's where your strength is. We are going to the fight." Pete gave his laconic salute, restrained by duty, a slight trailing off as if to say, *Go and do what you must; I will stay*. Jack turned as his brothers and their column of tagalongs moved at double time toward the fray. Pete stopped the third man from the end of the column and pulled all three to him. They were limping, above-average weight, weighed down with gear, and worn, and he had need of them. "You will work with me," he declared. Pete turned to the nearest guard, who had observed the passing column. "Anyone in charge? Any prisoners interrogated?"

"Not that I know of," the man said, his throat parched and tone cracked and raspy from the fine particles of pollens, grasses, fibers, and gunpowder residue that scraped his esophagus.

"Okay. I'm Pete. I answer directly to Andy. I'm going to separate the sheep from the goats, starting with these men at your feet. Any suspicious moves—shoot. They outnumber us. We must instill a righteous fear. Anyone rising, tell them to sit and ask what they want. They can piss and crap right where they are at. Water will be coming and, in time, food."

"Yes, sir," the raspy-voiced one said, pleased to have purpose.

"These two are yours," Pete said, moving two of his recently acquired men over to the guard.

Pete saw two others of his new charges, the guards, standing by, seeming disconnected from the fray. He approached them with his lone remaining man. “I’m interrogating. You will signal for a prisoner. One of you holds a rifle to the prisoner’s lower stomach and watches his eyes, and the other secures his hands behind his back. I’ve got ties in my pack. One movement, even a testing movement, and you shoot him in the thickest part of the leg—the quad muscle—so the bullet doesn’t hit your buddy behind him. Don’t hit the femoral artery; hit the outside quad muscle. But don’t panic if he bleeds to death—let it happen. No acceptance of any movement. The others must know there is zero tolerance. Once he’s cuffed, take him to his knees, search him thoroughly, strip him of coat, vest, packs, cut the straps—even the coats, if you have to—and throw them in a pile. All weapons should be removed at first cuffing and thrown over into a pile far from reach.” Pete saw another straggler soldier and waved him in. “Join us. They’ll get you to speed. You will take the firearms—” Pete abruptly stopping talking when he saw prisoners rising from the subdued ranks before his new guard and the two men assigned to him. The guard had not shot; perhaps the group of men rising all at once had confused him.

Pete began shooting with his pistol, hoping his rounds all found marks, as the area behind them was full of moving and sitting men. The guard began to shoot. Those not hit sat quickly.

“Leave them where they are,” yelled Pete to his guard.

Pete turned to the nearest prisoners. He spoke to his men. “Take that man and do as I have instructed.” Pete watched as his orders were followed. He noticed some hesitancy, a lack of forcefulness, but the sequence was correct. “Okay, you will get faster, be more forceful, assertive. Don’t fear their anger. For me to know they are angry tells me something and is a good tool for my use. But don’t abuse. We don’t need them alive. Clouds of angels stand among us, waiting to take these souls to Hades or Paradise, and they will not make a mistake. So you stop worrying about making a mistake.”

Pete reached down and physically pulled his first prisoner away from his three men, dragging him downhill fifteen feet by the collar. He would have no time to take notes or search for tattoos or any clues to the man’s true involvement. The man was not of robust build, Pete assumed, simply by the man’s weight. His hands were uncalloused, the nails cut and clean. The face held no fear, and a smirk was evident in the set of the lips. “Why are you fighting on the wrong side?" Pete asked. He had thought of saying, "with the forces of Satan," but *wrong side* would be more argumentative and encourage confrontation, which he needed.

"Just tired of the same old same old." The man spoke in a neutral tone of fact and emotion.

"What did you really want? Sex? Power? Wealth?"

"Nothing; just change," the man said in the same neutral tone.

"Nobody wants just change. Pick one of the three—sex, power, wealth."

"I'm not going to answer that." The voice held a quiver.

"Why?" Pete spoke angrily, the anger a ruse.

"You got no right." The man's tone held indignation.

"You've been asleep. This is the choosing time. It's why you were born, the sole purpose of your life. Christ or Satan?"

"I don't see it that way." The voice spoke of supreme confidence.

"Your choice." Pete took him by the collar and dragged him fifteen feet to his left. Pete noticed the rough treatment had not dented the confidence upon the man's face. He saw more Christian soldiers just standing, watching. "Over here." They came. "This is a bad guy. Find some heavy piece of scrap metal, more hand ties, ropes, or chains, and attach him to the metal. That burned-out chassis over there. Be ready to receive more. I'm Pete and Susquehanna Andy is my boss. You are now under my command." Andy had become "Susquehanna Andy" to distinguish him from a colonel whose surname was Andy.

"Next!" Pete called to his crew. They already had another prisoner ready. Pete grabbed one of the nearby men. "Go drag that man down here. That will be your job today."

***

Pete looked upon the captive. No fear in his eyes. He wondered if any would have fear or a healthy respect for the import of the times. Did they think they could challenge Holy God and He would not be angry? This man had more weight upon him. Evidently, food had been readily available to him.

"Why are you fighting on the wrong side?"

"Stupidity…I guess."

"I don't want your guesses. Were you fighting for sex, power, or wealth?"

"Probably all three."

"Explain."

"I was given rank, and women are attracted to rank, so I had women. The rank gave me power over others. The wealth would come once we won—although we could take anything we wanted."

"What about Christ?"

"What about him?"

"You must have been asleep. Right now, is the choosing time. Christ or Satan?"

"Well, Christ, of course. My side is losing." The man laughed.

Pete laughed with the man at his honesty. He knew what he was—an opportunist, no desire for values, just living to feed his carnal desires. "You chose hundreds, if not thousands, of times in your life for your flesh, and in turn, for Satan, the master of flesh—so much so that you are irredeemable. Christ was upon His throne. The goodness of life was apparent, the Holy Spirit talked to you daily, and no impression was made." Pete spoke to his assistant. "Take him over there with the other man. Make sure he is secure."

The man spoke loudly. "God gives second chances."

"You presumed the second chance would be your ace in the hole? Second chances are for the contrite of heart. I find none of that in you."

The man yelled, "Wait…wait…wait!" as he was dragged away.

"Next man," Pete yelled to his crew above him.

***

The Burnells had raced to the scene of battle, and gaining the lip of a rise, found bodies massed, packed tightly for half a mile on a continuation of the wide plateau that wrapped around the steep reservoir hills. The hills themselves were covered with fighting men, up one-third of the slope. On the vast flats, men were pushing, punching, stabbing, shooting, falling. Men grappled, tumbled, and slipped on the steep, bare hillsides. On the shale incline from the flat plateau to the even wider plain of Harrisburg, men stumbled, fell, crawled on hands and knees, died before they could reach the flat ground of the ancient riverbed, where Harrisburg had been built.

The contending forces seemed a living thing, like some giant, disturbed caterpillar nest upon the earth, advancing and retreating, pulsing with fisticuffs and stabbings, wrestling, and bayonet thrusts. Small-arms cartridges popped; bombs, grenades, and suicide vests exploded. The sound rang in the ears; black smoke blossomed and filled the air as the few lasers streaked the darkness of smoke with brilliant light. The smoke hung just above the heads of the combatants like the presence of death. The changing winds held clamorous shouts, yells, death throes, orders, cries, whimpers, and sounds of the flesh, of alien life, of subhuman creatures.

They saw Andy in the center of it, and John and Diana on either flank. Tuck and Robin covered the rear of the advance, walking backward, reaching out with their weapons. The Burnell brothers could still see the trail of Andy's advance through the mass—a trail of bodies, of the dead, of the wounded, and bodies of the living attempting to stop the scythe-bearers as they reaped. Jack took point, and Sammie and Robbie, the flanks. They walked the same course, the trail of the fallen. Grenades came at them, and these men died. Suicide vests exploded as the brothers found the bulky vests of the wearers in the crowd. Ammunition was used sparingly; the dead were searched for rounds. Christian soldiers who had been handcuffed and beaten were set free and joined behind; the wounded enemy soldiers capable of fighting were killed.

The brothers held only the moment: reaction and action; eyes picking out the immediate threat, and arms moving the weapon, the rifle barrel, the rifle butt, the bayonet. Sometimes they would lose sight of Andy and his band, and sometimes Andy and his band would crest a rise. On one such rise, the sun burst through the clouds, then the smoke of the battlefield moved away, and Andy and his crew seemed like angels sparkling in the column of golden light of God's favor. Victory.

The brothers waded through ongoing struggles of savagery, quiet pools of rest, and the turbulence of seething hate yet to be expressed. All emotions were upon the battlefield; all men were sucked into the violence of the brothers and the trailing band of God's soldiers. Jack saw Andy's band stop. They were looking backward and upward. Jack turned. Harrisburg was burning. The tall buildings were pouring out yellow flames and dense smoke. Detonations were heard and felt, rumbling through the earth. Buildings were collapsing. From the south, using the river as their guide, huge transoceanic jets, flying near stall speed, low to the earth, were leaving the airport. It seemed they could be touched. Was this a show of victory? Satan's men and women on their way to Israel to remove Christ from His earthly throne? Then, among the Harrisburg buildings, the brothers saw small specks, like gnats. They were air platforms from the Christian forces, and they poured their fire on the black-clothed forces of Satan.

The black-clothed forces upon the plain of Reservoir Park began to disengage, to walk, run toward the burning city below them. Many believed they were being left behind when they saw the jetliners leaving. Many believed the city was open for looting, killing, raping. Many believed that once they made the city a smoldering ruin, the jets would return for them. Many fled the fighting in fear and exhaustion, bearing hideous wounds.

Pete had glanced behind, between interrogations, and saw the city burning, heard the bombs exploding, the air platforms pouring destruction on the satanic forces, the jet liners cruising low. He looked over the prisoners yet to be interrogated and felt their collective thoughts of perverse mirth, cynicism, and hate. They were enjoying this. He saw one man among them who was different, his aura was downcast, and he began to weep, then sob.

"Bring the crying man." He pointed; the man was brought to him. Pete handed the man an unopened packet of tissues from his pack. "Why the tears? Is anyone else crying? You are a man. You made your choices. Live with them."

"Yes, I am a man…a special man. I am a fool." His voice was talking to the man within him. His eyes were wet, his nose ran, his throat was choked with phlegm.

"How so?" Pete observed an average-sized man, with neatly cut hair, wearing not boots but leather street shoes.

"I allowed a liar and thief to take from me all that was good." The man struggled to match his labored breathing with the exhalation of his words.

Pete spoke loudly, "What was good?" *This answer will be interesting,* Pete thought cynically. A composure seemed to wash over the man, a peace, and joy. Pete recognized the Spirit of his God.

"My wife, my children, supportive family and neighbors, interesting work, a peaceful life, a God I could talk to and who loved me and gave me good thoughts and hopes. Now, the city that I helped build burns, and my wife and children are gone—where, I don't know. My God has left me alone… nothing but evil occupies my mind."

"Turn around," said Pete. The man seemed confused. "Turn around," Pete demanded. The man turned. "Look at the faces of your comrades. See any of them crying and sad?"

The man studied the faces of the waiting. "No."

Pete forcefully turned the man's head back to his own staring eyes, then held the head in his hands. "Do you think your God, who died for you upon a cross, would abandon you the way you abandoned Him? Have you not heard of His faithfulness?" Pete's voice was charged with emotion at the faithfulness of God and the stupidity of men. The Lord was here to save this man. Pete had not let go of the man's head. He shook the man, not to hurt but to awaken. He prayed his emotion into his words. "Ask for His forgiveness, repent of your sin, then give Him the glory due Him for His faithfulness."

Pete saw the visible Holy Spirit of God come from above and lay His presence like a blanket, a prayer shawl, upon the head and shoulders of the man. Pete bent down and moved his hands to the man's shoulders and spoke softly into his ear. "He wants you to proclaim aloud your appeal."

Words gushed from the man's mouth quickly, trippingly, gaining strength. "Forgive me, Lord; forgive me for my turning away, for my sin. I want to come home. I want what we once had. I want you...as my friend, my leader, my God!" The man sobbed. "Please take me back; oh God, please."

Peter looked at his orderly. "Release this man. Put him to work." As he spoke, he saw a continuation of the low-flying aircraft from Harrisburg International moving almost at stall speed across their view. Pete helped the man to his feet as the guard cut away his restraints. Pete grabbed the man with his two hands upon his neck. "Look at me." The man looked. "Your sins have been forgiven. Live and fight for your God!" The joy of salvation passed between the two. Pete's hands pushed the man to the guard in joyfulness. Pete scanned the faces around him. He looked at the faces of his prisoners and saw anger, rage. He felt their strength wishing to lift them to their feet. He saw their faces portraying full betrayal; they knew the number and type of aircraft they had been told would leave, and now all the aircraft were leaving.

Pete's eyes had wandered to the north, where the high mountain ridge that ran northeast stopped at the Susquehanna River before starting again on the west shore. He was ten years old, on a high ridge before the mountains, and looking south to this place, on that trip with the some of the oldsters—Carl, Tim, Mat, DC Jones, Katie, Ling. He had cried in sympathy when the adults had cried, remembering the trauma of the Tribulation. Young and immature as he was, he still realized a price needed to be paid. He had wished to do some important and heroic act for his God who gave him Jesus, who had taken away his sin and had given him clean new life every moment. Mat and Tim had fought on that ground he had stood upon that day. Now the time had come to do that important and heroic thing. He would not fail. He would do that thing. Promise fulfilled; price paid.

Pete began searching the ground around him. He spoke to his orderly. "Help me to find a rifle and ammo as quickly as possible. He looked at the men he had detained, nearly fifty; all were attached to the skeletal frame of a burned-out personnel carrier. The faces of the men were enraged; they were pulling at their cords, ropes, chains, cuffs. *The storm will soon begin*, thought Pete.

"Here we go, sir." The orderly handed Peter an automatic-cartridge machine gun with a chest-mounted sling for belt-fed ammo.

"Put this on me. Quickly." The orderly complied, and then attached an ammo belt with two more boxes of belt-fed ammo.

The uninterrogated prisoners had begun to stand. The guard, without hesitation, began to fire his bolt-action rifle at the standing men. All of the prisoners rose and charged downhill toward their captors. The band of guards formed a defensive line. Pete stepped before them and raked the mass of prisoners with repeated passes of his barrel. More of Satan's men welled up behind the slain prisoners. He emptied an entire ammo box. That would give his men time to regain control—dominance. His barrel overheated; the warning indicator showed three minutes of cooling time needed.

He turned to the cuffed and chained interrogated prisoners to his left. Some had broken free and were freeing the others. Peter aimed his pistol and began shooting center mass or head shots, as a last resort. He stopped three times to reload new clips. He dodged lunges with knives, open and closed fists, grasps at clothing or arms. All were seething with rage and supremely confident they would kill him in their efforts. They were committed to their evil, that deep welling up of life called *self* was a drug they could not live without.

All were dead. He looked up the hill, where the uninterrogated prisoners had been. The area was littered with dead or dying. He saw the backs of men running away. The friendly forces that had held positions around the gathering were gone, too, running down the hill and escarpment to the city. He looked to the east longingly, to where the Burnells had gone; he wished them to return. He saw the enemy running toward his group of twenty men; the penitent sinner had remained, and others had joined. The enemy running down the hill, around and over the ranks Pete had just mowed down, were few at first.

Then, from over a swale, the enemy appeared as ranks of men dressed in black, armed, determined faces, striding in the confidence of victory secured. To his left was the main road, the corridor into the city, a sloping ramp from the high ground onto the flat plain of Harrisburg. To enter the flat plain from any other point, the steep escarpment forced single-file men onto sharply sloping trails of loose sandstone flakes; men tumbled and rolled; some did not rise, others rose dizzily with broken arms and legs. The ramp's height gave dominance of these trails to anyone with a rifle.

Pete walked the line of his twenty men, meeting their eyes, he called out, "Find a rifle, search for ammo. We're going to the ramp. Search for barrier material, once you are near it. Move out." Pete, who loved Grace, and who always wished to fill his guests with good food and drink and Bible quotes and conversation, who liked thought—a good book—more than the action of a pickup soccer game, was determined to kill the black-clothed men till he was dead or victorious. The thought of the degradations, carnage, torture they would inflict on helpless people increased his determination.

***

Andy and his squad had dissected the mass of rebels just as the flight of jetliners roared through. He was one-third of the way up the hill before him, when return scouts said the crest held no enemy forces. The scouts would remain on the crest as an overwatch. Andy turned to the west, saw the black-clothed soldiers gawking at the jetliners in the air, watching and wondering why they were not aboard, sipping alcoholic drinks, eating dainty little snacks, headed for the grand finale, the big event, the storming and sacking of Jerusalem. Andy spoke sharply. "Quick! Aim lasers on suicide packs and bolt actions on the nearest enemy. Conserve ammo. Fire when ready."

John, Diana, Tuck, and Robin had been piling dead enemy to form a wall, when the Burnell brothers and their men came over a swale and joined them. John and Diana began firing lasers, first reaching into the mass of blacked-clothed figures that seemed to be hesitating, unable to choose between moving to Harrisburg or attacking the remaining Christian forces on the battlefield. Bodies with midsection bulk were targeted. Bombs began to detonate, sending the survivors into a run toward Harrisburg. Then the bolt actions began to speak, and the enemy fell. The stampede to Harrisburg increased until the entire mass was moving. When the mass hit the escarpment, it swerved north for the elevated ramp.

Andy had oculars on the ramp. The commanding figure looked like Pete. Where was Grace? He gave his oculars to Tuck. "Look at the ramp. Where's Grace?"

Tuck spoke as he observed the ramp. "She's gone to paradise, Dad. Happened this morning on the far side of the heights. Her body has been retrieved."

"Oh," Andy said softly and sadly. "We've got to move to the ramp, or Pete and his men will be next to go. Tell half of our people to stuff some food in their mouths and drink, while the others fire, then flip the script. Five minutes, then we go." He caught Diana's attention. "You and John fly down and help out Pete at the ramp. They've got no lasers." She saluted and dashed toward John.

***

Pete believed his death would be soon. Rounds were pinging off the metal railing of the pedestrian sidewalk and the cement road surface and lighting poles. There were just too many of the enemy and not one laser in his possession. He felt a hand on his shoulder, he turned, and there were John and Diana, crouched behind him. He had forgotten their special skills of invisibility and flight. John shouted, "Andy's coming down the slope to join us. You want us reaching out with the lasers?"

"Yes!" Pete shouted, as the stampeding enemy raised a pall of dust and gunpowder smoke. How much they appeared as a vast herd of cattle or buffalo. He had seen such events early in his life, when the land was still uncrowded, and herds of animals ran free over the meadows near his cottage home. Back when Gracie was just a friend and life was new. He thought back to his childhood—he'd always wanted to be a hero, fighting against overwhelming odds. Just his skill with his weapon and his resolute determination to overcome, with God as his power and his calm within the maelstrom. And now, it was real. He thought himself a lucky man, and the absurdity of that thought weighed against the pain of being wounded, of dying, made him chuckle at his all-for-Christ attitude; it was 100 percent genuine and pure, and it pleased Him, his ever-present God.

He saw Andy's group rising from their position, moving down the slope, angling toward the ramp. He found an alcove of quiet between two trash receptacles and three dead enemy bodies and methodically loaded his weapon with the last box of belt ammo. He tightened the belt that held the box to his sternum. He reloaded his pistol with the last clip. He slipped the sheaf upon his combat belt nearer to his midsection, so he knew exactly where to reach. He peeked around a receptacle—just twenty yards before the enemy closed in! He turned his body and looked behind, around, three dead enemy bodies. His vision was filled with enemy soldiers.

The living, attacking enemy had gotten behind his position! They loomed above him, and a boot was coming to his face when he pulled the trigger and fell on his back. The boot missed. The man died. Pete twisted to a crouch, then stood, spraying the avalanche of bodies. He smelled sweat, urine; the sticky, coppery blood smell stuck to the gunpowder smoke. He sprayed above his position, then gained the top of the heap of dead and debris and swept the rounds in a one hundred eighty-degree arc.

John and Diana were by him, and five of his men. He thought of retreating away from their position, across the strewn field of the dead and dying enemy, but then saw Andy coming with his band, moving quickly down the slope. John and Diana heaved smoke grenades, fragmentation grenades. The enemy just wanted to get across the ramp to downtown Harrisburg, and perhaps the airport farther south. The highway to the city was filled with black uniforms. Pete and his group waited and rested, scanning the battlefield. Before them came Andy and his crew.

The Burnell brothers were alive and unwounded. The advance pushed the last group of enemy soldiers from the slopes and directly toward Pete's forces. Pete's field of fire had been pinched shut by the approach of Andy's forces and by the firing of his own men in front of him. He ran out from the fortress of debris and dead bodies, onto the slope, and flanked the onrushing enemy so that he was parallel to them. He fired at full auto into the masses. Men fell heavily, tumbling from their run ins with death. In the rear of the falling masses, a suicide bomber separated and calculated a path to the machine gunner killing his men.

Pete's machine gun was empty. He dropped the weapon, cut the harness from his frame, and pulled his pistol. He shot a suicide bomber, the man falling as his vest exploded downward into the ground. The force of the explosion lifted him high in the air as his black blood became a mist. Pete saw others had been hidden behind this man's rush and continued toward them. Pete's pistol was empty, and he pulled his knife. Jack, Sammie, and Robbie were in the lead of the rescue forces and were moving toward Pete. They could not shoot in fear of hitting their friend. Jack, on the outside, strained to gain the flank of the enemy, so a clear shot could be had.

Jack knew he must shoot—Pete could not kill five assailants with his knife. Jack, on the run, shot from his hip and dropped an outside man. Pete dropped to the ground and rolled. Sammie and Robbie fired, and another assailant crumbled. Jack hit another. Pete was forced to regain his feet just as an assailant thrust a bayonet that Pete trapped between his arm and body. Pete then moved forward, delivering a knife thrust to the man's neck, just as a bayonet from the fifth assailant pierced his neck. This enemy was shot by Sammie.

It was too late. The blood was spurting wildly, even as the three gathered, and Jack crammed coagulant into the massive wound. With a desperate hope, Sammie glued and stapled the wound together. Pete was looking at them as they worked. His eyes seemed to smile. He saw each one of them. *I will be back soon*, was his last thought as a final breath would not come. His spirit was gone. Andy saw the angelic blur gather up Peter in one easy motion and shoot into the sky.

Jack fell back on his haunches. "So close…so close…."

***

Pete wondered why he was not dizzy—the angels were moving at incredible speed. Earth was gone, it seemed, in seconds. He was not cold as stars and galaxies streamed past. The angels didn't seem to mind his weight—then he realized that his body wasn't with him, yet he could feel his body. The angels exuded compassion and a satisfaction at their work, knowing the importance of this bridge from death to life.

Then, he was there. Don't ask how, or what he had passed through, or even where he was. It seemed like Earth—a sizable spread of mown lawn, kids, playground equipment, chalked fields, tracks, tennis courts. There was Grace, his Gracie, surrounded by children, standing on a field near playground equipment. He was deposited beside her. "Hey, lady!" he said happily.

Grace turned. "What are you doing here so quickly? Well, look at my kids, Pete. I'm a teacher at this daycare. They are waiting for their parents."

Pete looked at the eager faces, not one over seven. Name tags said *Johnson*, *Burnell*, a few of the line of Tanya, Anya, Flo, had their father's last name. Only seven kids. He was happy at the low number and happy at their happiness, the ordeal that had brought them to paradise already forgotten. "That's smart. Keeping them with someone who knows their family tree, at least," he said.

Grace spoke. "Yes, I do know them. The Johnson kids came from the relatives who settled in South America. The Burnell kids came from Thomas Jr.'s lines and Thomas Sr.'s daughters' lines." She turned to the kids. "That's my former husband, by the way," she said to them. "You can call him Pete."

The kids happily replied, in tattered synchronization, "Hello, Pete."

Pete looked into Gracie's eyes—she was so happy. She took his hand and spoke. "Help me serve lunch. Are you hungry?"

"Why, yes, as a matter of fact," he said. The kids were holding hands in their column of twos. He liked kids, but he was better at other work. Gracie's happiness calmed him and satisfied him. All was well. He would stick with her for the afternoon, even if he was a former husband. He laughed.

***

Andreas, hidden in the forest, surveyed the terminal, hangars, repair and maintenance buildings of the airport complex. Beyond these buildings, past the flat plain, he surveyed the long, grassy ridge two to three hundred feet higher than his position. With an ocular device, he could see the Christian forces beginning to increase, and positions being dug. He had sent a drone over and pictures had been taken before it was shot down. His command was now formally reattached to the satanic forces, and mortarmen had come and set up positions in the trees.

He had not been asked to take his forces to the city of Harrisburg, to fight on some high ground of significance. He had well over two hundred men; stragglers and the unattached had preferred joining his command. Probably for the reputation as deadly fighters, the raffish lifestyle, and loose women. He did not wish to participate in the city fighting. The airport was where, in the end, he needed to be for a flight to the Middle East. Likely, he would need his men to secure a flight out. Technically, he was part of a retreating force, with significant pressure being placed upon that force. The big shots, the generals, had asked for it by wanting a last battle, and now he and his men might be the victims of the foolish policy. They should have peacefully exited—which was what the Christians had wanted.

One of his sergeants and a fighter from a command outside of his approached. They both were nearly crawling; their hands touched the ground. The black shirt of the fighter bore a fiery yellow and red patch with black smoke. The sergeant spoke. "Orders from above."

"Give them." Andreas addressed the fighter with forcefulness but no terseness.

The thin, lanky, sweaty-faced man with yellow hair spoke. "The general is sending a unit to hold this position. He wishes you to move toward Harrisburg and set up an ambush on the road to the airport."

"When does he want this to happen?"

"Now, as your replacements are already moving toward us," said the lanky man.

Andreas held his anger. In fact, he smiled. His men might pull off a successful ambush, but they also might lose their perfect placement for forcing ownership of a transport out. They might be counterattacked and wiped out during that ambush. "I am not happy with that plan. Why don't you remain with me? We will get you a meal and a woman."

"I would like to get back and report your answer. The troops coming can then return to their positions," the man suggested mildly, even as his mind was churning furiously to discern the machinations of this captain. How could he profit from this captain's intent?

"I intend to keep them with me. Stay; it will be safer for you." Andreas spoke with concern for the man.

The lanky messenger thought the proposal through and found his answer. He said, in a voice rough with overuse and tobacco and alcohol, "I will remain, but give me a guard so I can say it was against my will. Or better yet, tie me up until that time the forces are integrated with yours." He paused and gathered his courage. "And Captain, take me with you on the flight to Jerusalem."

"So be it," said Andreas. He admired the analytical foresightedness of the man. He would not compliment the man or ask of the trail of deduction that led to knowing. He needed no more conspirators and, as the saying went, silence was golden. Andreas addressed his sergeant. "Give him a meal if he wants it and a woman, then tie him up and place a guard. I am going to the left flank of our line and greet our new men."

"Yes, sir," the sergeant said, a cunning smile coming to his face as he understood the cunning of his commander.

***

Andreas stood on the extreme left flank. Trees and thick undergrowth hid him from observation by the enemy forces on the ridge. His replacing unit, sent by the general, halted before him as he greeted their commander, a captain.

"Good morning, Captain…?" Andreas's voice exuded cheeriness.

"Herbert," the captain replied crisply.

"Captain Herbert, a change in plans. You will remain with us, of course, but we are not sending any forces to the general's proposed ambush," Andreas said.

"Why?" asked Captain Herbert, his voice neutral.

"There is no advantage in it for our side, or my men, or me, or even you." Andreas matched the neutral tone.

"Explain your reasoning." Herbert's tone held curiosity and no rancor.

"Are there enough planes to take us all to the Middle East? Will the cease-fire hold as we are departing? Seating may be decided by proper staging and brute force. With your unit added to my men, we will be assured seats. An ambush on the road serves no purpose—it is an excuse to get rid of my men."

Herbert listened and thought. Internally, he agreed with the young captain's thought process. The general was thinking of his own departure. The question now was whether this Captain Hahn would be loyal to him and his men. Of course not. One eye would have to be kept on Captain Hahn. In the meantime, Captain Herbert and Captain Hahn had the largest force of soldiers on the battlefield, and when the fleeing, broken forces of Reservoir Park flooded the airport, the captains would have control.

"I agree with your thought process. Let us be the strongest fighting force at the airport. But I will not give up command of my men," said Captain Herbert.

"Of course not." Captain Hahn extended his hand; a salute might be infer that he was the lesser ranked. "And of course, we will share future decisions."

"Certainly," replied Captain Herbert.

CHAPTER 20

Jack, Sammie, and Robbie rested at the ammunition resupply station. Early evening; supper had finished an hour ago, the portions not stingy but not generous. At least a hundred fighters were resting or restocking ammo pouches or loading clips, drums, and belt-fed ammo. Some had broken down their weapons for field cleaning; some sharpened knives and bayonets. Some were still eating from their disposable plates and drinking from their throw-away cups. Leaf was head chef and organizer of the food service. As they rested, they smelled flatbread and corn muffins baking, their midevening snack, and they hoped to grab a handful of muffins or a piece of bread before pulling out. The portable packets of honey, jellies, butter, hummus had already been presented. Coffee could be taken with them if they provided the container.

The gathering still retained the pattern of the small groups that had come in, squads, platoons, the single soldiers on some special assignment or simply wandering in search of their units. Jack glanced over at the moderately sized family utility vehicle that had become Andy's traveling command post. Andy sat upon the opened tail gate. John, Diana, Emily, Dan sat on the portable lawn chairs that had been found in the vehicle. A communications man had set up his equipment on a portion of the back end, and he stood listening. Standing, by choice, to stretch his legs. The day was still warm, even though at 6:00 p.m., a drop in temperature should have been noticed. *What a long day*, thought Jack, as he studied his brothers.

He was proud of them—they had fought hard for their God and their country. They had given unselfishly to their fellow soldiers, sharing water, food, ammunition, bandages. They had carried others' packs, ammo containers, stretchers, rockets, mortar tubes. They had pushed stuck or broken-down vehicles, given food and bandages to wounded civilians, carried frightened and hurting children to safety, propped up the wounded parents under their arms and escorted them. They directed lost people. In truth, all the soldiers of God's army had done the same, without complaint—with joy and even contentment in their actions. Everyone ached or had sprains; most had been wounded or contused, or their minds concussed. Many were out of the fight with immobilizing wounds; but if they could help, they did. Leaf's crew found work for these soldiers.

He was proud of his brothers, because at one time, they had almost left the flowing, life-giving Spirit of Jesus, the Christ who sat on His throne in Jerusalem, who had taken the time to visit them along the banks of the Susquehanna. His brothers would be with him in eternity now. Perhaps they would separate and live their particular courses, their walks with the Lord. But always, they could meet again, share life's experiences, hug and encourage. He wondered who, within his extended family—aunts, uncles, cousins—would not be seen again. He knew his brothers believed, had given full control of their lives to Jesus, by their actions this day, by the wording and emotions of their remembrances of Grace and Peter, and their unmoving faith in seeing that faithful couple again.

Sammie spoke. "Look over at the vehicle. The resurrected barely look winded. They could fight all night and the day after."

Robbie smiled and said, "And the days after that." Robbie took a sip of his coffee and added, "We will soon have one of those bodies."

"And be able to fly, disappear, and pass through material objects," added Jack, as he rose suddenly, seeing Leaf bringing a tray out of the portable oven. She began dumping the muffins into the food pans. He was upon her in seconds. "Permission to take one, Leaf?"

“Take three. You might even get a second helping.” She smiled as she noted his worn countenance.

“Thanks, Mother,” he said as he grabbed butter and honey packets.

She smiled at his expression of love and appreciation. He walked back to his resting place, passing his brothers going to the food truck. He was tired, and the muffins might send him into sleep. Maybe, he could catch an hourlong nap. From the Reservoir Park battle, they had swept through the city. Anyone in black clothing had been shot—a back shot was as good as a frontal shot. Every Christian knew the pain, the degradation the Satanists would inflict if given time to organize and rest. The Satanists had upped the violence and degradation of their acts. No more rape or strippings or—newly added—immolations. No more eating of feces and unnatural sex acts, no more children watching their parents die or vice versa. They had come across an enemy platoon changing from black clothes to civilian clothes under a carport and had shot them all, even as they had protested and begged. Civilian clothes on combatants made them spies, at best, or guerilla fighters. Had they kept their uniforms on and surrendered, they would have lived. None of Satan’s forces had resisted in the city; they were just passing through to the bus station and the airport. Likely, some had hidden in apartments, duplexes, condominiums. The streets would be on lockdown tonight.

At the bus station, they had seen Dan and Emily, who had collected a score of repentant Satanists and a greater number of abducted Christians. These Christians were to have been taken out of the city and eventually flown to Jerusalem to serve as hostages. The Satanists, realizing the last flights were leaving, had voluntarily released the captives, because they took seats away from loyalists who wished to depart. Tuck and Robin had remained at the bus station, and Emily and Dan had joined the forces moving to the airport.

Jack noticed Andy rising, as his immortal entourage, too, began to rise. Andy saw Jack watching, and in response, gave a gathering signal with his arm. He then gave this collecting gesture to the gathered, and they, in turn, moved loosely toward him, slowly, still worn and tired.

Andy spoke, reaching into his diaphragm, where his resonance lived, near to his soul. “All is under control in the city and the county, except for the airport. The Satanists are organized in ranks, their leaders strutting, moving freely in their leadership positions, unafraid of snipers, or future judgment. They give the appearance that they expect more aircraft to come and pick them up. They have defensive positions around the airport, and they have reversed their course of action with hostages. Many were retaken before they could leave and are hostages again. We don't know if aircraft are coming for them. Only time will tell.

"We will further tighten our positions around the enemy, contain them. But if they make a break, we will kill them. If they shield themselves with hostages, we will send our invisibles in and kill the captors.

"The resurrected will be in the front ranks and will be the forces used in any counterattack or first strike. We wish to save you, the mortals, the pain of death, however transient. Any questions?"

Jack raised his hand.

"Yes, Jack."

"Any estimate on the length of time it will take to end Satan's designs and return to peace?"

"Jerusalem just issues the word, 'Patience.' But we know from scripture it is a short time, and it happens quickly and decisively. 'Fire came down from God out of heaven and devoured them.' Revelation 20:9. Satan, too, knows scripture, but apparently his countermeasure will fail. Here, in Harrisburg, this airport standoff should be decided within twenty-four hours."

Andy searched the crowd. "Any more questions?" No hands were raised. "Okay. Rest here one hour more. Grab more food and drink and move toward our vehicle, as more men will be coming in."

***

Andreas Hahn, captain, sat at rest among his command, hidden by concrete barriers, at the entrance to the airport. One road in, and one road out. Only the hardcore were left, and he was pleased with this. Much easier to command. Captain Herbert made no demands, and his men seemed capable soldiers. Everyone had a rifle and one hundred rounds. Five had laser rifles. Their pantry and cooks, traveling with them, had food for five days. All the wounded had died or been left behind, so another responsibility was gone. All objectives had been met. One: to piss on all these god lovers, to show them their powerlessness before the true power—the human will. He thought of Satan as a power to be used by men and discarded when victory was achieved. Two: to distract the local opposition, tie up forces and supplies. So damned simple—everyone else had bled and died except his men. They were his assurance that he would be leaving this unimportant, provincial war.

Personally, he was on the ascendant. He had started as a private and now had the power of a captain. He had killed people—men and women—and had enjoyed it. He had screwed all the women in his command, and they had liked it. He had not failed to meet his objectives on the battlefield, and he had enjoyed the mental discipline necessary to win. He had had plenty to eat and drink and liked the rough, outdoor life. Now, the Jerusalem campaign filled his mind with future pleasures. Exotic women, foods. The pleasure in destroying a rich and prosperous city. Maybe his command would catch that sneaky Christ on his throne and torture Him—all being recorded for posterity, including His death. Fuck god, fuck Christ and shimmering spirits.

The goal, now, was solely to be on one of the aircraft flying out. First, they had to fly in. He knew the Christian forces would allow them to fly in, and he knew, at least by intercepted communications, that they intended to allow the aircraft to fly out. Probably because they feared the killing of hostages. Two large craft carrying a thousand apiece would be needed for everyone to be transported. If only one came back? If only a smaller aircraft returned? He needed a strategy to ensure he was aboard. He could go alone to the open-doored aircraft, a bomb in his backpack, and try to con his way in or threaten to blow the aircraft apart. He could go with his company—two hundred of his men, or his combined force totaling 440, at this point, and fight his way onto the aircraft. Probably others would be using the same strategies; training had always stressed the survival of the most cunning and daring. Collectively, the satanic forces had no compunction to maintain discipline or adhere to a plan. Satan had business elsewhere.

***

Andy watched the sun set from the top of the long slope that ended at the ancient riverbed's flat flood plain. Beyond the flood plain was a second narrow belt of flatness, with woods and then the river. Occasional laser bursts came from the enemy perimeter. When an enemy form was seen, his own lasers answered back. In the rapidly descending dusk, the lasers held a brief, intense beauty, much like the heat lightning in the sky around them. Nighthawks cruised by his ridgetop position, searching for insects in the updraft of the high ridge. They gave their laconic call, "Cheech, cheech." He longed for this battle to be over, for normalcy, the return of peace.

Then he heard a jet engine rumbling, shaking the air and earth, portending violence, and the certainty of catastrophic change. Really, it was an interstellar rocket engine in an air transport, and with seats added in all available spaces, it could probably carry five hundred additional passengers over the normal carrying capacity of one thousand. For Andy, who had lived and died before mechanical flight, the immensity and noise truly were mind bending. Within his millennium life, he had rarely visited the airport south of the city. The aircraft he had seen in the past were not falling like rocks from the sky, consuming the limited vision of the eyes, stalling, roaring as if the earth would split. The largest objects in the air during his first earthly life had been eagles or vultures. In paradise, they had been kept in touch with earthly life through books, pamphlets, newspapers, and then radio and TV, and finally the electrascreen. So many mortals thought those in paradise were clueless about life on Earth, even though they were to return and would meet the present Earth dwellers every time one came to paradise.

Would another air transport follow this first one? It made sense it would not come till the first had departed, although the airport could accommodate six of the latest, supersized models. He sensed the Satanists would misbehave in the belief that no other flight was due—that was their mind-set—they were distrusting people, only interested in their own welfare, and had no faith in others, because there was no faith in God. Their lines would collapse, the hostages would be killed, and they would turn on each other. It made sense for him to order an assault at that time—to save hostages. But then, he could be accused of breaking the orders of his king to allow all to leave. And what if another jet did appear? Accuse? His God did not accuse; that was Satan's game. The pressures of accusations no longer existed.

Let the Satanists condemn themselves by their own actions. Lucky for Andy, the hostages below sat in one large group on the runway cement, under guard. He already had a unit designated to free them—or rather, to erect concrete barriers to surround them, keep them safe while a rescue attack was set in motion. The airliner did not appear to be making a circling pass; the wheels were down. The wheels shrieked from the air velocity streaming through; the craft was closing fast on the runway.

***

What a mess, thought Andy. His mind twisted into a knot as he attempted to calculate the scenarios. Ten minutes since the aircraft had landed, stopped, directly beside the hostages, who were sitting on the runway, evenly spaced, a solid square, easily two hundred people. The aircraft was being refueled with highly flammable rocket fuel; he could see the translucent vapor lifting into the air. The airport lights shone from their tall poles. He could not speculate on how long the refueling would last. He had no idea where the aircraft had come from or how much fuel remained in the tanks. He did know that completely full tanks were needed to reach Europe. Various men had come from the enemy perimeter to the open door and steps and had met with someone in the aircraft. He assumed the leadership was deciding who was going and when and how to load. He assumed they had decided on the fate of the hostages. He could not send a quick-reaction force to their rescue. One stray round, and all would be lost—engulfed in a ball of flame and heat. He wished to save them the pain of a fiery death, even though they would live again into eternity.

Call the enemy's bluff, said a voice within. *Call their bluff now. Send in the resurrected invisible warriors, some to kill the hostages' guards and some to guard the perimeter of the hostage gathering. Send in the convoy of trucks carrying concrete barriers, a mobile fort to surround the hostages. Secure the hostages behind the concrete. Then, begin a comprehensive assault upon the airport.*

What if the jetliner was struck by rounds and the fuel tanks hit? Would the hostages survive? The wind was at his back, blowing across the aircraft to the river, away from the hostages. Small advantage; maybe none at all. The explosive force of the fuel could easily counter the slight breeze and engulf the hostages. What if his convoy of trucks and barriers were decimated by enemy fire before reaching their objective? His plan had risks, but it was better than inaction; boldness and determination sometimes carried the weakest of plans to victory. It wasn't much of a plan, but it was all he had. He must take the initiative.

The refueling was about to end, he could surmise by the motions of the refuelers—their impatient waiting for the uncoupling of the fuel hose. Andy watched as his platoons of resurrected soldiers (men and women) formed ranks for the insertion behind his ridgetop position, unseen by the enemy. Some faces held an anxiety, but even these had resoluteness and confidence. They were in the hands of their God, and their God said, "Set the captives free." They did not need to apply logic, philosophize, debate, think—that had all been done the day Christ became the center of their lives. They simply had to do the Lord's will. Just to do was all He asked. Tuck and Robin, Emily and Dan were within the ranks. The refueling ended, the refueling hose was still being retracted when he ordered, "Go."

The immortals gave quick glances to their right and left, and they were gone. "God's speed and His protection," Andy spoke over them, raising both hands in praise and direction as he watched the giant white aircraft, surrounded by the ranks of the enemy, a half mile away. Andy set his stopwatch. He had thirty seconds to breathe deeply of the humid night air traced with a coolness. He looked straight up; the starry sky was thick. To imagine in 1765 he would be here, before a mechanical bird that could hold 1,500 souls, the forces of evil arrayed against his people, and the God of the universe sitting on an earthly throne. He looked at his watch, thirty seconds.

The radio handset was given to him. "Send the convoy in now." He knew his immortals, unseen, were already with the hostages.

In the lead armored strike vehicle, John Johnson replied into his handset "Convoy, a go." The mission had begun. Diana was beside him, laser rifle in hand. In front of the strike vehicle, an old bus, remote-controlled and filled with concrete debris, sped into the closed front gate surrounding the fenced airport. The gate flew open, metal fence posts were ripped from two consecutive rows of fencing. The bus pulled over, and the strike vehicles shot ahead. The thumping of the concrete on the hard, bullet-proof tires drummed into his mind—1,009 years ago, on his first war mission, on the Polish frontier, God had planned it all.

Andy watched the insertion unit materialize among the hostages and quickly subdue, disarm, cuff, and shackle the enemy forces as the screening force created a perimeter and faced outward toward the enemy. The enemy had been distracted by the forcing of the gate and the strike force now speeding toward the aircraft. Enemy forces were running to their defensive positions. John's convoy began its encirclement of the hostages. John ordered the dropping of the cement barriers around the hostages and, seeing the shock and confusion of the enemy, he deviated from the planned exiting of the empty trucks from the airport. He halted the trucks and began loading hostages onto the empty beds and then sending the trucks into a circling pattern at a safe distance away from the aircraft.

John saw that Satan's forces from the gate's defensive position were coming toward him. John studied their movements. Would they shoot into the still-loading hostages or the loaded trucks, circling, preparing to pass and exit the airport gate? Would their shots strike the jetliner and engulf everyone on the runway in yellow flames? He ordered his driver toward the enemy forces approaching, then realized as he neared the forces that they had no interest in the hostage trucks; their facial expressions screamed survival. Revenge was absent; they could think of nothing but the open door of the aircraft. Other units had broken from their defensive lines and were streaming across the barrenness of the runways and open fields to the jetliner.

John's convoy waited, waited till every hostage was in a truck, then slowly passed through the unguarded, broken gates without incident and raced on the road up the long slope to Andy's command center. As the trucks unloaded, the resurrected became visible in the air and landed in the encampment and positions of the command center. The hostages had been freed! No casualties taken by the Christian forces! John, Diana, Tuck and Robin, Dan and Emily—all participants in the raid—sought each other as they arrived and smiled in thankfulness. They searched for Andy. His nerve, his gamble had brought success.

They found him on the protected north slope, where Leaf had set up her food station. He was hugging Leaf; she was embracing him. They saw his face was tear stained and heavy with emotion and the unknown drama he had borne alone. The ache that had been his for the hostages and his men in harm's way found release. It had been his plan, and the thought of death among the hostages and lengthy disability to the immortals would have been like a knife thrust to his heart.

Dan spoke to his halting group. "Let's go to him now, lay hands upon him and Leaf, and pray for the peace of the Lord." They went and they touched

Andy and Leaf together, and they placed hands upon the couple's shoulders. The Lord was gracious to the gathered, and the Holy Spirit touched Andy with such power that the resurrected saw the presence of the Lord like a clear, cool whirlwind of love twirling through them and above them. From somewhere, a shofar sounded deep and long, and the children of God raised their voices in thanksgiving and praise.

***

Andreas Hahn was one of the first to reach the aircraft from his position at the front gate. Andreas had seen the striker vehicle bristling with weapons and knew it would not fire. The Christians just wanted his forces gone. His battle was to get onto the jetliner that had a maximum capacity of 1,500 souls. Satan's forces wishing to depart were three times that number. Captain Herbert's men were beside his. Their combined four hundred, with new stragglers added, totaled five hundred men. Enough to secure the craft. Hahn knew that once his men entered the craft, they must take off before the remaining thousands gathered at the steps and forced their way aboard or shot at the departing craft. Something else had to be done; Herbert had to be eliminated. Andreas Hahn needed to land in the Middle East the undisputed leader of five hundred troops, if he was to survive the political intrigues of command status and commensurate prestige and rewards, within the gathered army.

With a plan firmly rooted in his mind and shared with two of his most loyal subordinates, Andreas stormed the steps with his men, jamming a metal sign-post pole into the closing aircraft door. By force of bodily strength in shoulders and arms, the door was fully opened. Flashing knives subdued those by the door, who stubbornly resisted. Andreas entered the aisle, and though small of stature, his voice bellowed deeply. "Andreas Hahn, captain of Harrisburg's revolutionary guard, takes command of this craft. You aboard are welcome to remain."

A scuffle was heard behind him as Herbert's arms had been grabbed and a knife plunged into his heart. Andreas's loyal supporter spoke loudly to Andreas. "Sir, Captain Herbert pulled a knife and was about to stab you."

A look of shock swept over Andreas Hahn's face. "I trusted that man." His voice held a despondency. A dutifulness entered his next words.

"Nonetheless, invite his troops on board. Tell them of his death. I will make an announcement and give an explanation as soon as we are in the air." Andreas leaned out the door, waving his arm in inclusiveness to the waiting soldiers of Herbert's command.

When all five hundred men were accounted for, Andreas oversaw the closing and locking of the door. Just before the doors were closed, last-minute rounds were shot into a collection of soldiers possessing shoulder-fired missiles. They were all killed. His staff sat in the front-row seats, nearest the door to the cockpit. He had loyal followers interspersed among Herbert's men. The rocket engines were already roaring, screaming, and the aircraft sprang forward, knocking all unseated to the floor. He sat silently, looking inward, waiting for rockets to slam into the metal fuselage and yellow heat and flame to engulf him. From the window, he saw they were airborne. The thrusters kicked in; the craft kept low to the ground till it was out of the airport's hand-held rocket range. Then, upward went the craft as stomachs and equilibriums were left behind.

Captain Andreas Hahn stood, faced the long corridor of seats, raised his hands in celebration, and then quietly, with a downcast face, lowered his hands to his sides. "A moment of quiet for those who died for the freedoms of individuality we honor, and for those left behind. Captain Herbert was a brave and good man, but he feared losing control of his men, whom he loved. He felt the need to remove me, seeing me as a threat. I never was and assured him many times through the last weeks. Let us free ourselves of paranoia and work together as a team. I loved your captain as much as you, and I will treat you as my own." Andreas's eyes came out of their fixed inward gaze and lit with joy as he surveyed his men. He bellowed, "Onward to Jerusalem!"

The passengers clapped and cheered. Captain Hahn understood that he was a guiding light, a man who uttered words that had import and caught the collective desires, consciences of the masses. In summation, he was a leader.

***

Within weeks, the country known as the United States of America had rounded up the battlefield stragglers from the forces of Satan, and, finding their numbers so great as to overflow temporary housing, they built a prison. Spiritual reeducation was offered, as well as work in prison industries, where salaries were paid. Men and women graduated from the spiritual reeducation courses, but the results from polygraph tests and even more sophisticated "truth tests" seemed to indicate the knowledge was indeed learned but not absorbed. Satan's people were loaded onto planes and sent to the Middle East.

Americans cleaned up the debris and destruction of the four-month rebellion upon their land. New homes, churches, offices, factories were built to replace the destroyed. The damaged buildings were rebuilt. Communications were restored. Everyone kept a watchful eye upon the electrascreen on the developments in the Middle East, where Satan and his horde of worshippers found compliant countries to house their developing armies. And the Lord, still on His throne, refused the help of men and materials from the lands recently freed from rebellion, even as he was surrounded by an enemy army of millions. He was confident, unperturbed, and spoke of the New Jerusalem coming, the new and final resurrection of worthy mortals, and the Great White Throne of Judgment, where those who had rejected the authority of God and Christ from the beginning of time to the present would receive judgment in their earthly immortal bodies.

An eager expectation gripped the United States. It seemed to crackle in the air as summer faded. When would Satan's rebellion be crushed? So many questions—when would the righteous mortal dead, the Tims and Marys, the Toms and Tishs of the millennium, return in their resurrected bodies? When would the living righteous mortals, like Jack, Sammie, and Robbie, who had lived through Satan's rebellion, receive their new bodies? When would the judgment of the unrighteous begin? When would New Jerusalem come?

CHAPTER 21

John and Diana had invited Emily and Dan for a "hang out" on the deck of their rebuilt mountaintop cottage. The cottage had been burned by Satanists while John and Diana were on military assignment in the city. "Hang out" was an appropriate term, as John had rebuilt the deck so that it hung out from solid ground. An unobtrusive safety net of fine mesh hung underneath; it was strong enough to support the stoutest man and fine enough to catch a fallen ring. The middle-of-August weather was warm and would have been hot if not for the constant, easy, fragrance-filled air currents playing hide-and-seek in the treetops. The brilliant-blue sky, the sparse wisps of white clouds with gray bottoms made for a vast view of a land at peace and in love with the God of Creation. The four gathered were in love with God; their Great I Am, their Yahweh, their Jehovah with so many titles denoting His powers and benevolences—well, where could it end? He had upheld them each, protected them, given them guidance, given them hope and courage in these past and sometimes desperate days. I Am Who I Am—He had given them everything they possessed! They sang to Him from the deck because, really, what else could they do but love Him with all of their being?

In time, they talked of the deer and elk, of the buffalo herds still roaming about, of the waters of the sparkling Susquehanna, nearly a mile wide and teeming with fish—huge sturgeons, slippery eels, shad. A mountain lion had discovered the long, high ridge of the mountain chain. In the nights, he or she would scream at the wandering bands of wolves or coyotes. None had an interest in man and certainly not to harm. Predators had become content with using the old and/or gravely injured mammals as food and rarely attacked the seemingly healthy. Fish, nuts, fruits, tubers, grains were a greater part of the menu now. The gardens and fields had given bountiful crops of perfectly textured and tasty fruits, grains, and vegetables, as they did every year. The gathered wondered if Tuck and Robin would stop in after work. Diana was about to mention their departed friends Pete and Grace, when the electrascreen snapped on.

John noted the time: 10:00 a.m. Eastern Standard Time. He spoke quickly. "It's programmed for automatic ON for news of the war." The hologram appeared on top of the large picnic table. Surround sound clicked on, and the size of the hologram went to maximum (ten feet). No one moved. The date and time in Israel was given at the bottom of the screen—5:00 p.m., same day as in Harrisburg. "This is live action," John said. Cold shivers embraced their skin.

They saw drone footage of the city of Jerusalem, beginning at the rebuilt temple. The drone flew above the belt of military fortifications, friendly armies, which girded the city. Miles of soldiers in ranks, gun emplacements, encampments. Then, no man's land—empty grazing land, war debris, and alert and anxious soldiers in small groups. The drone scanned the horizon in all directions. Satan's armies touched the Dead Sea in the east and the Mediterranean in the west, Syria to the north, Jordan in the south. Missing were the demonstrators who wished to petition Christ for eternal sexual rights. Satan had given them the choice of a weapon or a bullet in the head—most had chosen a weapon. Enemy rockets, bullets, laser beams whizzed past the drone. When the drone hovered, John and guests saw enemy munitions being deflected by an invisible shield around the drone.

The drone accelerated at incredible speed, moving toward a solid concrete, windowless building. The drone suddenly stopped, and the drone's camera lens closed on figures on the building's roof. John yelled out, "That's Satan! That's Satan!" They saw a turbaned man with a long, dark-black beard and piercing eyes surrounded by men. He did not recognize any of the men. Undoubtably, Satan's generals and staff members. The beast and the false prophet were locked up in Hell.

Then it happened. Suddenly. Played in slow motion? Or had God slowed time so that all could see and understand? A brilliant flash of light from above, then a tendril of fire, falling like ticker tape from a skyscraper. A heavier downward end, and a tapering, fluttering tail. Living fire, with tendrils coming from the main stem, yellow, white, orange. A piece of the sun, a solar flare, taken from the sun and brought to Earth? Seemingly slow, it fluttered downward, growing in size and brightness. The drone slowly retreated upon its previous course as the object grew in size.

The drone was gone. The camera was high over the city, catching the entire city within its lens. The fiery tendril touched the earth and wound itself around the city and the allied armies of Israel, falling only within the massive belt of Satan's collected followers. As the fire laid upon the earth, flashes of light appeared within—ammunition, vehicles, supplies, and bodies popping, hissing, and exploding in the now billowing fire. The shimmering heat distorted images. It was so intense there was barely any smoke to rise. The sound was shaking the table, the flesh of the gathered friends; the sound of burning was a roar. Another camera caught the fallen fire spreading, billowing out over the enemy forces, and before the eyes could adjust to the magnitude of destruction, the flames were gone; the earth—just recently scorched—was still, silent, unmoving; the structures of former inhabitants were whole and standing; grasses, crops were unburned; civilians, alive. The forces of Satan, their encampments, their supplies of ammunition, food, vehicles were gone—incinerated to powder.

Seven times God had called down fire from heaven, upon the earth, in the days before Christ was upon the earth. Had not Elijah called down fire from heaven upon the soldiers of Ahaziah? What was too difficult for God?

A hush was on the soundtrack, then the labored breathing of the newscaster and camera crew, struggling to comprehend the great destructive power that had seemed to threaten them with death, and yet now there was peace and stillness—life. "My God! My God!" were the awestruck whispers of the crew as they clumsily directed their drone to search the former camp of God's enemies. Not one could speak a sentence. Evil was gone—the task done as quickly as it had begun.

The familiar newscaster, a kind man of fatherly demeanor, with great faith and love for his Lord, spoke. "Satan and his armies have been destroyed—totally destroyed. Fire from heaven. No one left, not even a corpse. Here is a pronouncement from our King."

Christ was sitting upon His throne. The people of His kingdom revered that picture, that snapshot, that representation of who He was. Had a mere man, an elected official, a president, a premiere, a politician, a general sat upon a throne, they would have toppled him from power. THIS WAS THE SON OF GOD, WHO HAD LOVED THEM TO THE CROSS AND VICTORY. He saw what they could be when they were rebellious—hateful, cruel, depraved, and twisted images of what they should have been—and He had counted them as redeemable, as having worth. What else could He sit upon but a throne?

"Today, Satan inhabits hell—the great lake of fire—never to exist anywhere else. Today, his human followers begin their trials at the Great White Throne of Judgment. Judgment not for guilt or innocence, not for captivity or freedom, but for punishment commensurate to the depth and duration of the depravity they inflicted upon the innocent and helpless. If it were possible that a man or woman existed who had never hurt another, his or her guilt would remain—for not recognizing and worshipping our Father. They would have been worthless in helping to lead others to My help.

"In the courts of heaven, God our Father will pronounce judgment and punishment. No jury, no defense lawyer. God has seen in intimate detail even the inner thoughts of the guilty, from their births to their deaths. There is nothing to argue and no doubt in His pronouncements. Within weeks the cases will be made public, presented electronically or through tangible printed matter. Or even by your mind's inquiry, the Spirit of God will hear and provide the answers you desire."

Jesus stepped off the throne; his royal robe slipped from His shoulders and was placed on the throne. In a business suit, He walked over to a lectern. "The people of the millennium who left us will be returning in the next few weeks in their resurrected bodies. The people who lived through the millennium in their mortal bodies will be called to paradise to receive their resurrected bodies. Embrace Rosh Hashanah and the following holy days in a new way, with a new perspective, for soon I will relinquish my earthly spiritual and political power to my Father. I came to redeem the world and to rule, and those goals have been accomplished. The Holy Spirit, the

Advocate, Teacher, and Comforter came to you in my absence. His work has been accomplished—the mind of God is known to you and is in you. The New Jerusalem is to come."

The screen faded. A panel of news commentators were upon the electrascreen. No one on the mountaintop paid attention. They could hear the fire sirens of distant towns and beyond, to Harrisburg. Fireworks were popping. Rams' horns were sounding from backyards, pastures, mountaintops. John ran to the cottage to retrieve his horn, and Dan followed. Emily grabbed Diana's hands, saying, "Tim and Mary, Mat and Barb, Katie and Paul, Hope and William, and the Burnells—Tish and Tom, Tanya, Anya, Flo, Tom Jr., and their spouses and kids are returning. I wonder if Robbie, Jack, and Sammie have left yet?" When Emily paused, Diana inserted her names: "Carl, Ling and family, and Pete and Grace."

"And DC Jones will come back to visit her old friends," added Emily. Dan sounded the shofar; tall and thin, he produced the resonance from lungs and diaphragm of a marathon runner.

Diana spoke softly to Emily as the men sought the four cardinal points to blast their happiness, their awe at their God's power and faithfulness. "Finally, it is over…completely. We've lived the last pages of God's book, His Holy Word. The final chapter for all people born. All will be judged, all with eternal life either in heaven or hell. Never, never could I have believed as an eighteen-year-old Parisian streetwalker, bereft of hope, that I would be here…loved by God in a resurrected body with an eternity of fulfilling life ahead of me. Loved by God…it is so overwhelming." Diana wept and Emily, once a beaten and abused child with both parents dead, who had wished for death as the Tribulation raged, till Matthew touched her heart when the Johnsons took her burden to the Lord, wept with Diana at the love of their Father.

John and Dan came back from their mission to sound the victory of the Lord to all Creation and find their most beloved friends in tears. John immediately took Diana's hands. He knew she was thinking back to the beginning of this journey and realizing who she had been and what the Lord had made her. He spoke. "My Diana, once my only earthly hope—me, as a scared Enslaver, wanted for murder and mutiny. With your help and love, I made it, and we did something good, along with Gramps. We…no, you…filled with the Spirit of the Lord…found the satanic bible. Think of it, woman: you're in the history books! Played a key role in exposing the corrupt church. In this millennium, you were right there in every fight."

Diana answered, "From April 15 to August 15—four months that seemed like two years. Oh, Johnny boy, we did do good things together. If I had never met you…never felt sorry for your withdrawn mind and scrawny, pathetic body…." She laughed, and he laughed, and they felt, emanating from one another, the deepest oneness and satisfaction that they had not only survived the times but had conquered…simply by trusting in Jesus.

Dan and Emily had withdrawn to the picnic table. Dan, who had lived longer, had his arm around Emily's shoulders and his free hand in hers, encompassing her with his warmth. "Little Emily, you and I have survived much, but we have lived deeply…don't you think, for two lives that seemed over before they began? You, the mushroom admirer, and me, standing dumbly while the bullets zinged. But He used us…and that gives satisfaction. What can we say about a thousand years of peace, knowledge, contentedness, the curse of Satan broken? I'm glad I had you for company."

Emily corrected him. "We had each other."

Diana called over, "Let's make a cake for this celebration!"

John added, "And eat lunch." They laughed in joy at humanity's liberation from slavery and for the absurdity and inconsequentiality of that desire called hunger.

***

Andy and Leaf strolled silently down the river trail before their homestead. Andy would stop and listen, watching the birds in the trees, the mammals on the ground. The river water was cooling, but the sun's heat kept the temperature agreeable to hungering fish. This was their first real day to unwind. They had heard the sounding horns, the firecrackers, and had turned on Andy's forearm electrascreen, with flat view only, and caught the commentators saying the war was over, Satan was destroyed, and judgment was coming to the evil.

Andy spoke softly to his wife. "This is near your lucky time of the year... the time when Leaf became your name."

She smiled. "Yes, a blessing to be hitched to an arrogant cuss like you."

He laughed then spoke in a serious tone. "Why did He choose me?"

She smiled wryly. "Probably the same reason I did…you were the only one left." She referred to the state of marriageable Native American men when they courted—most dead, wounded, alcoholic, beset by disease and vengeance.

Andy laughed deeply at her simple but profound wording. He spoke coaxingly. "For real."

She shook her head. "You really do know…you saw two crippled, worthless kids...the seed of your loins…and were disgusted, seeing no help or glory in them. You were about to do what the world would have done… kill them. But you didn't listen to Satan's voice—they and I, the bearer of cripples, were not worthless. Why, you did not know, but you listened to the voice of God…His nature…His character. That is why He chose you for eternity, and that is why He chose you to lead during the rebellion. You had broken away from yourself, your people, from the world, and in truth, from Satan. You were His man…only His, a man of compassion."

"Is that it?" Andy asked, not in anger or frustration, but in a thoughtful need for finality. He was puzzled.

Leaf's eyes gathered tears for her silly man. "That is enough. The more the world ground you down to dust, the more the armor of God shone through. You can't break a broken man's spirit when it is replaced by the Spirit of God." She stopped his walk, forcefully hugged her man, who could not see his nobleness, his loving heart.

They were at their sitting stone, a long, smooth river rock that sat two comfortably. They sat. The view was of the island and the river past the island, to a far western shore unseen. Yellow river-birch leaves spun to the water.

"Our boys are coming," said Leaf, looking into the sky.

Tuck and Robin stepped down from their flight onto the rocky shoreline as smoothly as if upon a carpeted floor. Tuck shouted up the bank, "Did you hear the news?"

Leaf answered, "We believe we did."

That was just like Mom, always covering wide spaces with few words. The men propelled up the slope as if possessing springs in their legs. Andy watched their fluid movements and the power in their legs. They sat beside him. God was good, and all the sufferings his little family had endured had been worth it. Life was everything, and it never should be thrown away, even in the face of overwhelming challenges—he knew this without doubt. Andy then did something he didn't often do; he hugged his boys. It seemed forever, and he cried with a sense of duty fulfilled, mission accomplished; he cried, for his God had heard his prayers and had carried him, and the burden given from the day of his birth—to protect that which was good—and the burden carried since the day his boys were born—to honor life and protect that which was weak—had been lifted. His boys were so wonderful, so beautiful. His boys sat beside him and kissed his cheek, rubbed his back, held his hands, and told him what a great man he was and is. Behind them, Leaf gathered them all into her embrace, and they praised their God together in humble, almost whispered, prayer.

***

Grace pressed the OFF button on the computer. It was the right thing to do—to come back to their little cottage and rest before seeing friends. The judgment of the damned was happening now. Her heart felt light and free. All her kids and her kids' kids were safe. *Home sweet home*, thought Grace as the quietness of her cottage living room wrapped around her. The light was fading as she looked out her large window at the eastern mountain and the stars that were appearing. Pete entered the room from the kitchen, carrying a tray with light-snack goodies—cheeses, warm breads, spreads, cuts of smoked chicken and ham. To drink, homemade root beer.

Grace spoke. "Petee, (her name for Pete Jr.) and Gracious (her name for daughter, Grace) are okay. No armies landed or beached in their part of the world. But a hundred miles east was different. None of their kids or their offspring answered Satan's last call. Our Holy God kept our family intact, Pete. Faith undefiled by the passage of years—we all held firm!"

He heard her satisfaction and gratefulness in the quiver in her tone and the lightness of her voice. He thought of his son as a child, Peanut Butter—Petee, he was called. And he thought of his little girl as a toddler, Goodness Gracious was her moniker. He sat, expecting to eat, till his emotions compelled him to kneel before the couch. Tears streamed from his eyes. He sobbed as he saw his children and their families for two generations flash before his eyes—such precious kids. The Lord had covered them with His wings, had gathered them tightly to His bosom and protected them. "Give praise to our God, Grace. Let us pray for all those who lost their loved ones to eternal death and damnation."

Grace moved down to her knees beside her husband, grabbed his arms and hands. Then one hand went around his waist, and she hugged him tightly. "Yes, it is finally over—the testing time. The children of God fully revealed. Some will have remorse, but it will be a short season, as we value who we have around us, and the new Jerusalem coming, and eternity before us."

Pete confessed. "I hold onto the negative...just on the trip back...all those who disappeared before our eyes...on their way to judgment and eternal hell."

Grace answered. "Well, some might have been going to paradise for their resurrection bodies. But the rebellious—the Lord knew what was in their hearts. Most had enough daring to follow Satan but no love for our Savior. The final judgment...it's all over." She thought for a moment. "Tomorrow, let's go downriver. Tim and Mary, Mat and Barb, Katie and Paul, Hope and William, even Tom and Tish may be back in their resurrected bodies...and Tanya, Anya, and Flo. Maybe Tom Jr. will show. Everyone and their kids."

"What about Carl, Ling and family, DC Jones, and our precious war buddies, Robbie, Jack, and Sammie?" he asked.

Grace kissed him and whispered, "Let's pray, dear."

Pete smiled, and they poured out their hearts to their God.

In time, when all had been given to God and nothing withheld, Pete rose and offered his hand to Grace, who accepted and was pulled up and onto the couch. Pete sat beside her. "Hearing how our friends and relatives spent their days in paradise, how they lived on Earth while we were gone—sitting by the river, eating good food—holds my interest."

"A little food, sleep and tomorrow will be as exciting and bright as the past one thousand years," Grace said. "We can keep the doors unlocked again."

"Amen," said Pete.

***

The new day came in cool and with a gentle quietness. God's presence was palpable and satisfying, and Grace's radiance could have lit a darkened room. She noticed Pete's radiance. Pete held Gracie's kayak steady as she delicately placed both feet in. Her form, her hips were still youthful and supple. *The resurrected body is an amazing bit of engineering*, he thought. Once in place, she sidled her kayak up against his and used her paddle to keep it tight against a log buffer on the shore. Pete adeptly transitioned from earth strider to river glider. The late-summer water was cool, and the river was on a slight rise. The weather indicated an early fall and winter. The rocky *V* of their eel corrals could be seen above the water and had inches showing. The eel traps had been taken out, as they had no idea how long they would be visiting. Pete had already caught a basketful, and the eels were waiting in the freezer for their return.

"You know, Grace," he said, and then his voice trailed away.

"What?"

"I could have left the baskets in place. I can fly. I could have easily checked them each morning." He had flown in from paradise with Grace, but he didn't have many hours in, other than the training in paradise.

"But hauling the eels out and gutting them—and our freezer storage isn't great. And smoking them takes care," she reminded.

"I guess I did the right thing." As his eyes scanned the river, his mind held amazement at the ducks and geese in great flights or feeding in quiet eddies by islands and shore. The wind, brisk, was at their backs or upon their right shoulders, from the northwest. The sky was overcast. A coldness of great force, suddenly struck their backs, and bent island trees. The view of the river ahead, showing the great width and expanse that always amazed him, seemed convex. He saw a hunting blind on an island's stern. He saw no one and heard no shots anywhere on the river. The millennial humanity had had enough shooting recently, and even avid hunters just wished to rest, sit this season out. As a newly resurrected man, the desire to hunt had disappeared when Pete knew any living form would gladly come to him to be slaughtered—the "have dominion over them" now unimpeded by the world, the flesh and Satan. With the mortals now immortal, perhaps hunting would cease.

He remembered the story his grandfather Mat had told him of crossing a lava ash and sludge-choked river during the Tribulation. He wished to hear it again, and of the temporary death of Emily on the other side. Maybe he could hear the story from Tim, Mary, Katie, and Emily. Would be interesting to hear their perspectives.

Grace spoke. "You want to hear the sludge river story again?"

"How'd you know that?" he exclaimed in amazement.

"I'm not sure. Maybe it's because now, not only is Satan gone, but also the last vestige of the world system, and the people of the flesh are no longer creating noise in our world of peace."

"That's deep and may be correct!" He marveled at the implications.

They floated in silence, and then he headed, and she followed to the center of the river, where the islands were thickest with overhanging trees, and stream-like runs cut the islands. Kingfishers splashed in still waters, holding trophies in their glistening beaks; and herons, treading lightly, with studious grace, turned their heads, saying with their eyes, "Leave me alone." Deer were caught in surprise, drinking from the streams, as was a skunk searching for good things under the leaf litter. Then, they headed back toward the eastern shore. Drifting in their thoughts, gazing at bluffs with sedimentary layers exposed by the early falling leaves, watching elk and even a moose and a herd of buffalo, drinking from the river's eastern shore.

Pete's thoughts turned to Andy, Leaf, and Tuck and Robin, who had seen this river before in a pristine state and lived among the first men, the hunter/gatherer ideal. The women were fulltime farmers, mothers, cooks, clothing makers. Andy, once, in a long dialogue of the heart, had dispelled the persistent myths cast by the deceiver about that state of human economic growth where, supposedly, all was peaceful, and everyone loved one another, and their only enemies were outsiders.

They were as hateful as any human flesh stained by original sin. Siblings fought violently, lies were told easily. Property was taken at will, but that was not called theft, because all things belonged to all people. Marriages were fluid; the sick, forgotten; perfect and imperfect infants were killed; mockery and ridicule would only cease if retaliation occurred. And yet Andy had thought of them as his people, thought they loved him or at least respected him—till his crippled boys were born. That was his first forsaking of the world, when he knew he would walk alone with only God, somewhere out there, to show the way. Then, the Holy Spirit had come to him and a new world.

"There's Andy and Leaf," said Grace, who had moved closer to the eastern shore. Without warning, the thick back of a long sturgeon, perhaps eight feet, arched between their kayaks; both were looking at each other when it happened. They said nothing, as each knew the other's thoughts of delight. He could barely make out human forms till he shifted to his left. In their old bodies, their eyes would never have discerned their friends. Upon the river, they suddenly spied Tuck and Robin.

They were in a long, low, wooden, flat-bottomed boat, emptying their eel baskets. They were far from Andy's farmstead, above even Katie's cottage (the farthest north of the homesteaders). No doubt, it was a perfect corralling area, perhaps even known from the 1600s. Fifteen hard strokes with the current and the wind directly at his back, and he was looking into the deeply ladened boat. The eels were squiggling and squirming; the shades of browns, grays, and grass green to lettuce green blended so beautifully that Pete thought the scene worthy of an oil painting.

The sun-darkened, weathered faces of Tuck and Robin flashed white with teeth. They had not seen their neighbors since that awful day almost three weeks ago, and their joy was immense. In truth, seeing anyone—even a stranger—brought joy. Each person was a gift. No more people were being made, and these people you saw were the best made. All had hearts and souls for their God. You would never be misunderstood; you would never be impugned with false and hateful motives—not in speech or actions. Everyone wished the best for everyone else. No evil thoughts, no craftiness, no cunning, no desire for evil. The freedom was exhilarating—you could actually share your heart with another, even a stranger, and the "why are you telling me this" face, the coldness would be nonexistent. The release from bondage was truly palpable. Every breath was a sigh of release from the tension and anxiety of the world, the flesh, and Satan.

"Back from paradise. We'll go flying together soon," said Tuck, smiling happily.

"The last time I saw you two, my heart ached," said Robin. "But I knew this day would come. So glad to see both of you."

"And we, you," Grace's lilting voice revealed her heart. "Robin is bobbin with the eels in the boat. And Captain Tuck's countin' the bucks."

"And rhymin' Gracie is no disgracie…to poetry." Tuck began to laugh at his own wan performance. They all joined in laughter so giddy with happiness that they would have laughed at anything. Life was truly a gift.

As they quieted, Pete spoke. "To think that colloquialism 'buck' is from your time on Earth so many hundreds of years ago." He paused. No reply was needed; they heard each other's replies, ruminations, and thoughts without words spoken. "We're going in to see your folks. See you on shore."

Leaf and Andy were contentedly sitting by a small fire, heads hatted, deerskin jackets with a woolen lining buttoned tight. They worked the location of their spitted eels upon embers they had pulled from the flames of the burning wood. "Half for each of you. And we will make more," said Leaf. "Hey, haven't we seen you before?" Her face seemed to glow as the corners of her mouth turned upward into a shining grin, as did Andy's.

"Yes, I think we were friends before we died and went to paradise," said Pete, playing along. To be so casual about death? Should he be? Yes, it was gone forever now. He remembered his Gracie's face as she had died and that feeling of loss but not aloneness, for the Spirit of God had always filled him. Even as he had died, he had not felt alone. He had really felt satisfaction in knowing he had given it all, his very life, to Christ. Grace had told him she had felt the same, with just a momentary regret that she was not there for him.

Andy spoke from his heart. "You died bravely, Pete, fighting to the end against overwhelming odds. Jack, Sammie, and Robbie made a valiant effort to kill your attackers."

"I remember seeing them coming toward me," Pete said. "I am honored to have had the opportunity to fight with you, your sons, John, and Diana, the Burnell brothers, Emily and Dan. I had always wanted to give Christ everything."

Andy spoke quietly. "Spoken like the loving man and warrior you are. Yes, it is good to give it all…as He did for us."

"Are we done fighting…do you think?" inquired Pete.

"Who knows what work we will do in the future, but God. Are there worlds out there that will need us to fight for them or with them? Did not angels do the same for us?"

"Eels are done," said Leaf. "Grab a leaf—but not me." She had collected the large, flat, wilting leaves of some unnamed plant to use as plates.

"What kind of plant is that? Is it safe?" asked Grace, wondering if some acrid taste was possible.

"I don't know, but it's large," Leaf said dumbly. Leaf laughed at Grace's shocked expression. "Yes, I have used them many times, as have my people."

Grace was just reacquainting herself with "Leaf humor," and was a little slow. She laughed—quite an actress.

They ate the flaky, sweet flesh as they enjoyed the now-chilling cold wind through the trees, the raining leaves of color, the smell of smoke, the heat, and the vista of a primitive river and islands. Tuck and Robin came ashore and enjoyed the impromptu feast with them. God reigned, the worst was past, the history of Earth complete, and new adventures awaited.

CHAPTER 22

Andreas Hahn was in a net; he sensed he was hurtling through space. Others were in the vast net, their collective weight forcing the sides of the rough, bristly, rope net into those unfortunate enough to be on the outside. His body was burned to a black crisp—like a piece of meat accidentally fallen through the grate of the outdoor grill or cast into an open fire. All the forms around him were burned. He remembered leading his columns into the front-line trenches, bullets whizzing over the embankments, parapets. How proud and eager he had been. He had risen to the rank of major—a thousand-plus troops followed his orders. He had felt a heavy wind pushing him down, a rushing sound.

He had been pounded only once, into the earth, then ground into the soil. The air had been sucked from his lungs; he had watched his body turn to charred, flaking flesh. He was naked, without toes, without fingers; his genitalia did not exist; his ears and nose were gone, and certainly, his hair. He realized his eyes were gone, yet he could see and feel his stinging flesh, and he could think. He was living from his soul and his mind, separate entities from the flesh.

His internal organs had dried up from the searing heat; they hung inside, shriveled by the intense heat—dried-up lungs, heart, bowels. He could hear his brain, shrunk to the size of a small potato, dully rattle in his skull. Fire from heaven had caught them all, rendered them incinerator rubbish. As the almost-weightless body had been sucked into the vortex of rushing sound, a giant net dragged by angelic beings had caught them up.

He was beyond terror, he verged on hysteria, and yet he knew that if he did not remain in control, if he did not struggle to keep his burned flesh together, he would be cast into the four winds in an excruciating agony. His will would surge and weaken, over and over, creating even greater pain. Death throes… the struggle to be. He felt himself willing the burnt, seared flesh and internal organs to remain as one.

He saw an orb in space, a blackened orb, burned, with dark clouds surrounding the sphere. Thunder pounded his ears and lightning, horizontal and vertical, dashed through the clouds. He felt dry heat penetrating with excruciating pain. He saw a circle, an amphitheater carved into the ground, made of fitted stone, and a huge central stage. Beings were arranged—humans in white robes, sitting in various circular patterns. His net passed over. An angel dropped one corner, and the contents fell onto the huge amphitheater.

He was retching as he fell. It was all in his mind, he told himself; but he was spinning, and he wished he could die; he wished for nonexistence, complete annihilation. He hit the stone floor. The impact turned him into a pile of dust. But he had cognizance and sight. A man in a white robe was walking toward him. Suddenly, he felt the absolute terror and helplessness of one to be raped; he would be touched and fondled and had no strength to resist. The white-robed ones would mock him and laugh at his puniness, mock the sound that came as his voice as weak and frail. He would be stomped on and entered, defiled. They would ravage his private places, his weaknesses. He would no longer be a man, a being with dignity. Or would they just sweep aside the pile of ash that was Andreas Hahn with the broad side of their feet?

The white-robed man stopped before the pile of ashes that was Andreas and spoke. "That is not us. That is one of your victims speaking through your emotion. 'Do onto others as you would have them do onto you.' Or if you please, 'love your neighbor as you would yourself.' Rise in your immortal body, Andreas Hahn."

His emotion leaped with joy—immortality! He had found favor with them. It would soon be over, this pain gone.

He stood in his fleshly body, fully whole and healthy, clean, clothed in a robe as clean as his flesh.

"Follow me," said the robed man. He passed other captives and their white-robed guides as he approached a half circle of men, sitting high around a mini amphitheater. Andreas stood in the center, looked up, and studied the faces of the men. They had kind faces, and he felt he could wrest mercy from their souls. He did not sneer at kind faces now. The kind-faced people had won.

The man with the kindest face spoke as the white-robed guide left. "Be certain of this—you are in the court of the White Throne of Judgment. You will have everlasting life, lived in hell. Your name has not been found in the Book of Life. You have rejected Christ—I might add, repeatedly and consistently. We are here to render a judgment of punishment that befits your bestial and depraved actions and thoughts while upon Earth. We are not here to torture, nor are we here to refine your thoughts and character for the goal of repentance. You had a lifetime to repent, and you did not.

"Your actions and attitude toward the Godhead and toward humanity will be turned upon you for eternity. You have embraced the law of the carnal in life. You have shunned the Spirit of God. You shall be judged under the law—an eye for an eye, a tooth for a tooth. As matter is neither created nor destroyed, should it surprise you that the soul of a human lasts for eternity?"

Andreas erupted in hate. "That's smug. What of forgiveness and grace?"

"You rejected forgiveness and grace when you rejected Christ. You will be silent."

Andreas's throat tightened; he could not speak.

"You wish to argue and manipulate. You had a lengthy and healthy lifetime for that. The word of God was in the air, within your mind, evident and overpowering. That was the time to choose correctly. Christ had paid your sin debt, you simply had to consent to His truths, and acknowledge His death and resurrection. You were not even asked to use your will to not sin. You were simply asked to yield to the voice of the Holy Spirit. Simply yield. You loved your hate, and you loved your sin. Watch the hourglass before you; in a minute of time, you will see the sin of your life paraded before you, and the punishments for the same."

A bright light came down from heaven and transfixed Andreas Hahn to the stage. The hourglass that contained a minute of time was turned. He was compelled to go into his mind, his past; a mechanical clock was ticking, running time, pages from a calendar were turning to certain dates, his age; from his birth, it sped. Comments were spoken by the Holy Spirit, not addressed to him but to the Book of Judgment, a narration of sin. His input would not be needed or tolerated.

The narration gave no hint of his inner thoughts or of others' attitudes and behavior toward him. The narrative addressed lies and willful refusal to obey parents and godly authority. He had been a slanderer from an early age and enjoyed creating confusion and disobedience. He gave no respect, no kindness. Hate, dissatisfaction, strife, impatience, rudeness, championing of all that was bad were his goals. He was unfaithful to God and man and cruel in action and word. He was a volatile spirit, uncontrolled. He worshipped himself. He was proud, arrogant, abusive, ungrateful, unholy, heartless, unappeasable, and brutal, and he hated goodness. Treacherous, reckless, a lover of sexual domination. Scenes from his life streamed on, the exact year, day, time of every event. Every event was marked with the exact violation or list of violations.

Andreas smirked—no use pretending or attempting to hide his true feelings behind sadness, shame, repentance. God, evidently, did know everything. Who would have thought? Who would have thought He kept track of it all—every damned second? Where had that ability come from? The life before him was his life. He had enjoyed it. He had hurt many—that's what life was about; it was unavoidable. He had to have an argument, a counterpoint. Ah, he had done good things, acts of sharing and kindness. He would hide behind these—that would even the score! He could hide behind his goodness. He had to speak up now—now, before it was too late. He could not speak. He was physically unable to speak.

Then the streaming presentation was done, finished. He tried to utter a word. No word came from his lips. He had been sealed up, unable to speak—what a devilish trick. It appeared God and Satan were the same. The sentence: to the tenth level of hell, and there were only ten levels. If there were only ten, then he would have as his companions serial killers, child molesters and rapists, sadists, sadomasochists, murderers of all kinds. *In a way, it's a compliment.* He humphed. He came out of his mind. The men were looking at him. He saw the timer. He saw the last grain of sand fall. It seemed that at least a day had passed. He was still expecting a chance for a last word, or to place his appeal. He attempted to speak again—to tell them of his goodness. No word was allowed to form.

He was gone. He didn't remember leaving; darkness was around him, total darkness. But there was the feeling of falling in the pit of his stomach. Those men didn't even want to talk to him, the rude bastards. What about his side of things, his feelings? What about his goodness? What about a second chance?

***

Tim and Mary toured River View Plantation—the acreage, the outbuildings, the river shore, their home, Tim's farm equipment and tools. The evidence of struggle and destruction were still visible on the land and the home. New repairs stuck out, and downed trees and new growth, as well. Still, Mat, Katie, Hope, John and Diana, Pete and Grace had done well to keep the homestead together over the years. A fireplace fire warming the inside of the home satisfied them and gave assurance that life would be good again. The family had come back together: Katie and Paul were at Katie's cottage; Mat and Barb, at New Canaan. Hope and William had gone with Katie and Paul. Tuck and Robin were not at home, and Leaf and Andy, too, were out somewhere, no doubt eel trapping. Tom and Tish were back at their homestead, Beulah Land. They had all remained together in paradise.

Paradise had been wonderful as the name suggests. Relaxing yet stimulating—so many classes in how to use the resurrected, immortal body; classes on the heavens; on future projects that might be implemented by their God. They heard nothing about the earthly life of their living friends and relatives and this was good—to trust their sovereign God in His redemptive work. New arrivals at paradise were reported and routed to their families. When the final harvest was complete, all returning resurrected were sent to their last known addresses. Jed (father to Pete), the only one of Mat's kids to remain in the area, had opted to go to South America, where most of his kids lived. He and Pete had met and conversed in paradise and had planned to meet later. In time, back upon Earth, Pete and Grace would visit, as would Carl. In time, DC Jones and Ling and his family would make the pilgrimage to central Pennsylvania. Tom Jr. and Lana had returned to China, as did the Burnell brothers, temporarily. Tim knew of the Burnell brothers through his brother, John; they probably would return to Beulah Land at some point, with Tom and Tish.

Tim and Mary focused their perusal of their homestead on the foodstuffs and found that someone had resupplied the cold cellar with locally bagged potatoes, sweet potatoes, onions, turnips, beets; jars of tomato sauce and blueberries had been procured. Local maple syrup was found in the same area. In another storage area, they found large bags of flour, corn meal, salt, yeast packets, sugar, baking powder. "Looks like someone was anticipating us," said Tim. "Tomato sauce and blueberries from Pete and Grace, I bet."

Mary said, "So kind of them to think of us, when so many other concerns must be on their minds. Let's check out the refrigerator and freezer—the last place anyone would put food." The last sentence was spoken without guile, for these storage places implied more immediate use, and their return date had been unknown.

Tim opened the refrigerator door and gasped. "Eggs by the dozens, bacon, sausages, loaves of store-bought bread, butter, grape jelly, flat breads, hummus. Lunch meat—turkey, ham, Lebanon sweet bologna." He looked at Mary. "Call the kids and see what they have. Let's meet at the river for lunch and discuss food issues, if any. I intend to make a quick sandwich."

Mary was already on her wrist phone. Whoever had stocked the refrigerator wanted a luncheon, and so did she.

***

Tom Sr., Tish, Tom Jr., and Lana, all in rain boots, slowly walked hand and hand as they toured Beulah Land. The clouds spoke of rain. They had planned this return together in paradise. Tom Sr. looked up at the mountain to his east—the size, the vastness of the tree-covered slope had shrunk in his memory. Now, the sheer volume of rock two thousand feet above them reaffirmed the awesome power of their God. Tom Sr. remembered the earthquake of the Tribulation that had heaved the mountains a thousand feet higher. That quake should have killed them.

Tom Jr. spoke as he pointed to the tip of the ridge before it plunged almost straight down to the river. "There's John and Diana's cottage. I see sunlight reflecting from solar panels."

Tom Sr. answered, "Yes, I see it too."

Tish glimpsed the cottage before her eyes were diverted to the graveled country road leading into their lands from the highway. "Who are those characters approaching from the road?"

"That's Robbie, Jack, and Sammie," said Tom Jr. in surprise—he wasn't expecting them for weeks or months.

"Those are our boys," said Lana with pride in her voice and remembrances of when she and Tom Jr. had brought them to Beulah Land for one last try at turning them to the Father. They had succeeded—no, the Lord had succeeded. She remembered it had been a mild, wintry day like this one, smoke coming from the chimney of the house. John and Diana had dislodged the intruder, Stan. A light drizzle began.

Tom Sr. and Tish were expectant—they had never met the boys. The expectancy disappeared; the boys were approved by God Almighty, redeemed, sanctified, in immortal bodies. Without a prompting thought or word Tish said, "Forever family…for eternity." Then she added, "My only emotion is joy!"

"That's the same phrase that went through my mind," said Tom Sr. "Amazing, Tish. We hear each other's thoughts and the voice of God shaping our language."

Tish tightened her hand upon Tom Sr.'s hand. "Yes. Amazing."

Jack's face was beaming as he approached the group. "I was showing Robbie and Sammie where my first contacts with Satan's forces occurred."

Robbie added, "A destroyed commuter bus on the road, then farther back, in caves along the mountain."

Sammie, not speaking, had grabbed Tom Jr. and Lana and hugged each in turn. "Thanks for caring about us. We wouldn't be here, if not for your love." Sammie smiled broadly and moved to Tom Sr. and Tish, hugging them firmly, with great affection. "We wouldn't be anywhere if not for you two—our family's Adam and Eve."

Tom Sr. laughed, and Tish smiled as broadly as Sammie was smiling, and they hugged him tightly.

Lana laughed. "Our quiet Sammie, so full of goodness." She remembered how sullen he had first appeared when they had met years ago. Now, his inner, loving heart was full upon his mind and his words. That was a miracle comparable to making a blind man see.

Robbie and Jack, prompted by the rightness and goodness of Sammie's actions, gave hugs to Tom Jr. and Lana. They followed Sammie to Tom Sr. and Tish, who were hugged as well. Tom Sr.'s eyes became moist, as did Tish's eyes, for three young men, who had never known them, yet were part of them by heredity of the flesh, but more importantly—all importantly—by the Spirit of God. This was the fulfillment of Tom Sr.'s work during the millennium—of teaching the young the story of Christ and the power of Christ to take the god-hating, rebellious know-it-all sinner to the foot of the cross. Then, to watch a debased and depraved piece of flesh become a human in every way that God had first imagined and created humanity to be.

A man of unselfish desires, a man who nurtured others, his children, his family, even the unknown and unloved of the streets and offices. A man whose mind always returned to his mind's home base—to the reality of the Creator, of God the Father in that home within the mind in which men and women dwelt. Tish had heard her husband's thoughts, and she commented, "Tom Jr. heard you, and he followed, and here is the reward."

Tom Jr. heard; he had heard all the silent thoughts, as did everyone within the group. Tom Jr. spoke. "Mat was a part of it all. At a bad time in my life, he reminded me of your words, Dad. *It is knowing your evil is an affront to God, and this God you affront is the only good in the world. When you hurt God and are ashamed of your hurting Him, then you are on the threshold.*

"When Robbie, Jack, and Sammie were struggling, and I took them in, it was this saying that guided me, was my marker, to tell me if I had succeeded. If they reached that understanding, it would mean they knew absolutely that God lived and God loved. Righteous shame tells us we are the bad guy, the kink in the plan, the problem—not God."

Tom Sr. spoke. "I remember when Mat and I spoke. It was a rainy day like today, and I had just encountered a mother bear with four cubs by the chestnut tree on the south lawn. We went inside and sat by the fireplace. It seems like yesterday, and every minute detail is remembered."

Jack spoke. "The three of us made a commitment at the end of that first visit. Christ even took the time to exhort us to endure. But not till my brothers came back during Satan's rebellion did the commitment become real."

"It's totally real now," said Sammie. "Resurrected bodies!"

"Amen," said the gathered.

CHAPTER 23

Even though the day was cloudy, and the wind carried a chill, and even though many had had contact in paradise, the Johnson clan, Tim and Mary, Mat and Barb, Katie and Paul, Hope and William were upon the riverbank, enthused, talkative, with two fires working side by side. John and Diana, Dan and Emily saw the fires from the mountain cottage, dropped down from their heights, landed among the party, and were absorbed into the love of the gathered. Blankets were around shoulders, and the potluck lunch was still being held, when Pete and Grace quietly swooped in on the back of the broad waters of the Susquehanna. The exclamations of happiness and delight were vibrant and heartfelt as William and Paul went down the bank, made shorter by the rising water, and steadied the landings of their family members.

Pete pulled a heavy mass from the back of his kayak and held it in the air. "A very heavy ham, ready to slice, if someone is still hungry."

Paul spoke determinedly. "Slice it up."

William added, "I second that."

As they gained the riverbank, Pete and Grace made the rounds for hugs, handshakes, and kisses, their faces lit by the passion of seeing faces long gone but every bit the healthy and loving countenances they once knew. "Praise God, praise God," came from Grace incessantly as she gloried in His handiwork—the people she loved in eternal bodies; all the gathered, within a life unending, with their Savoir and their Creator.

From the river trail came Tom and Tish, Tom Jr. and Lana, Robbie, Jack, and Sammie. Shouts of greetings, praises for God, the father; God, the Son; and God, the Holy Ghost, resounded as the Johnsons gathered around the Burnell family. Tanya, Anya, and Flo were with their families, thousands of miles away. Warm drinks were put in every empty hand, and a plate to fill.

A "halloo" came from the river, resonating over the water as two boats shored—Andy and Leaf and Tuck and Robin in their eel boats. A great shout of acclamation came from the riverbank. Spontaneous applause resounded with shouts of "Andy!" led by those who had so recently fought against Satan's rebellion. They came up the bank into tumultuous praises for the Lord of Lords, the God of Banners, the God who knew only victory. Andy and his family were, like the others, absorbed into the aura of love and friendship.

A cold wind came from the northwest, carrying sleet. Then snow began to fall in September. Conversation became difficult, and the conversing groups decided to move into Tim's home. The quiet stragglers, absorbed in the cold and snow, the beauty of the scene, slowly followed. In every fireplace, a fire was built. The living room collected the veterans of Satan's final rebellion. Pete and Grace, John and Diana, Andy and Leaf and their sons, Tuck and Robin. Robbie, Jack, and Sammie. Mat and Barb, Tom Jr. and Lana gathered near the veterans, as did Tim and Mary, Tom Sr. and Tish, Katie and Paul, and Hope and William.

A knock was heard at the door, and suddenly Carl, Ling, and DC Jones appeared in wet clothes specked with ice and snow. A shout of greetings and approval rolled out from the gathered. Carl, Ling, and DC Jones looked behind themselves at the door they had just entered. To the crowd, this was a humorous act of real humility, as if they did not deserve such a greeting and thought someone of importance was coming behind them. When they were in through the archway, Tanya, Anya, and Flo appeared with their husbands, Tobe, Keith, and Rickee. Another roar of welcome rose from the gathered. They were complete—the chosen, the beloved of God, their Daddy God, who had redeemed, sanctified, given eternal life, brought them through the world, the flesh, the deceptions of Satan, into hallowed life.

Within a minute, the newcomers had mingled, and conversations returned. Tim stood in the center of his living room, upon a low, sturdy coffee table he had made hundreds of years ago and raised his hands. The crowd focused upon him and quieted. Tim spoke. "You may remain all night, even sleep here, if you wish. Eat and drink whatever you like—our God will provide more. I thank you all for being here.

"As Satan is now gone to his place of suffering, never to take another person hostage; as his world is dead, never to arise; as our resurrected bodies will never make another carnal demand and temptation upon us, we should give thanks and praise to the veterans of this last conflict—the final conflict of the world of humanity, the last harvest. First, to our leader, Andy, a bush fighter from the beginning, and his wife, Leaf, who kept the home fires burning, and who fed our army. Also, their two sons, Tuck and Robin, dogged warriors always ready to fight. Then, to John and Diana—John had military experience from before the Rapture; Diana had none. They were in the fight all the time. To Pete and Grace, who fought in the worst battles, had no military or combat experience and who died in combat. Dan and Emily, who worked the streets for intel, fought with weapons in hand. And lastly, to the Burnell brothers, Robbie, Jack, and Sammie, who fought the entire four months. They had no prior military experience in their mortal bodies, and all three were wounded at one time."

Robin stood shyly, raising his hand. He caught the approving nod of Tim. Robin spoke. "I'd like to say that the Burnells were literally all wounded at one time—the same time—in battle on these very grounds. It was a desperate time—all three hugging the earth in shallow trenches, enemy fire ripping overhead, eating up protective stumps and downed trees. John and Diana were there, too. I dropped in among them. Told Jack they could surrender, but he didn't like their chances in surrendering. He wanted to fight to the end if need be. He said…" Robin paused to concentrate the hearing of the gathered; but in his wait, emotion passed upon his heart and vocal cords. He stifled tears. "He said, 'Death has no sting.'"

The crowd erupted in the loudest praise, a roar of victory and thankfulness to their great and eternal God, who was never at a loss, never confused, always ready to claim His victories. Robin held his hands up, wishing silence, and said, "Jack had the presence of mind to give me orders—a strategy, and it worked. Likely, our victory saved these homes from burning." Those who could barely hear his words over the shouts of acclamation, heard them within their minds and roared all the louder in praise.

Mat rose, and Robin pointed to him in acknowledgment. Mat spoke. "They fought for us. They suffered for us. They won for us. We owe them eternal gratitude. They will be the first to recognize the efforts of all those in this room who wrote their life stories down, who wouldn't allow the future generations to forget the sorrows of Satan's rule and the Tribulation's suffering. They made real the awful consequences of living without God. Tom Sr. and Tish, my dad and mom, Katie and Paul, through her songs, my Barb, Dan, Emily, DC Jones, Carl, and Ling all published their stories, even me. For a thousand years, we kept the remembrances alive so that men and women who had never known danger and war would run to the call of their Savior, put their lives on the line."

The room erupted in praise and the clapping of hands, and when the tumult should have stopped, it simply began again with greater vigor and zeal each time another attribute of God was voiced in heartfelt gratitude and emotion. They caught each other's overwhelming love for their God—their God and the inexpressible import of their time on Earth. Pete hugged Katie as he went from person to person, and she felt his overwhelming joy. The joy of the Spirit swept over everyone.

Pete called out, "Listen." The crowd stopped their tumult in a supernatural immediacy. "Every promise fulfilled. We have eternal life. Eternal bodies. We were chosen—the unimportant to the world, the not-so-charismatic or talented, the broken bodied, the deformed, the people just not quite right, the people of fairy tales—Enslavers, we were once called. We chose to love our God, and here we are. The offscouring of the world, the mocked and abused, the resolute, the enduring, the come-from-behind winners. Here we are! The last pages of written history are almost done. Just the New Jerusalem waiting and God's presence as our light. Soon, we'll be stepping off the pages of what was, and a new book will be written of what is to be. I love you all and can't think of any people I'd rather be with."

Someone from the crowd (some say it was Tom Sr., some say Carl) yelled, "That's good, because you're stuck with us forever!" The gathered laughed.

There are times of impromptu worship when the human heart, with nothing but thankfulness and praise, rises to the highest levels of the soul and transcends emotion to a higher realm. This was one of those times. Greatly amplified by the absence of the world's system, the fleshly appetites, and Satan's presence, God's chosen people reached the abode of God. A glory encircled them, lit upon them, and Jesus, as Savior, was among them, hugging and shaking hands. He spread his arms, and they fell to their knees. Eternal God, who passed before Moses, came to them. The Shekinah glory danced among them, and their holy voices sang, intertwined in celestial music; and time was lost, thought was lost. Only praise for the holiness of their God prevailed.

EPILOGUE

Andreas Hahn did not know the time of day or night. A dull blackness pervaded his sight at all times. He did not know the day of the week, the month, or the year. He did not experience seasons. He did experience physical sensations; the stages of his burnings came with calendar regularity, the rising and falling of his lungs, the beating of his heart, the opening and closing of his eyes, the hot air upon his burning nasal passages, the touch upon his skin of heat greater and lesser—but always heat.

He could move his arms and legs throughout his life cycles, and at one time thought he could find the limits of his hell. A wall to climb, where Eden lay on the other side; or a ladder, or a narrow beam that would lead to the other side of the chasm; a vast water he could swim to another land. He failed to find it. He then searched for a place to hide from the heat—a cave, an outcrop of rock, an abandoned building. He found none. He found others on his journeys, men and women in various states of distressed flesh—whole or burnt to crispy blackness or gray ash that turned to dust, some with appendages and others with burnt stumps, all naked and horrible. They followed the same cycles of burning as he.

He feared the whole, fleshly cycle, when he had appendages, full movement, healthy skin and internal organs—his former Earth body restored.

Within this cycle of life, his fellow travelers would overpower and abuse him in ways that sound minds could not comprehend. The stages of burnt flesh would culminate in ashes lying piled by bones. He would be outside his body then and would pick up his bones, rattle his skull or hold his femurs in religious awe. Then the cycle began again, and he was of sound flesh.

God had not taken what was good from the heart, soul, mind, and strength of Andreas on his day of judgment: Andreas had had no good within. For what was good in a man was the Spirit of God. The Spirit of God was God's. Man had created no goodness within his mind or his flesh. Man without God was a depraved being that could not comprehend that he was depraved. When he had possessed goodness, he had thought he was the author, creator of that good, and he had perverted it. In truth, Andreas and all the creatures of hell lived only because of their memories of life lived in the flesh within that true and real world of the Spirit. As true good had been taken from their memories, but not the deceitful memories of good created by Satan, all of hell's creatures lived in hells created by their own memories. They were living what they truly had been and were and always would be. They had made their own hells.

In time, a thousand years or two thousand, Andreas would attempt to destroy the piles of dust that were his flesh and the skeleton that was his body. At those times, he stood outside in his ghost. No success. In time, Andreas reasoned that he had good within, for he knew that his existence was depraved and futile. If he could only hold onto that fleeting good within the self-awareness and collect it and build a construct of good and enter into it, might he escape the torment for moments of time? The wisp of good was too fragile and fleeting to offer shelter or succor.

For all eternity, Andreas had done to him that which he had done or would have liked to do to others. He was raped, physically abused, exploited. He was hectored and harassed, conned, belittled, embarrassed, shamed, and pranked. He was stabbed, punched, beaten, shot, and tortured. Not a kind or encouraging word was sent his way. He was the weakest of the weak. Andreas had no rest from his depraved brethren and spent his eternal existence in fear, hysteria, anxiety, and dread. His loneliness was unremitting—no conscience to talk to, no self, no friend, and no God. God did not hold Andreas to account for what he had done to the Godhead—the curses, the lies, the tricks, and slanders. But for humanity, both Christian and non-Christian, who had suffered under Andreas, the pain was doubled.

***

The eternal people of God spent their unending days in constant adventures of the mind and body, in learning and exploring, in creating and implementing, in teaching, in caring for one another, and in loving their Father, God, through prayer, exultation, exhortation, song, and the works of their minds and hands. Their devotion was always heartfelt and powerful. They remembered—through histories and autobiographies, songs, paintings, photos, films, and dramatic arts—their years in Satan's kingdom, during which they were frustrated, lost, or confused with questions, such as What is the point? Is God love? How could He do this to me? Where will I find the strength? How can I face my enemies? Is this a book of fairy tales? They had endured and persevered and found in the millennium that their God was faithful, all His book was true, and His rewards were extravagant and deep in love.

Praises to the Creator God, who has set before man only one task: to choose good or to choose evil.

Praises to our Loving God, who seeks, affirms, and exalts those who seek truth.

www.ingramcontent.com/pod-product-compliance
Lightning Source LLC
Chambersburg PA
CBHW071411200726
48294CB00002B/355

* 9 7 8 1 9 6 0 0 0 7 1 2 4 *